HEAVEN CAME DOWN

HEAVEN CAME DOWN

BOOK ONE IN THE OCULUS GATE SERIES

BY

BRYAN DAVIS

MOUNTAIN**BROOK**FIRE

Heaven Came Down
Published by Mountain Brook Ink under the Mountain Brook
Fire line
White Salmon, WA U.S.A.

The website addresses shown in this book are not intended in
any way to be or imply an endorsement on the part of Mountain
Brook Ink, nor do we vouch for their content.

This story is a work of fiction. All characters and events are the
product of the author's imagination. Any resemblance to any
person, living or dead, is coincidental.

Any scripture quotations are taken from the King James Version
of the Bible. Public domain.

ISBN 978-1-943959-82-2
Published in association with Cyle Young of the Hartline Literary
Agency, LLC.
© 2020 Bryan Davis

The Team: Miralee Ferrell, Alyssa Roat, Nikki Wright, Cindy
Jackson
Cover Design: Indie Cover Design, Lynnette Bonner

*Mountain Brook Fire is an inspirational publisher offering worlds you can
believe in.*

Printed in the United States of America

Chapter One

Summer shivered. Sitting on a rickety wooden pew, she stared at the carnage—her parents lying motionless in front of the kneeling altar, the shadow of angel wings spreading across their smoking bodies. The scene was surreal, impossible, yet the very outcome they had feared for so long.

The angel, blonde and beautiful, crouched in front of her, her face glowing. "I'm sorry you had to witness this." Her pupils seemed to blaze. "It's all for the best. If we are to live in perfect unity, all must agree to the common worship."

Summer looked away. Although the angel spewed lies, disagreeing with her might incite another blast from her deadly eyes.

The angel set a hand on Summer's knee. "Since, by law, you're too young to execute and old enough to survive on your own, I will leave you here to fend for yourself. Just be sure to warn others to heed the instructions of the holy angels." She rose, flew to the exit, and closed the door behind her.

Summer knelt at her mother's side and lifted the cross she always wore, the coarse wood scorched by the twin lasers that drilled holes through her chest. She untied the leather cord and held the cross in her trembling hand. As she caressed it with a fingertip, her face warmed, then blazed. *Unity.* An angel's buzzword. A patriot's obscenity. What good was unity if everyone united around evil? It was all wrong, so very wrong.

The door opened again. Summer stuffed the cross into her skirt pocket. At the entry, framed by midday light, a man strode in and took off a military-style cap. Dressed in camo and carrying a rifle, he bent his lanky body and stooped at Summer's side. "Do you know who I am?" he asked, kindness in his tone.

She nodded. "The resistance commander."

His eyes, as gray as his hair, sparkled. "I apologize for arriving too late. I came as soon as I heard from our regional watchman."

"I understand. It's not your fault."

"What's your name, and how old are you?"

"Summer. I'm seventeen."

"Old enough." He threaded his cap through his fingers. "Would you like to join us?"

"To battle the angels?"

"The so-called angels. No real angel would murder your parents."

"I know." She sniffed and brushed a tear away. "But why me?"

"I need someone to help me expose them for the monsters they really are, and you're perfect for the job."

"But I'm just a—"

"Just a kid. I know. But if you join us, we'll make you into what you need to be. And even if you don't, you're welcome to live in our farming community."

Summer gazed again at the faces of her parents, both noble, both peaceful. They were such good people—loving, giving, and kind. The commander was right. The angels were monsters. They had to be stopped.

"I'll send someone to take care of your folks." He rose and extended a hand. "Will you come?"

She took his hand, and they walked out together, leaving the carnage behind.

Summer stood in a line of ten new recruits, all dressed in boots and camo. She glanced at Jack Garrison standing at her side, tall and muscular, eyes straight ahead—the portrait of courage. How could she, a scrawny teenager, ever be a true soldier like him?

She clutched the scorched cross dangling at her chest. She could do this. She had to do this. Nothing else mattered.

Commander Barks stood in front of the line and raised his right hand. "Repeat after me."

The recruits raised their hands and recited the resistance oath, ending with, "And I swear to give all that is necessary, including my life, to rid the world of the angel scourge."

Twenty camo-clothed onlookers applauded. Handshakes spread all around. A few greeted Summer, though no one except Jack's sister, Trudy, asked for her name. After most had filtered out, Jack, Trudy, and their brother Ben remained, talking to Barks. Ben, speaking to the commander with a confident stance, was obviously the leader of the siblings. Although he and his wife, Kat, had been part of the resistance force for quite a while, he had joined Jack and Trudy in taking the oath. It seemed that this family trio did everything together.

When their group broke up, Barks strode to Summer and extended a hand. "Welcome to the resistance."

"Thank you, sir." Summer shook his hand. "So what's next?"

Barks glanced at the Garrisons, then looked again at Summer. "Follow me."

As they walked past the trio, Ben whispered something to Trudy. She stomped on his foot. "Don't be a jerk. She can be trained. She's the same age I am, so it's possible."

"Ignore Ben," Barks said as they walked toward a folding table with a deck of cards on top. "In his eyes, a female soldier has to … well …"

"Prove herself?" Summer asked.

Barks nodded. "And you'll certainly get a chance to do that."

They sat at the table across from each other. Barks picked up the deck and fanned the cards. "Pick four and place them face down."

Summer did so. "Telling my fortune?"

"In a way, but it's really a magic trick." He set a finger on one of the cards. "I need a spy who can memorize complex codes that will allow for secure communications. Therefore, this spy must become a jack of all trades." He turned the card over, revealing the jack of spades. "You will need to be a quick study."

He touched another of her selected cards. "I need a spy who can infiltrate angel headquarters and get close to the angels' hive queen. She is the key to everything." He turned the second card over, revealing the queen of spades. "You will need to learn extraordinary stealth."

He touched the third card. "I need a spy who is beautiful, charming, physically fit, someone even a king would desire." He turned that card faceup—the king of spades.

"But I'm none of those things," Summer said. "I'm a skinny scarecrow."

Barks smiled. "Beauty is in the eye of the beholder, and you're certainly a lovely young lady in mine."

Her cheeks warmed. "Thank you."

"You're welcome." He cleared his throat. "In any case, you will go to a training camp to develop whatever skills and fitness you're lacking. My plan is long-term. It might take years to play out."

He set a finger on the fourth card and pushed the others to the side. "Finally, I need a spy who hates the angels as much as any patriot in our fold." He turned the card over, this time slowly, a slight tremble in his hand. The ace of spades now lay alone on the table. "Long ago, this card was considered a symbol of death. It means you must be willing to die for the cause, just as you swore in your oath. And since you have no living close relatives, I'm giving you the opportunity to become the spy I need." He paused for a moment, a hint of wetness in his eyes. "What do you say?"

As Summer stared at the card, the church scene returned to mind—the angel flying into the sanctuary, demanding that those who stood with the angels exit immediately. Two dozen worshipers ran out, leaving only her parents standing firm. The angel shot both with her laser eyes, killing them instantly, a cold and callous execution.

Now it was time to pay them back.

She picked up the ace. "I'm your spy, Commander."

Chapter Two

Four years later

Ben set his plasma rifle on the ground and propped the angel's corpse in front of a tree, pressing her leather-like wings against the trunk. In the filtered moonlight, a glow emanated from under the bill of her military patrol cap. When he flipped it away, golden tresses fell to her camo-covered shoulders, and her serene face shone brightly, though she had died several minutes earlier.

"Are you there?" Jack's quiet voice came from Ben's earbud. "What's the delay?"

Ben adjusted the bud. "Got a patrol angel. Female. Older teen. Maybe early twenties." He eyed the gaping hole in her chest, still smoking at the edges. "Took just one plasma shot to kill her."

"Then she's a grunt. Probably first generation."

Ben touched the angel's cheek, smooth and radiant. No wonder so many people were fooled by these phonies. The so-called angels often chose attractive, youthful humans, and the radiance added to the deception. "More likely Gen Two. She's got the glow and wings. And I hit her in the heart. Close range. That'll kill a Two."

"True, but if Gen Twos are patrolling this area at night, we've got more trouble than we bargained for. We're far from headquarters. Maybe someone tipped them off."

Trudy's voice filtered through the earbud, even quieter than Jack's. "Don't be such a pessimist. I found the jeep at the coordinates. Everything's inside, including the medical bag and vaccine cooler. Our mole came through. We've got this."

"Good." Ben glanced around for any sign of movement. Nothing stirred. "I'm at the pickup site, and I checked the locker. The security IDs are in hand."

"What're you going to do with the angel?" Jack asked. "We have to be to HQ's security gate shortly after dawn. Not enough time to remove the implant in the field or take her to Doc."

"I didn't bring an extraction kit," Trudy said. "This isn't a mission of mercy. Not for the angels, anyway."

Ben pushed a strand of hair from the young woman's ghostly face. "Mercy mission or not, I can set this poor girl's soul free."

"How do you know she's not a volunteer?" Jack asked. "And maybe her soul's not even there anymore."

"I have an AngelScan. Hang on." Ben withdrew the palm-sized disk from a belt pouch and set the electrode side against the girl's forehead. The screen lit up, showing an image of her brain. A red blob with snaking tentacles surrounded and impaled a white, radiant sphere embedded in the brain stem, like scarlet serpents spearing an innocent dove. "Her soul's there. The implant has it trapped. Even if she was a volunteer before, she isn't now."

"All right," Jack said. "Your call. I doubt I can talk you out of it."

Ben turned the girl's head, withdrew his handgun from its hip holster, and, pushing her soft locks to the side, set the barrel at the base of her skull. Her smallish nose and fair complexion made her look like a younger version of Kat, but he couldn't let sad memories stop him from doing the right thing. "Sorry, young lady, but it's for your own good."

Trudy stood at the dark roadside and stared at the pavement, her muscles tense as she waited for the inevitable. As the mission's point man, Ben made the final decisions, even some that bordered on suicidal.

A gunshot rang from the earbud. Trudy flinched. As she imagined a soul escaping from a ruptured skull and sailing into the air, she blew a sigh. Another tragic casualty. But at least the girl was no longer a prisoner of the implanted slave master.

"Bugging out," Ben said, breathless, apparently running. "With any luck, the gunshot will draw the patrollers here, and I'll be long gone." A hum blended in, Ben's electric motorcycle. "Be there in about twenty. Watch out for SkySweep drones. When that angel doesn't report in, they'll search for her."

Trudy scanned the sky through the tree branches, mostly bare as a cool breeze rattled the remaining dry leaves and prompted her to zip her jacket. In the distant valley, a light blinked over the city skyline, maybe an airplane, too fast to be a landscape-scanning angel drone. So far, so good. But from this elevated perch, blinded by the mountain to her rear, it was impossible to be sure.

The gibbous moon hung low in the pre-dawn hours, and the usual stars dotted the blackness along with the new celestial lights that drew an eye-like disk of glittering specks across a fourth of the visible sky, a cluster that appeared when the angels arrived several years earlier.

The angel-driven media dubbed it the Oculus Gate, an eye in the sky through which the universal deity watched the planet. Ben, however, gave it a different label during their first resistance meeting—"Hell's Gate." To this day, no one in their rebel faction could be sure why it was really out there, though the theories and rumors chilled the bravest of souls.

"I found the tech gear," Jack said through the earbud. "We're set. See you in ten, Sis."

"Roger that." Trudy's words emanated in twin puffs of white. "No bogeys in sight. I'll prep the jeep." She attached the radio to her belt, opened the vehicle's rear swing-out door, and flipped up the cooler's lid. A cloud of vapor rose into the humid air, adding to the morning's growing fog. She lifted the cooling blanket. Underneath, several trays of fake vaccine vials lay stacked in tiers, five hundred doses. She set the blanket back in place and closed the lid. Perfect. Enough to stop the border invasion. Now if only she and Ben could infiltrate angel headquarters without getting caught.

She unzipped a suitcase lying next to the cooler. Their physician disguises lay folded neatly inside. Once again, perfect. But could they really pull it off? After months of preparation, now that the mission was finally underway, nothing seemed certain. Fooling the security drones and getting into angel headquarters would be hard enough, but the rest of the plan?

She shook her head, casting away the doubts. Confidence was the key. Ben and Jack never showed fear, at least not while she was around. She had to avoid being the protected kid sister and display the bravado and medical skills that convinced them to assign her this role. Otherwise, they would abort the mission and send her packing.

And, worst of all, every remaining patriot in the region would die.

Trudy fished a band from her pocket. After tying her hair back, she pried the jeep's inner side panel away and set it on the cooler. She grabbed a flashlight from her belt and shone the beam into the newly revealed compartment. Inside lay an unlabeled toothpaste-like tube—probably skin-glow cream—and a plastic case no bigger than a ring box, both hidden carefully for good reason. If captured, the driver who brought the jeep here could explain away the vials in the cooler as rejected medical supplies, but these two items had no purpose besides deception.

She removed both, pushed the tube into her pocket, and drew the case closer to her eyes. Inside, a pair of tiny glass containers glimmered, no bigger than one-milliliter vials. How could these nearly invisible capsules hold a monster? Yes, the experiments had worked, but those test monsters were dead. Whether or not these capsules could contain a supernatural captive who was desperate to escape remained to be seen.

A hum drifted on the breeze. She pushed the capsule case into her pocket next to the glow cream tube, snapped the jeep's panel back in place, and turned the flashlight off as she pivoted toward the sound. Seconds later, Jack, seated on his electric motorcycle, careened around a curve, one of many on this winding forest road.

As usual, he rode much too close to the edge, only inches from the nearly vertical drop, probably just to scare her. Making her shudder had been a favorite hobby of his ever since her toddler years. But she couldn't bat an eye. Not this time.

After stopping next to the jeep, he shut off the motor and dismounted, wearing black leather from his jacket to his boots. He slipped off his helmet, releasing his dark, curly locks and revealing a smiling, angular face, clean shaven for a change. "Everything ready?"

Trudy nodded. "Ready to kick some angel butt, if that's what you mean."

"Well, that and some much dirtier business." He rolled his motorcycle off the road and into the forest. "Gonna hide my bike and ditch some stuff I don't need. Back in a minute."

With Jack out of sight, Trudy let herself shudder. That dirtier business would be far dirtier than anything she had ever been a part of, but there was no way around it. It had to be done.

When Jack returned, now without his bike, helmet, and leather riding gear, he stood with Trudy as they looked down the road. "Any idea what Ben's thinking?" she asked. "About the dirtier business, I mean."

Jack brushed off his camo cargo pants. "He's conflicted. As usual. But he'll get the job done. Always has."

"They chose the wrong side." Trudy crossed her arms tightly. "They deserve it."

"No need to convince me. It's kill or be killed. I vote for staying alive. And I don't think we have to convince Ben. He has too much invested in this."

"You mean he hopes to find Kat."

Jack smiled in a sad sort of way. "He'll never give up. But don't worry. His head'll be in the game. Trust me, I know what he's going through. It takes time to get over it."

Trudy averted her eyes. The words "as if *you've* gotten over it" came to mind, but no use stabbing a wounded heart. She retrieved the capsule case from her pocket and handed it to him. "Let's see if they hold a charge."

"When Ben gets here." He pushed the case into his pocket and again watched the road. Soon, a new hum drifted in on the gentle breeze. Ben appeared, his bike skidding around the curve and heading for the ledge. At the last second, he leaped off and hit the pavement running, his rifle strapped to his shoulder and his helmet nowhere in sight. The bike flew over the ravine in a plunging arc and disappeared.

Ben sprinted the rest of the way, his camo jacket flapping, and halted in front of Trudy and Jack, gasping for breath. "Bogeys on my tail. SkySweep's coming."

"This way!" Trudy hustled to the jeep, flung open the cooler, and pulled the blanket out. When her brothers joined her, the trio huddled low behind the jeep and wrapped themselves in the blanket's frigid material, leaving a small gap to look through, Trudy in the middle.

In the forest, the treetops shook, blown about by the drone's massive propellers, aimed at the ground to keep the craft aloft. A red light flashed, bathing everything in a crimson wash. It stayed on for far too long.

Jack whispered, "My bike was still warm. Maybe they spotted that."

"Small heat signature," Ben said, a bead of sweat trickling into his five-day beard. "It'll look like an animal. The bike's no bigger than a deer."

"Not even that big." Jack shuddered. "A wolf, maybe."

"Jack?" Trudy nudged his ribs. "Are you afraid of the big, bad wolf? You're shivering."

He hissed, "I'm shivering because I'm covered by a liquid-nitrogen blanket."

She grinned. "Yeah. Right. Uh-huh. I believe that."

"Well, believe what you want. We'll see who's shivering when—"

10

The red light flicked off. The area darkened, and the treetops settled. Seconds later, the light flashed on again far from the jeep.

Ben pulled the blanket away, used a sleeve to mop the remaining sweat from his wide brow, and ran a hand through his closely cropped hair. With every move, vapor rose from his overheated body, barely cooled at all by the blanket. "No time to lose. They won't stop looking, not with a Gen Two missing."

Trudy took the blanket. "I'll stow this."

Ben tossed his rifle into the back of the jeep, leaped into the driver's seat, and started the engine while Jack slid into the rear compartment in front of the supplies.

After closing the cooler, Trudy hustled to the front passenger's seat and jumped in. "Let's roll."

"Rolling." Ben shifted into gear and drove onto the road, headlights off. As hoped, the moon provided enough light. The forecast for clear skies had held true. "Time to check for updates."

Trudy turned the radio on and set the frequency to 87.7. The speakers emitted a mechanical voice. "Thumb scans required."

Trudy set her thumb on the dashboard scanner. A light passed from left to right beneath it. When she lifted her thumb, Ben set his on the sensor, then Jack took his turn, leaning over the seat and reaching a lanky arm to the dashboard.

A moment later, the radio returned with a man clearing his throat.

"Commander Barks," Jack said. "I'd know that sound anywhere."

"Why him?" Trudy asked. "Recording updates for field agents is below his pay grade."

Ben huffed. "As if any of us gets paid."

"Greetings, Ben, Jack, and Trudy Garrison," Barks said in his usual low, commanding tone. "If everything is going according to plan, you are listening to this message less than one hour after I began recording it, and you might be wondering why I am personally providing your last-minute instructions."

"He knew you'd ask," Jack said to Trudy. "Kind of spooky."

"Recent radio transmissions indicate," Barks continued, "that other pockets of resistance are in deep trouble. Our Eurasian allies have been blitzed by tanks and strafed by attack helicopters. Only a handful of fugitives remain to report the atrocities. The angels have besieged patriots in neo-Africa, and they are near starvation, lacking the farms that we have in our community."

"He told that group they should pose as farmers," Jack said. "He's probably still ticked off that they didn't."

"Shhh!" Ben and Trudy hissed at the same time.

"Our mission is, therefore, crucial. We have an opportunity to punch a hole in the heart of angel headquarters and make them hemorrhage, perhaps fatally. Even if they survive, they will likely call for reinforcements from other regions, thereby giving relief and hope to our beleaguered allies. The benefit will be great, but the danger is high, the most perilous mission we have ever undertaken. If we fail, everyone in our community will die, and the angels will have no force to oppose them, either in this region or in any other around the world. Therefore, I am personally in charge for the duration."

"Good," Ben said. "He needed to dump that ultimate-weapon project. It's doomed."

Trudy firmed her lips. Ben meant that without Kat, the weapon project was doomed, but he didn't want to say it out loud. Too painful.

Barks cleared his throat again. "Your contact at angel headquarters is a woman named Chantal. She's been working undercover as a security tech for more than a year. Because of how deep her cover is, we don't know her alias, and she has not provided any updates. During the planning of this mission, we have been sending her encoded communiqués through a courier who drops them off at a secret site. We know only that the messages disappear without a response, which means that either she has read them or they have been intercepted by the angels. We are operating on the assumption that she knows her role. If the messages have been intercepted and decoded, then your mission will likely lead to your capture and death."

Jack blew through his flapping lips. "Thanks for that. A real boost to our confidence."

Trudy shushed him. "Be still."

"After the implantation," Barks said, "Chantal will meet Ben and Trudy on level one. We are not certain what she will be wearing, but the tech uniform includes a white polo shirt with an angel logo on the left breast pocket. A drone will likely be accompanying her, and she is to lead Ben and Trudy to the authentic vaccine. Your code phrase is 'the building seems quiet today.' This will not raise an alert if you speak it to the wrong person because it is Angel Sabbath, and most people will be going to the worship service at the city's temple. Chantal's response will be 'angels are always on call.'

"Since we are not certain that Chantal has received these passcodes, if your escort does not answer in this way, it might not be reason for alarm. She still might be Chantal. Yet, proceeding with the mission could be dangerous. Whether or not it should be scrubbed will be up to your discretion."

"He means," Jack said, "don't you dare screw this up. Do it or die trying."

"Your next step," Barks continued, "is to meet your temple contact in town, which necessitates a pass through a checkpoint. You should have your ID passes by now."

Ben reached into his jacket pocket and withdrew a trio of gray disks the size of an ancient silver dollar. He handed one each to Trudy and Jack.

"As you have experienced, there are more checkpoints traveling to the city than to angel headquarters. We believe the angels are preparing for a big event at the city's temple, but we haven't yet learned what it is. In any case, the purpose of your city visit is as follows: We received a cryptic message from our spy at the temple requesting a face-to-face meeting with a field agent to facilitate a message handoff. We have no pass phrases for that meeting. You will have to use your skills to find the spy and gain the knowledge she wishes to transmit."

Trudy glanced at Ben and Jack in turn. Their narrowed eyes made them look as puzzled as she felt. A spy in the temple? That was a revelation. At least they now knew the spy's gender.

"That is all the information we have at this time. If you encounter obstacles that require immediate assistance, contact satellite outpost seven using the newest security codes. I will be monitoring the transmissions."

Something clicked, and low static replaced the broadcast.

Trudy whistled. "Three words—what in blazes?"

"Yeah," Jack said. "This Chantal chick is buried pretty deep."

"Super deep. No contact in a year? I've never heard of that. What if she got discovered?"

Jack set a finger gun to his temple. "Then she's dead, and this mission's already shot."

Ben adjusted the rearview mirror to get a better look at Jack. "Already shot. Funny."

"It's not funny that Barks has this thing for female spies," Trudy said. "Ever since his granddaughter died in the first plague, it seems like he's trying to replace her. I wonder about his judgment sometimes. You know, too easily trusting someone who reminds him of her."

"And who's this mysterious spy in the city?" Jack asked.

"I've heard about her," Ben said. "Not sure what level she is, but most of the hierarchy are women, so it's no surprise that our spy is one as well."

Trudy clutched her throat. "Gag me. Can you imagine pretending to be an angel sycophant, sucking up to those monsters, kissing their *blessed* feet at the altar?"

"To keep from barfing," Ben said, "let's focus on what we know. Like the passcode. The building seems quiet today. Easy enough."

"Any idea who Chantal really is?" Trudy asked.

14

"Must be from another rebel base," Ben said. "Trudy's the only female field agent I've heard of. No. Wait. Remember when we took the resistance oath?"

"Yeah," Jack said. "Seems like forever ago."

"Anyway, there was another female in the line. Anyone remember her?"

Jack chuckled. "The skinny teen. A sure wash-out."

"Her name was Summer," Trudy said. "And don't be so mean. She had a good heart. Hated the angels with a passion."

Ben nodded. "She did have passion, but I guess she flaked out. I never saw her after Barks took her to the side, probably to tell her how tough the first PT drill would be. So back to the original point. Trudy's the only female I know of who made it. Not that they would tell me about others who trained elsewhere."

Trudy poked Ben's ribs. "You'd be the last person I'd tell. You're way overprotective. Too chivalrous."

"Wait. Just because I open a door for a woman, it doesn't mean—"

"Get real, Ben. I'm not talking about opening a door. Being a field agent is life or death, and you think a woman's life is worth more than your own. You can't do that. In the field, we have to be equals."

Ben rolled his eyes. "Stop parroting the training video. I know the spiel. But I have yet to meet a woman who walks that talk. When it comes to acting like a soldier, getting down and dirty, sleeping in fly-infested mud, washing in a cold river, and … and …"

"Peeing in a bottle," Jack said.

Ben and Trudy both turned and frowned at him.

He shrugged. "Just trying to help."

"Anyway," Ben continued, "in the first angel raids, every woman soldier I worked with flaked out. Every single one."

"Not Kat," Trudy said. "Well, she probably never peed in a bottle, but you know what I mean. She got down and dirty."

Ben nodded. "Okay. One exception. I'll give you that. Kat's one in a million."

"And me. I haven't flaked out."

"You haven't been tested. Let's hope it doesn't get that bad."

Trudy folded her hands tightly in her lap. After biting her lip, she whispered, "Don't worry. I won't let you down."

For the next couple of minutes, all was quiet as Ben drove the jeep into the valley. In the rear compartment, Jack took the containment capsules from their case, set them in a rectangular analyzer the size of a matchbox, and plugged it into the laptop computer provided by their mole. "I'm pushing an electronic signal into the capsules. We'll know if they're viable in a couple of minutes."

Trudy leaned over the seat and watched the operation. "They'd better be. Or we're sunk."

Now in the valley and on a wider road, Ben turned on the headlights. "You're not wrong. The only option would be to retreat and come up with a new plan before the invasion."

Trudy frowned. A new plan? The scouts said that angel forces would send invasion soldiers into their farming sector within days, not weeks or months. When the invaders finished spreading the contagion, every man, woman, and child would die. There was no time to come up with a new plan. This had to work.

She muttered under her breath, "Retreat is not an option."

Ben sighed. "I hear you, but those implant capsules are critical. With any other glitch, we can improvise."

"Not with the vaccine. If we can't get the real stuff from the angels—"

"Yeah, baby!" Jack pumped a fist as he stared at his laptop screen. "They're holding like champs."

"Good." Trudy gazed out her side window. Dawn's first rays appeared on the horizon, casting red highlights across thin clouds. "Looks like the show's on."

Chapter Three

Commander Barks descended the creaking stairs, a hand on the knotted pine rail to help his sore knees endure the effort. The aroma of freshly brewed tea filled the air, both a pleasant scent and a malevolent odor. Although humans enjoyed "angel tea" without harm, the angels' obsession with the concoction always raised reminders of their foul presence on earth, good enough reason to hate the stuff.

When he arrived at the bottom, he scanned the tiny chamber. Disguised as a tea storage room, it had changed somewhat since his previous visit a month earlier. Burlap bags of tea lined every wall from the rough concrete floor to the six-foot-high ceiling, not quite high enough to stand under without bumping his head. No casual visitor would guess that this was actually an anteroom leading to humanity's last hope for survival, that is, if the Garrison team failed.

A door on the opposite wall stood ajar, allowing the brew's aroma to pass through, much stronger than the dried leaves in the bags. The good doctor was likely working feverishly, as usual, and forgot to latch and lock the entry, a potentially fatal mistake.

Barks entered the narrow hall and closed the door behind him.

"Barks?" Doc called from the weapon room on the left. "Is that you?"

"Who else would it be?" Barks set the lock. "But if you leave the door open, no telling who might show up."

"Oh. My mistake." Doc walked into the hall, his gray hair disheveled and his flannel shirt and khaki cargo pants wrinkled. "Why are you here?"

"To give you an update. And to receive one."

"Oh. Good. Good." Doc let out a wide yawn and scratched his head. "I was wondering if there was some sort of surgery need that Trudy couldn't handle. Maybe an extraction."

"Nothing like that."

Doc gestured with a hand. "Come in."

As Barks walked toward the weapon room, he glanced through the open doorway on the hall's opposite side. A cot with a pillow and wadded sheet sat next to a wall, along with a nightstand and chair, Doc's meager accommodations when he spent the night, which had become more frequent of late. Urgency demanded his presence as the expected invasion drew near.

Barks entered the weapon room, about twice the size of the tea storage chamber. A desk with two large computer screens abutted the far wall, one showing the Oculus Gate and the other, columns of data. To the left of the desk, an alcove ran from floor to ceiling, more like a shallow pantry without a door than the housing of the weapon they had christened "Liberty."

He sat in one of two wheeled chairs while Doc sat in the other. "You first," Doc said, nodding.

Barks cleared his throat. "Well, the vaccine mission is proceeding today, even as we speak. The Garrisons are on their way to angel headquarters."

"Terribly dangerous." Doc folded his hands tightly. "I will be praying for them."

"Pray, yes, but finishing the weapon would be an answer to my prayers. I hope you have good news."

Doc rose from his chair. "Are you finished with your news?"

"Yes. The details of the mission are unimportant. You've been briefed on them, and nothing of significance has changed."

"Very well. I have news of one advance." Doc pushed a hand into Liberty's alcove. Light flashed on within, illuminating a missile-like object that stood with its nose as high as Doc's shoulder. "The connection with the angels' conduit is now secure. The missile will have no trouble flying into their source of power."

Barks gave him a thumbs-up. "Congratulations. That's excellent news."

Doc withdrew his hand, shutting off the light. "I suppose it is, but tests on the warhead have been inconsistent. Since it's based on photo neurons instead of gunpowder, it takes a neural component to maintain its charge."

Barks chuckled. "You lost me. I have no idea what you're talking about."

"Trust me, if not for Kat's notes, I wouldn't either. When she designed the weapon, I asked her to document everything so that a third-grader could understand it."

"Smart move. But do you have a solution to the problem?"

"Maybe. Since the human body has a neural capacity, I can be the catalyst myself and create a photon explosion here in this room." Doc slid his hands into his pockets and shifted uneasily. "A much smaller one, of course. Otherwise, it would disintegrate me. But during tests, when I let go of the warhead, the neural network always began falling apart. I don't think the missile can make it to the Oculus Gate before the network deteriorates too much."

"Can you make the missile fly faster?"

Doc sat in his chair. "Not a chance. You see, when I open the conduit, whatever is in the chamber is pulled at a set speed, no matter the size of the projectile we tested, and it's already much faster than what we could accomplish with traditional rocketry."

"So, in theory, could someone hold the warhead and take it to the Oculus? Would that keep the network active?"

"Almost certainly, but it would be a suicide mission. First, the volunteer would need a pressurized space suit to fly that high, though I don't think he'd require an air tank for the short journey, because, second, when the warhead is activated, it would obliterate the flyer. If I am unable to come up with a solution to the neural component issue, I will be the human missile."

Barks lifted a hand. "I was about to volunteer myself."

Doc smiled. "Two old widowers vying for heroic immortality. Perhaps we should flip a coin."

"You're on. But do we have a pressurized suit?"

"Working on it. I should have one by the end of the day. Since we're approximately the same size, it should fit either of us."

"Excellent. But what about your other tests? Are you sure that destroying the Oculus will destroy the angels as well?"

"Without a doubt. We know the connection to the Gate gives angels their power, so my theory, and Kat's, has always been that cutting off the source will cause them to shrivel and eventually die. The last time we captured an implanted human and I extracted the angel, I isolated it in a small capsule that repels the frequency at which the angels communicate with the Gate. Indeed, it did morph into a dry, wrinkled mass, much like a raisin. It was quite dead."

"And what happens to the human host?"

Doc waved a finger. "Therein lies another problem. The angel transforms from a massless light to a physical form. With its tentacles implanted in a brain stem, it would surely kill its host. We couldn't possibly extract them in time. Maybe we could save a few people close at hand, but not the number of humans we believe to be implanted."

Barks nodded. "Last estimate is twenty-three hundred."

"Way too many, but wouldn't it be better for the world if they gave their lives for the greater good?"

"They wouldn't be *giving* their lives. Some volunteered to be implanted. I don't care what those traitors suffer. But many were abducted. They have no choice, whether to be implanted or to be martyrs later. It's not like they're soldiers doing their duty."

Doc sighed. "Yes. Of course, you're right. It's a ghastly predicament they're in."

Barks laid his hands on his aching knees and massaged them. "I can't worry about that. I have to save millions of lives and leave the rest to God. I don't know what else to do."

Doc gave him a grim nod. "I concur."

"And we shouldn't be the only two who know about that option. The suicide mission, I mean. In theory, something might prevent us from completing it. Then all would be lost."

"Whom should we tell? The Garrisons?"

Barks shook his head. "Their plates are full. And they're locked undercover in the field. Getting a message to them would be difficult."

"What about the girl you brought here blindfolded? The young redhead. What was her name?"

"Iona. And I didn't intend to bring her here. It was my only option. She was close to finding the weapon. And, no, I won't tell her. She's proving herself useful as our agent now, but since she worked for the angels in the past, I can't trust her with this information. It's too important."

"Chantal?" Doc asked. "If the message is properly encoded, an interception wouldn't do us any harm."

"Nor any good if she's been compromised. We have to be sure that someone knows our options. Besides the two of us, I mean."

"Then send a coded message to Chantal and leave another for the Garrisons, somewhere they're sure to find it. I'll write the instructions on how the warhead works. I'll leave it to you to encode everything."

Barks nodded. "Like I said, contacting the Garrisons will be difficult, especially in the near future, but it's probably the best solution. I'll see to Chantal's message right away."

"Good." Doc rose from his chair. "I should go home. The batteries are running low, and the angel guard isn't due to start the water pump's generator for a few hours." He tapped a key on the keyboard. "Maybe I'll return when the batteries recharge, though I'm not sure banging my head against the wall is going to solve the neural-component problem."

"Then let's end the head banging now. No more work on Liberty. One of us will take her to the Oculus Gate." Barks pushed a hand into his pocket and withdrew a quarter. "Heads or tails?"

"That's not one of your magic trick coins, is it?"

"No. It's real. Make your choice."

"I often feel like the butt of a bad joke, so I will choose tails."

"Okay. Heads I take Liberty to Hell's Gate. Tails you take her."

Barks flipped the quarter into the air. Both men watched it sail in a fast spin until it hit the floor.

Ben drove the jeep slowly toward the checkpoint station and stopped behind a van, the only vehicle waiting to be processed. He, Trudy, and Jack held their pass disks, their thumbs on the ID face. When the van drove on, Ben lowered the driver's window, pulled closer, and stopped next to a uniformed guard holding a computer pad.

"Disks," he said as he scanned the interior.

The trio passed the disks to him. At the center of each flat surface, a thumbprint glowed, indicating that its owner had pressed the ID sensor within the last thirty seconds. One at a time, the guard fed them into the tablet, read the screen, and took them out. When he finished, he handed them back to Ben. "What's in the cooler?"

"Vaccine for the temple." Ben nodded toward Trudy. "She and I are doctors. Our assistant's in the back."

The guard looked at Trudy, then at Jack. "I'm going to the temple for my vaccination when I get off duty. The angels know best how to avoid a third plague, right?"

Ben spoke through a tight smile. "Right. The angels know best."

The guard waved an arm. "Proceed."

"Thank you." Ben raised the window and drove away on a main thoroughfare. "What time do the vaccinations start here?"

"Noon," Trudy said. "Everyone in the city will be at the temple."

"Right. Angel Sabbath. Explains why traffic is so light."

As he motored on, they passed a series of churches, the windows and doors boarded. A sign posted in front of each bore the familiar message in block letters— "To ensure spiritual harmony, all worship will take place at the central temple. We are now free of divisions. We are one."

"We are one," Ben whispered. "The second biggest lie the angels tell."

"Okay," Jack said. "I'll bite. What tops that lie?"

"I'll show you."

Seconds later, they passed a billboard that read "Violent crimes committed year to date." A number in an electronic display showed a numeral three. Then more text followed. "Security is the greatest blessing."

"There it is."

Jack peered at the billboard through the window. "What's wrong? Crime *is* way down."

"Don't be a jerk. Of course crime is down. When you crush people under your heel, they'll obey. The lie's the second part."

"Just pushing one of your many hot buttons, Bro. You're an easy mark."

Ben eyed Jack in the rearview mirror. "As if you don't have any hot buttons."

"Yeah." Jack averted his eyes. "I'm busted."

After another minute or so, Ben drove under the temple's portico. Three men stood next to the doorway, one tall and two short. Dressed in black from their dusty cloaks to their mud-caked hiking boots, they looked like they had recently arrived from a long journey.

"Huntsmen," Jack said.

Trudy turned toward him. "Who are they?"

"A bizarre cult. They always travel in threes. Tall one's the alpha, the one who tracks the scent like a bloodhound. If he's like the others, he took the name of a constellation. Angels probably wouldn't let them in. If they were on a hunt, they haven't bathed recently."

"I've heard they're relentless." Ben eyed the tall one. His shaggy, nearly shoulder-length hair, protruding brow, and perpetual scowl gave him a menacing aspect, and his three-day scruff meant that his journey had been relatively short. He was probably good at his game. "Any idea how the alpha gets his talent?"

"Sensory-deprivation training. Candidates shut off all sensory input except sense of smell and then live their lives that way. The ones born with the talent take only a few days to train their noses. Others take weeks. Most fail completely."

"Interesting."

Trudy shoved Ben's shoulder. "Go on. The longer you wait, the more they'll think you're intimidated by them."

"I'm not intimidated. I'm sizing them up."

"They're mercenaries," Jack said. "They won't bother you unless they get paid to do it. Just focus on finding whoever wants to hand off a message. Then we'll scram."

"That's my plan." Leaving the engine running, Ben got out and strode directly to a pair of massive glass-paned front doors. As he passed the trio, the tall one, his arms crossed at his chest, spoke in a gruff tone while chewing on a toothpick. "Are you my courier?"

Ben halted and faced the alpha, tilting his head upward to look him in the eye. "Are you expecting a delivery?"

"I am. Name's Leo. The boys and I rounded up a fugitive. They wanted him alive, but he won't be alive for long."

"So you're expecting the bounty." Ben shook his head. "No, that's not why I'm here."

Leo sniffed. "I should've guessed. You're from the farmlands, not the city."

"Oh? What gave me away?"

"Your scent, Farmer Jones." He shifted the toothpick from one side of his mouth to the other. "Camp stove heating oil, traces of chicken manure, alfalfa hay. The usual. Most likely from the next county to the east, though. They don't grow alfalfa around here."

"That's impressive. I'm sure you're worth every penny they pay you."

"Yep. I always find my man … or woman. Gender doesn't matter to me, as long as I get paid."

"A skilled laborer deserves high compensation." After giving Leo a friendly nod, Ben opened one of the doors and entered. Inside the spacious, carpeted lobby, a security camera perched near the ceiling at every corner. From a side room, a young woman approached, silky red hair draping her shoulders and a sea of freckles dotting her cheeks. Wearing a white robe tied at the waist with a black sash and standing barely taller than five feet, she had the stature of a young teen, though her serious countenance made her appear at least twenty.

"I am Priestess Iona," she said as she smiled and folded her hands in front. "May I help you?"

Ben raised his brow. "I thought you might already know why I'm here."

"Oh. I apologize. It's too early for that."

He studied her youthful face and bright eyes. Too naïve to be a mole. Still, her ambiguous reply invited further probing. "Too early for what?"

"For the vaccinations." Her smile wilted. "What were you hoping for?"

"What else is available?"

She folded her hands behind her and rocked back and forth, again appearing younger. "Well, we have information about our holy angels. The temple holds a wealth of knowledge. It's never too early for that."

Ben looked through the door at the jeep. Trudy gave him her hurry-up glare.

He nodded and faced the priestess again. He had to go for broke. "Do you have any secret information that you normally don't divulge to commoners?"

Her brow lifted. After a furtive glance at the nearest camera, she gave him an exaggerated nod. "Oh, you mean the esoterica."

"Maybe. What is it?"

"I'm sorry, but I'm not allowed to provide that to any outsiders." She extended her hand. "It's too bad that you had to come here for nothing."

As he reached toward her, something slipped out of her sleeve into her palm. He grabbed her hand and allowed her to transfer the item, then pull away.

He closed his fingers around the object, a small disk. "Thank you for your help."

Worry in her eyes, she whispered, "Don't let Commander Barks know."

"Understood." Ben pivoted and walked toward the door at a casual pace. Outside, the huntsmen were nowhere in sight. Maybe a temple agent paid them for their work, and they had no reason to stick around.

When Ben reached the jeep and boarded, he drove out of view and gave the disk to Jack. "What do you make of this?"

He turned the watch-face-sized disk over a couple of times in his fingers. "Magnetic media. Old school. We don't have anything with us that'll read it."

Ben turned down a road leading out of town. "Where can we get a reader?"

"Home, for sure. Maybe at angel HQ. Risky to try to read it there, though."

"We might get a chance. The way the girl—Priestess Iona— acted, it has to be important. And she said not to let Barks know. She was young. Scared."

"Okay," Jack said. "That's mysterious. Barks is a patriot. Why would this girl want to keep a secret from him?"

Trudy eyed the disk. "Sometimes Barks carries too much on his shoulders. Maybe another rebel faction thinks this data needs to get into the hands of other patriots."

"She took a big risk." Ben extended his hand. "That's a plus on her side. We'll figure out a way to read it and then decide what to do."

"Sounds good." Jack dropped the disk into Ben's palm. "Keep me informed."

After getting checked at the city limits again, they drove into a hilly forest. This rural area, like their farming region, stayed free of checkpoints, though they would soon have to get past a much stricter security screening—and face certain death if the plan failed.

Chapter Four

Ben drove within a half mile of angel headquarters and stopped at the side of the road on a hilltop. From their vantage point, the complex lay in view, a network of buildings that ranged in height from one to three stories. With treed courtyards, a swimming pool, and four tennis courts, it looked like a resort, which it actually once was, though the razor-wire-topped chain-link fence surrounding the campus made it look more like a prison.

Ben twisted in his seat toward Jack. "You're on foot from here."

"Yeah, I get the fun jobs because you two are so pretty." Carrying a laptop computer and a briefcase that held his communications equipment, he got out and looked in through the open door. "Don't forget your earbuds." He closed the door and quick-marched on a trail that led into the dense forest.

"Our turn," Ben said. "Time to get pretty."

Trudy smirked. "Easy for me. We'll have to work on you, though. Good thing you brought a razor."

After getting their white medical lab coats and green scrubs from the suitcase, putting them on, and inserting their earbuds, Ben quickly shaved his scruff with a battery-operated razor. He then shifted the jeep into gear and drove down to the valley where he turned into an outer HQ lot, mostly vacant because of Angel Sabbath, and parked next to the wooded path that led to the security gate. "Game face on, Sis."

"Born that way."

"I gotta admit. That's true."

They exited the jeep and stood on the path. Ben straightened his shoulders, filling out his lab coat. "So do I look like a brilliant doctor?"

"Doctor? Yes. Brilliant? I guess we'll see about that."

He rolled his eyes. "Thanks for the vote of confidence."

"Not a problem." She scanned him. "Earbud's out of sight. Glad you got a haircut yesterday. Crew is a good look on you. And bonus points for smelling good."

He sniffed an armpit. "That huntsman said I smelled like chicken manure and alfalfa hay, but I can't detect it."

"Me neither." She rotated slowly. "See anything off kilter?"

As she turned, Ben scanned her strong yet lithe form, nearly identical to Kat's five-foot-seven frame. Trudy's long, dark hair also matched, but her brown eyes looked nothing like Kat's sparkling emeralds.

He reached for Trudy's lab coat pocket, withdrew her stethoscope a few inches, and let the earpieces hang out front. "There. Perfect."

"Good." Trudy touched a fender on the jeep. "Jack has the other key, right?"

"He'd better. It's a long walk to the rendezvous point."

"Do you have the disk from the temple?"

Ben patted his pants pocket. "Right here. Shouldn't raise a flag."

"Okay, then." She nodded toward the security gate. "Ready, Dr. Kidd?"

Ben took her hand and intertwined his fingers with hers. "Ready, Dr. Kidd."

She glanced at the hand clasp, then eyed him. "Fine. But don't you dare try to kiss me."

"I'd rather kiss a cactus. Less prickly."

Trudy half closed an eye, failing to suppress a grin. "Oh, you're so funny."

"I try to be." He strode forward, pulling her along. "Let's go."

As they walked toward the gate, they entered the main parking lot and passed a black airship moored with a chain to a thick post near the access road. Large enough to carry ten passengers, the ship boasted huge swiveling, drone-like propellers, probably a luxury transport for angel royalty, like the queen and her entourage.

Although no one outside of HQ knew what the queen's current host human looked like, since she shed her human and implanted herself in another from time to time, word had it that she always traveled in style.

Ben shook off the thoughts and touched his earbud. "Comm check."

"Loud and clear," Jack said. "I'm in position. The passwords checked out. Got a computer link to the operating room and control of the security cameras."

"Are our handprints in the database now?"

"Locked and loaded, but there's a problem. A pretty big one."

"What?"

"Turns out that the handprints and names are matched as primary keys."

"What does that mean?" Trudy asked.

"It means that I had to use your real records. I altered them to match the histories we cooked up, but I couldn't change your names."

Ben grimaced. "But our fake personas are the ones scheduled for implantation."

"Not anymore. I hacked into the surgery database. You and Trudy are now on the schedule under your real names."

"The angels are expecting two doctors named Kidd. This will never work."

"You said yourself that we can improvise if we run into a glitch. Well, this is a glitch. It's time to improvise."

"Easy for you to say. You're not walking straight into the jaws of hell."

"For me it's more like the jaws of heck," Jack said, "but if I'm caught, I'm still a dead man. I've got the plasma rifle, but how long will that last against a dozen angel assassins and their laser eyes?"

Ben nodded. "About ten seconds."

"Or less. I feel like I've been hung out to dry. Not enough leaves around to hide me in this tree. We did the trial run during the summer. Lots of leaves then."

Ben drew a mental picture of Jack sitting with a laptop in the treehouse built weeks ago for this mission, a platform high enough to send a line-of-sight signal to the angel compound's receiver without passing through the fence and getting scrambled by its built-in jammer. The idea was primitive, but apparently it worked. "All right. We'll improvise."

"Yep," Jack said. "No turning back now. Give me an okay, and I'll go silent till I hear from you again."

"Okay. Might as well go silent now." Ben halted at a high chain-link gate attached to a fence lined at the top with razor wire.

A security drone hovered in front, its tiny propellers whirring. The size of a dinner plate and shaped like a storybook flying saucer, it scanned their clothes with a spotlight beam. "Metallic items found," it said with a robotic voice. "Two stethoscopes, and one metallic box. Open the box to allow inspection."

Trudy withdrew a small first-aid kit from her coat pocket and opened it, revealing their stash of medical supplies. After the drone's quick scan, it said, "No weapons detected." The beam shifted to Ben's face. "Human male with no implant. What is your passcode?"

Ben blinked at the light. "Four, one, x-ray, golf, seven."

"Expose your palm."

He opened his hand. The drone's light scanned his palm from base to fingertips. "Identification match. Benjamin Brock Garrison, MD. Implantation scheduled for eight a.m." The drone shifted to Trudy and flashed its beam in her face. "Human female with no implant. What is your passcode?"

She glanced at Ben for a split second. "Seven, six, delta, Oscar, nine."

"Expose your palm."

She complied. After scanning her hand, the drone's light dimmed. "Identification match. Gertrude Elmira Garrison, MD.

Implantation scheduled for eight a.m." The gate clicked and crawled to the side along its ground runner. "Proceed to the surgery ward, second level."

As they walked on, again hand in hand, Trudy spoke softly. "I wanted my new name."

"You heard Jack." Ben focused on the building straight ahead, barely moving his lips. "He changed your history. You're a twenty-five-year-old doctor now. Deal with it."

"Easy for you to say. You like your name."

"True." He glanced at her face in profile. Her features tightened, much like Mom's did during pain spasms not long before she died in the second plague. "You should be proud. You're named after prominent ancestors."

Trudy grumbled. "Their ghosts must've held a gun to Mom's head."

"Don't be a name bigot." Ben passed between two of several Corinthian columns and stopped at the complex's entry, a pair of metal-framed glass doors embedded in marble walls. He pulled one of the doors open. "Game face on, Gertrude."

"It's on, Benji." Trudy breezed in and marched across a cavernous lobby with a high arched ceiling, much like the interior of a cathedral. "Get your butt moving. We're going to be late."

Ben caught up, grasped her wrist, and slowed her pace. "Let's be a little late. If we put them behind schedule, they'll be in a hurry, less likely to ask questions."

As they walked together through the empty chamber, their footsteps echoed. "It's like a mausoleum in here," Trudy whispered. "I wonder if they all go to the city temple for angel worship or if they have an altar in the building."

"It might help to know. Keep your eyes open for clues."

As they approached the bottom of a spiral staircase where a statue of a winged angel peered at them from each side, Ben gazed at one of the marble faces, at least three feet higher than his head.

"Biblical archangels. Michael and Gabriel. The warrior and the herald."

Trudy stopped at the staircase, reached up, and touched one of Michael's intricately carved wings. "It's weird. Practically no one questions why the fake angels never talk about God. Just the media references to someone watching us through the Oculus."

"Right," Ben said. "The emperor has no clothes, and the people are afraid to mention it."

"And no wonder. Easy way to get the axe."

"Or implanted."

They strolled up the curving stairway, then along a hall while scanning the direction signs on the walls. When they found the surgery ward, Ben opened the door and ambled in, Trudy close behind.

A tall, round-faced woman wearing green scrubs and staring at a clipboard stood in the reception area, most of her auburn hair tucked under a surgical cap. A badge on her pocket read "Donna Elder, M.D." She looked at Ben and Trudy, then at her wristwatch. "I was expecting you five minutes ago. We should never keep angels waiting, especially those who have just been drawn from the hive."

"The security drone delayed us," Ben said. "Apparently our names were entered incorrectly."

Dr. Elder ran a finger along the clipboard page. "Aren't you Dr. Jonas Kidd and Dr. Michelle Kidd? Husband and wife?"

"We're husband and wife and both doctors, but we're Benjamin and Trudy—um, Gertrude—Garrison. Your printout is probably old."

Dr. Elder withdrew a mobile phone from her pocket and ran a thumb along the screen. After staring at it for a few seconds, she nodded. "Checks out. Your names are on the schedule."

"Good. And sorry about the delay."

"Sure. Sure. Whatever." She opened a door behind her and waved them on. "Like I said, we shouldn't keep angels, especially these, waiting. They're from the Sixth Level."

Ben took Trudy's hand and walked into a hallway. An open door marked Operating Room #1 led to a spacious chamber. Inside, three surgical beds stood under adjustable spotlights hanging from the ceiling, and various computers and lab equipment sat on counters and tables around the perimeter.

Dr. Elder joined them and gestured toward the operating room. "Take your shoes and lab coats off and choose a bed. I'll bring the angels here in a moment." She walked down the hall, then turned out of sight.

Ben stepped into the operating room, followed by Trudy. "We're in, Jack," he said in a low tone. "We don't have much time. Surgeon is Dr. Donna Elder."

"Got it," Jack said through Ben's earbud. "I found you on the camera feeds. I'm searching for a recorded surgery in that room now."

"Sixth Level?" Trudy whispered. "I guess that means Gen Six. I've never heard of anything higher than five."

"Same here." Ben slipped off his shoes, shed his lab coat, and laid it on a bed rail. "Let's hope our capsules can contain them. If they leak, we're implanted for real."

"And *that* would take improvising to a new level." Trudy kicked off her shoes and laid her coat with Ben's. "But no turning back."

"Nope. We're past the point of no return." Ben climbed onto the first bed on the left and searched the room for a camera. So far, nothing obvious.

Trudy chose the bed next to his and lay on her side, facing him. "Jack. We probably have only a few seconds left."

"Cool your jets," Jack said. "I've been watching an implantation at triple speed. Dr. Elder operates without a nurse. She injects the angel into the capsule with a hypodermic needle, just like we thought. She makes the incision behind the right ear, which is good to know. I've seen scars on the left side. Now we don't have to guess. Not that you care, but the probe she uses looks like a number eight. It's thin enough to push the capsule deep. Then the angel's tentacles will break through the capsule, and it'll squeeze past any tiny gap in the skull it can find, then it'll wrap around the brain stem. And I count three stitches to close the incision."

Trudy repositioned her earbud. "Perfect. That's all we need."

"Do you have the sedative ready?" Jack asked.

"Oh. Right. She'll probably start with Ben. He's on the first bed." Trudy passed a pen across the gap between the beds. Ben took it and slid it into his shirt pocket.

"By the way," Jack said. "I see you from your right side. Block the camera as soon as your surgeon's knocked out. I turned off the recorder, but I can't shut off the passive view like we hoped. That means the security guards can still watch, but the audio is off on both sides unless they intentionally turn it on. I'm distracting them with a feed of a gorgeous woman in the rear parking lot primping in her reflection in a car window. Let's hope they stare for a while and can't tell it's a loop I made when I did recon last week."

"How'd you manage that?" Ben asked. "You said you can't shut off the passive view."

"I passed by that camera on the way in. Easy change. Put it on a timer I started a few seconds ago. Had it planned for a while."

"Good thinking."

"Thanks. But the timer's set to stop the loop real soon. So get that camera blocked ASAP. When you do, they might think it's just a glitch. At least it should buy you some time."

To the right, Ben spotted a hole in a picture frame carrying a portrait of Imperial President Natalie Logan, the queen angel's first choice as a host. Her deep brown irises and dark eyebrows stood in contrast to her golden hair and fair skin. In person, her glowing face made the contrast even more striking. It was hard for anyone to take his eyes off her. But that was before the queen shed her, like a viper that outgrew its old skin.

Dr. Elder entered, wearing gloves and a mask and carrying a stainless-steel tray that held a few surgical instruments and two small syringes with attached needles. Liquid inside the syringes glowed bright red. "Dr. Benjamin Garrison, you will be hosting Ejardi, and Dr. Gertrude Garrison, you will be hosting Joquile." She set the tray on an overtable and rolled it next to Ben's bed. As she transferred the tray's items to the table, she glanced between them and Ben. "I'm sure you're honored that you have been chosen for this blessed task."

"Indeed," Ben said. "We took the prep classes, but no one said anything about Sixth Level. What's new about them?"

Dr. Elder frowned. "That's odd. The information is in the new instructional video."

Ben looked at Trudy. "Hon? Did I miss something?"

She shook her head. "Maybe ours wasn't updated."

"The Sixth Level," Dr. Elder said as she transferred the now-empty tray to a counter, "has only one enhancement over the Fifth Level. Your wings will sprout in hours rather than days. You will be flying tomorrow."

"Excellent," Trudy said. "That's exciting."

Dr. Elder nodded. "I requested hosting myself, because I've always wanted to fly. They told me to wait a while longer for a higher generation. Being a stronger angel will be my reward for my faithful service here. Maybe now that Level Six has arrived, my application will finally be approved." She set the needle closer to Ben's arm. "Are you ready?"

"Wait." Ben took the pen from his pocket and lifted it close to the doctor's face. "Will you put it on the counter for me?"

Dr. Elder raised a gloved hand. "I'm sterile. We don't want contamination."

"Sorry. You're right." Ben clicked the pen's button. The tip sent a stream of gray smoke into the doctor's face. The moment she inhaled, her eyes rolled upward, and she collapsed to the floor.

Chapter Five

Ben leaped out of the bed, grabbed the instrument tray from the counter, and leaned it against the portrait, blocking the camera. Trudy retrieved the lab coats, withdrew the first-aid kit from hers, and set it on the table.

When she flipped it open, they each took a pair of sterile gloves and a syringe filled with a topical anesthetic and injected each other behind the right ear. Trudy plucked the capsule case from the kit, opened it, and used Dr. Elder's syringes to infuse each capsule with an angel. She then picked up the scalpel and took a deep breath. "Now the fun part, though I might not be sterile anymore after opening the capsule case."

Ben lay on a bed, his back toward Trudy. "Just do it."

She set one hand on his head and pushed the blade against his skin with the other. "Cutting now." Pressure followed but no pain. "Assuming the labels are correct, I put Ejardi inside, and you are now officially implanted." She picked up a suturing needle and thread. "You don't need more than two stitches, but I'll add a third in case someone counts."

While she worked, Ben, moving only his eyes, scanned the room for a device that might read the disk the temple priestess supplied but found none. When Trudy finished, they traded places. He made a tiny slice behind her ear, inserted the other capsule, and began the stitching process, dabbing at the blood with gauze as he pushed the needle into her skin. "You bleed a lot more than the cadavers did."

"Hard to get living volunteers for practice." She winced. "Too deep."

"Sorry."

"It's all right. Just hurry." As he continued stitching, Trudy stared at the doctor's unconscious form. "If Gen Sixes get their wings as fast as she said, we've got problems."

"Right. The other powers are easy to hide, like Gen Three's night vision and Gen Four's eye lasers and mind reading." Ben tied the third stitch. "If people know about a Six's abilities, they'll question why we're wingless. We might have to shorten our timetable."

Something beeped. A voice came through a hidden speaker. "Is everything all right there? The camera's gone black."

Ben whispered, "Security guard."

"Fine," Trudy said, trying to imitate Dr. Elder. "I'll check it out in a minute. I'm in the middle of an implantation."

"Dr. Elder? Is that you? You sound different."

Trudy coughed. "I caught a bit of a cold. Good thing for the patient that I'm wearing a mask."

"And for the blessed angels," the guard said. "I'll be up there in a couple of minutes to have a look at the camera."

"Give me ten. I'll be done with the procedure by then."

"Ten it is."

The moment the voice clicked off, Trudy rose from the bed and smacked herself on the forehead. "I can't believe I said ten minutes. I should've said twenty."

"We can do it." Ben stripped off the gloves, retrieved the skin-glow tube from the box, and squeezed a white dollop onto his fingers. "Hold still." He spread the cream across Trudy's face, neck, and under her shirt to her shoulders.

As she did the same to him, she kept her voice low. "What if Gen Sixes glow in other places, like their hands?"

"We'll just say the glow hasn't spread that far yet."

When she finished, they scanned each other. Trudy's face was already emanating a slight radiance. "It's working," Ben said.

She touched his cheek and smiled. "Now *that's* the brother I remember. The glow whenever Kat walked in the room."

38

Ben allowed that image to enter his mind for a moment, then pushed it away. "Yeah. I suppose so." He capped the tube and set it back in the box. "Let's grab anything that might be useful."

Trudy collected a scalpel, forceps, and a clamp and put them in her lab coat pocket, then removed smelling salts from the supply kit, closed the lid, and slid the box into her pocket. "Sorry about the Kat remark."

"No, no. Not your fault. You'd think after eight months I'd have a tougher skin." Ben nodded at the doctor. "Time to wake her. Remember our training. We're angels now."

"Smug and pretentious. Got it." Trudy knelt next to Dr. Elder, removed her surgical mask, and passed the smelling salts under her nose.

She jerked and snapped her eyes open. "What happened? Why am I on the floor?"

Ben and Trudy each grasped an arm and helped her rise. "You are on the floor," Ben said in an even tone, "because your legs would no longer support you."

"And the force of gravity pulled you downward," Trudy added. "The mystery lies in the cause of your malfunctioning legs."

Dr. Elder blinked at them in turn. "You're glowing. The procedure's already done."

"It is." Ben tilted his head. "Is your memory failing as well?"

Dr. Elder massaged the back of her head and scanned the room. "It seems so, but everything is out of place." She pointed at the tray leaning against the portrait. "How did that get there?"

"Another mystery has arisen," Trudy said. "If you want us to consult the stars, you may beseech us now."

"Oh! Pardon me, blessed ones!" Dr. Elder dropped to her knees. "I have been speaking as a mad woman. I am not in my right mind. Forgive me, I beg you."

Trudy touched the top of her head. "Rise, good doctor. Your deficit is obvious. No harm has been done."

"Thank you, Ejardi." She climbed to her feet and faced Ben. "And you, as well, Joquile."

Ben read the doctor's eyes. They seemed skeptical. Maybe her misuse of names was a test. "Why do you call me Joquile? I am Ejardi." Ben nodded toward Trudy. "She is Joquile."

Dr. Elder swallowed hard. "Yes, of course. My brain is still woozy. But if you will pardon me one last time, I must finish the post-operative exam." She opened a drawer under a counter, withdrew a light-check wand, and turned it on, activating a purple glow. The moment she passed the wand in front of Ben's face, it beeped. She read a tiny screen on the handle. "Yes, Ejardi is definitely within."

When she shifted toward Trudy, Trudy grabbed her wrist and twisted it, making her drop the wand. As she grimaced, Trudy's face hardened. "You take too many liberties, Doctor. If he is Ejardi, exactly who do you think I am? Only one identity remains."

"You're right. You're right." Dr. Elder leaned to the side as if trying to see around her. "At least allow me to check your stitches. Since my state of mind was crippled, I'm concerned that—"

"No!" Trudy twisted harder. "You will cease the suspicious behavior immediately."

Gasping, Dr. Elder nodded. "Yes. Of course. Please forgive me."

"Only if you make no more mistakes." Trudy shoved her away and looked at Ben. "It is time to conduct our mission."

"Yes, Joquile." Ben turned toward Dr. Elder. "Where is the vaccine stored?"

She rubbed her wrist, her expression tight. "In the vault downstairs. I will send a drone to guide you when you reach the first floor. It will scan you for access to the vault."

Ben patted the doctor's cheek and spoke in a kind tone. "I suggest that we all forget what happened here. It would not look good on your record."

She nodded vigorously. "Consider it forgotten. And thank you."

Ben and Trudy marched at a quick angel pace out of the room, through the waiting area, and into the second-floor hallway. As they descended the stairs, Ben whispered, "Why did you get rough with her?"

"She was trying to look at the stitches. She might know they aren't hers. And, besides, I wanted to give her a show of physical strength. Angels endow their hosts with extra power, and I'm stronger than the average woman, especially one my size."

"Without a doubt." Ben adjusted his earbud's position. "Jack, we're heading toward the first level, and we figured out a way to get to the vaccine if Chantal doesn't show. Everything's good here so far."

"Not as good as you think. The doctor entered a security alert. You're going to be shadowed by an angel. Be ready. They know their own kind."

"Understood. You're done here, Jack. See you at the rendezvous point."

"You bet. When I get there … Uh-oh. Bogey spotted me. Five others with him. Erasing everything. Scrambling signal. Heading for the refuge. Good luck."

Ben halted on the stairs. "Jack?" The earbud emitted static. Ben plucked it out and slid it into his pocket. "If they catch Jack, we're compromised."

Trudy removed her earbud. "Do we abort?"

"No. We're too close. Maybe we can escape with the vaccine before they figure out what's going on. It's time to watch for Chantal. Remember. The building seems quiet today."

"Are you going to say it? Or am I?"

"I will."

They hurried down the staircase and rounded the final turn. The first level came into view, still void of people—angels or otherwise. "No sign of anyone yet," Trudy said as they neared the bottom. "Let's take it easy."

They slowed their pace, looking in every direction. When they stopped at floor level, a security drone buzzed toward them, carrying a tray holding three cups filled with some kind of steaming brew. A tall, dark-haired woman followed. Wearing a form-fitting navy-blue blouse and a tan knee-length skirt over a near-perfect figure, she looked like a supermodel dressed for office work, except for the huge pair of wings spreading behind her as if she were posing to impress the newly implanted angels.

A spherical pendant hung from a thin chain around her neck. A trio of thin metal bands encircled a glowing marble, like ribbons of electrons orbiting a nucleus, as if protecting a fragile treasure within. Touching her skin an inch or two below her throat, the pendant cast a white aura across her chest, eerie and alluring.

Ben glanced at Trudy and whispered, "Chantal?"

Trudy spoke through a fake smile. "I doubt it."

The woman halted in front of them and smiled, adding to her face's radiant glow. "Welcome. I am Novada."

"Greetings, Novada," Ben and Trudy said at the same time.

"First, the traditional toast to our newest arrivals." Novada lifted two of the cups from the drone's tray and handed one each to Ben and Trudy. "Angel tea. Freshly picked in our own plantation."

"Excellent." Ben took his cup and inhaled the earthy aroma. Rumors said angels drank it because it was supposed to strengthen their attachment to their hosts, but Doc said the idea was nonsense. It caused no effects whatsoever, except for a huge caffeine boost. "The scent is pleasant."

"And the taste is even better." Novada took the third cup and lifted it. "To Joquile and Ejardi, may you serve the hive queen with honor and loyalty."

Ben and Trudy lifted their cups as well. Not knowing what to say, Ben kept his cup high, waiting for a cue from Novada. Trudy followed suit.

When Novada lowered the cup and sipped the tea, Ben did the same. A spicy tang ran along his tongue and down his throat, warm and soothing. "It's very good."

Trudy sipped hers and nodded. "A refreshing treat."

"Then enjoy." Novada downed the rest of hers and set the cup on the tray.

Ben and Trudy did the same. As Ben set the cup on the tray, he eyed Novada's wings. Unlike the white feathery representations depicted in Renaissance artwork, they were similar to leathery skin—supple and smooth, somehow more humanlike, though even thinking that way seemed contradictory.

Novada cocked her head. "Is something wrong? You're staring."

Ben blinked. "Oh. I apologize. I was admiring your wings. They are lovely."

"Thank you." She flapped them slowly. "It's natural for you to admire them. I'm sure you are looking forward to getting your own."

"We both are."

Trudy gestured toward the sphere. "I was admiring your pendant. What is it?"

Novada touched one of the pendant's surrounding bands. "I call it a homing orb, but this is no time to explain its meaning."

"Are we in a hurry?" Ben asked as he scanned the area once more. "The building seems quiet today."

"True, but that will change after worship hours." Novada nodded to the drone as it hovered nearby. "Proceed."

The drone's front light turned on and scanned Ben's face. During the identification procedure, he resisted the urge to look at Trudy to gauge her reaction to the missing passcode phrase. They were in trouble, but a decision to abort the mission or continue could wait. For some reason Novada believed their tale so far. Maybe Chantal had briefed her with enough information to make her believe they were angel allies but didn't get a chance to relay the planned phrase response. On the other hand, maybe Chantal had been captured and now sat in prison, or worse.

When the drone finished, it floated to Trudy and scanned her. During the process, Ben studied Novada's eyes. Her pupils were too large for the amount of light in the room. She was a mind reader, which meant she was Gen Four royalty. Trudy was sharp enough to notice—no need to tell her to guard her thoughts and avoid eye contact if possible, because of Novada's mental powers and her laser-shooting pupils. Fortunately, so far it seemed that she hadn't looked directly into his eyes or Trudy's.

The drone's light flicked off. "Joquile and Ejardi are implanted."

Novada offered an apologetic smile. "Forgive me for this extra verification step. It seems that our surgeon has succumbed to suspicion without cause, a typical human weakness." She bowed her head briefly before focusing on Trudy. "Joquile, as I said, my name is Novada. I am the heir princess of the hive mother, and a Fourth Level offspring. It is my duty to brief you two on developments that have arisen since you were infused with information in the hive."

Trudy bowed her head in return. "Thank, you, Princess Novada. Please go on."

"I will show you the update in the vault." She touched Ben's shoulder. "Ejardi, from your appearance, it is clear that your host's genetics are superior to most. When your wings grow, you will be an intimidating specimen, indeed."

"As the hive queen lives," Ben said. "I am looking forward to the blessing."

Novada's hand lingered on Ben's shoulder for a moment, her eyes piercing, inquisitive. Ben resisted the urge to turn away. Doing so now would be too obvious. Instead, he trained his thoughts on the strangeness of the surroundings.

After a moment, Novada smiled again. "I understand your trouble adapting. After so long in the hive, it takes some time to acclimate." She turned and walked toward a hallway adjacent to the lobby, the drone at her side. "Come with me."

Ben and Trudy followed, saying nothing as they closed the gap. At the end of the hall, a huge metal door blocked the way. Bearing a wheel that resembled the steering mechanism on an old ship's helm, the door looked like the entry to a bank vault.

Ben nudged Trudy. "The vault. So far, so good."

Keeping her stare straight ahead, she nodded.

The drone set its beam on a sensor next to the wheel. After a moment, something thudded inside, and the drone backed away. "Mechanism unlocked."

Novada turned the wheel several rotations, then pulled the massive door open. She extended an arm. "You may enter. Proceed to the terminus. I will meet you there after I close the door."

As Ben and Trudy walked into a massive corridor, red lights flashed on from the flat, ten-foot-high ceiling, bathing them with warmth for a few seconds before turning off, perhaps another identification procedure. They walked on. Drawers embedded in the side walls and stacked in rows, much like corpse coolers in a morgue, seeped white vapor from their edges. A label marked each drawer, but the lettering was too small to read.

At the end of the corridor, a massive projection screen, almost as big as a theater screen, displayed an oval of tiny, flickering lights, denser at the perimeter and thinning to almost no lights near the center except for a vague, hazy aura. A long table with three chairs stood in front of the display, with a trio of computer monitors on top, maybe control units.

Gazing at the displayed spectacle, Ben whispered, "Hell's Gate."

Chapter Six

"So they're monitoring the Oculus," Trudy said, also staring. "But why?"

"Mesmerizing, isn't it?" Novada walked up behind them and stood next to Trudy. "To answer your question, we're monitoring the Oculus because of recent activity in the cross-dimensional plane. In other words, an entity of some sort is trying to gain passage. We are analyzing data that is coming through in order to determine what sort of entity it is and how to stop it if necessary." She touched the back of an empty chair. "Our scientists will return soon to continue their monitoring duties. They are attending worship services at the city temple. While there, they will also receive the vaccination against the contagion. Yet, this is redundant information, since we told you about the temple and the need for the vaccine in your data infusion before you left the hive."

Ben gave her a nod. "You said there's an update."

"Correct." She tapped on a keyboard. The display changed to a set of barracks-like buildings, void of people. "This is Camp Rogers, the base where you will deliver the vaccine and inoculate the soldiers who will take part in the rebel roundup. In our trials, we discovered that the vaccine causes severe headaches and joint pain that subside in a few hours. For that reason, we included a sedative that will help the soldiers sleep until the symptoms fade. By the time they awaken, the side effects will be gone, and they will be protected from the contagion. The speed of the vaccine's efficacy is the greatest advance our scientists have accomplished, functional antibodies in less than an hour instead of days or weeks. We expect that the soldiers will invade the rebel compound shortly thereafter."

The screen altered to an animated diagram of Novada's explanation, showing tanks, missile launchers on flatbeds, and a squad of about a hundred soldiers. "They will approach the compound with artillery vehicles while their aircraft spread the contagion over the entire area. Our soldiers will be unaffected while the rebels contract the disease and expire within an hour."

As the animation unfolded, Ben looked at Trudy. She met his gaze. Her impatient expression likely mirrored his own. This was exactly the same information the mole's intel provided. They needed Novada to wrap this up. With Jack in danger, the entire mission was at stake.

"Since the contagion is vulnerable to fire," Novada continued, "our soldiers will burn the corpses and surrounding vegetation, thereby destroying the contagion and creating a quarantined area."

She walked to a waist-high drawer in the wall and pulled it out. Vapor billowed from within, creating a cloud that quickly dispersed. After taking two sets of tongs from a hook on the wall, she used them to draw out a silver cooler and set it on the floor. "This container will protect the vaccine vials for twenty-four hours."

"Excellent," Ben said. "I assume our transportation is ready."

"Yes." Novada returned the tongs to the hook and closed the drawer. "A military vehicle is already waiting for you at the gate. It is fully equipped with medical supplies, including four vaccine jet injectors."

"Good. Then we should be on our way." Ben folded his hands at his waist. "Soon, the rebellion will be squashed without a shot fired. Whoever came up with this idea should be commended."

Novada tilted her head, eyeing him intently. "The idea was mine. You knew that. It was part of your knowledge infusion."

Ben forced a steady smile, working hard to believe his lie. "It's my way of complimenting you, Princess. A rhetorical pat on the back, if you will."

"I see." Her gaze intensified. "What, then, is the actual purpose of the contagion?"

"The actual purpose?" Ben waved a hand toward the display. "As we just witnessed, to eliminate the rebels at the base."

On the screen, the animation stopped, and the Oculus Gate returned. Novada walked toward Ben, her arms crossed over her chest. "We have had the power to eliminate their pitifully undermanned forces at their so-called farm for a long time. Instead, we have been strategically pushing them into a sequestered corner for a specific purpose."

Trudy stepped closer. "Are you sure our infusions included that information? I have no knowledge of strategic maneuvers beyond killing the rebels with the contagion."

Novada narrowed her eyes at Trudy. "Interesting. You really don't have knowledge of our plan, do you? How could the scientists have omitted that from the infusion?"

"Maybe you should tell us now," Ben said. "Not knowing the goal could be crippling."

"Indeed." Novada stared at Ben once more. "How convenient that you're missing this particular piece of information, a plan that the rebels would surely want to know."

"Convenient? Rebels?" Ben half closed an eye. "Novada, what are you talking about?"

"Your feigned ignorance is wearing thin." She raised her voice. "How did you fake the implantation?"

Ben drew his head back. "Fake the implantation? That's impossible."

"Or so we thought." Fire crackled in Novada's pupils. "But I will find out how you did it when I split your skull open and examine your brain."

Lasers shot from her eyes. Ben leaped to the side. The beams singed his hair and burned into one of the control-panel chairs. Armed with a scalpel, Trudy attacked. Novada spun and fired twin blasts again. One missed while the other zapped Trudy's wrist. The scalpel clattered to the floor. Trudy collapsed, writhing.

Novada aimed her eyes again, this time straight at Trudy's head. Ben grabbed the scalpel and charged. He plunged it into Novada's neck and shoved her toward the wall. She slammed into a drawer and slid to the floor, blood oozing from her neck into her blouse. Seconds later, her eyes closed.

Ben helped Trudy rise. As she held her forearm, smoke rose from a small hole in her wrist. He grimaced. "That has to hurt."

"No kidding." She nodded toward the cooler. "Let's get the vaccine and go. We can't count on Chantal's help. She might be dead for all we know."

Ben looked at Novada as she quivered in apparent death throes. "We have to dispose of the body. We'll put her in the drawer where the cooler was."

"What about the blood?"

"Her blouse caught it," Ben said. "None on the floor."

Working quickly, they carried Novada to the empty drawer and hoisted her inside, stuffing her wings in at the edges. "Okay," Trudy said, "let's go."

Ben set a hand on Novada's forehead. Somewhere inside, a suffering girl might be trapped, begging for escape.

"Ben?" Trudy touched his arm. "Volunteers get no quarter."

"We don't know what she is. Sometimes they abduct the most beautiful women as trophy implants."

"But there's no way to check. We left the AngelScan in the jeep. Besides, we're in a hurry, and we don't have a gun to blow her skull open."

Ben heaved a sigh. Jack was in trouble, and the mission balanced on a knife's edge. Not only that, there was no time to search for a reader to access the disk from the temple priestess. "All right. Let's go."

He slid his lab coat's sleeves over his hands, grabbed the cooler, and hustled with Trudy to the door. After finding and using the unlocking mechanism, she pushed the door open, then, the moment they left, she shoved it closed.

The drone, hovering at eye level, scanned them with its light. "Joquile and Ejardi accounted for. Novada is not present."

Trudy gestured with a hand toward the door. "She stayed inside, I assume until your scientists return."

"Acknowledged." The drone's light blinked off. "Your transport awaits at the gate."

Ben and Trudy walked toward the front door at a brisk pace. When they exited and reached the security gate, the drone stationed there scanned them and let them out. Beyond the sidewalk, an M-ATV sat at the curb, emblazoned with a winged angel and the words "Official Business."

After setting the cooler in the back, Ben hustled to the driver's seat while Trudy boarded on the passenger's side. A silver cylindrical key with metallic wings protruded from the ignition switch, typical of angel vehicles, whether ground or air transports. Ben turned the key, starting the engine, then shifted the ATV into gear and took off.

Trudy gazed out the rear window. "If Jack's been caught, who'll drive the real vaccine to our base from the rendezvous point? We don't have time to do it ourselves."

"We'll have to call the outpost to send someone to pick it up, but you make a good point. If Jack doesn't bring the jeep, we won't be able to get the fake vaccine or our other stuff." He turned toward the outer parking lot. "We'll get everything now."

"Risky." She straightened in her seat. "But we have to do it. If Jack's a no-show, it'll mean a big delay getting our people inoculated before the invasion."

"One potential disaster at a time." Ben raised a finger with each of his points. "First, we know Jack won't give up any information no matter how much they torture him. Second, if they implant him, the angel will read his mind, and they'll know the entire plan. Third, that process will take some time. We can stay a step ahead of the angels and get this done."

"And four," Trudy added as Ben parked the ATV next to their jeep, "we have to—"

"Hold that thought. I'll get the fake vaccine. You get what you need, and we'll talk on the way."

"On it." They both jumped out. While Ben retrieved the fake-vaccine cooler, Trudy transferred her medical bag from the jeep to the ATV. The moment she settled back in place, she slapped the dashboard. "Let's move."

Ben took off and drove onto the access road to the highway. "As I was saying," Trudy continued, "we have to figure out what Novada meant about the actual purpose for the contagion. She gave away a lot of intel, like the reason they're monitoring Hell's Gate, but not everything we need. And since Chantal apparently got caught, she might get implanted. Then the angels will soon know everything."

"Maybe not." Ben accelerated to the speed limit. "Chantal's an undercover agent. She's been trained to block her memories, so she might be the least of our worries."

"You mean Hell's Gate is at the top of the list?"

"Right. We've known all along that the angels came through the gate, but now something else might be trying to get here." Ben shook his head. "Things could get even uglier really quick."

"Yep. If the angels are worried, it's got to be bad news."

"Unless Novada was lying."

Trudy wrinkled her nose. "Yeah, I got the impression the she-devil was testing us all along."

"Back to what we know. The only purpose for their contagion is to kill. Maybe it's a trial run to see how effective it is against our rebel force. If it works, they'll use it to kill a lot of other people. Millions or even billions they deem expendable."

"That's a nightmare scenario, but it makes sense. We've been wondering why the angels haven't just bulldozed us. Now we have a good guess. We're lab rats."

"So, if all goes well, we'll ruin their experiment, but it'll be a temporary setback. They'll try again. We have to figure out how to sabotage the idea for good."

"One problem with the theory," Trudy said. "If they want the contagion to kill millions, why are they giving the vaccination to so many people at the temple?"

"Good question. We'll have to think about it."

They veered onto an unmarked dirt road and into a forest, plowing through saplings and underbrush. A few hundred feet in, they arrived at a clear spot where Jack, if everything had gone according to plan, was supposed to eventually meet them with the jeep, though that now seemed impossible.

Ben and Trudy got out and scanned the forest. "No sign of him," Trudy said. "Let's hope he holed up at the refuge."

"I'll get a better look." Ben climbed on top of the ATV and rotated slowly—nothing but trees and brush.

After a couple of minutes, he looked down at Trudy and shook his head. "Nothing."

"I guess it's time to call the outpost," she said.

"No other choice. We have to get the vaccine to the farm." Staying on top of the ATV, Ben inserted his earbud and spoke into the air. "Outpost seven. Outpost seven. Can you hear me?"

Static filled the reply. "This is outpost seven."

"This is satellite one. Security code seven, four, kilo, delta."

"Satellite one, you are verified. Return code, niner, six, alpha, foxtrot."

"Satellite one requests emergency rendezvous. We need a driver to pick up our payload. Provide a location in our mission region previously unknown to the satellite team. Time is of the essence."

"Roger. One moment."

Ben sat on the ATV's roof and studied Trudy's face. Her worried expression said it all. They were abandoning Jack to the winged wolves, and there was nothing they could do about it. "He'll be all right," Ben said. "The emergency refuge isn't far. He's found it by now. And Jack's a survivor. You know that. He'll—"

"Can we change the subject?" Tears glistened in her eyes. "Please?"

"Yeah. Sure." He nodded toward her arm. "How's the wound?" She showed him the dime-sized burn on her wrist. "Not bad. Hurt like the devil at first, but it's shallow. No permanent harm."

"Good." He concealed a smile. "Still, it looks pretty painful. I was going to ask you to drive the M-ATV. Do you think you can handle it?"

Her lips wrinkled into a grin. "Better than you."

"Prove it." Ben tossed her the cylindrical key. When she caught it, he smiled. "And put your earbud back in. You can listen to the outpost's instructions with me."

"You got it." She inserted her earbud, opened the door, and hopped into the driver's seat. "Ready when you are."

Ben's earbud crackled. "Satellite one, proceed southeast on highway seven. In five klicks you will see a restaurant called Aunt Millie's Diner. The commander will meet you there in thirty minutes."

"Commander Barks?" Ben said. "Why would he come?"

"I'm not at liberty to say. Ask him when you see him."

"Understood." Ben climbed to the ground and boarded the ATV on the passenger's side. "Did you hear?"

"I did." Trudy started the engine and barreled toward the highway, the ATV again mowing down the vegetation. "I guess Barks really is watching this mission closely."

"To make sure we don't screw things up."

"Like we've already done. I mean, no offense, but we lost Jack. It's a major screwup."

Ben rolled his eyes. "As if I didn't know."

"Sorry to kick you in the head, but I'm the realist." Trudy gripped the steering wheel tightly as they bounced on the rough terrain. "And I'm sick to my gut that we're leaving Jack with those cockroaches."

Ben grabbed the handhold above the door. "Trudy, the second we get this job done, we'll go back and rescue him. Got it?"

She sighed. "Got it. No choice, though. I have to accept it."

"Listen. If this mission was just for the commander, I'd tell him to shove it, but we've got—"

"Women and children who'll suffer and die. I know. Like you've told me a hundred times. But if you want to keep venting, go ahead. Bend my ear."

Ben exhaled heavily. "Yeah. I'm venting. Sorry."

"No problem. Pressure release is good for you." After a short pause, she pushed his shoulder. "Hey. Are you all right?"

"What do you mean?"

"When Novada had me in her crosshairs, you shifted to warrior mode. No pause. No questions. You cut her throat in a split second."

"Yeah. So? It was the only way to save you."

"Exactly. And thanks for that, by the way. But this mission needs Warrior Ben twenty-four-seven. Otherwise, we'll fail. We can't have you stalling. Like when you wanted to set Novada's host's soul free. You made the right decision. We couldn't afford the time. You didn't go soft on me. It was perfect. So stay that way. All right?"

Ben laughed under his breath. "Keep me in line, Sis. Keep me in line."

"Trust me. I will. And I have more to tell you, but I'd rather do it when we have time. I think we're almost there."

"We are. About thirty seconds."

When Trudy parked the ATV in the diner's lot, they scanned the other spaces—empty.

Ben turned toward her. "It might be a while before Barks gets here. What's on your mind?"

She settled back in her seat and faced him. "The reason you've gone soft other times."

"All right, Miss Realist." Ben leaned his head back but kept his gaze on Trudy. "Lay it on me."

"You sure? It's a sore subject."

Ben smiled. "Now who's going soft?"

"All right." She inhaled deeply. "Simply put, you always have Kat on your mind. You want to see her again, I don't know, in some kind of afterlife, I guess. And if you stay in kill-first-ask-questions-later mode, you think maybe you'll miss the train to heaven when the time comes. Cold-blooded killers aren't allowed through the pearly gates."

Ben gazed into her sincere, sparkling eyes. She knew him so well, better than any living person. "You're right. Guilty as charged."

"Thought so." She slid her hand into his. "Listen, Ben. This world's in trouble. Huge trouble. The angels, whatever they really are, probably have a plan to kill billions. And the rebellion is on its last legs. After all the post-plague defections, we're down to what? Two hundred who can handle a gun? Maybe ten who can drive a tank? And how many who are willing to risk their lives on a crazy suicide mission like ours?"

"Am I supposed to guess?"

"No. Be still and listen." She pointed at him. "Not a single one except you, Ben. You're pretty much the world's only hope. Yeah, Jack and I are with you, but mostly to keep you alive. Because if you die, we'll all die. And Jack and I follow your lead. You inspire us. We'd be scared kids without your courage to prop us up." She tightened her grip on his hand. "So be the warrior the world needs. Kill the monsters that want to slaughter the innocent. No quarter. No mercy. No retreat. Then someday, maybe fifty years from now, when the train comes that leads to wherever Kat is, I'll bet the other passengers will cheer when they see you. They'll make the engineer stop the train, and they'll carry you aboard on their shoulders. Because they'll know you're the one who set the world free."

"Thanks, Sis." Ben chucked her under the chin. "How long did you rehearse that speech?"

"Well …" She offered a sheepish smile. "Maybe a couple of days."

"It helped. Thanks again."

"No problem. And sorry to rip open the Kat wound."

"You didn't. No harm done." Ben closed his eyes and leaned his head back. As memories of that midnight mission returned once again, the explosion flashed below the bridge, toppling the support. Kat's scream followed as she fell into the raging river and tumbled down the waterfall. Although they never found a corpse, no one could have survived that plunge.

Tears welling, he released Trudy's hand, turned to the side, and tapped on the passenger window. "Barks will probably come from that direction."

"Yep. And I'll be right here." Trudy massaged his shoulder. "I've got your back, Ben. Always."

Chapter Seven

Jack ran through the woods, keeping his gasps quiet, but the thick undergrowth answered his footfalls with loud crunches. Each noise sounded like an explosion. Any angel could track him, even a Gen One.

He halted, leaned against the wide trunk of a huge oak, and peeked around it as he forced his breathing to slow. A breeze swayed the nearly bare treetops, making the dappled sunlight dance on the forest floor. A twig popped here and there but nothing consistent, no telltale signs of anyone giving chase.

Jack took a cleansing breath and let it out slowly. The lack of a pursuer made no sense. This escape was too easy. Blasting at the bogeys with his rifle's twenty plasma spheres kept them at bay for a while, but when he'd ditched the empty weapon to run faster, they could have given chase. Maybe they were prepping SkySweep to search the forest for his heat signature. But if he could get to the refuge, SkySweep wouldn't be a problem.

He scanned the landscape in the direction he had been running. About a hundred paces away, the terrain sloped upward to a ridge. He could probably see the stream from there, maybe even the waterfall.

Just as he flexed his legs to run, the sound of labored breathing rode the breeze. The crunching of leaves followed, consistent and drawing closer. Grunts joined in—a female in pain.

Jack spun toward the sound. A woman came into view, following the path he had blazed in the undergrowth and fallen leaves, stumbling and limping heavily. Although her lowered head hid her face, camo pants and shirt gave away the truth. She was a rebellion soldier, probably an escapee from angel headquarters. Maybe she had taken advantage of the chaos and found a way to sneak out. And if she was being held at HQ, she had to be an important prisoner.

Jack edged around the tree and hissed, "Over here!"

The woman stopped and stared at him, now only fifty feet away. "Jack?" She swallowed, trembling. "Is it really you?"

Jack squinted. Her dirty face clarified into an impossible visage. "Kat?"

"Yes!" She hobbled to him, grabbed his arm, and pulled him behind the tree. "They're after me." She gasped between halting phrases. "Angels. Gen Twos. Four of them. And their hounds."

"Drone hounds?"

She nodded, her eyes wide as she licked her cracked lips.

"How are you here? We thought—"

"Hold your questions. We have to run."

He grasped her arm. "Wait. You have to give me something. Prove to me that you're really Kat and not an imposter. I mean, for eight months we've thought you were dead."

She pointed at her face. "This isn't enough?"

"You could be implanted. An angel in Kat's skin."

"As if an angel would stoop to getting this dirty." She let out an exasperated sigh, then glared at him, shooting daggers with her eyes. "Ben has a birthmark on his butt that's shaped like a kidney."

"Okay. I'll hope an angel can't mimic Kat's trademark stare that well. Stay close." Jack marched up the slope, Kat trailing, her limp forcing him to slow his pace. As they climbed, they kept scanning every angle, but no sign of the angels appeared.

Soon, they reached the top of the ridge and looked back. Below, trees covered the undulating ground with angel headquarters nestled in a low-lying glen. The closest road lay beyond the building, the highway that provided access to HQ. In the opposite direction, a narrow stream snaked through the forest at the base of the downslope, maybe three hundred yards away. That had to be the location of the refuge.

"Look." Kat pointed toward a spot between them and angel HQ. "The angels and their hounds are chasing the woman I escaped with. We split up. I got lucky."

Jack eyed the group—four winged humans following a pair of drones that hovered a few inches off the ground, their scent detectors as good as any bloodhound's. Not far ahead, a short, thin woman staggered away much too slowly. Her pursuers were closing in. "Who is she?"

"A scientist they wanted for implanting. Brilliant but rebellious. She would rather die than host an angel."

"Same here. Too late to help her, though." Jack pointed toward the stream. "We'll head for water, mess up the scent trail, then find our refuge. We'll hide there till the heat's off."

Kat pushed a strand of dirty hair away from her eyes. "Refuge?"

"Yeah. It's new. Tell you more later. We'd better scoot."

They descended the slope on the opposite side, sometimes sliding on damp grass as they avoided protruding rocks and roots. When they arrived at the water, Jack pointed downstream. "That way first. We'll deposit forensic countermeasures and double back."

They walked into the cold flow and waded downstream in knee-deep water until they came to a beach of soft gray sand. They stepped out, leaving obvious footprints on the beach, then continued walking over harder turf. Jack found a thorny smilax vine, tore his sleeve, and left a fragment hanging on a thorn. They then hurried as quickly as Kat could travel parallel to the stream about a hundred feet, stepped back into the water, and walked against the flow.

"That should do it," Jack said.

Kat offered him a pain-streaked smile as she trudged. "Classic. Just like in training."

As Jack gazed at her, questions blazed to mind. How had she survived? Why did the angels keep her alive? Had she been locked up at HQ all of these months? But the questions had to wait. The angels wouldn't rest, and drones never grew tired.

After several minutes of walking on the streambed's sand and pebbles, they came upon a ten-foot-wide waterfall that spilled over a rocky ledge thirty feet above. "This has to be the place," Jack said.

"The refuge?"

"Right. Follow me." Jack walked through the curtain of tumbling water to the face of the cliff and stood knee deep in a pool, Kat at his side. He ran his hands along the face's slick, wet surface. "The entry's supposed to be at waist level to keep water from getting inside." His fingers touched an indent. "Wait. I think this is it." He shoved the wall with both hands. A three-by-three square of stone gave way and slid inward. After a few feet of sliding, the stone toppled into a dark room inside. "Yep. We're in."

Jack withdrew a penlight from his pocket, flicked it on, and squirmed through to a low tunnel. Crouching to keep his head from hitting the ceiling, he helped Kat snake her way in. Together, using a pair of iron brackets embedded in the stone, they heaved it back into place.

Hunching over, they walked into a cavern with a higher roof, allowing them to stand, though darkness veiled the surrounding walls. His clothes and hair dripping, Jack guided his penlight's beam around. They stood in an eight-by-eight-by-eight cube, some of the walls natural and some carved with power tools.

He swept the beam across a battery-powered lamp. "Ah. This will help. No idea how long it's been here, though." He sat on the floor next to the lamp and turned it on at a low level. The dim glow illuminated the cavern, allowing him to flick his penlight off.

Kat settled next to him and wrung water from a drenched sleeve. Her hair, cropped shorter than usual, glistened with droplets. "Okay. Your questions first."

He gazed at her, scarcely able to believe that a living, breathing Katherine Garrison sat within reach. "Well, first of all, how are you alive? You plunged down a waterfall. We thought you were dead, drowned, or dashed against boulders."

"I guessed that. Actually, a winged angel caught me on the way down. I suppose it was too dark for you to see him."

"An angel? Why was one hanging around ready to grab you?"

"He was there on a mission to kidnap a high-level member of our group, and he took the opportunity when I fell. I think he might have staged the accident, so he was ready."

"Why go through so much trouble to kidnap you? What information did they want? And did they torture you?"

She nodded. "First, it was torture the old-fashioned way. You know, whips on the back, hot pokers, even stretching on a rack."

Jack winced. "Ouch! And you never broke?"

She shook her head and shifted to a southern accent. "I'm just little old Emily James, a rabble rouser from Alabama. My fingerprints said so."

"Right. The backstop we created for you. But what did they want to know that was worth torturing you for?"

"They heard about the weapon project." She lifted her brow and paused, as if waiting for him to comment.

"So … uh … what did you tell them?"

"That I didn't know anything about it. That we're a ragtag bunch of disgruntled survivalists causing trouble here and there. No organized plans. Even though they didn't believe me, they stopped the torture. I couldn't figure out why until I heard they put me in line for an implant. They figured an angel in my head would get the information they wanted. It was supposed to happen today. In fact, I was already in the surgery room, and they dosed me with a mild sedative, something to relax me before the stronger juice. When I pretended to go to sleep, they untied me, and I listened in on some of the chatter. Anyway, a bunch of alarms went off, and they left me alone with the other prisoner. I untied her, and we took off. We were both kind of groggy, but the adrenaline rush gave us a boost."

"Whew! That was close!"

"You're telling me. But waiting a few weeks for the implant worked out. I had time to heal, except my hip flexors from all the stretching." She wrung out the other sleeve. "So how long did you search for me?"

"All night that night, then for days afterward. Calling your name, following tracks, asking locals if they'd seen anyone, you name it."

Kat dabbed at a chafed spot on her neck. "Worrying that you guys were worried about me was almost as bad as the rack."

"I can imagine." Jack shook his head. "No. I really can't. Eight months!"

"Eight long months." Tears sparkled in her eyes. "My turn for questions?"

"Sure. Absolutely."

"How's Ben?"

Jack smiled. "He's the only one who never gave up on you. He invented a hundred hopeful theories. You know, about how you might still be alive. The river swept you downstream for miles. You crawled to shore with a head injury that gave you amnesia. You wandered to a wilderness shack and survived on nuts, berries, and trapped animals. Or a rural family took you in, and you were still living there with a new name to this day."

Kat smiled. "That sounds like Ben."

"And you getting captured and taken prisoner was another theory, so Ben sent spies to all of the known holding areas. Although we didn't know they kept prisoners at headquarters, we tried getting in touch with our mole there just in case she heard anything about you, but every search came up empty. Still, like I said, Ben never gave up the hunt, though he's been quiet about it lately."

Kat brushed a tear from each cheek. "I can't wait to see him."

"And I want to be there. I'll be glad to hear him say 'I told you so' a thousand times just to see you two together again."

"Where is he now? What's he doing? And why were you at angel headquarters?"

"Long story. Short version is we were on an infiltration mission, Ben, me, and Trudy."

Kat's brow lifted. "Trudy? Really? Well, good for her. She's come a long way."

"Yep. Tough as nails now. And Doc Calhoun trained her in surgery. Anyway, Ben and Trudy went into HQ as husband and wife to pretend to get angel implants …"

Someone tapped lightly on the dormitory door. "Iona?" a woman called. "Are you in there?"

Standing at the side of her cot, Iona stared at the door, staying perfectly quiet as she slowly loosened her robe's sash. Priestess Anne was always suspicious. One false move and this charade would be over in a hurry.

"You weren't in line for your vaccination." The knob rattled. "And why is the door locked?"

Iona shed the robe, leaving only her knee-length nightgown, and pushed the robe inside her pillowcase. Although the pillow now looked a bit fuller than those on the nine other cots in the dorm room, maybe no one would notice.

"I'm calling Mistress." Footsteps clopped on the wooden floor, fading.

Iona whispered, "Mistress." That meant about five minutes to certain doom.

She stripped off her nightgown, grabbed her backpack from the floor, fished out her disguise—torn jeans, canvas shoes, and a loose-fitting, long-sleeved jersey—and threw it on, leaving her shoes untied for the moment.

With the pack still open, she pulled the revolver from the bottom next to a bar of soap and checked the ammunition. Only two bullets. That would have to do. She set it back in place and covered it with her wadded blanket.

Looking in the mirror, she grabbed two bands from the attached dresser and quickly braided her hair into twin pigtails. She scanned her reflection. Baggy shirt and no makeup made her look young enough. Now for the escape.

After checking the tiny microphone adhering to the back of the mirror, she inserted a listening bud into her ear, slung the pack on, and hopped on one foot toward the window, tying one shoe, then the other. She slid the sash up and climbed out to the narrow ledge below, then closed the window and slid her feet toward the corner of the building, intentionally not looking at the thirty-foot drop to the temple's courtyard.

A noise rattled in her ear, the dorm's door unlocking. Then a voice came through. "Where is she?" Mistress asked. "I don't see her."

Iona grasped the drainpipe at the corner and began sliding down.

"I know she was here, Mistress," Anne said. "The door was locked."

"Did you see her go in?"

"I saw someone go in and close the door. Iona was the only one missing from the vaccination line. It had to be her."

"I'll check the washroom," Mistress said.

Nearing the bottom of the pipe, Iona smiled. "Cue the scream."

Mistress shrieked. "Roaches! Thousands of them!"

Stomping footsteps followed, then the slamming of a door.

Iona jumped the rest of the way to the grass and ran to the pink bicycle with the flower-decaled basket in front, parked exactly where it always stood during worship services. She straddled the bike and rode out of the courtyard, then onto the road that ran alongside the temple's social hall.

As she accelerated, Mistress called, "Look, Constance. See? Roaches."

Iona gulped. Constance wouldn't be fooled, not in a million years. She had seen it all. Iona pedaled even faster, now zipping through a residential neighborhood.

"It's a diversion," Constance said calmly through the earbud. "She's escaping."

"Escaping from what? The vaccination? Does she believe that absurd rumor?"

"The vaccination rumors are irrelevant. Iona fears being exposed and punished. You see, she was working for the angels as a spy to gain intelligence from the rebels. Now that she has departed in a stealthy manner, it's clear that she has become a traitor and must be terminated."

"But how?" Mistress asked. "She has to be far away by now."

"Send for Leo. The huntsmen will find her."

Iona shuddered. Huntsmen. Expert trackers. What kind of countermeasures would work against their bloodhound-like pursuit? They would probably find the microphone, but could they trace the listening frequency?

She pried the earbud out and threw it into a flowerbed as she passed. She turned onto a forest trail and bounced along its rugged surface into the depths of the woods, her surroundings darkening as she rode on and on. She had to find the rebel agent from this morning's meeting. Since he had been sent on such a dangerous mission, he would be the one to contact. Her own life and maybe the fate of the entire world depended on it.

Chapter Eight

Commander Barks arrived in an unmarked royal blue sedan. When the car parked next to the ATV, the commander exited on the passenger's side, and Dr. Calhoun climbed out from the driver's seat, both men dressed in full camo. Tall, wiry, and wearing a sidearm low at his hip like an ancient gunslinger, Doc was a good choice to accompany the commander.

Ben looked at Trudy. "How old is Doc now? Seventy something?"

"Seventy-five, two years older than Barks. They fight like cats and dogs, but they respect each other. Figures they'd come together. Barks has an implantation phobia."

"He wants Doc around to do an immediate extraction?" Ben winked. "That's not a phobia. That's just being prepared." He opened the passenger door, jumped to the pavement, and nodded toward Barks. "Commander."

"Garrison." Barks nodded in return, pulled off his patrol cap, and ran a hand over his crew-cut gray hair before putting the cap back in place. "We'll wait for everyone to gather before we talk."

When Trudy circled the ATV and joined them, Doc gave her a genial smile. "How's my favorite protégée?"

She stood straight, hands behind her back, and smiled in return. "Your *only* protégée. And I am fine, thank you, considering the circumstances."

Barks scanned the area, his brow bending on his narrow, withered face. "Regarding the circumstances, I count two Garrisons, not three."

"Yes, sir." Ben shifted his weight from foot to foot. "Jack had to hightail it. Bogeys spotted him. We haven't seen or heard from him since. We had to keep moving. Even now we're in a hurry to get to the base."

"You mean, the fox has to stay ahead of the hounds." Barks gave them a grim nod. "Counting on your brother's skills to make it to the refuge. Your confidence in him is warranted."

"We think so, sir. But we plan to search for him as soon as the mission is over."

"Of course you do. And we'll check the refuge and relay any intel." Barks glanced at the ATV. "Do you have the vaccine?"

Ben nodded. "Both the real and the fake."

Barks turned toward Dr. Calhoun. "You and Trudy get the vaccine and put it in the car. Wait for me there while I talk to Ben."

Doc grinned. "Keeping secrets from me, Roland?"

"Every day, from everybody, Doc. Now get your butt in gear."

After shaking Ben's hand, Doc walked with Trudy toward the ATV, chatting quietly.

Barks leaned close to Ben and lowered his voice. "Garrison, you got the vaccine. That was the most critical step. We'll be protected from the disease. If you want to abort the rest of the mission, I'll go along with it. You might have already lost your brother. We can't afford to lose you or your sister. We can take this win and move on. That'll free you to hunt for Jack with Trudy right away."

"But what about the invasion? Do you think they'll scrub the mission because they're not vaccinated?" Ben firmed his lips. "Or maybe they'll go through with it anyway."

Barks slid a hand into a pocket, his head tilting. "What do you mean?"

"We have an idea. A guess, really, that the contagion's primary purpose isn't to annihilate the rebels. They could've done that long ago. It's a test run to see how effective the contagion is."

The commander nodded. "I see where you're going. Even unvaccinated, they might send their soldiers after us, spread the contagion, kill everyone, including their own soldiers. More victims. Better test."

Ben's ears warmed. The commander's affirmation of the theory painted the angels with a murderous brush, making the idea ring true. "Yeah. I wouldn't put it past them."

"Either way, we'll be protected. Thanks to you."

"Your plan, sir. We just put it into motion."

"Perhaps so, but the next move is your call. Be sure to keep me informed. We'll have someone close enough to pick up your signal and relay the message to me. I need to know as soon as possible if we're marching in to occupy their base or hunkering down at home."

Ben nodded. "Will do."

"And one more issue." Barks glanced at Trudy and Doc as they put the vaccine cooler in the car. "Even if all else fails, we still have the weapon we've been developing."

Ben furrowed his brow. "I thought you abandoned that project since you lost the inventor."

"The inventor, as you call her, finished the prototype but never tested it. I asked Doc to take over. We think we found a way to deliver the warhead, but it's a last resort. A suicide mission."

"What? How?"

"No need for details because it's not your mission."

Ben nodded in an exaggerated way. "Oh. It's *your* mission. You're planning to give your life to make the weapon work."

"Not necessarily mine. But, like I said, it's a last resort. If your mission succeeds, the need is far less likely, at least for a while. Of course, if we could find another scientist as skilled as Kat, we might be able to use the weapon without any danger."

"Yeah, well, good luck with that."

"I know, I know. Sore subject." When Trudy rejoined them, Barks grasped Ben's shoulder. "Good luck, Garrison. You and your siblings are the best hope for this world." With that, Barks pivoted and walked toward the car.

"Let me guess," Trudy said. "Barks gave you the option to abort and look for Jack."

Ben smiled. "You know him well."

Trudy stepped in front of Ben and spoke rapid fire. "Listen, I know it's your call, but there's really no choice. We have to do the vaccinations. Finish the job. Searching for Jack is a shot in the dark. This is our chance to—"

"You're right. We'll go. Like you said. No quarter. No mercy. No retreat."

"Oh." Trudy shifted uneasily. "Well, okay, then." She hopped into the ATV's passenger seat. "Come on. The hounds might be closing in."

Ben climbed into the driver's seat and took off at a high rate of speed, following a memorized route toward the military base. "New idea. Once the soldiers are incapacitated, our men will come for the weapons and ammo, like we planned. For now, we'll keep some for ourselves, maybe a tank, and head back to angel headquarters. With more firepower, maybe we'll have a chance to spring Jack."

Trudy clenched a fist. "Love it. And that reminds me. The update Novada gave us. She verified what our mole said, that the vaccine is supposed to make the soldiers sick and put them to sleep. Ours does the same, but they won't wake up."

"Right. That's the plan. Once everyone is dead, we call our men to collect the weapons, including the biological ones."

She lifted her brow. "Did you forget the next step?"

"Attack angel headquarters with the contagion. Give them a taste of their own med—" Ben slapped his forehead. "But we'll be there looking for Jack."

"Which is why ..." Trudy slid a vial from her pants pocket. "This one's enough real vaccine for the three of us. You, me, and Jack."

Ben smiled. "Did I ever tell you that you're a genius?"

"Nope." She grinned. "Lay it on me."

"Trudy, you're a genius."

"I am, for sure, but not enough of a genius to use this stuff without an instruction manual." She reached over the seat, retrieved their medical bag, another vaccine vial, and a box labeled Jet Injector. After setting the bag on the floorboard, she placed the box on her lap, opened it, and read the pamphlet. After a few seconds, she pushed the vial into the ammo chamber of a handgun-like device. "Our fake vials fit the angels' injector."

"Good. What about dosage?"

"The gun's delivery dosage is adjustable. According to the pamphlet, we're supposed to inject a quarter of a vial into each soldier, so four doses per vial. That matches our specs. Our mole came through perfectly."

"What about soldier size? Does that make a difference? I mean, maybe not for creating antibodies, but it might for killing a guy. Takes more poison to kill a horse than a mouse."

"In the briefing, Doc assured me that the recommended dose will kill anyone, horse or mouse. He was kind of anal about it. Showed me a chart with death probabilities ranging from a hundred percent for a full dose to nearly zero percent for half a dose."

"What would half a dose do? Just make them sick?"

"And sleep. The fake vaccine is really a sedative plus a nausea inducer. With half a dose, you wake up. With a full dose, you don't." She squinted. "Why do you ask?"

"Just thinking if someone's suspicious, we can show them it's safe by using it on ourselves. We'd be all huffy and arrogant about it, of course. It's the angel way."

"I see what you mean. If we cut the dose in half for ourselves, we'd all get sick together. Then you and I would wake up, but they wouldn't." Trudy smiled. "Pretty smart. Not genius caliber like me, but pretty smart."

"Glad you approve." Ben nodded toward the bag on the floorboard. "Did you happen to put our AngelScan in there?"

"Yep." She reached into the bag and lifted the disk partway out. "Just one of the million reasons you need me."

"You got that right."

Along the way, Trudy took the blanket out of the cooler and left the lid open to allow the vaccine time to warm a bit. According to the instructions, the vials needed to reach room temperature before injecting a dose. As they neared the base, Trudy applied the glow cream to Ben's face as well as her own, checking herself in the visor mirror to touch up every spot.

When they arrived at the entrance, a black-and-white striped gate bar blocked their way. A short, clean-shaven uniformed man walked out of the guardhouse with a computer pad in hand.

"Turn on angel mode." Ben lowered the window and leaned his head out. "Greetings, sir. We are here to provide the inoculations."

The guard looked at the pad. "Jonas and Michelle Kidd?"

Ben shook his head. "It seems that there has been a communications error. Our human hosts are Benjamin and Gertrude Garrison. I assume the Kidds were disqualified. We have not been informed of the reason."

The guard studied the pad another moment before focusing on Ben. "I understand. It happens sometimes, but I have to call HQ to verify."

Just as he turned toward the guardhouse, Ben called, "Wait." When the guard pivoted back, Ben pointed at the pad. "Do your records show our angel names?"

The guard squinted at the screen. "Yes."

"And I assume scanning us for our angel identities is part of security protocol. Correct?"

"Of course. Security is top priority, especially in this case."

"Then it would be more efficient to scan us now and verify our identities. There is no need to call headquarters and wait an exceedingly long time to talk to the right person. Such a delay would be unfortunate, considering the urgency of our purpose."

"You're right. I'll get a scanner." The guard walked into the guardhouse and returned with a scanning wand. "Please exit your vehicle and stand side by side."

When Ben and Trudy complied, the guard passed the wand around each of their heads, read its tiny screen, and studied the computer pad. "Joquile and Ejardi. You're verified. Proceed to the medical center, fourth building after the barracks. You'll see the sign. Report to Major Livingstone. I'll radio ahead to let her know you're coming."

"Thank you." Ben and Trudy re-boarded the ATV. When the bar rose, they drove slowly along the wide, paved road. As they passed the barracks, dozens of uniformed soldiers walked here and there, some serious, some smiling, all with fresh, youthful faces.

"They're my age," Trudy said.

"Or younger." Ben studied her deep frown. She was what Mother always called *born old*. Now at the age of twenty-one, she acted more like she was forty-one. "What did you expect?"

"I'm not sure. I didn't really think about it. But they're so young."

"Same age I was when I enlisted. To me they look almost like children now."

Her shoulders sagged. "They're going to die. Every single one of them. And we're going to kill them."

"They're volunteers. They're planning to use biological weapons to murder innocent civilians."

"And volunteers get no quarter." Trudy kept her eyes averted, still looking at the soldiers. "I remember."

"Trust me. I know exactly what you're feeling. These kids think they're doing the right thing. They believe they'll be stopping a menace. They've been bamboozled, sold a bill of goods. And soon they'll die for it."

"Yeah. That pretty much sums it up." Trudy shrugged. "But what can we do? Like Jack said to me this morning, it's kill or be killed. And these soldiers want to kill people who haven't hurt a fly."

"Maybe we can get a better picture of their attitudes when we talk to the major." Ben parked the ATV next to the medical center, a three-story brick building with five white columns in front. "Let's do this."

Ben carried the cooler while Trudy brought along her medical bag stuffed with the four vaccine injectors. Stationed at the front, a male private opened the door and stood at attention. Another private rushed out and extended his hands toward the cooler. "I'll run that upstairs for you while you ride."

Ben pulled the cooler back. "No need, soldier. I am quite capable."

The private straightened. "Then please proceed to the elevators on the right. The car is waiting for you."

Ben and Trudy walked in, found the open elevator car, and entered. A third private standing inside pushed the button for the second floor. When the doors closed, he stared straight ahead, saying nothing.

Ben eyed his tight expression. He seemed scared, or maybe nervous. The presence of angels obviously had a dramatic effect on these young soldiers.

The doors reopened. A thirty-something, fair-skinned woman wearing military fatigues stood in the hallway. She bowed her head briefly, her dark hair pulled back in a bun. "Welcome, Joquile and Ejardi. I am Major Carol Livingstone. It's always an honor to have blessed angels at our base."

Ben and Trudy stepped out of the elevator and bowed their heads in return. "We are glad to provide this service," Ben said. "Your young soldiers are taking a great risk to preserve our system of justice, and they deserve to be protected with all speed and diligence."

"Thank you." Major Livingstone extended a hand to her right. "This way, if you please."

Ben and Trudy followed her to a double door that opened automatically. Inside an enormous room, a long table stood several steps away, blocking further progress. A five-gallon water cooler sat on one end of the table with stacks of paper cups next to it. Jars of cotton balls and bottles of alcohol covered the remainder of the surface. Behind the table, hundreds of cots sat side by side, filling the rest of the space.

Major Livingstone turned and stood in front of the table, her hands folded at her waist. "I trust that you'll find everything you need here. We set it up this way so our soldiers who are awaiting their turns could see the others resting comfortably."

Ben placed the vaccine cooler on the floor. "Are some frightened?"

The major smiled. "A few are. They're practically kids, still nervous about injections, getting sick, feeling less than heroic while they recover."

Trudy set her medical bag on the table. "We have a connection to the emotions of our hosts, so we understand. We hope that our presence will provide comfort and boldness as they prepare to march out against those who dare to rebel against our cause."

Major Livingstone's expression tightened. "Not to be too bold myself, but I hope you'll avoid mentioning the invasion while in the presence of the soldiers."

Ben cocked his head. "Why is that, Major?"

"Most have been told that they are participating in a police action to round up the rebel leaders and take them to our base where they will stand trial for treason. They think the purpose of the inoculation is the threat of a biological attack from the rebels. Except for a few officers who are preparing the contagion for deployment, our men and women have no knowledge that we are the ones who will introduce it to the battlefield."

Trudy's brow arched but only for a split second. "Interesting. Do you think they would balk at their assignments if they knew the truth?"

The major shook her head. "They're soldiers. They'll follow orders."

"Then why the pretense?" Ben asked.

"It's for the media. If we told the truth to so many soldiers, it's inevitable that the information would leak. We don't want bad press for the angels. The major outlets would spin the story in our favor, but the underground media wouldn't."

"Ah," Ben said, nodding. "An ignorant populace is a content populace."

The major nodded, as if in robotic mimicry. "In any case, the soldiers will be told the truth on the morning of the invasion. When the operation is over, leaks might still happen, but the media cycle about this event will have ended. Victory is the ultimate blinder. No one will pay attention to how it was accomplished."

Ben forced a fake smile. "I appreciate your clever handling of the matter."

The major bowed her head again. "No sacrifice is too great for our blessed angels."

"That's ..." Ben cleared his throat. "That's a strong expression of loyalty." He looked at the door they had entered. "Shall we begin the process?"

"Immediately." Major Livingstone strode toward the door, calling back, "I'll summon the soldiers. Make yourselves comfortable. With so many people coming in, it's bound to get warm."

The moment the major left, Trudy rolled her eyes. "No sacrifice is too great for our blessed angels?"

"Yeah." Ben shed his lab coat and laid it on the table. The short-sleeved scrubs felt cool in the air-conditioned room, but like the major said, that would change. "My BS meter hit the red zone. She's a bootlicker."

"Yep." Trudy took off her coat as well, revealing her scrubs. She loaded vaccine vials into two injectors and handed one to him. "We'll have to keep an eye on her."

Chapter Nine

Jack exhaled. "So that's the plan. And as far as I know, they'll go through with it."

"Kill the soldiers?" Kat's brow knitted. "Ben's going along with that?"

"The soldiers are volunteers. Not forced. Not implanted. They're marching out to murder men, women, and children with a terrible plague. So Ben bought into the plan."

"Not the Ben I know. He'd find another way."

"Maybe he's not the Ben you know anymore. Your death skewered his heart. Hardened him."

"And he thinks revenge is going to make him feel better?" Kat shook her head. "I don't believe it. He'll find another way to stop the invasion and the disease."

Jack set a hand on her shoulder. "Listen, Kat. The plan is the plan. I know it. He knows it. Trudy knows it. Everyone's on board. He can't deviate. If he does, a lot of innocent people will die. You know Ben wouldn't let that happen. And, besides, he's not the old Ben. Wishful thinking isn't going to change that."

"Wishful thinking? We've been married ten years. I know my husband. He wouldn't change, at least not about slaughtering people who haven't done anything wrong."

"But *they're* planning to slaughter people. This is a preemptive strike. A protective one. He knows if he doesn't do it, innocents will die."

"No. There's always another way." Kat's cheeks reddened, and her voice took on a plaintive tone. "Take me to him, Jack. Together we'll come up with a new plan. We always could before."

Jack waved a hand. "All right. I'll try to figure out how to get you two together. In the meantime, we'll wait here maybe another hour or so, dry off a bit. The angels might give up by then. They'll think we're long gone."

"Good. And now I have another question. I've heard rumblings that the angels are worried about a new entity trying to get through Hell's Gate. Have you heard anything about that?"

"Rumors. No evidence. Why?"

She pulled her knees up and wrapped her arms around them. "I'm hoping the new entity is divine help."

"Divine help?" Jack rolled his eyes. "Not that again."

Kat frowned. "What do you mean *again*? We haven't talked in eight months."

"Not from you. From Ben. Well, not recently, but he prayed like crazy when you …" He drew quote marks in the air. "Died. He stopped after a while. I assumed he gave up. Anyway, it's a pipe dream. Anything coming through Hell's Gate is bound to be trouble, maybe worse than the fake angels."

"Okay. Maybe help won't come from Hell's Gate. But there's got to be light in all this darkness. God would never leave us without hope, without a hand to reach out to."

"Kat, ninety-nine percent of the world fell for this insanity. Invited it. Welcomed it. Nearly every church, synagogue, mosque, whatever gladly joined in." Jack lifted his hands and spoke in a preacher-like cadence. "Peace and unity. Peace and unity for everyone. We are angels of God who have come down from heaven to give you what you need, what you crave. Peace and unity." He snorted. "If I were God, I would be disgusted. People traded their freedom for this so-called peace. And unity? Yeah, everyone's the same, enslaved to the whims of the angel overlords. Sure, crime is way down, but only because of instant death to anyone who steps out of line. And the worst crime is to say a word against the system or the angels. Then you're an enemy of the people, a villain who opposes peace and unity."

Kat nodded, her head low. "Yeah. I remember."

"But it's worse now. They're cracking down more than ever, and people are blind to the cruelty and bondage. Willingly blind." Jack clenched a fist. "Maybe God decided to let the fake angels have their way. You know, punish the world for their stupidity. He's done it before. Killed nearly everyone in a flood."

Kat's shoulders slumped. "And there's no ark in sight."

He pointed at her. "Exactly right. God's cleaning house. So we have to resort to our instincts. Fight the real villains. Kill or be killed."

"No, Jack." Kat's eyes sparkled in the lamp light. "We can't see an ark, but that doesn't mean it's not out there. Not necessarily a boat, though. Something to expose the fake angels for what they are. Maybe real angels can help us."

Jack resisted the urge to roll his eyes again. "Right. A thousand real angels with drawn swords will come and mow down the fake ones. I don't think so."

"I'm not asking for a thousand." Kat raised a finger. "Just one could make it right. You know, show us what to do. Lead us. Guide us. Give us hope that we're not doing this alone, that it's not a crazy suicide mission."

"Yeah. Well, you keep hoping. I guess someone has to. Ben gave up a long time ago."

"He'll find the light again. Maybe it's dormant inside, but it can be stoked." Kat slid her hand into his. "Like I said. Take me to him. You think he gave up because my death hardened him. Seeing me will restore hope, relight the fire. You'll see. He won't slaughter those soldiers. We'll find another way."

Jack eyed their hand clasp. To this point, her speech sounded like the Kat of old, but the affection signaled a change. "And like *I* said, I'll figure out how to get you to him. But it's tricky. By now, he and Trudy are on their way to Camp Rogers. Maybe already there. I'm not sure how long it'll take to get the soldiers together for the immunizations, but probably not long."

Kat rose to her feet. "Then let's go. Now. The angels are probably gone."

"Not yet." Jack pulled her back down. "Like I said, we have to give it at least another hour. Besides, you look exhausted. When was the last time you slept?"

She settled into a cross-legged pose. "Not sure. Maybe a day and a half. My bed is a concrete floor."

"Then take a nap. I'll let you know when I think it's safe to leave. If we have to run, I want you fresh."

"All right." She leaned her head against his shoulder and hummed as she spoke. "You're the first pillow I've had in months."

"Yeah … sure." Jack forced himself not to fidget. "I guess I'll catch a few winks myself."

"Sounds good." Kat closed her eyes. Within seconds, her breathing became heavy and rhythmic.

Jack smiled, though this pose, like the holding-hands gesture, was odd. Maybe being imprisoned for so long changed her somehow. Ben wasn't here, and she desperately needed comfort.

Jack dimmed the lamp, closed his eyes, and tried to sleep, but a buzz from Kat's nostrils kept him awake. He smiled again. She sounded a lot like Sophie when she slept after an exhausting day.

Trying not to move his shoulder, Jack withdrew the dog-eared photo from his shirt pocket and gazed at the portrait—himself, Sophie, and Alana, all smiling while sitting on the living room sofa. He ran a thumb along Sophie's face. She was so beautiful. And so happy. Those were much better days, before the plagues, before the angels arrived. Before their joy-filled home fell apart.

"I didn't know you still had that photo," Kat said.

Jack slid it back into his pocket. "I thought you were asleep."

"I was."

"Then go back. I can turn the lamp off if that'll help."

"Not yet." She sat up straight. "How old was Alana then?"

"Two."

"And when she died?"

"Three. Well, three and a half, like she always told us."

Kat smiled. "I can hear her saying it. Her voice is still in my mind even three years later."

"Four years. A little more, actually."

"Oh. Right." Kat's smile turned sheepish. "Eight months in torture will do that to you."

"No worries. I get it." Jack sighed. "Listen, if you're going to keep talking about Alana ..." He waved a hand. "Never mind. Sorry. Say whatever you want."

"Go to sleep, Jack." Kat curled her arm around his and nestled close. "Pretend I'm Sophie. Let your mind think she's here and try to rest. Can you do that?"

"Pretend you're Sophie? Are you serious?"

Kat studied his face for a moment as if unsure what to say. Then she pulled away and averted her eyes. "I'm sorry. I'm not myself. Living in a cage makes you wonky."

"Wonky? Since when did Katherine Garrison, vocabulary queen, use that word?"

Her hands trembled. "Just ... just go to sleep. I have to get my bearings."

"Hey. It's all right. It's some kind of trauma stress thing. You'll feel better after you sleep awhile."

"Right. Let's both sleep." Kat curled on the stony floor, using her hands as a pillow. "Let me know if I say anything else that sounds ... well ... off."

"Will do." Jack closed his eyes. Soon, his thoughts wandered into a dream, the same one he had dreamt a hundred times—Sophie and Alana standing at a gate of pearls, their arms extended as he ran toward them. But he could never get there. An invisible force held him back. And the dream always ended the same way, Sophie and Alana drifting high into the sky, waving as they called, "Come to us soon. We love you."

Something shook him. He blinked his eyes open. Kat stood nearby, holding the lamp. "It's been long enough."

"All right. We'll go." Jack rose and gave her a mock salute. "You're in take-charge mode. That's the Kat I know."

"The nap helped a lot. But remind me if I get …" She smiled. "Wonky again."

"Got it." Jack looked at the blocking stone leading to the waterfall. "We'll have to hoof it to the outpost. Maybe thirty minutes. I couldn't go there earlier. I didn't want to lead the bogeys to it."

He took the lamp from her and, hunching again, shuffled to the stone. After setting the lamp down, he grasped the brackets and pulled. It slid out slowly and toppled to the floor.

Light poured in, filled with sparkling dots—spray from the tumbling water outside. Jack turned the lamp off, crawled out, and waited in the pool while Kat took her turn to exit.

When they broke through the falls and blinked the water out of their eyes, two angels stood at the stream bank, their wings spread, plasma rifles in hand, and four drone hounds hovering at their sides.

"Split!" Jack shouted.

The moment they turned to run in opposite directions, the drones shot bolts of electricity. Pain stabbed Jack's neck. He toppled into the stream, barely catching sight of Kat doing the same.

As his limbs stiffened, he thrashed to keep his face above water while trying to crawl toward Kat. His vision blurred, though every sound magnified—Kat's own thrashes, a drone's hum, and the splashing of boots tromping toward them. He couldn't possibly escape.

A sense of dragging ensued. Someone, maybe a pair of someones, pulled him faceup to the shore.

"Your tracking worked perfectly," a man said.

A woman responded. "Of course. Now we must hurry. Time is of the essence."

Jack felt his body drop to a floor, maybe at the back of a vehicle. Prickly rope slid across his wrists, fastening them together, then the same sensation crawled along his ankles and pressed them side by side. Kat's grunt landed nearby, only inches away. A motor rumbled. As his vision cleared, he scanned the surroundings. Kat lay on her side, facing him with her eyes closed, though her rapid breaths proved the presence of life. Thick rope bound her wrists and ankles as well. Try as he might, he couldn't twist his neck to see his captors, though the edge of a huge beige wing fluttered into view for a brief second.

He tried to blink away the blurriness. How could the angels have tracked them? By planting a device on Kat? Maybe she was more sedated than she realized. Was her escape staged somehow?

Jack struggled against the ropes to no avail. Every joint felt locked tight. Torture or death was sure to come, maybe even implantation. And if that succeeded, the angels would learn their plan, and Ben and Trudy would be walking into a death trap.

Jack lay on a hospital bed, his vision blurred and his mind dizzied. Close by, Kat stood next to another bed, her hair brushed and neatly tied back in a ponytail and her face washed and glowing. Wearing the same camo clothes as she had earlier, she smiled. "The implantation was successful. Your angel is Zeebach. If he has not already taken over your mind, he soon will."

Jack touched a sore spot behind his ear. A series of stitches tickled his fingers. As his cheeks warmed, he growled, "Zeebach is in for a fight. I won't go down easily."

"Fight if you wish. The end result will be the same. He will conquer you. And if you anger him, he might inflict more pain than you can imagine."

Jack glared at her, ready for more verbal sparring, but her words, the facial glow, and serene expression suggested that an angel had already taken control. It might be better to work a different angle. "I assume you're already implanted."

"Have you had such keen observational skills all your life, Jack?" She laughed softly. "Yes, I am an angel, Laramel by name, and I have read this human's mind. Now we know your plans, and we will adjust ours accordingly."

Jack pushed to a sitting position. "Not if I can help it."

She smirked. "Your bravado is futile. You are in no position to help yourself, much less your allies."

"I can die trying." He lunged at her.

In a flash, she leaped to the side, grabbed his arm, and wrenched it behind him, adding a twist with incredible strength.

Pain ripped through his arm and into his skull with throbbing peals. As he bit his lip hard to keep from moaning, she laughed. "You were saying?" She shoved him, making him tumble to the floor.

As he tried to climb to all fours, a voice entered his mind as if spoken from somewhere close.

Pretend to be controlled by Zeebach and say nothing about my advice. It is your only hope.

Jack whispered, "Who are you?"

Silence. You may speak to me with your mind. I can hear your unguarded thoughts. But do so later. You must rise now and be Zeebach, a first-generation angel, a lowly servant. You have been infused with no information, so any questions you ask will not be considered strange.

Jack rose slowly to his feet, rubbing the back of his head and forcing a smile. "Laramel, thank you for helping me tame this human's rebellion. He is a spirited one."

"You're welcome, Zeebach. And you're right. Both he and the human I possess are strong willed. It is difficult to keep mine under control, so I put her soul in a confusing vortex for a while. I advise you to do the same for yours if he becomes troublesome."

"I will." Jack massaged his wounded arm. "I heard your name. What is your generation?"

She cocked her head, the emanating aura pulsing. "Did you get that question from the human? The rebels often refer to generations."

"I did. His mind is spewing questions at a rapid rate, but I am unaware of some of the answers, so I asked using his vocabulary."

"Interesting." A pair of wings emerged behind Kat and spread out. Leathery and infused with struts and sinews, they resembled dragon wings from fanciful illustrations. "I do not belong to any of the generations the humans have encountered. I am the hive queen, the most powerful of our race."

The voice returned to Jack's mind. *Don't ask why, but you must leave her presence as soon as possible. Your life depends on it. Give her homage, learn your part of the plan, and ask permission to go.*

Gladly. Jack straightened and squared his shoulders. "My queen, I am greatly honored by your presence. Now if you have gained the information you need from our humans, please tell me my role, and I will do whatever is necessary to aid our cause."

"We have the information we needed from you." Kat crossed her arms, her expression taut. "You are to rejoin the rebel forces at their farming community. By the time you arrive, our soldiers will be ready to attack them with a deadly contagion. Since our soldiers will have received a fake vaccine, they will die. The rebels will have the real vaccine. You are to receive it along with them. It will allow your human to survive. Once our soldiers are dead, you will lead the rebels to our headquarters here. They will follow you without question. You will find automotive transport outside, labeled number forty-one, and directions to the rebel base are already programmed in the vehicle's GPS unit in case you have trouble getting that information from your host."

Jack kept his face slack, though questions flew within. Why would the angels allow their soldiers to die? Why would the rebels follow him to headquarters without question? What diabolical plan were the angels hatching? His expression still blank, he gave her a nod. "I will go as soon as you give me leave."

"One moment. Someone is coming. I want her to meet you."

Another winged woman entered. Dressed in fashionable jeans and a white polo, she appeared to be younger than Kat, her skin flawless except for a three-inch scar across her neck, red and freshly stitched. A pendant with an inner radiant sphere dangled from a necklace. Although her face glowed, an ashen hue made her appear somewhat ill. Yet, in spite of the sickly appearance, she was stunningly beautiful.

Kat smiled. "Welcome, Novada. This is my first chance to congratulate you. Your tracking ability proved itself, exactly as you predicted."

Novada smiled in return. "My connection with you is as strong as ever. I was worried for a while, though. I sensed the general area you were in early on, but it took some time to pinpoint the exact location."

"I was worried, as well, but I shouldn't have doubted. In any case, I'm glad you're here. I need your mind-reading skills. My interrogation of the rebel leader has not gone well of late."

Novada drew close to Kat and grasped her hand. "I'm sure we can work together to break her resolve."

"She almost made me stumble," Kat said. "She planted false memories and uncharacteristic words, and she caused me to think that she was affectionate toward Jack." She nodded in his direction. "Her husband's brother. When the memories she fed me turned to something more than a sisterly affection, I became suspicious, and I stopped believing her."

Novada nodded slowly. "I see. The affection was a way to warn him. Raise red flags in his mind."

"Correct. Fortunately, I saw through the scheme before I raised too many flags."

"Kat is a clever one."

"Cleverer than I first realized. Now I think she probably lied to me about many things. She might not know the weapon's location after all."

Again, Jack forced a slack expression, though the mention of the weapon piqued his interest.

"You could expel her," Novada said.

"I thought about it. She seemed pliable at first, which gave me reason not to expel her right away, but now I feel her infusing falsehoods into her memories. If I expel her, I won't be able to tell what's true. We need to proceed with a probe soon."

"Of course. Whenever you're ready."

"Which tactic do you plan to use?"

Novada gazed into Kat's eyes. "It would be counterproductive to give her a warning, but I don't sense her listening."

"She is in a dizzied state," Kat said. "When you're ready to probe, I will release her from the vortex."

"For this stubborn woman …" Novada stepped back from Kat. "I think the best method would be to go into her mind with a conciliatory tone, to tell her exactly what she wants to hear, to confess that we have done her wrong, that I am actually her secret ally, a friend among enemies. This approach appeals to humans who want to believe the best about people. Since she assumed Jack would respond to her warning, obviously she believes he is smarter than he really is."

"An excellent point." Kat looked Jack over. "He is rather unintelligent. Strong and handsome, to be sure, but his IQ likely barely achieves room temperature level."

Once more, Jack steeled himself. Staying quiet had never been so difficult.

Novada turned toward him. "Unintelligent or not, might he know where the weapon is?"

The inner voice returned. *Make an excuse to go. Immediately. And do not look at Novada. Her beauty enhances her mind-probing gifts.*

"He does not," Jack said. "After the queen threw him to the floor, his will broke, and I was able to probe him with ease. He is no more than a grunt who obeys orders."

Kat waved a hand. "Then take your leave. You know what to do."

"Right away." As Jack headed for the exit, he cast a stealthy glance at Kat before focusing on his path. Apparently, she had been implanted a long time ago, proving that this Laramel witch was quite an actress. Her defense of Ben and his merciful ways was so convincing.

Also, his rescue of her had been part of her ploy from the start, and he missed every clue, every red flag. And what about the wings? Could she make them sprout and contract at will? Could she repress the angelic glow? And what memories did Kat have that they would try to extract? If they were hunting for her anti-angel weapon, nothing they could dredge from her brain would do them any good. She never had a chance to finish working on it.

Jack quick-marched into a vacant hallway and followed signs to the building's exit, likely the same doors Ben and Trudy had entered earlier. As he walked out and headed toward a portico curb where a jeep sat, the number 41 emblazoned on its side, he spoke quietly. "Okay, voice in my head, I think we can talk safely now. What's going on? What's this all about?"

Regarding what this is all about, I am implanted in your brain, but I have not taken over your faculties.

"Why not?" Jack opened the jeep's door and sat behind the steering wheel. "Isn't that your job … um … Zeebach, right?"

It is not my job, as you say. And I am not Zeebach, as they have called me. My real name is Zachariel.

"Zachariel. Got it." Jack found a winged, cylindrical key protruding from the ignition and started the engine. "Whose side are you on? Mine or theirs?"

Neither, but I will continue to help you meet your goals to vanquish the false angels and to protect your human allies. And while I am inside you, I can protect you from physical harm in various ways, though not from the contagion, which is why you will need to administer the vaccine as soon as possible. I can also endow you with abilities that you never had, but I will not speak of those yet.

"Okay. I call that my side." Jack turned the jeep's GPS unit on, shifted to drive, and began following the map's directions. "You call them false angels. If you're not one of them, how could you be inside my brain? What exactly are you? And why did you tell me to scram when Novada asked about probing me?"

Novada would have discerned quickly that you are not under my control. Other than that, I will not explain further at this time. For now, you must proceed with all haste to the farm you call your rebel base and report what you have discovered about Katherine Garrison, that they plan to extract from her the location of a certain weapon.

Jack nodded. "Kat's the inventor, so I guess she does know where it is—or was—but she never finished it. At least, it was never tested, as far as I know. Commander Barks would be a fool to try to use it. It could blow up in his face."

Considering the angels' fear of the weapon, perhaps it is more of a threat to them than you realize. I assume that you have not kept up with its progress or whereabouts.

"Nope. Only Kat had access. She even kept the secrets from Ben. Only she and Barks knew. And maybe our doctor, though I'm not sure about that."

Then the subject is not your concern for now. Since your siblings are marching straight into a trap, you must hurry and protect them from disaster. In fact, you might already be too late.

Chapter Ten

Ben stood with Trudy at the vaccination table. A young, redheaded male soldier walked in wearing a white T-shirt and camo pants. He stopped next to the table and stood erect, his face expressionless, though a gleam in his eye gave away excitement. A female followed, dark-skinned with bright brown eyes that reflected the same enthusiasm. Soon, more than a hundred soldiers had arrived, all dressed the same.

The line of soldiers coiled around the hall and into a stairwell, some of them older men and women, including those who probably wouldn't go to the battlefield. They all had to be vaccinated in case anyone in the strike force returned with the contagion, maybe on their skin or attached to their clothes.

Ben studied the faces within view. Most really were kids—naïve, impressionable, idealistic youngsters who were eager to do what was right, at least in the perception of the media-manipulated mindset, a kind of groupthink borne of angel miracles and a world made less chaotic by brute force. Were they really noble-minded? Or were they killers for hire, ready to follow an order to slaughter innocent people? That remained to be seen.

He stared at the injector gun, his fingers tight around the handle. He was here to kill these soldiers, ready to follow orders of his own and take so many lives himself. Hypocrisy? That label was hard to dodge. He was a killer for hire, noble in his own mind, ready to terminate hundreds who trusted in his benevolence, unaware of his treacherous goal. How different was he from these kids?

At this point, was there any way out of this trap? A way to accomplish their mission without being as murderous as the pseudo-angelic tyrants? Maybe. If the soldiers' deaths came at their own hands and not his, he and Trudy could save their people and their own integrity at the same time.

"Ben," Trudy whispered, leaning close, "you're zoning out. What's cooking?"

"This." He switched the gun's delivery setting to half. "Do it."

Trudy's eyes widened. "What? Why?"

"Just trust me."

She switched the setting on her gun. "You'd better know what you're doing."

"We're all set," Major Livingstone said as she reentered the room and faced the line of soldiers. "When each of you gets the injection, take a cup of water and choose a cot. You'll find barf bags at the end of the row in case you need one, but you'll probably fall asleep before the nausea hits. When you awaken, we'll be ready to round up the rebels."

The soldiers responded with a loud "Hooah!" in unison.

Major Livingstone turned toward Ben and Trudy. "Shall we begin?"

Ben withdrew two more guns from the bag, switched the dosage level to half on each, and set them on the table. "I assume you know how to load vials, Major. We'll count on you to keep us supplied with vaccine and cotton balls. It will speed up the process."

"Certainly." She lifted the vaccine cooler to the table, removed a tray of vials, and began loading the guns. "Have you two been vaccinated?"

Ben shook his head. "We are not going to the battlefield, and we will be gone before you return."

"That was the original plan," the major said, "but I received a new communication from headquarters that might alter your orders."

Ben retightened his grip on his gun. "What did it say?"

"The plans are premature, but you will probably need to be vaccinated." She set both loaded injectors on the table. "Proceed, doctors. I will take my shot last, then vaccinate you two."

"We can do each other," Trudy said. "Not a problem."

"I hope you'll allow me. It's an honor I will never forget."

Ben nodded at her. "Thank you. The honor will be ours."

When the major glanced away for a moment, Trudy pivoted toward Ben and spoke with tight lips, barely audible. "BS meter's in the red zone."

"No kidding. We need hip boots. She's a sycophant to the max." Ben lifted his gun. "Let's do it."

Trudy turned toward the soldiers. "File past us. Halt by twos. Make sure your upper arm is exposed. Keep the line moving."

As they swabbed the soldiers' skin with alcohol-soaked cotton balls, injected their arms, and swapped out guns as needed, Trudy kept glancing at Ben, her expression a blend of curiosity and anger.

Ben concealed a sigh. No wonder she looked that way. He had changed the plan without her knowledge or approval. She was in the dark.

Noise in the room grew—soldiers choosing cots, chatting, and laughing. Ben took the opportunity to whisper to Trudy, "Where's the good juice?"

She glanced down at her pants pocket, then continued injecting arms.

After a couple of hundred soldiers had filed past, yawns drifted through the air, then snoring sounds along with a few moans as some felt the sickness before conking out.

Once the final pair had received their vaccinations, Trudy set her gun in the medical bag and exhaled as she reached into her pants pocket. "That was rather taxing."

"I agree." Ben set his gun in the bag beside hers and gave her a stealthy wink. "Do you need to use the restroom?"

Trudy nodded and picked up the bag. "I'll be right back."

"Vaccinations first," Major Livingstone said as she rolled up her sleeve.

"What's the hurry?"

The major handed Trudy one of the other guns and a wet cotton ball. "To get over the side effects as soon as possible."

Trudy gave the bag to Ben, then swabbed the major's arm, taking extra time in the process. "You know, Major," Trudy said, obviously trying to keep her distracted, "we are quite interested in accompanying you to the battlefield. Maybe you could tell us how to prepare for the experience."

While they chatted, Ben set the bag on the table. The real vaccine vial now lay inside. He loaded it into one of the guns. When he finished, Trudy vaccinated the major, then stepped back and eyed the injector she had used. "Well, this gun's empty now."

"I have a fresh one." Ben handed the newly loaded gun to the major and pushed up his sleeve. "We thank you for your service."

"It's my pleasure." The major swabbed Ben's skin with a cotton ball and injected the vaccine, then did the same to Trudy. After finishing, she set the gun on the table and scanned the remaining fake vaccine vials. "I wonder why we have so much left over."

"We weren't sure of the number of soldiers," Trudy said as she collected the injectors and set them together on the table, stealthily unloading the vial with the real vaccine from the gun. "Unfortunately, we have to incinerate the rest, including the guns. Once the vaccine's been at room temperature, it can't be cooled again without ruining it."

"I'll get an orderly to take care of that." The major set one of the injectors to the side along with a few vials. "But we'll save some doses for the soldiers guarding the gate. We can't have everyone sleeping at the same time." She nodded toward the common area. "Why don't you choose a couple of cots? I'm sure you'll need them soon."

While the major handed the other three injectors and the extra fake vaccine to an orderly, Ben and Trudy found side-by-side cots and sat facing each other. Trudy leaned close and whispered sharply, "What in blue blazes are you thinking?"

He folded his hands and wrung his fingers. "I'm thinking that these kids deserve a chance to make a choice. If they go along with the orders to slaughter the rebels, then they deserve to die, but they'll die by their own hands, not ours."

Her whisper turned into a hiss. "Did you ignore what I said? No quarter for volunteers. We need to be killers, not trial judges."

"They're going to die. We guaranteed that. We've given them the rope to hang themselves with."

Trudy shook her head. "I don't like it. I don't like it at all. Barks is expecting to march through the front gate in a few hours and overpower a couple of guards, thinking everyone else is dead. And we still have to rescue Jack, but we'll be conked out with the rest of them."

"It's going to work. We just need to tell Barks before we fall asleep. Give him enough time to get everyone inoculated before the soldiers show up at our base."

"I'll make the call." Trudy withdrew her earbud from her pocket. "I said I have to hit the can, so I'd better go. And with only a few women here, I'm more likely to be alone."

"Good point. And I'd better go, too."

They rose, found the restrooms in the hall, and entered their respective doors. With the two urinals occupied by soldiers, Ben chose a stall and stayed as quiet as possible, hoping to listen to the men. One of them spoke up. "Yeah, I heard the rumor. The major's tight-lipped about it, but it's all the same to me. We're vaccinated, so no problem."

"Pardon me for having a conscience," the other soldier said. "I mean, if they attack us, I'd mow 'em down, but us attacking first? They have women and children."

"So what? People die in wars, including women and children. You'll do what you're told. Case closed."

"Yeah, but putting a kid in the crosshairs will give me nightmares."

"Suck it up, soldier. If you turn tail, I'll shoot you myself."

"Is that supposed to scare me? You couldn't hit a ..." Their voices faded as they exited the restroom.

Ben shuffled out behind them and met Trudy in the hallway, her arms tightly crossed.

"What's up?" he asked.

"Barks okayed the change. He'll still get all the weaponry they bring with them to the farm, every frontline soldier will be dead, and we'll have no casualties on our side. He says it should work fine. They'll just hunker down somewhere safe until the contagion kills the invaders."

"Good. But you're still bothered. What's eating you?"

She set a hand on his chest, pushed him against a wall, and whispered with a new hiss. "You flushed our plan down the toilet without telling me. I'm risking my life with you, and you don't trust me enough to ask my opinion. I'm not your kid sister anymore."

Ben's ears burned. As he gazed into her fierce eyes, her words struck home. She was right, absolutely right. He grasped her hand in a thumb lock and pushed away from the wall. "You nailed me. I was wrong. I should've asked you first."

"Fat lot of good that does us now." She heaved a deep sigh, her eyes sparkling. "Just trust me from now on, okay? I trained for this. I know what I'm doing."

"I will. I promise."

"And I have news. Barks said they checked out the refuge. It was empty, but it's clear someone was there recently. Two puddles next to a wall."

"Two? Jack and who else?"

"No clue, but at least we have hope for Jack now." She nodded toward the two soldiers as they resettled into their cots. "I saw them come out before you did. Hear anything interesting?"

"Unfortunately. They're ready to slaughter everyone. Doesn't matter if they're women and children."

Trudy crossed her arms again and took on an I-told-you-so pose. "Is that another way of saying I was right? That we should've killed everyone? Because it's too late to administer a second dose. The orderly already took the supplies."

Ben blinked. "A second dose?"

Trudy hooked her arm in his and walked toward their cots. "Right. What about it?"

When they sat, he touched her arm, keeping his voice low. "We got half a dose, just like everyone else. The instructions for taking the real vaccine call for more. I'm wondering if half a dose will protect us."

"Doc didn't say anything about the real vaccine's dosage requirement, but our vial has some left. It's back in my pocket. We can juice up again, but we have to make sure no one's watching."

"I have news," the major said as she strode toward them. "The queen herself ordered you to come to the battle with us."

Ben gave her a nod. "Of course we will obey, but did she communicate a reason? Something we can prepare for?"

"None. Maybe she's concerned about relying on an untested vaccine and wants to make sure doctors are on hand." The major pulled pins from her hair bun and shook out her tresses. "Though that's doubtful. If anyone contracts the disease, nothing can be done. It's a fast-acting strain. Death occurs in minutes."

"Yes, that was my understanding as well."

When the major left, Trudy leaned close. "It's simple. They're suspicious of us because of the name change, so they're sending us to the battle to make sure we suffer whatever fate the soldiers do. If we're really angels and everyone is vaccinated, no problem. If we're not, then we die with the soldiers."

Ben stroked his chin. "More test cases, and they execute two angel impersonators."

"Either way, they get what they want."

"It's like we're prisoners without cuffs on."

"Right. We couldn't escape even if we tried."

Ben raised a finger. "Unless we wake up first. Our half dose probably has less of a sedative than their half dose."

"Because their full dose was designed to kill them, and ours wasn't. Good thought." She let out a wide yawn. "But I'm already feeling it anyway."

"I guess we'll give in and go to sleep. Then we have to wake up and get out of here. It won't take long for them to question why our wings aren't growing."

"Another good thought. And then we won't need the second dose, because we won't get exposed."

"And we don't want to fall asleep again."

"Right." Trudy narrowed her eyes. "I suppose they'll go through with the invasion without us. Too much is at stake for them to abort it."

"Agreed. We can try to monitor it from a safe place." Ben scanned the room. Nearly everyone was asleep, though Major Livingstone stood near the door whispering to an armed guard, a man nearly as big as a bear, probably not yet vaccinated. She was likely giving him orders to watch two potential angel imposters closely. But why wasn't she getting groggy? Her dose of sedative was stronger than his or Trudy's. Maybe she was good at resisting the influence.

A wave of dizziness flooded in. Ben reclined on his cot and looked at Trudy. "Lights out."

"Yeah. I'm going dark." She yawned again and lay on her side. "See you in a few hours."

Ben allowed the dizziness to take control and fell asleep.

Chapter Eleven

Iona pedaled with all her might across an open field, bouncing with the bicycle on the uneven ground. The huntsmen were less than a minute behind, riding horses, fast ones. How could she possibly elude them now? Leo seemed able to sniff out the bike, maybe the grease on the axle or the rubber in the tires, but if she dumped it, she'd never be able to stay ahead of them.

She looked back. Framed by the setting sun, three horses broke out of the distant forest, galloping, their hooves raising a cloud of dust.

Breathless, she pedaled on. After cresting a ridge, she sped downhill, the bounces worse than ever. Ahead, a barn stood at the edge of a cornfield, the stalks brown and spindly. Beyond the barn, several horses grazed in a grassy meadow bordered by a corral fence.

She rode to the gate and eyed the horses. Could she take one of them? Maybe, but it might be impossible to ride bareback faster than the huntsmen could in saddles.

A foul odor assaulted her nostrils. A huge manure pile sat just inside the fence, probably a resource for fertilizer. She turned toward the ridge. Although the sound of galloping hooves drew closer, the huntsmen hadn't yet reached the crest.

Still wearing her backpack, she leaped off the bike, leaned it against the fence, and untied a short rope holding the gate closed. After fastening the rope around her waist, she opened the gate and padded toward a horse that looked like a young gelding. "It's all right," she said in a gentle tone. "I won't hurt you." She clutched a fistful of his mane and jogged with him through the gateway, then turned him in the direction she had been going and slapped his flank. He took off at a fast gallop.

Hoofbeats drew closer. Iona hurried back into the corral and lay on her stomach with her face at the edge of the manure. Holding her breath, she dug into the pile, pushing manure back into place behind her. Once she reached the middle, she stopped. Breathing through her mouth, she quieted herself and listened. Fortunately, horse manure was light and porous enough to allow air and sound to pass through.

Soon, the galloping hooves made the ground tremble, drawing closer and closer. When they stopped, Iona stiffened.

"That's her bike, Leo," one of the huntsmen said.

"Or course it is, Prince Perceptive." Leo's voice seemed only a step or two away. "She decided she couldn't stay ahead of us on a bicycle, so she stole a horse. Smart girl."

"But a horse is easier to track than a bike. That's not so smart."

"Except that we don't know which horse. The gate is open. Several could be gone."

"Oh. Right. And the ground is dry and hard. I don't see any hoofprints."

"Which means that we'll have to rely on my nose."

"The smell of a horse? But you don't know which one to track."

"We won't be following the scent of a bicycle or a horse. We'll follow the scent of a young woman, Iona herself."

"But you've never been in sniffing distance. You don't know what she smells like."

"How little you know, Pisces. Just trust me. I can find her."

Footsteps struck the ground nearby. Iona held her breath as she imagined the three men searching the area. "She walked here," Leo said, his voice near the edge of the pile. "Maybe she mounted a horse at this spot."

"Could be," one of the other men said. "The manure pile's been disturbed. She's short, so maybe she stood on it to mount."

Iona clenched her fists. They were getting close to the truth. Too close.

"No," Leo said. "If she stood on the pile, the manure would be flattened, and her footprints would be obvious. This loosening is due to the farmer recently digging a supply of fertilizer."

"But the corn is finished. What would he need fertilizer for?"

"Potatoes. In that field over there. They're still growing."

"Oh. Right. I didn't see them. They harvest those much later."

"Correct. But we're spending too much time here. Let's get back to the chase."

Seconds later, the sound of hooves resumed, fading. When the noise settled, Iona exhaled. That was way too close. She had fooled them for now, but what would happen if they found the gelding? Maybe they would think she rode a different horse, or maybe they would double back and search the farm area again.

Either way, it would be better to stay put, get some rest where her own odor would be shielded by the manure, a warm blanket for the night.

She rolled to her side and closed her eyes. Exhausted by the escape, she quickly fell asleep.

After what seemed like only a few minutes of sleep, something throbbed in Ben's head. He shook himself awake and sat up on the cot. His skull felt like someone was trying to crack it open.

In the adjacent cot, Trudy slept on, her eyes tightly shut as deep creases wrinkled her brow. She seemed to be in pain as well.

Ben checked a clock on the wall. It was now evening, several hours after they finished the vaccinations. Throughout the rest of the room, the soldiers slept on, some snoring, most quiet.

He touched the incision behind his ear, the pain's focal point. Something was going on in there, and it couldn't be good. He leaned close and studied Trudy's incision, now red and swollen. She was suffering the same effects.

Ben walked to the guard and whispered, "My fellow doctor's implantation incision is breaking open. I need to re-stitch it, but I am low on sterile gauze. I assume you have some in your supply room. A few pads will do."

The guard nodded. "Sure. I'll get it."

When he left, Ben grabbed the medical bag from the table and hurried to his cot. With his back toward the door, he withdrew the scalpel, forceps, and stitching supplies from the bag. With no anesthetic, it would be better to do this while Trudy was still asleep.

He cut her stitches, then sliced into her skin. She cringed but stayed quiet. Using the forceps, he grasped the capsule, a bit deeper than expected, and pulled it out. Tentacles protruded through holes in the glass. The angel implant had been burrowing out, already crawling toward the brain stem to take control. Once it completely broke the capsule, it could squeeze the rest of the way past the skull.

Resisting the urge to gag, Ben found a zip-lock pouch in the medical bag and sealed the squirming capsule inside.

Footsteps approached. Ben stuffed the bag into his pocket and turned. The guard walked up and set a box of sterile pads on Trudy's cot. "Can I get you anything else?"

"No. These will do."

"I'll be at my usual place if you need me." The guard walked away.

Ben opened the box and pulled out a pad. As he cleaned and re-stitched Trudy's incision, he imagined his own implant crawling toward his brain stem, the tentacles snaking along millimeter by millimeter.

When he finished, he grabbed the tube of glow cream and reapplied it to his face and to Trudy's. She smiled during the process but stayed asleep. After putting the tube away, he carried the medical bag to the exit door and nodded toward the restrooms beyond, the doors within view. "Been sleeping awhile. Gotta take a dump."

The guard glanced at Trudy before refocusing on Ben. "Go ahead."

As Ben walked toward the restroom, he winced. Take a dump? That was no way for an angel to talk. Maybe the guard didn't notice.

After entering, he set the bag on the edge of a sink, looked in the mirror, and repeated on himself the same procedure he had performed on Trudy, working quickly to keep the guard from getting suspicious. Although cutting and stitching himself proved to be awkward and excruciatingly painful, he finished in only a few minutes, and the throbbing eased.

He dropped the zip-lock pouch, now containing two angels, into the toilet and flushed it, then looked at the mirror again. The glow had brightened. Maybe the change wouldn't be too noticeable.

The guard walked in. "What's taking so long?"

Ben lifted the needle and thread. "A stitch came loose. I was trying to tighten it."

The guard eyed the incision. "Looks like you got it. Some blood smeared, but not too bad."

"Thank you." Ben set the needle and thread into the medical bag and zipped it. "I should return to my cot. I'm still not feeling well."

"Sure." The guard opened the door. As Ben walked past, the guard set a hand on his back, then pulled away. "Sorry. I should know better than to touch an angel without permission."

"No harm done." Ben strode toward the cots. It seemed that the guard's eyes drilled into his back. Was the touch a check to see if the wings were sprouting? Obviously his suspicion was growing.

When Ben arrived at the cot, Trudy sat up and offered a nod, wincing as she touched the stitches. "I dreamed I had the surgery again. Stings like crazy."

"You did. Our implants broke through the glass. I had to take them out." Ben set the medical bag on the floor. "I flushed them down the toilet. And more news …" He gestured with his eyes toward the guard. "He noticed that I don't have any wing sprouts."

Trudy kept her gaze averted. "So we're exposed. Naked. When the major wakes up, we're cooked."

"Maybe." Ben glanced at the remaining injector gun on the table. "Let's vaccinate the guard with the fake stuff. I'll distract him."

"Double dose to the neck," Trudy said. "If he's on to us, we can't take any chances."

"The juice has to put him down fast. He's a big guy."

Trudy grinned. "You can take him. No problem."

"With a surprise attack, but we have to put him down quietly, then go to the major and inject her again."

Trudy shifted uneasily. "Uh ... yeah. Sure."

Ben tilted his head. "Something wrong? I thought you wanted me to consult you."

"I do. It's just that your sudden killer-Ben mode took me by surprise. It's all good."

"Let's go before I change my mind." Ben rose and walked casually toward the guard while Trudy picked up the injector and a vial and concealed them behind her.

"Private," Ben said as he drew near. "Have you seen angel wings sprouting before?"

He nodded. "Couple of times."

"Can you look at my back and tell me what you think? My wife's not sure."

"No problem." The guard chuckled. "Actually, you asking me to look is kind of a relief."

"Oh?" Ben lifted his brow. "Why is that?"

"Never mind. Not important." The guard gestured with a finger. "Let's take a peek."

While Ben stripped off his shirt, the guard moved behind him, and Trudy positioned herself at the guard's side, the injector ready.

Ben twisted the shirt into a thick rope. Trudy would inject him at any second. "See anything familiar?"

"Not yet. Maybe your back muscles are hiding—Hey! What did you do?"

Ben spun, leaped behind the guard, and wrapped the shirt around his throat. As he gagged, Ben pulled him to the floor. The guard flailed. His meaty hand slapped the injector from Trudy's grasp and sent it flying. It clattered and slid away. Ben banged the guard's head against the floor. Finally, he fell slack.

Ben released the shirt and checked for signs of life. The guard's chest rose and fell in a steady rhythm. "Alive, but knocked out."

"He'll be dead soon." Trudy retrieved the injector and looked it over. "It's broken. Now what are we going to do about the major?"

Ben twisted the shirt again. "I'll take care of her."

"Really?" Trudy set the broken injector in the medical bag and put it on the table. "In her sleep?"

"You got another idea?"

"Uh … no."

"First, let's get Private Grizzly Bear to a cot." They carried the guard to an empty cot and laid him on it. Once they had set him in a natural sleeping pose, they found the major on a cot in a far corner, sleeping on her side.

Ben knelt next to her. Her hair had fallen back, exposing her ear as well as a scar behind it. He pointed at the scar. "Check this out."

"Implanted?" Trudy whispered.

He nodded. "Get the AngelScan."

She hustled to the table and retrieved the bag, withdrawing the scanner as she returned.

Ben took it and set it on the side of the major's head. The screen displayed her brain as well as the red, octopus-like angel within, its tentacles embedded in the brain stem. Yet, no sphere of white floated anywhere.

He kept his voice low. "No soul."

"What?" Trudy studied the screen. "I've heard of that possibility, but I've never seen it before."

"Same." Ben lifted the shirt with a tight grip. "And it gives me an easy out for my conscience. This is not a real human being."

Trudy nodded. "Do it."

Ben pushed the shirt under the major's neck and twisted it into a tight tourniquet. She gagged softly, quivered for a few seconds, then relaxed and fell limp. After several more seconds, he released her and checked her pulse. She was dead.

He rose, put the shirt back on, and smoothed the wrinkles. "Having no soul is new. This could be huge."

"I'll look for a medical log and see if I can spot anything." Trudy hurried to an adjacent examination room.

Ben took the broken injector gun from the medical bag. Now if they wanted a second dose, they would have to find another injector. He dumped the gun in the restroom's trash receptacle and returned to his cot. Trudy joined him, sat on hers, and opened a file folder on her lap. "I found this in a locked drawer. Her keys were on the desk." She flipped a page. "Okay, she got implanted almost two years ago."

"Two years. Mostly Gen Ones back then. Explains why she didn't glow or have wings."

"Right." Trudy blinked at the page. "Strange. It says here that she got the vaccination two weeks ago."

"What?" Ben shifted to her cot and looked on.

Trudy set a finger on the date. "See?"

"Yeah. Exactly two weeks." He looked at Trudy. "Then why would she let us vaccinate her again?"

Trudy shrugged. "To keep us from knowing she was vaccinated before?"

"So it was being kept a secret."

"You mean she was a guinea pig to see if the vaccine was a success before giving it to the soldiers? She didn't even know she had been vaccinated."

"Right. They were willing to sacrifice a Gen One."

"Ben." Trudy set a hand on his knee and squeezed. "Does success mean what I think it means?"

His throat tightened. "The vaccine destroys a person's soul. Nothing there but a body controlled by an implant."

"And Commander Barks is going to inject the vaccine into everyone."

Ben licked his drying lips. "Or he already has."

"And it got injected into us." Trudy's voice shook. "Ben, a vaccine does the same to a person's body whether or not it's implanted with an angel."

"Makes sense. What's your point?"

She bit her lip. "Are we going to lose our souls?"

He tried to infuse his own voice with confidence. "We got half a dose. Maybe not."

"I have to call Barks." She leaped up and hurried toward the restrooms, a finger touching her ear. "Outpost seven. Come in, outpost seven."

Chapter Twelve

With Trudy gone to contact the commander, Ben leafed through the pages in the major's file and stopped at a handwritten note. *Major Livingstone's vaccination worked as planned. She is now in a servile state. As expected, not only does the vaccine kill the contagion, it also purges the soul in a few hours, thereby eliminating all obstacles to perfect obedience— no boundaries, no morals. The ideal soldier. It remains to be seen how an added payload will affect a human. That will be tested during the invasion.*

He closed the file. So all of the major's angel praise wasn't pure BS. And no wonder the record was locked away. The angels didn't want anyone to know they were using the vaccine to make soulless robots. And maybe her robotic condition explained why the sedative didn't affect her as quickly.

Novada's question returned to mind. *What, then, is the actual purpose of the contagion?* An excuse to create the soul-killing vaccine and enslave everyone. But what could the payload be? Since he had been injected with the invasion version of the vaccine, that payload was probably now coursing through his veins.

The throbbing headache returned. Was it the start of the soul-killing process, or was it just stress? Unfortunately, if the vaccine worked as designed, he might never know.

Trudy appeared at the door, shuffling slowly, her face pale. She sat at his side and wrapped both arms around him, sniffling as she whispered, "They've already been vaccinated. Everyone. Full doses."

Ben trembled, then quickly steeled himself. "How did Barks react?"

"He got quiet. Then his voice shook. He said he would prepare everyone."

"Prepare? What does that mean?"

"He said something about deploying the weapon, but he had to take care of our community first."

"A suicide mission with Kat's ultimate weapon." Ben massaged his aching temples. "I read in the file that the vaccine purges the soul in just a few hours, making the victim a pliable zombie. If that happens too soon, and Barks knows where the weapon is …"

"Then the angels will be able to find out. And if the vaccine works as expected, the rebellion will end. Our own people will be zombies for the angels, even the children. And everyone who got vaccinated at the temple. They're creating a perfectly obedient army. We are screwed to the wall."

"The temple. That reminds me. We need to look for a way to read that disk." He withdrew the disk from his pocket and scanned the room. The desk computer was an old model. Maybe it would work. After finding the computer's media port, he slid the disk in. The reader hummed for a moment, and a file folder icon appeared on the screen.

He tapped the icon with a fingertip. A message popped up: "Enter Password."

"Password?" Ben pounded a fist on the desk. "She didn't tell me about a password."

"That doesn't make sense." Trudy drew closer, eyeing the screen. "Why would she give you the disk without a password if she knew you needed one?"

"Thanks for spelling it out, but it doesn't help."

"Maybe she gave it to you, but you didn't pick up on it. Think about everything she said from the moment you saw her."

Ben stroked his chin. "Well, she asked if she could help me, and I said something about maybe she knew why I was there. Then she said it was too early for that, and I said too early for what. She said for the vaccinations and asked what else I could have come for. So I asked what else was available, you know, to give her a chance to reveal who she was."

"But you didn't know yet that she was the mole," Trudy said, "so you were playing coy."

"Right. I asked her if there was any secret stuff she normally doesn't tell anyone. And she said ..." Ben scrunched his brow. "She used a word. Something odd. I can't remember."

"That was probably the password."

"Eso something."

"Esophagus?" Trudy asked.

"No, not medical."

"That's my field. I can't think of any other eso words."

"This computer probably has a dictionary." Ben switched to the computer's program options, found a dictionary, and opened it to the letter E, then browsed to ESO while Trudy watched. "There's esophagus," he said.

Trudy pointed. "Esoteric."

"It's the next word. Esoterica." He read the definition out loud. "Items intended for a restricted number of people."

"That has to be it."

"Yep." Ben switched to the password screen and typed the word in. The computer responded with "Password Accepted."

Trudy crossed her arms. "Clever that she inserted it into your conversation."

"Yeah. More to her than meets the eye."

A map filled the top half of the screen with a document underneath. Ben read it out loud. "To the rebel field agent. My name is Iona. I am a priestess in the temple, and the angels forced me to become a spy for them. I infiltrated your ranks and became a spy for you, a double agent, but I don't have time to type out that story. My task for the angels was to learn if a secret rebel weapon is real. As an angel worshiper at the time, I accepted the mission gladly. While I was snooping at your farming community under the guise of a shepherdess, Commander Barks discovered my real identity. Instead of executing me as a traitor, he asked me to infiltrate the temple and learn whatever secrets I could that might help his cause, though he wouldn't trust me with any rebel secrets until I proved myself. This mission was more vague, but it gave me the opportunity to look into rebel files, both physical and electronic, to sniff out the weapon.

"Being young and innocent looking, I gained access that others likely could not have gained. I learned that the weapon was, indeed, real. I informed angel headquarters, and they told me to keep digging to learn its location. One day when I was searching an area, Commander Barks found me. He had some heated words for me, and I thought he was going to shoot me on the spot. Instead, he blindfolded me and took me to the weapon's location because that's where he was heading. Anyway, I didn't see the weapon. I know only that it is in the region shown on the attached map.

"While I was there, I discovered that Commander Barks has delayed the deployment of the weapon. He didn't say why, but he told me about your mission to help the rebels become immune to the contagion. He wants to get the vaccine in hand and test it on his people as a way to ensure its safety for others. One huge problem. I learned that, although the vaccine will stop the contagion, it also has a dangerous side effect, though I don't know what that effect is. I suggest that you warn Barks about the potential dangers of the vaccine, but don't tell him that I learned about the weapon.

"You see, after my final meeting with Barks, Queen Laramel grilled me about what I learned so far. She is obsessed with destroying the weapon. Her interrogation included forms of torture that I won't describe here. I will just say that she forced me to endure a lot of pain. That's when reality hit me like a sledgehammer. True angels would not treat their loyal subjects like that, and I determined to keep the weapon's approximate location to myself. Then I delved more deeply into the angels' secrets and learned that they are an alien race, and they will do much more to control humans than they have so far.

"That's why I give this information to you now. I believe you must bypass your commander and, assuming that the weapon is designed to eliminate the angels, deploy it immediately. Destroy the angels before they destroy you. Every man, woman, and child in the world is counting on you.

"Also, as you might guess, I am risking my life giving you this information. If I die, maybe my efforts will not be in vain. Only you will determine that outcome."

Trudy blew out a long breath. "Wow. That's intense."

"Tell me about it." Ben studied the map. It showed a region a hundred miles square about eighty miles to the east of angel headquarters. The area included a mountain ridge, a deep canyon, and a spread of meadowlands. "Pretty big range. I wish we could narrow it down."

Trudy crossed her arms again, this time in her analysis pose. "Okay, let's focus on what we know. The angel queen wants to find the weapon and destroy it. That means we have to, number one, keep the information out of her hands and, number two, protect the weapon at all costs."

"Right, but if Iona's forced to take the vaccine, she'll become one of the zombies, and the information will still be in her brain. An angel implant could unlock it and eventually track down the weapon. Then it's toast."

Trudy lifted three fingers. "That's number three. Find Iona and keep her safe."

"And since we're sure Barks is compromised now that he's been vaccinated, we have to bypass him. Deploy the weapon without his say so. Exactly like Iona said."

"You're right." Trudy cursed under her breath. "If we had read the disk before we delivered the vaccine, Barks and the others would be safe. Iona got the intel to us early enough. We just didn't process it in time."

Ben stared at the disk, still in the computer's drive. He was the one who delayed reading it, choosing other priorities instead. Iona had risked so much to get the information to him. Why hadn't he put the brakes on the mission to see what she had to say? It was a stupid mistake, and likely a fatal one.

He heaved a sad sigh. "No use whipping ourselves over wrong turns. We just have to stay on task. Get this mission done. Then we'll move on to the next."

Trudy sighed as well. "Right again. The vaccinations at the temple are done. Thousands of zombies in the making, and it's too late to stop it."

"Let's shift to what we have right in front of us." He tapped on the major's file folder. "This is interesting stuff. Maybe the medical info will give you some ideas."

"Read it to me. I need to get my mind off all these screwups."

"More likely to burn them into your brain." Ben read the file's contents to Trudy, taking the time to let her absorb the information. When he finished, he exhaled heavily. "So there's the proof. We committed the ultimate screwup."

"But maybe we'll have time to finish the job. Make sure the disease kills the invading soldiers. Take their equipment and hide it somewhere so they can't use it."

"Not much time for all that." Ben tapped the file on his knee. "Just a few hours to soul purging."

"Purging. That could mean expelled, not destroyed."

"How could a soul be expelled?"

"Medically, I can't be sure, but maybe the brain's environment becomes toxic to the presence of a soul, and the soul has to leave."

"Like when the body dies," Ben said. "So maybe the vaccine forces the brain to mimic death somehow, and the soul leaves for the afterlife. And we have no idea what the payload will do to the zombie that stays alive."

"But with only half a dose, maybe we have more time than we think. If we have, let's say, eight or ten hours, we can make sure the contagion kills these soldiers and then try to rescue Jack." Trudy laughed under her breath. "I don't know about you, but this news will turn me into an ultimate warrior."

"You mean, more reckless? Ready to take life-threatening chances?"

"Exactly. If the rebellion dies, we have to destroy as much of the angel hierarchy as we can."

"And we'll find the weapon. Do whatever it takes to deploy it."

"Brother and sister demolition team." She offered a quivering smile. "Not a great way to bond, but what choice do we have?"

"No choice. And I think we've waited long enough. Let's do this." Ben rose and clapped his hands. "Wake up, soldiers. We have urgent news."

The sleepers stirred. Some sat up, and some stretched, yawning. When they had all awakened and turned their bleary eyes toward Ben, he continued in a loud voice, waving the file folder. "We have learned that Major Livingstone had taken the vaccination before. For some reason that we have not yet determined, she took another dose today, which put far too much vaccine into her body. Unfortunately, the second dose killed her."

Murmurs spread across the room before quickly subsiding.

Ben gestured toward the big guard. "This private also succumbed. We suspect that he suffered an anaphylactic seizure from an allergic reaction."

More murmurs arose, this time continuing as Ben went on, even louder now. "We checked everyone else, and it looks like we have no other negative reactions. This is a tragic result, but such is the risk with medical breakthroughs. And since you are soldiers, I know you will gather courage and do your jobs." He lifted a hand. "Who will take charge in the major's absence?"

A forty-something man with shaved head and muscular, tattooed forearms rose to his feet. "I'm Captain Nelson. I was second in command of this operation. I'm in charge now."

"Excellent." Ben walked to the captain and spoke with a low tone. "Are you aware of which side will actually deploy the contagion?"

He flexed an eagle on his right forearm. "The payload is already in the aircraft, and I will inform everyone soon. But how do we know the vaccinations worked?"

"While you were all asleep, we took blood samples from twenty soldiers, and all twenty had active antibodies."

"Good. We can leave right away and attack under cover of darkness."

"What will be the method of deploying the contagion?" Ben asked.

"Low-flying drops, like crop dusting."

"And the range of coverage?"

"We have an informant who identified a twenty-square-mile region. We plan to cover all of that area and fifty percent more to make sure every rebel rat dies."

Ben raised his brow. "Is this informant one of their higher-level officers?"

"My understanding is that the informant actually lived within the community. We're certain the information is accurate."

Ben gave the captain a nod. "Let's proceed."

While the captain barked orders to the soldiers, Ben sidled to Trudy and whispered, "A spy at the community."

"Iona?"

"I doubt it. Since the major said we had to join the invasion, I'm thinking they know our plan."

"Jack's been implanted?" Trudy asked. "They caught him after he was in the refuge?"

"I can't think of anyone else who could tell them. Barks is at our base."

Trudy scowled. "Then the angels knew about the fake vaccine. They altered their plans to let us test the real vaccine on our people, not these soldiers. They're manipulating the invasion's movements as we speak."

Ben gestured toward the soldiers as they folded the cots and carried them out, though they left the two dead soldiers on their cots. "And they kept everyone here in the dark because they're all going to die, whether from our fake vaccine or from the contagion."

"So how can we use this information to our advantage?"

"Well, they didn't know we would kill the major. Maybe we can send updates to them in her name. Get some intel that way."

"Then we'd better scramble. The captain's bound to send news to HQ about her death."

"I'll speak to the captain." Ben pointed toward the adjacent office. "You figure out how the major communicated with the angels. See if you can take over that link. Pretend you're her."

"I'm on it." Trudy jogged into the office.

Ben looked at the stairway. The tail of a line of soldiers was just about to leave with the captain at the rear.

"Captain," Ben said as he hustled to join him. "May I have a word?"

The captain pivoted. "Yes. Of course."

"The major's demise is a setback, but I think it would be best to keep the news to ourselves. We wouldn't want headquarters to abort the mission, not at this late stage."

"Agreed. She was a valuable asset, but we can continue without her." The captain glanced at the empty stairwell. "Is there anything else I can do for you? I need to get an orderly to pick up our fallen soldiers."

"No." Ben patted him on the shoulder. "Go ahead."

"Thank you." He pivoted again and hurried down the stairs.

Ben jogged across the nearly vacant room, dodging the dead private's cot as well as the major's, though hers was now empty. When he strode into the office, Trudy stood next to a desk with the major's corpse seated in the wheeled chair. "What are you doing?" he asked.

"I need her print on a scanner." Trudy set the major's thumb on a pad attached to a computer. "That should do it." She pushed the chair away and leaned over the keyboard, speaking as she typed. "All is proceeding according to plan. Invasion will begin on schedule. Do you have any updates for me?" She hit the Enter key. "Let's see what happens."

Seconds later, the computer beeped. Trudy read the message out loud. "We learned moments ago that the rebels switched our vaccine with a fake one that is designed to be lethal. Since you're alive, should we assume that all is well?"

Ben nodded. "Send an affirmative. HQ will figure that out soon enough."

Trudy typed, "We had only one death, and that was from anaphylaxis. Perhaps their fake vaccine was not as lethal as the rebels hoped."

Another reply came though. "This is not a surprise. Proceed with the invasion as planned. Make sure the two imposters come with you. They will die along with the others."

Ben blinked at the screen. "Not a surprise? They guessed we wouldn't kill the soldiers?"

"Jack knows you can be soft-hearted." Trudy backed away from the desk. "Could that be it?"

"Maybe we can find out." Ben nudged Trudy to the side and typed, "Did the spy give you any new information?"

"Risky," Trudy said.

"I know." Ben tapped the Enter key. "I think it's worth it."

While they waited, Ben and Trudy glanced at each other, then at the monitor. Trudy pressed her lips together. "I don't like this. It's been too long."

"You're right. Whoever is on the other side is thinking about their response. It'll be calculated."

A few seconds later, the computer beeped, and a new message came through. "Our spy has not been cooperative lately. Her interrogation is continuing."

Trudy squinted at the screen. "Her? So Jack's not the spy? Then who is it? I'm the only woman in the inner circle. And Iona couldn't have known about our plan."

"Something's not right." Ben drummed his fingers on the desk. "They delayed the answer. Maybe they changed the spy's gender for some reason."

"But why? The major wouldn't care one way or the other."

"They might suspect someone else is communicating on this end, and they're fishing. I don't think we can take any more risks." Ben typed "Understood" and sent the message.

Trudy began raising fingers as she spoke each point. "Okay, we might be immune to the contagion. Our souls are in danger. A spy, probably female, is ratting on us. And Jack is in the wind. What's the plan?"

"Like we said before, we go with the invading army. They'll all die, and we'll take a couple of tanks to angel HQ, try to find Jack, do as much damage as we can, and die before we can lose our souls and become zombies for the angels."

Trudy blew a breathy whistle. "Things are pretty bleak when that's our best option."

"Death in battle's not so bad. We knew it could happen."

"But now we're planning on dying. That's just twisted."

Ben stared at Trudy. She stared back, her eyes filling with tears. Firming her jaw, she spun, grasped the back of the desk chair, and began wheeling the major out of the room. "Let's go. We've got angels to kill."

After they laid the major back on her cot, they collected their medical supplies and hurried down the stairs to the first floor. Captain Nelson met them at the exit door, a belt with a holstered sidearm in each hand.

He gave one to Ben, the other to Trudy. As they strapped the belts on, the captain forked his fingers. "You two will ride with me. Reconnaissance tells us the rebels are in camp, probably asleep. Now's the time to strike."

"Have the soldiers been informed about the strategy?" Ben asked.

"They have. A few seemed hesitant, but they'll follow orders." As Trudy checked the handgun's ammo magazine with practiced hands, the captain squinted at her. "You seem experienced with a weapon. Do you have military background?"

Trudy slid the gun into its holster. "My human host spent three years in the army. Her brain's muscle memory is quite helpful for weapon handling."

"I see." The captain scanned her from head to toe. "I wonder what else she can do with that muscle memory."

Trudy whipped the gun out and pressed the barrel against his forehead. "She could put a bullet through your brain if it weren't such a tiny target."

"Whoa!" The captain raised his hands and backed away. "No offense intended, Dr. Garrison. I was just admiring your skills."

"No, you were lusting. And you seem to be too stupid to remember that my host's husband is here." Trudy slid the gun back to its holster. "But, no matter. You are a mere pawn for our cause. Your usefulness will soon come to an end."

Captain Nelson bowed his head. "You know best, I'm sure."

Ben cleared his throat. "Okay. Now that you two understand each other … Captain, lead the way."

Chapter Thirteen

Jack stopped the jeep at the forest road's dead end. From here, he would have to hoof it the rest of the way to the community. So far, no checkpoints had slowed his progress, and that meant trouble. Every rebel soldier had been called in, probably to receive the vaccination, and so far, no one had returned to man the outposts. There was no time to lose.

He trudged into the woods, trying to keep his footfalls as quiet as possible, though the crunching undergrowth spoiled his hopes.

Zachariel's voice buzzed in his brain once more. *Your progress is too slow and noisy. I think it's time to provide you with a new benefit.*

Jack halted, breathless. "Okay. What benefit?"

You will soon see. Allow me to take over your body for a few moments. The experience will be painful but brief. Although I could take control by force, I prefer to have your permission.

"All right. If it'll help me get there faster. Go ahead."

Pain shot through his shoulders. More pain knifed into his back—hot, searing torture. Muscles seemed to be ripping apart. Groaning, he arched his back as reddish shadows streaked across his vision.

He dropped to his knees and looked back. Wings had sprouted, tearing through his shirt and growing at an impossible rate. Soon they were as big as any he had seen on other angels, leathery and powerful.

Stand, Zachariel said to his mind. *Try to move them.*

With pain still knifing across his shoulder blades, Jack rose to his feet and adjusted his shirt, now ragged with two gaping holes in the back. He mentally focused on the newly formed muscles and flexed them. The wings drew closer together. Then he reversed the muscle movement. The wings expanded as if in gliding mode. Although the pain continued, it diminished as he flapped the wings slowly.

Well done, Zachariel said. *I am impressed.*

"Will they actually carry me?"

They are big enough. The rest is up to you and your muscles. Bend forward. Allow them to lift you on the downbeat, then fold them in on the upbeat.

Jack bent and flapped the wings. As they drew downward, his feet lifted from the ground, then, when he raised the wings, his feet replanted.

Draw your wings in more on the upbeat. Work harder. I know it hurts, but we have no time to lose.

"Okay. Here goes." Jack flapped the wings with more force, grimacing at the pain. This time, his feet lifted higher and stayed off the ground. Soon, he flew above the treetops in a yo-yo motion, nearly breathless.

Now angle the wings. You'll learn quickly.

Again, Jack did as instructed. At first, the angle he chose sent him backwards, and he dropped several feet before altering the angle and rising. Then, he shot ahead, rising higher and higher with each cycle of up-and-down beats.

He sucked in a breath. "This is amazing!"

Yes, flying is a blessed gift. It has been far too long for me.

Jack searched the forest below for a landmark. "Have you flown on earth before?"

Many times, but not in recent years. When humans accepted the fake angels, we were called back to heaven.

"Why? We needed you. I mean, not all of us accepted the phonies."

The inner voice seemed to sigh. *I do not have all the answers, but I do know that God sometimes allows people to suffer the consequences of what the majority demands.*

"But then the innocent minority suffers. How can that be fair?"

It is not fair. Not at all. And, of course, some people attempt to right the wrongs, as you and those in your community are doing, but when the vast majority chooses slavery, the masters rarely allow exemptions. He paused for a moment before adding, *By the way, I think you are able to fly faster.*

"I'll try." Jack beat the wings harder, grunting as he spoke again. "So why are you here? And why now? Not to offend you, but your name's not in the Bible. My sibs and I studied angels in depth, and your name is associated with a lot of weird mystic stuff."

The way the ignorant humans use my name is unfortunate, and, as you noted, my name is not in the Bible, but it is in the Book of Enoch, though it varies based on the translation you read. In any case, I have dominion over the earth. I am an archangel.

Jack gulped. "An archangel! And you're inside my brain?"

Indeed I am, and it is a most interesting dwelling place. Your memories are quite an intriguing study.

"No. Don't go there. My memories are private."

So you think. They are more open than you realize.

"What do you mean?"

Your grief is evident to those who care to notice. Your longing for Sophie and Alana is spelled out in your sagging shoulders, your tight fists, and the cry of your voice.

"So you read my mind to learn about Sophie and Alana?"

Although I could have learned about them in your mind, I already knew about them. I have seen their souls myself.

Jack's heart thumped. "So they are in heaven." A smile came unbidden. "And you saw them."

I saw them, but I did not say they are in heaven.

Jack's tongue dried out. "Then are they …"

Ease your mind, Jack. They are not in hell. They are in a temporary holding place. You see, the fake angels have managed to seal off the gateway to heaven for the time being, and this blockade is one of the main reasons I have come to earth, to destroy the blockade and allow the safe passage of souls, whether to paradise or to perdition.

"A soul blockade? How is that possible?"

It is possible in a number of ways. In fact, it has happened before, but that is long-ago history that I need not recount at this time. The present blockade is the important issue, and it is associated with what you call the Oculus Gate.

"We also call it Hell's Gate."

An apt moniker. Currently, every soul that emerges from its body flies away from earth in the spiritual plane. The Oculus Gate has a traction mechanism that tries to pull souls in. If not for the blockade, souls could escape the pull, but they are all eventually sucked into a vortex, a spiritual whirlpool of sorts that plunges them into the depths of torment that I call the Never-ending Highway. Although it is not the biblical Lake of Fire, souls who suffer there might believe it to be, which adds immense mental and emotional suffering, as you can imagine. They think there is no escape from the torture, though it's not a physical torture. It is a suffering of mind and spirit invented by a fallen archangel.

"Are Sophie and Alana there?"

Unfortunately … yes.

Jack's heart thudded again. Heat surged through every muscle and sinew. "What can I do to get them out?"

We are already working on that goal, and I will reveal my plan as we progress. For now, stay the course with me and be patient. We have a lot to do, and it will take a good deal of time.

A hammer seemed to pound Jack's skull. How could he be patient while his wife and daughter were suffering? "Why so much time? If you're an archangel, why don't you show up with a huge sword, mow down the phonies, blast the blockade, and be done with it?"

Jack, your speed is flagging. This revelation about your family has strongly affected your emotions. You must concentrate on the matter at hand, and you must fly as if the entire world depends on your efforts.

As Jack pumped the wings, new pain roared across his back and shoulders. "I don't think … I can fly any faster."

You are doing better. Continue at this velocity.

"What about … my questions?"

Ah, yes. Your questions. Let's start with why I do not blast the blockade. The answer is simple. I do not have the power to do so. And why not a brandished sword? Several reasons. Because then faith would be made sight far too plainly, which is a complicated matter. In any case, I am the archangel of mercy, the messenger of last chances. I do not mow down anyone, human or otherwise. In short, I am a counselor, not a warrior.

"So you're no Michael. No offense, but we could use his sword right about now."

No offense taken. I think, however, that you would not like the results. Michael's swath might be much wider that you suspect. You see, he is an avenging angel. His destruction would be broad and catastrophic, and nearly every human on earth would fall to his blade. I am here to give mankind a final opportunity to realize the truth, to amend their ways, and you and your siblings have been chosen to deliver that opportunity.

"Will humans accept it?"

I do not know. Free will is an unpredictable beast. It is the greatest of blessings and the foulest of curses. Some use it to foster peace, ease suffering, and bless their neighbors, often to their own hurt. Others use it to incite war, inflict pain, and oppress their fellow man, always to their own benefit. In moments we will learn how your commander will use the information you bring. Will he leave on a quest to deploy his anti-angel weapon? Or will he stay home to make sure his own people survive the coming scourge?

"What do you know about that weapon?"

Very little. Only what I have been able to piece together from your memories.

"You're right. It's very little."

And, of course, your lack of knowledge is not your fault. Your commander kept most people in the dark, likely to protect them as well as the weapon. And now his next choice will be an interesting phenomenon to witness. The human will is fascinating, especially in people who are truly altruistic. They are rare, indeed. From what I have seen, your commander is one of them.

"Yeah. He's one in a million. That's for sure. He's the reason Ben and Trudy and I signed up. He was like a father to us after our parents died in the second plague."

Yes, I know. I studied your family thoroughly before coming to earth.

"Okay. That's good, I guess. But how did you know you would be put into me? That was pretty risky, wasn't it? I mean, the fake angels have free will, too, right?"

Most matters are left to free will. Some are not. I will say no more about that. Again, turn your attention to the matter at hand.

"Fly faster, right?"

Correct. You decelerated again, though I must say that you are doing well for a human's first effort.

"Yeah. Whatever. Let's just get this done." Jack's shoulder muscles throbbed with spastic peals of pain, but he ignored the torture. The farming community now lay in sight. A few dim lights dotted the valley, like dying campfires. Strange. With the recent SkySweep forays into rebel territory, all outdoor fires had been banned for weeks. Something was wrong.

Jack angled his wings, fluttered toward one of the lights, and landed on the run, stumbling, but avoiding a fall. After folding his wings in as tightly as he could, he walked toward the light, passing the infirmary, a one-story cabin. He stopped, reversed course, and eyed the infirmary's open door. Lantern light glowed within. He entered, padding with soft steps on the wooden floor.

The usual dispensary items sat on wall shelves—bandages, pill bottles, cans of nutrition drinks, and the like. At a table near the far wall, a case of vials lay open, and an injector gun sat next to it. A label on the case read "Vaccine for Angel Contagion." Obviously Ben and Trudy had succeeded with this part of the mission.

Jack strode to the table and looked the gun over. A full vial had been loaded, the dosage already set. He pushed his sleeve up a few inches and pressed the gun's barrel against his forearm. Although it had been several hours since they retrieved the vaccine, according to the specs the mole provided, it would still be effective for a while.

He pulled the trigger. The injection stung for a second, then eased. Breathing a sigh, he set the gun back on the table. At least that was done, but would it work before the contagion showed up?

He exited the infirmary and continued toward the light he had seen earlier. It was, indeed, the remains of a campfire. A family lay near its dying warmth—father, mother, and two preteen children, all huddled together.

Jack let out a "Psst!" but no one stirred. He knelt next to them and listened. No breathing sounds rose. He checked the father's neck pulse—no response. He checked the other three. They, too, were dead.

His heart racing, Jack hustled to another campfire. Multiple families lay near it. A quick check confirmed that they were all dead.

He bit his lip hard, holding back a sob. What could have happened? A reaction to the vaccine? He picked up a hefty stick, still burning at one end, and flung it back to the embers. "Arrgh!" Sparks shot into the sky, dancing as they rose.

"Who's there?" a man called, his voice shaky.

Jack crouched. He felt around the waist of one of the dead men and found a handgun. After quietly cocking it, he spoke slowly and evenly. "A friend, I hope."

"Jack?"

The voice registered—Commander Barks. Jack rose and slid the gun behind his belt. "Yes. It's me."

A flashlight beam flicked on and shone into Jack's eyes. As he blocked it with a hand, he waved toward the corpses with the other. "What happened here?"

The beam lowered to the ground, tracing a trembling line to a flashlight about thirty paces away. As Commander Barks approached, his outline clarified—the flashlight in one hand and a gun in the other. "I'm glad you escaped from the …" He gasped and drew back, raising the gun. "You're one of them!"

He fired, missing. Jack charged, boosted by his wings. He grabbed the commander's arm and wrestled the gun away. "Listen,"

Jack hissed. "I'm not one of them. This is ... well ... a disguise. All right?"

"A disguise?" The commander blinked, his features vague in the dimness. "Explain."

Jack returned the gun to the commander. "You outrank me, but I think you should explain first. It looks like everyone but you is dead. What's going on?"

The commander shook his head, tears glimmering. "The vaccine was a Trojan horse. The angels tricked us into taking it, and it purged everyone's soul. I volunteered to be vaccinated last, so it hasn't happened to me yet. It's only a matter of time."

Jack concealed a hard swallow. That meant his own soul was in danger. "So not having a soul killed them?"

"I wish it were that simple." The commander heaved a sigh. "When the first vaccinated man lost his soul, he began attacking the others. He was like a wild savage. The others tied him up, but by then, the rest of us had already been vaccinated. It was too late to change our minds. Then we got word from your sister that the vaccine might destroy a soul." He withdrew an AngelScan disk from a belt pouch. "So we checked that man's brain, and, sure enough, his soul was gone."

"And no fake angel was inside?"

"No, but there was something else strange. Sparkles of red light. Nothing like any angel we've seen, but it was the same color."

A guiding principle, Zachariel said in Jack's mind. *The vaccine must have implanted it. I will explain more later, but when there is no soul, the mind has no direction. It will heed any influence. I suspect that the angels put some kind of seed for violence in the vaccine to cause these poor people to attack the others.*

Jack repeated out loud much of what Zachariel said, though he kept the angel's presence a secret.

Barks nodded. "We concluded something similar, especially when the man's wife reacted in the same way, and their young son."

"And then they died?"

"No." Barks shifted uneasily. "We took a vote. It was unanimous. I shot that family to put them out of their misery, and the others drank poison and gathered around campfires to die together."

Jack gasped. "Mass suicide?"

"Not suicide, Garrison. You know better than that. This is war, and in war you kill your enemies and protect your allies. We all would've become angel robots and a danger to the innocent. If dying to prevent that is suicide, then so is diving over a grenade to protect your buddies in a foxhole. Besides, the other option was to wait until we killed each other. And whoever survived would become the angels' robots, like I said."

"But diving over a grenade is the choice of a brave soldier. Most of these weren't soldiers. And some were children. They didn't choose. Not really."

Barks let out another long sigh. "I can't argue with that. Won't even try. But tell me, Garrison. What would you have done? Let the children suffer horrible pain, feel their souls burn inside, and then attack their families as angel zombies? Or would you give them a quicker death and send their souls to heaven?"

"I ... I don't know." Jack's throat tightened, nearly choking his words. "I just don't know."

"Now you understand how much torture I felt making the decision."

Tears blurred Jack's vision. "Did you drink the poison?"

"Not yet. I was to be the last. It was my job to make sure everyone was dead. I was just about to drink my dose when I heard you."

"But maybe the vaccine doesn't purge everyone. Maybe it was just that family—"

"No, son. We waited till we were sure. Our people began turning one by one exactly in the order they were vaccinated." Barks extended a wrinkled scrap of paper. "This has my password for using the anti-angel weapon. Doc has one as well, but I don't know where he is. He won a coin toss to deploy the weapon, so he said he would try to get to it. I told him he couldn't possibly make it, but he insisted, so I gave him my password. I had to stay here to take care of our people. If you find him alive, he can give you the other password and tell you where the weapon is."

"I didn't see him in the infirmary." Jack took the paper and pushed it into his pocket. "I'll find him if I can."

"If he's dead, then the weapon is useless. You can't deploy it without both passwords." Barks winced.

"Is it getting worse?" Jack asked.

"Much worse."

"Is there anything I can do?"

He extended the gun. "Take this. Put me down. I don't want to drink the poison and wait for it to work."

Jack took the gun and stared at it, his hand shaking. "I … I can't."

The commander backpedaled three steps and squared his shoulders. "Jack Garrison, I command you to shoot me. If you're not an angel, and you're really still on my side, you'll obey. Don't fail me now."

Jack raised the gun and aimed it at the commander's head. As he set his finger around the trigger, he bit his lip hard. "Commander … I …"

"Shoot me!"

"But I—"

"Now, Garrison! Don't screw this up!"

Jack whispered, "Zachariel?"

It is too late to help him. I cannot intervene in your decision.

Tears welling, Jack swallowed, then pulled the trigger. The gun fired. The bullet seemed to fly in slow motion. It punctured the commander's forehead, drilled a hole, and exploded out the back. He collapsed in a heap and moved no more.

Jack threw the gun down, knelt at the commander's side, and wept. Spasms rocked his body. Tears flowed. How could everything have gone so wrong? Their plans had crumbled into dust. Backfired.

Exploded in their faces. Now the entire rebel faction at the farming community was gone, except for Ben, Trudy, and himself. And soon he would become a battle zombie, ready to do the will of the angels. And there was no way he could find Doc, assuming he was alive, get the other password, learn where the weapon was housed, and arrive there to deploy it before he succumbed. Impossible.

His hand shaking violently, he picked up the gun again and set it against his temple. As he curled his finger around the trigger, he looked to the sky. "Sophie. Alana. I'm coming. Maybe together we can figure out how to escape that place."

Chapter Fourteen

Captain Nelson walked to an ATV at the front of a line of vehicles—eight tanks, five flatbeds with missile launchers aboard, and at least thirty M-ATVs. When he jumped into the back, Ben and Trudy circled to the other side.

Ben whispered, "Now that Barks knows what the vaccine does, do you think he'll set an ambush instead of hunkering down?"

Trudy nodded. "If they're still alive and aren't zombies yet, they'll go down fighting."

A prop plane flew over, then another, as if leading the way for the invasion.

She added a sigh. "There they go. Death in their payloads."

Ben and Trudy boarded the ATV. As a private drove the vehicle past the gate, the others followed. A waning moon provided a view of the bumpy terrain as they drove off-road, cutting across stream-filled valleys and cresting low ridges.

Ben looked out the window. Progress was slow through the backcountry as they dodged trees and plowed through underbrush. They probably chose this route to stay out of sight of any rebel scouts. A smart move, but if the disaster in the community had already come to pass, they had nothing to worry about.

After nearly an hour, the ATV stopped. The private turned off the headlights. "We're at the coordinates."

The captain nodded. "Radio the pilots to spread the contagion. We'll go in at dawn."

The private spoke into a radio handset. "Deploy."

Jack! No! You must not kill yourself!

Jack loosened his trigger finger. "Why not? I'm not going to let myself fight for the angels. Never. Not a chance."

You can let me fight inside you. I will use your warrior body.

Jack lowered the gun. "What do you mean?"

If you kill yourself, I will have to leave your body and go to heaven. I don't know whether or not I can return to earth. Then Ben and Trudy will have to finish the mission alone, without you, without their commander, and without any help whatsoever from earth or heaven. The final chance to save all of mankind will be lost, squandered.

"What'll happen to my soul if I don't kill myself?"

The vaccine will force your soul out of your body, but before that happens, I will put you in a special container, a shield that will allow you to escape the Oculus Gate's vortex. Once you are in spiritual flight into the ethereal cosmos, you can allow yourself to be drawn into the Never-ending Highway. You will be able to seek your wife and daughter there.

When you find them, you can offer comfort by telling them escape is possible by destroying the vortex and the blockade, but you will have to return to earth to do so. You will not be able to bring them out with you. I expect you will want to try to transfer your shield to them, but I warn you not to. If you manage to strip it off, it will dissolve, and you will be trapped in the Never-ending Highway with them, unable to depart and do what is necessary to help them escape. Do you understand?

"Yes … well … sort of." Jack set the gun on the ground. "But why can't you give a shield to every soul? Wouldn't that solve the problem?"

It would, indeed, but I have only one. Angels are limited. Only God is not.

"Right. No-brainer, I guess. But if that's true, can't God just fix everything—blast the fake angels out of existence, destroy the Oculus Gate, and restore peace on earth?"

Your understanding of God's purposes is faulty. God can, as you say, fix everything and create a perfect universe, but that would not achieve the desired purposes. In short, you cannot have real love and worship without the opportunity and reality of hatred and rebellion. Suffice it to say that God often chooses to work in this world through devoted followers. If that is not enough of an explanation, then your curiosity will have to continue begging for answers.

"Okay. Whatever. But back to the real world. How do I return? My soul, I mean."

The protective shield I will give you allows you to resist all forces that attempt to pull on your soul. You can simply leap away and will yourself to go in any direction you choose. When you are ready, retrace your path back to your body. I suspect that you will be gone long enough for the vaccine's toxicity to decrease to a sufficient level for your soul to survive.

"But what will my body be doing while I'm gone?"

My own presence can survive the vaccine's influence, and I will remain because your body will survive, thanks to the vaccine. I will take control, and with your brain and its memories intact, I am confident that I can mimic your patterns of speech. I will, in a sense, become you.

Jack licked his dry lips. "Will you tell Ben and Trudy who you really are and what happened to me?"

I plan to keep my identity to myself until the proper time. Stopping the fake angels and destroying the blockade are the highest priorities, but you can trust me to take care of your siblings' feelings. By the time you return, I expect to be at angel headquarters. Find me there, and I will restore your soul to your body.

Tears still trickling, Jack rose to his feet. "How long do I have before the vaccine purges my soul? Do I have time to try to find the weapon and deploy it?"

Definitely not. You have minutes, not hours. You can, however, find any records your community has concerning the weapon's location and use, including the scrap of paper your commander provided. Read them, then burn them. Perhaps we will be able to use that information when you return.

Jack nodded. "That makes sense." An airplane engine hummed nearby, coming closer, then a second one. "The invasion?"

That is likely. We have to hurry.

Chapter Fifteen

Ben closed his eyes, imagining the deadly rain spreading across the area. Soon, every invading soldier would die, including the hesitant ones, kids who felt they had no choice but to join the invasion.

"But they still made the choice," he whispered to himself.

Dawn's first rays illuminated a valley ahead. A narrow river ran through it from left to right, the community's water supply. The encampment itself lay half a mile beyond it.

A strange odor wafted in, musty and infused with sulfur. "That's the contagion," Trudy said. "I heard it would be carried in a sulfur-based powder."

Ben coughed. "Vile stuff. I guess we'll soon know how well the vaccine works."

"What are the first symptoms?" the captain asked.

"Headache," Trudy said. "Then severe nausea. Projectile vomiting. After that, high fever and death. It kills in less than an hour."

"Good." The captain flexed his forearms again. He seemed to enjoy showing off his tattooed muscles. "It'll soon be daylight. Maybe we should call them out so we can watch them drop like flies. Better than wasting missiles on them. Funnier, too."

Ben gritted his teeth but said nothing.

The captain smirked. "What's the matter, Dr. Garrison? Do you get worked up when I talk about humans that way? I thought you angels considered us vermin."

"Some are, and you're proving yourself to be in that category."

"Is that so?" The captain reached over the back of the seat and motioned toward the ATV's glove compartment. "Private, get me the AngelScan. It's in there."

"Right away." The private popped open the box.

"Captain," Trudy growled, "if you dare subject us to your insulting test, I will strangle you with my bare hands."

He touched the handgun at his belt. "Afraid to prove yourself?"

"Captain," Ben said, "your gate guard verified who we are with a scan. If you wish to subject us to another ID test, you will be marked as an angel doubter. Is that what you want?"

He scowled. "And if I find that you're really not—"

"Captain." The private pointed toward the front. "Look."

Ahead, someone crossed the river, coming toward them.

The captain narrowed his eyes. "What's this?"

"An angel?" the private asked.

Ben squinted. The man had wings at his back, fully spread as he trudged slowly, his head hanging low and his shoulders slumping.

The captain faced Ben. "Supposedly he's one of yours. You should talk to him. Warn him about the contagion. Find out if he's been vaccinated."

Ben nodded. "We'll both go."

He and Trudy got out of the ATV and walked toward the winged man. "I hope you know what you're doing," Trudy said.

"Not really, but I couldn't think of an excuse not to go. He's already suspicious. Since the contagion kills in under an hour, getting out of his sight for a while might be a good idea, especially when they start getting sick."

"True. But now we're caught between two potential killers."

"I know. Squeezed with no way out." As they drew near the winged man, Ben kept a hand near his sidearm. The wings indicated that this angel was at least a Gen Two. If he was a mind reader, he would soon figure out that they weren't implanted. They had to be ready to run. But where?

When the angel drew within a few paces, he halted, his head still low. Ben and Trudy halted as well. Wearing camo from ankles to neck, the angel resembled a rebel soldier, but the sinewy leather wings proved otherwise.

133

Trudy grasped Ben's elbow. "He looks like … No. It can't be." She took a few steps closer, then halted again. "Jack?"

Ben blinked. "Jack? What are you talking about?"

The angel lifted his head, his face glowing. He did look like Jack, exactly like him.

Ben sucked in a breath. "You've been implanted."

"Of course he has," Trudy said as she closed the gap. She set a hand on his shoulder. "Welcome to the angel forces. I am Joquile, and my companion is Ejardi. What is your name?"

Jack stared at Trudy, his gaze piercing. "You are not an angel." He turned to Ben. "Nor are you."

Ben slid a hand around his gun's handle. Jack had been implanted by a mind reader. Gen Four at least. What other powers might he have?

"Jack." Trudy touched one of his wings. "Just because we don't have these assets doesn't mean we're not angels."

"It's not the lack of wings." Jack looked past them at the vehicles. Ben and Trudy looked as well. Captain Nelson stood outside the ATV, binoculars at his eyes. He was watching carefully. "I apologize for this." Jack extended a hand. Ben's gun lifted from its holster and flew to Jack's grasp. With his other hand he snatched Trudy's gun in the same way. "Now fall and close your eyes. Both of you. You have to trust me."

He fired a gun at Trudy, barely missing her. When she dropped to the ground, he pivoted and fired at Ben, nicking his ear. Ben held a hand against the wound, fell, and closed his eyes but left a slit to watch through.

Jack leaned over, pushed Ben's hand to the side, dabbed the blood with a finger, then straightened and displayed the finger for the captain to see.

The captain lowered the binoculars and nodded, then wobbled, dropped to his knees, and vomited. The private jumped out and set a hand on the captain's back. He, too, vomited. Behind them, more soldiers deboarded their vehicles. The sounds of their moaning and retching filled the morning's misty air.

"You can get up now," Jack said, extending a hand toward Trudy. "Ladies first."

Trudy grasped his wrist and rode his pull to her feet. Ben did the same and stared at him. "Are you really Jack?"

"I am ... kind of. It's hard to explain." Tears in his eyes, he pulled Ben into a tight embrace. "I love you. You know that, right?"

"Of course I do." Ben patted him on the back, unable to avoid touching a wing as he drew away. "But what's going on with the wings?"

"Just a sec." He hugged Trudy and kissed her on the forehead. "I love you, Sis. I'm sure you'll keep Ben in line."

"I love you, too, Jack, but what do you mean—"

He set a finger on her lips. "No questions. No explanations. Just stay focused on the mission." He stepped back, crossed his arms in front, and took a deep breath. His eyes flared, glowing for a moment before fading to normal. Then he lowered his arms and looked at Ben and Trudy in turn. "The contagion is in the air. Have you been vaccinated?"

Trudy nodded. "With the real stuff."

"That's not good. It will purge your soul."

"We know," Ben said. "But we got only half a dose. We're hoping we can stick it out, but we heard that it also has a payload of some kind. We don't know what it'll do."

"I know what the payload is. Maybe we can use it to our advantage."

When Jack took a hard step toward the captain's ATV, Trudy grabbed his arm. "Wait just a second, Jack Garrison. We're not doing anything until you explain the wings."

"And the gun-snatching trick," Ben added. "How can you be implanted and still be our brother?"

Jack sighed. "It's a long story."

"We have some time." Trudy nodded toward the captain. He and several soldiers lay in view, writhing on the ground. "They'll be in death throes for a while."

"Very well. First, there is good news to report." Jack set his hands on Ben's shoulders. "Kat's alive."

Ben spluttered. "A—alive? Are you sure?"

"I saw her myself. We talked for quite a while." Jack compressed Ben's shoulders. "You were the first person she asked about."

Ben trembled. "Where is she now?"

"That's the bad news. Well, part of the bad news. She's implanted."

The tremors worsening, Ben steeled himself. He had to stay calm no matter what. "Implanted?"

"Right. By some royalty angel. Calls herself a queen. And I got implanted, but my angel is a real one. From God, I mean. He let me stay in control. Gave me these wings and that snatching power, and he kept my body alive. I'm immune to the contagion."

Ben eyed Jack's glowing face. Earlier, he spoke with an odd formality. Now he sounded more normal … like Jack. Very strange. Gaining more information from him might be risky.

"What about our soldiers?" Trudy asked.

Jack gazed across the river. "That's the other bad news. They're all dead. Every one of them."

"Dead?" Ben's legs weakened. "Commander Barks?"

Jack nodded.

"Oh, dear God in heaven!" Trudy clutched her stomach. "Even the children?"

"I'm afraid they're all dead. The families were huddled around campfires. They drank poison so they would die before the virus could purge their souls."

Trudy leaned over and dry heaved, crying as spasms rocked her body.

Ben's throat tightened. "A suicide pact?"

"More like diving over a grenade to protect others, but, yeah." Jack nudged a pebble with his toe, his voice small and quiet. "Commander Barks told me the story. The vaccine's payload made them violent. They attacked each other. No way to cure it. That's why they made the pact. He was the last man standing, and he asked me to shoot him."

"So …" Ben's voice quaked. "So you did."

"The commander gave me an order. He said dying was the only way to keep him from becoming an angel zombie, and he didn't want to wait for the poison to work." Jack kicked the pebble, his voice spiking. "What did you expect me to do?"

Ben lifted a hand. "Hey, hey. Calm down. I'm not blaming you."

Jack inhaled and exhaled slowly. "Sorry. It's just that … you know … it was hard."

"Shooting our commander?" Ben swallowed, but it did nothing to loosen his throat. "Yeah. Nearly impossible. But you had to do it."

"Anyway, Barks gave me a password for using Kat's anti-angel weapon. He wants me to find it and deploy it. But Doc has a password, too … or had one. I couldn't find him, but he has to be dead by now. So the weapon's useless."

Ben half closed an eye. "Or the angels want us to think it's useless."

"Don't overthink this, Ben." Trudy spat a stream of saliva. After brushing tears with her knuckles, she took a halting breath. "Only the real Jack would know who invented the weapon. And he wouldn't tell an implanted angel about something the angel wouldn't know to probe for. He's legit."

Ben stared at Jack, his mind in a whirl. So many new revelations, and combined with the tragic deaths, it seemed impossible to think straight. "We were planning to attack angel HQ with tanks, you know, go out in a blaze of glory."

"Because we think the vaccine might strip our souls," Trudy said as she massaged her arm's vaccination point. "We took the real stuff but, like Ben told you, only half a dose."

Ben looked toward angel headquarters. "But now we know Kat's at HQ. We have to get her out, not just to rescue her. She's the only person who knows where the anti-angel weapon is and maybe how to get around not having Doc's password."

"That means we can't just attack the place." Trudy crossed her arms tightly, matching the firmness of her lips, obviously trying not to cry. "We could accidently kill Kat. Queen or not, her soul might still be inside."

"It is," Jack said. "I'm sure of it. So we need a strategic strike. I'll go in and learn exactly where she is. Gain her confidence. Then you two can cause a distraction by attacking a different section. Use your vaccine payload to go full Rambo on the place."

Trudy blinked at him. "Rambo? What are you talking about?"

"The vaccine's payload is an impetus to be violent. As long as your souls are intact, you should be able to control it, but it will also empower you." Jack gave her a curious look. "Was Rambo not an appropriate illustration?"

"It's an ancient flick. I saw it once when I was ten. And what's with the *appropriate illustration* stuff and *impetus*? That doesn't sound like you."

"Besides that," Ben said, "how did you learn so much about whether or not souls can control the payload?"

"Zachariel taught me. His thoughts come through. Bigger vocabulary, as you might expect."

"Zachariel?" Trudy repeated. "The angel?"

Jack spread his wings. "You might say that it's hard to figure out where Jack stops and Zachariel begins."

Ben looked Jack over. He seemed to have many of his normal mannerisms, but something was off. What could prove whether or not Jack was really still there? The AngelScan was in the ATV, but using that could come later if necessary. There was another way to test his story. "Zachariel was an archangel."

Jack nodded. "Yes. I have dominion over the earth. I am what you might call the angel of last chances."

"Last chances. I see." Ben probed his own mind, searching for something in the Bible that Jack or a fake angel probably didn't know, but a real angel should know. "Who is the Prince of Persia in the book of Daniel?"

"The earthly prince was Cambyses," Jack said without hesitation, "the son and crown prince of King Cyrus. There was also a fallen angel, a demon, with the same title."

Ben lifted his brow. "There were two?"

"Correct. I think, however, you are referring to the demon who wrestled with an angel sent to help Daniel. Since wrestling against angels has been your mission for a number of years, it stands to reason that you're interested in that topic."

Ben frowned. "That 'stands to reason' part. That's not Jack talking. I believe you're a real angel now. I mean, no fake angel knows so much about Bible details, but how can I know Jack's in there, too?"

Jack folded his wings, not quite hiding them. "You can't know. It's impossible."

"Not impossible. An AngelScan would tell us."

"True. You could scan me. But I assure you …" Jack breathed an exasperated sigh. "Listen. Are we going to stand around here yakking like chittering squirrels, or are we going to attack those monsters at HQ?"

Trudy pointed at him. "Now that's the Jack I know."

"What about the bodies of our people?" Ben asked. "We have to give them the respect they deserve. Vultures are bound to show up soon."

Jack looked at the dying invaders. "The vultures will have plenty to eat, and I salted our friends' bodies with something that will repel the scavengers. It will last until we return. I'm concerned, however, that you and Trudy won't last if the vaccine fails to work on you. And we must use your payload when it takes effect."

"Okay," Ben said. "Now I hear Zachariel talking again. Can you keep your mouth tuned to Jack's frequency? I have a hard time hearing angel words coming from that mug."

Jack punched his arm. "You got it, Bro."

Ben cracked a smile. "Close, but not quite."

"Let's get going," Trudy said. "I've been aching to drive one of those tanks. Our training is finally ready to pay off."

Ben gave Jack—or Zachariel—a long look. His attempts at being Jack were too obvious, even strained, but they had to work with him. "Remember, we're ditching Plan A and Plan B. This is Plan C. No. Plan D. Trudy and I will drive the tanks to HQ."

"And," Jack said, "if I remember Plan D correctly, I'll drive the flatbed with the missile launchers."

"Right. We'll park at the meadow two klicks east of HQ. Then Jack will scout for Kat and report to us." Ben withdrew an earbud from his pocket. "We still have our earbuds. Do you?"

"The angels took them from me, but I picked up a new stereo pair in our supply room when I was looking for Doc."

"Good. Let's put them in and get moving. You drive lead. If an angel patrol stops our convoy, you can vouch for us."

"Will do. Let's roll." Jack hurried away toward the military vehicles.

As Ben and Trudy jogged behind Jack, Trudy touched Ben's shoulder. "Jack dodged the AngelScan. That worries me. Maybe he's not as legit as I thought."

"I noticed the dodge. That private put an AngelScan on the front seat of the ATV. Maybe one of us should get it."

"I will," Trudy said. "And our medical bag. We have a scanner there, too."

When they arrived at the front of the convoy, Ben hustled to the first tank in line, opened the hatch, and checked inside. The odor of vomit emanated from within, and the tank's young female operator sat slumped over the controls, an X99 rifle leaning against her thigh.

Ben crawled in and hoisted the corpse up through the hatch, then climbed out and rolled her off the side of the tank. Her body lay with her face toward the brightening sky, a familiar face, the second soldier in line to receive a vaccination. Blood and vomit stained her shirt, her eyes no longer bright. Another life wasted.

Staring at her, he tightened his fist. Those cockroaches would pay for this slaughter. Even if he had to kill every last fake angel with his own hands, he would punish them and burn their headquarters to the ground.

He tore his stare from the woman and loosened his fist. Where did all that fury come from? He had to fight the payload and keep his mind on the goal, to save Kat. That was all that mattered now.

Chapter Sixteen

From behind his tank, Trudy called, "Ben."

He turned. She knelt atop a tank, its hatch open. "Nobody in this one. I'm taking it. And there's a sweet X-ninety-nine assault rifle inside. I'll be loaded for bear."

"Same here." He looked past her. Several vehicles to the rear, Jack pulled a driver from a flatbed truck, let him tumble to the ground, and hopped inside.

Ben climbed into the tank and studied the controls, exactly like the mock-up design on the computer training module. He could handle this.

He drove forward, dodged the ATV in front of him, and turned his huge vehicle around, bulldozing undergrowth. He passed Trudy's tank, then slowed as he waited.

Once Jack maneuvered in front and took the lead and Trudy rumbled into position at the tail end, they drove through the forest to the main road and accelerated to the tank's top speed.

Ben shouted to overcome the engine noise. "Jack, tell me more about Kat. How was she? Did she look all right?"

"As beautiful as ever." Jack's earbud answer sounded distant, though clear enough. "But, like I said, she's implanted. She goes by Laramel now, and she has some crazy angel strength. She put me on the floor in a heartbeat."

"And you said Kat's still there, right? In her brain, I mean."

"Oh, she's there, all right. Laramel puts Kat in a spin, or something like that, so she can't fight. I got the impression that when she's awake, she gives Laramel fits. Feisty as ever."

Ben nodded, trying to keep his voice steady. "Yeah. Kat's a fighter."

"Right. But she's got problems. Laramel called in an angel named Novada to interrogate her. I suppose Laramel will let Kat come to the surface and Novada will drill her with some kind of mind-reading powers."

"Novada? Gorgeous young woman with incredible eyes?"

"Yeah. That's her. You met her?"

"Met her? I killed her. Sliced her throat with a scalpel."

"Then someone has mad doctor skills there," Jack said. "I saw the scar. I was wondering how she got it."

"Sorry, Ben," Trudy said. "I guess I should've let you crush Novada's skull. You wanted to."

"Yeah, but it was my idea to put her on ice. That probably kept her body from dying." An ache at the back of his skull raised a wince. Maybe the soul purging had begun. "Hey, Jack, Trudy and I met a soulless officer at the angel's military base. She seemed normal. Couldn't tell any difference until she started spouting some angel-boot-licking nonsense. We scanned her and found an angel but no soul. Never seen that before."

"Probably the first," Trudy said. "Many more planned. But maybe they don't know their experiment worked. The expanded vaccine experiment, I mean."

Ben nodded. "Right. If the angels autopsy the bodies, they'll find the poison, but they won't know why the people took their own lives. They'll know the souls are gone, but with no angel inside, the souls would be gone no matter how or why they died."

"I'll use that knowledge when I infiltrate," Jack said. "By the way, do you two feel anything weird yet? Violent tendencies, maybe?"

Trudy laughed. "I've already daydreamed about slicing angel throats. So, yeah. It's like a boiling stew in my gut. If I don't bash some heads pretty soon, I think I'll bust."

"Same here," Ben said. "I'm ready to rumble. And I have a headache. That might mean something." The tank's engine coughed. He checked the fuel gauge—much lower than expected. "Hey, Trudy. How's your fuel supply?"

"Um … It's low. Real low."

"I'm close to empty," Jack said. "What's that all about?"

"I don't know. The soldiers had to notice. Checking fuel is part of prep." Ben's tank sputtered. "Let's call a halt. Bring your rifles." He killed the engine, grabbed the X99, and climbed out of the tank. As he sat at the hatch's edge, Trudy crawled out of her hatch. Behind her tank, trails of liquid drew squiggly lines back to the forest road.

"There's our fuel," Ben said, pointing.

Jack flew from the flatbed and landed next to Ben. "Sabotage?"

"Yeah. No other explanation."

Standing on top of her tank with her X99 strapped on, Trudy set a hand at her brow and looked at the trails. "They didn't want anyone else to have the artillery."

A distant engine sound came from somewhere above. As Ben searched for the source, he rose to his feet and pivoted in place. "Someone in the invasion force knew they weren't returning to the base. It takes only one person to puncture fuel tanks, but the timing had to be perfect."

Trudy turned toward the front. "Another zombie? Like Major Livingstone?"

The sound drew closer. Ben spotted a military plane coming their way, its angle and speed too severe to avoid a crash. "Kamikaze attack! Run!"

They leaped to the road and sprinted. To the rear, an explosion erupted. Metal screamed against concrete. A concussive force slung Ben and Trudy forward. They tumbled along the pavement, ending in a painful slide, both with X99s still strapped on.

Groaning, Ben sat up and looked back while Trudy did the same. Jack stood between them and the wreckage, facing the crash site, his arms and wings spread. A brilliant aura encompassed him, and debris lay scattered, though the field of twisted metal and melted plastic split where he stood, leaving the area where Ben and Trudy sat free of vehicle remains.

Flames crackled at the impact point, shooting into the sky. More fires burned here and there in piles of wreckage—airplane parts, tank tracks, and missile sections.

"Let's get out of here," Ben shouted. "We might have more explosions."

Trudy scrambled to her feet, grimacing. She pulled Ben to his, and they both backed away. "Jack," Trudy called. "Come on!"

He turned toward them and, flapping his wings, joined their retreat. When they had run about half a mile, Ben signaled a halt and pivoted. A new explosion shot more flames into the air, but it was too far away to send shrapnel anywhere close.

Ben shook his head. "They've been planning this for a while."

"Right." Trudy set a fist on her hip. "First, they knew we were swapping the vaccine. They let us do it. They didn't care who the vaccine's guinea pigs were as long as they could see how well it worked. Second, this plane's attack proves that they expected us to try to steal equipment long before we did it. And third, they obviously don't give a freaking flip about their troops." She crossed her arms tightly. "To our blessed winged demons, all humans are vermin."

"Bottom line," Ben said, as he checked a spot of blood on his knee, "someone leaked our plans."

Jack raised a hand. "That would be me. I spilled to Kat. I didn't know at the time that she was one of them. I mean, that she was really Laramel. My blabbermouth gave them enough time to spin everything against us."

Ben examined his X99's ammo. Everything seemed intact. "Looks like they didn't sabotage this. I can still do a lot of damage at HQ."

"Same here," Trudy said as she checked her weapon. "Like I said before, I'm itching to scalp a few angels."

Jack tapped Trudy's head. "Just remember, payload-powered sister, the goal isn't to kill angels. It's to rescue Kat. We need to stay alive to do that."

Ben looked down the road. "Any idea how far it is to HQ from here?"

"Let me check." Jack leaped and flew straight up. After a few seconds, he was soaring nearly out of sight.

Ben gazed skyward. "This is way beyond strange."

"You're telling me," Trudy said, also watching Jack. "And we didn't even mention how he blocked the wreckage from tearing us to shreds. He's got some serious powers we've never heard of."

"I guess the medical bags got roasted."

"Yep." Smiling, Trudy withdrew an AngelScan from her pants pocket. "But I grabbed this."

"Out of all the things you could've taken from the bag, you chose the AngelScan."

"Hey. He's our brother." She slid the disk back into her pocket. "We've gotta check eventually."

Jack floated downward, his wings fluttering. "I'd say HQ is about six miles, give or take. A little shorter if we leave the road and go cross-country."

"No choice there," Trudy said as she stared into the forest, fifty paces or so from the road. "We have to go cross-country. They're bound to show up here soon to check for bodies."

"And when they don't find us," Ben said, "they'll bring drone hounds."

Jack pointed toward the tree line. "We'd better get under cover now. I can do quick checks from treetops to map our route and see if we're being tailed."

When they ducked into the forest, Jack led the way. "We need to keep going this direction. Anyone got a compass?"

"Right here." Walking directly behind Jack, Trudy snapped a compass off her belt and studied it as she walked. "We're heading plus three degrees off north, northwest."

"Good. Keep an eye on it once in a while."

Ben trailed the other two by a few paces. As he scanned the area, Jack's revelations about Kat pushed their way to the surface. "Jack, what information do you think Novada is trying to get from Kat?"

"The weapon's location. Since Kat knows where it is, I don't know how she's holding it back. That Novada shrew has a bag of mental tricks, but I guess Kat's tougher."

"Did you talk to Barks about the weapon?"

"Briefly. He thinks Doc went to deploy it. That's why I couldn't find him. Like I said before, Barks and Doc each had a password. Barks gave me his, but he doesn't know Doc's. Barks says no way Doc could've made it in time, but you know Doc. He probably had to try."

"So the angels are afraid of the weapon," Trudy said. "They got enough intel from Kat to know that it's a real danger to them."

"Or Kat fed them enough to scare them." Jack halted, forcing the others to halt as he scanned the tree canopy. "And it worked, but their reaction to the fear turned into a nightmare for us. It's obvious now that they could've wiped our base off the planet long ago, but they opted for a different plan, something that would subjugate the entire world more quickly. They needed us alive, people who weren't already groveling at their feet."

"To test people who were resistant," Ben said as he caught up and walked abreast with Trudy. "See how well the vaccine worked on them."

"Exactly. That way, no rebellion could ever rise again." Jack marched on, speaking louder to overcome the tromping of boots on underbrush. "Listen. I'm thinking that maybe I should fly on ahead and prepare the way, like we planned. You know, make sure you two can cause a ruckus without getting caught. I'll tell the angels that I found the rebels dead after I gave myself the vaccination, which means they can't be sure it's safe for them to use on themselves. My own survival might be an anomaly."

"And not getting vaccinated makes them vulnerable."

"Right. I'm not sure how to use the idea yet, but once you're in earbud range, we can come up with a plan."

"Works for me," Ben said. "We got a good head start on any drone hounds. And Trudy has the best sense of direction of any of us. Six miles isn't much. We'll get there in a couple of hours."

"Perfect." Jack halted again and turned toward Ben and Trudy. "Try to contact me as soon as you can." He flapped his wings and launched into the air, zooming past the treetops. In seconds he was out of sight.

Trudy whistled. "I don't know if I can get used to that."

Ben switched his earbud microphone off and motioned for Trudy to do the same. When she complied, he stared at the sky. "Maybe we shouldn't get used to it."

"You mean because Jack's not there?"

"Right. No AngelScan needed. Jack wouldn't leave us like that. Too abrupt."

"It still doesn't mean Jack's not there at all. Only who's calling the shots."

"True, but I think we have to act like he's not our brother." Ben turned toward Trudy. "From now on, everything we learn stays between the two of us unless we both decide it's okay to let him know."

"I'm good with that." As they walked on, Trudy massaged Ben's shoulder for a moment before letting her arm drop to her side. "Are you ready to see Kat? Implanted, I mean. It's going to be hard feeling so helpless."

Ben slid a hand into his pocket. "I know. Well, I think I know. I can't take more than one step at a time. We're not even sure we'll have souls at the end of the day. Trying to figure out what to do about Kat isn't on my radar screen yet. First, we invade HQ. Take out as many as we can. Then we can focus on Kat."

"Or we could go stealth instead. Kidnap her. She's a high-order angel, but supposedly we have an archangel from God on our side now. That's a lot of firepower."

"Good thought. We'll wait on intel from Jack—or Zachariel—before we decide."

With Trudy constantly checking her compass, Ben picked up the pace. Saying Kat wasn't on his radar screen was a lie. He just wanted it to be true. Getting too worked up about her would destroy his ability to make decisions. He had already made too many wrong ones, maybe costing a lot of people their lives. It was time to be smarter. It was the only way to save the world from the angel scourge.

Chapter Seventeen

His soul now separated from his body, Jack flew away from earth and soared deep into a dark expanse. The confused expressions on Ben's and Trudy's faces when he left them at the farming community raised a haunting sensation. They had no clue what was really going on, that their brother was departing their world on a mission they knew nothing about, one that Zachariel insisted remain a secret.

As he zipped through the inky blackness, he set his hands in front of his face. Although they glowed, they seemed normal—five digits, complete with nails. He tried to tap the back of one hand with the index finger of the other, but the fingertip wouldn't make contact, probably because of the shield Zachariel mentioned.

Something flickered at the side, then an image—a baby dressed in blue. Images passed one by one, but so quickly they seemed to move, like flipping pages in a book of slightly different drawings. The baby altered to a little boy, Jack at five years old throwing a rock through a windowpane.

Jack winced. Was this his life passing before his eyes? Would he have to endure watching every stupid thing he ever did? If so, plenty of cringeworthy moments lay ahead.

The window's glass shattered, and the scene shattered with it. The fragments blew away, as if swept by a gust of wind. Other awful scenes appeared from his childhood days, then from his teens— lies, rebellion, betrayal. His father's anger. His mother's tears. With each event, he tried to look away, but he couldn't. He watched every episode through his own tears.

Yet, as with the first, each scene shattered and blew away. Then when he tried to bring the image back to mind, it wouldn't come, as if it had been wiped from memory.

Soon, the Oculus Gate came into view to one side with its oval cluster of stars. Straight ahead stood a rectangle of light, like a doorway of brilliance, as if someone had painted pure radiance on the black background. As he drew close, the light bathed him with warmth, not physical warmth but pure delight—ecstasy, comfort, joy. Whatever lay inside had to be wonderful beyond all imagination.

When Jack arrived, he willed himself to stop. As he floated in front of the radiant opening, he tried to look inside, but the glare was too bright. To the rear, glowing phantoms streamed toward the door, but when they drew close, they slowed. An invisible force stretched them toward the Oculus Gate. As they elongated, they reached toward him with groping hands, their eyes wide with fear. They, too, probably felt the warmth and craved to enter, but the pull from the Gate had caught hold and wouldn't let go.

He glided back and tried to grasp the wrist of one of the phantoms, a teenage girl with flowing dark hair, but when they touched, sparks flew, and she jerked away. Then the force sucked her into its grasp.

As dozens of souls zipped toward the Gate, they spun slowly as if in an outer-space eddy, the whirlpool Zachariel mentioned.

Jack looked again at the doorway. Pure bliss likely awaited inside. But could he possibly enjoy that bliss while knowing Sophie and Alana were suffering? Might memories of their travail be swept away like the images of the sins of his youth? Maybe. Such memory loss would guarantee bliss, but wouldn't that be a phony sort of bliss? Dancing like an ignorant fool while his wife and daughter suffered? That would be the worst eternity possible.

He willed himself toward the whirlpool and joined the spinning flow, slowly accelerating with the helpless phantoms. Maybe soon he would arrive at the Never-ending Highway, but how long would it take to find Sophie and Alana?

Closing his eyes, he let himself go. After all, he had no other reasonable choice.

Kat swam in the deep blackness that had been her lost-and-lonely world for far too long. As always, voices entered, and she had to sort through them, figure out who was talking, how to counter whatever Laramel might do or say. It seemed that planting the idea of an affair with Jack began to work, at least for a while, but the wicked angel figured out the plan and sent her deeper into a spinning morass of thoughts and memories, not letting her anywhere near the surface. Here in the depths, everything seemed warped, twisted, impossible to understand.

"She's coming," a woman said.

That sounded like her own voice.

"Good. I'm ready."

Another woman, but who?

A light shone. Kat winced at the brightness. Was she finally coming back to the surface?

"Katherine," the second woman said, "wake up. I need to talk to you."

Kat opened her eyes, then blinked several times. A lovely young woman with a fresh scar on her throat leaned close, staring. "My name is Novada. I am trying to rescue you from Laramel."

Kat scanned her surroundings. She lay on a hospital-style bed in a brightly lit area that resembled a doctor's exam room. "Rescue me?" she whispered. "How?"

"That's an excellent question. I assume you remember that you've been implanted by an angel."

Kat nodded. The motion felt strange, like her head hadn't moved in months, or maybe she had been disconnected from her muscles that long.

"I injected you with a drug. It sent that angel, Laramel, deep into your subconscious. She will be incapacitated for a while, and she thinks that I am on her side, bringing you out of her mental depths in order to probe you for information. While she is in the depths herself, she won't be able to understand our conversation."

"Okay. That's good."

"Unfortunately, however, the drug will wear off soon, and it's too dangerous to give it to you more than once a week. We have to converse quickly before she returns and takes control."

Kat's throat narrowed, forcing her to swallow. "I understand. What do we do?"

"I am a resistance angel. I believe that we are wrong to subjugate humans. I want us to leave the planet and find one where we can live in our natural states instead of as parasites. Also, there is another danger, the Oculus Gate. We recently translated a series of transmissions from the Gate that indicate an invasion is at hand. We don't know what kind of beings will break through, but since the angels are bound inside humans, they are dependent on humans for survival. We don't know if the new creatures will have the same limitations. They might be far more dangerous to humans than the angels are." Novada caressed Kat's hand. "Are you with me so far?"

"Yes." Kat slurred the word, her brain feeling numb. "Go on."

"Before we angels came here, we lived in a world covered with seas of warm water infused with protoplasm, and we inhabited protoplasmic globules suspended in the seas. When the Oculus Gate formed, the seas began drying up. The Gate's energy flow drew several of our species out of the sea and sent them to this world. How we eventually became implanted in humans is a lengthy tale, but I will tell you that the team that helped us included a medical doctor and a military commander. When the commander learned of the first implantation, he refused to go along with the plan. He would never allow an alien force to take over a human soul. Their strife was such that the commander vowed to stop the doctor at all costs. The doctor had to go into hiding to resume her work." Novada paused and looked Kat in the eye. "Have you guessed the identity of the military commander?"

"Barks?"

"Yes, he became the doctor's nemesis and searched for her everywhere. In the meantime, the doctor was able to successfully implant a living human, a brilliant scientist who helped her figure out how to harness the angels' abilities. You see, as light-energy entities capable of manipulating protoplasm and other pliable matter, they were able to somewhat restructure the bodies they inhabited, such as growing wings, though at first that ability remained at a theoretical stage. Because of the great potential, the species decided the most efficient way to gain acceptance in this world was to pretend to be supernatural beings, creatures the people would admire, even adore. Therefore, we have angels."

"And it worked."

Novada nodded. "Far too well. With each improvement in the angels' abilities, a new generation, as Barks and the rebels called it, the species became more powerful. Some could do works that seemed like miracles, and, of course, when a generation sprouted wings, nearly everyone was convinced that God sent his holy angels to bring peace to this war-torn world, order to the chaos."

"So why are you telling me all this?"

"As I said, I am part of the resistance. I am an ally of Commander Barks."

"Okay. What do we do now?"

"I have not been able to get in touch with Barks lately. Do you know how I can contact him? Obviously it would have to be through secret channels, and I have been undercover for so long and so deeply, the channels I knew previously are no longer operational."

"What do you want to tell him?"

"That the angels' greatest fear is a weapon the rebels created, but they're not sure exactly what it does."

Kat studied Novada's gaze. Her knowledge of the weapon's existence couldn't be a wild guess. "I see. Where did you get your information?"

"Actually, from you. Laramel has been probing your brain herself, but it seems that you have resisted her quite well. Yet, she was able to learn that you, Katherine Garrison, are the inventor of the weapon. Unless, of course, you fed her a lie, but she was certain it's the truth. That's why I want to talk to you about it."

Dizziness swept in. Maybe the drug was wearing off, and she would soon sink back into darkness. "All right," Kat said. "I'm familiar with this weapon. What do you want to know?"

"Laramel briefed me on what she learned from you. The weapon is supposed to travel through a conduit that will take it to the Oculus Gate. I want to know if the weapon is designed to destroy the Gate, the angels, or both."

"Why do you need that information?"

Novada touched a spherical pendant dangling from a thin chain around her neck. "This is a homing orb. It contains protoplasm from our world. If I were to break the inner sphere, the protoplasm would irresistibly draw every angel to it, and if I had a way to transport them, we could go to a world that is more hospitable to our species. And your world would be set free."

Kat nodded. "That would be perfect."

"Excellent. So let's start with the weapon's location. Where is it?"

"I'll take you there myself. First, extract Laramel, and—"

Novada's eyes widened. "Extract Laramel? No, I can't do that. I don't have the skill."

"But if you leave her in my brain, I can't help you. She'll send me to the depths again. There's no way you can operate the weapon without me."

"We have brilliant scientists who can help. Just tell me the location and—"

A door opened, and a winged man with a glowing face walked in. "Benjamin and Gertrude are on their way. I have earbuds, so we can listen to their chatter."

Novada spun toward him, her mouth dropping open. For a brief moment, she just stared, then she stammered. "Who ... who are you? And what are you doing here?"

Kat squinted. The man looked exactly like Jack. How could he have wings?

He glanced at Kat, then focused on Novada. "Who are *you*?"

Novada crossed her arms and huffed. "Never mind. No use pretending. She's seen too much."

The winged man walked to the bedside and stood next to Novada. "So what are you going to do?"

"I am considering my options." Novada looked him over. "I assume you're decontaminated."

He nodded. "From head to toe and to the tips of my wings."

"Good. I'll send her back to the depths and bring Laramel to the surface." Novada refocused on Kat and stared into her eyes. "Laramel, the interrogation is over. You can return now."

"No!" Kat shot to a sitting position and leaped out of bed. She shoved Novada, knocking her down, and rushed toward the door.

The winged man grabbed Kat's arm and pulled her close. Thrashing, she screamed toward his ears. "Ben! It's Kat! Run! Get away!"

The man held her around the waist with one arm and pulled his earbuds out. While Novada struggled to her feet, he lifted Kat to the bed and set her on it. "You recognize me, don't you?"

Kat nodded. "But I know you're not really Jack. He's been implanted. The real Jack would never be on the angels' side."

"That's right. He wouldn't." When Novada joined him at the bedside, he showed her the earbuds in his palm. "Nothing to worry about. I had the microphone turned off."

Novada eyed the buds. "Good. But keep listening."

He reinserted them. "I'll let you know if I hear anything important."

The room grew dim. A sinking sensation took over. Kat reached out, groping for something to hold on to. "No, no, no. Oh, Ben, help me."

As she fell into the dark void, Novada's voice seemed to come from far away. "Zeebach, when you do hear from them ..." Then silence blanketed her senses.

After studying the compass, Trudy gazed at the deep, down-sloping trench that lay ahead, leading to a narrow stream that meandered to the right. "I say we go straight down, cross the stream, and head up the next slope. Then we'll be on high ground and can try to contact Jack again. Better than following this ridge. It could take us miles out of the way."

"Good call." Ben crouched and retied one of his boots. "Ready. Let's do it."

As they tromped down the slope, she cast stealthy glances at him. With his chiseled jaw firm, a hand clutching the X99, and his eyes focused straight ahead, his determination blazed like an inferno. Kat was alive. Nothing could stop him. Yet, his sloped shoulders and slogging feet, which caused him to step on his own bootlaces from time to time, told another story.

The vaccine was likely shredding his soul. She felt it, too—headache, nausea, a sense of separation, like something was pulling her from her own body. It felt awful.

And for Ben, the deaths of so many friends and allies had taken their toll. Grief and regret gnawed at his mind. His pain had to be horrific.

"Ben," Trudy said as they began wading across the waist-deep stream, "giving the soldiers only a half dose didn't change anything. You know that, right? Same result."

"I know," he replied without inflection.

"Just making sure you're not blaming yourself." She shifted her weapon higher to keep it out of the water. "No one guessed what the real vaccine would do."

A trembling smile appeared. "My sister reads me well."

Their pants and shoes now wet, they trudged out of the stream and up the next slope. "Hey, someone has to prepare you for killer-Ben mode. Blaming yourself won't help. It's bull. You need to toss it. Now."

"You're right. As usual." He grinned. "Tossing it, as ordered, sir."

She punched his arm. "Don't be a jerk."

"Jerk mode terminated. Booting killer-Ben mode."

Shaking her head, Trudy smirked. Ben was being Ben. He would be ready.

After cresting the ridge, they looked across a flat expanse, far less forested, merely dotted with trees. The main road lay about half a mile away.

"Time to call Jack." Ben touched his earbud, turning the microphone back on. "Jack, this is Ben. Can you hear me?"

Trudy powered up her own earbud and listened in.

"Jack," Ben said. "I think we're in range. Can you hear me?"

A scratchy voice came through, as if shouted from afar. "Ben! It's Kat! Run! Get away!"

The voice silenced.

Trudy stared at Ben. He stared back at her, his mouth open. He set a shushing finger to his lips.

A new voice came through. "You recognize me, don't you?"

Trudy mouthed, "Jack?"

Ben nodded.

Kat's voice returned, still far away. "But I know you're not really Jack. He's been implanted. The real Jack would never be on the angels' side."

"That's right. He wouldn't."

As a pause ensued, Trudy licked her lips. The tension felt like electric shocks. What was going on?

"Nothing to worry about," Jack said. "I had the microphone turned off."

Another woman's voice piped in. "Good. But keep listening."

"I'll let you know if I hear anything important."

A mumble filtered through, maybe Kat's voice, but it was indecipherable.

"Zeebach," Novada said, "when you do hear from them, guide them to this room."

"Where will Laramel be?" Jack asked.

"She is the queen. That will be up to her. But I imagine that she will want to use her talents—and her face—to extract information from our guests."

"Understood."

"I see that Laramel has resurfaced," Novada said. "She will need some time to recover. While she does, I will accompany you to the vault, and we can monitor your earbuds from there. I want to get an update about activity in the Oculus Gate."

"Yes, I am interested as well."

"Give me one of the buds," Novada said. "I want to listen in on any conversations."

"Of course."

Something clicked. No more sound came through.

Ben pulled his earbud out. Trudy did the same. She turned the microphone off and slid the bud into her pants pocket. When Ben secured his bud, he faced her. "Thoughts?"

"Jack let us listen in. Then he turned the microphone off when Novada asked for an earbud. And since Novada called him Zeebach, she doesn't know he's really Zachariel."

"Or he's not Zachariel, he's not on our side, and he let us listen in to make us think he is."

Trudy drew her head back. "Wow. That's quite a stretch."

"No. Listen. If he's on our side, why didn't he rescue Kat? She was there. It sounded like Laramel was incapacitated. If he's so powerful, he could've done it. And then we wouldn't have to attack headquarters to get her out."

"Gotta admit, good points. But he might know something we don't. If he's really an archangel from God, we have to assume he has a lot of smarts."

"Fair enough, but like I said before, we trust each other. No one else. Even Kat is compromised."

"Right. Laramel might try to fool us with a Kat impersonation, like she did with Jack."

"Exactly." Ben shifted his rifle strap and marched on. "We need to get going."

Trudy hustled to catch up and walked at his side. "Got a plan?"

"Full frontal assault. They won't expect it."

Trudy imagined the scenario. Dashing in and killing people right and left would be amazing, but the feeling was probably the violence payload talking. "So we're just going to shoot everyone we see?"

Ben slowed his pace for a moment before accelerating again. "If they're at HQ, they're either angels or their sycophants. It's the only way. This is war."

"Okay. I get that it's war. But remember our ammo supply. Thirty rounds. A strategic strike might be better."

"I plan to try to get a plasma rifle. They'll have the newest models there. A hundred shots without a recharge. After we take out the gate drones and shoot the locking mechanism, guards with blasters will come at us. I'll relieve one of those guards of his weapon."

Trudy let a smile break through. "I've always wanted to try the newer ones. More rounds and more power. I heard you can punch a hole through an oak with one."

"Not likely, but it'll pack a punch. I'm sure it'll fry the winged cockroaches."

Trudy rolled a hand into a fist. "Let's crush them."

Once they reached the road, they stopped and looked toward headquarters. The entrance lay only a quarter mile away, the closed gate in sight. Ben's finger twitched around his rifle's trigger, and his face reddened. After a few seconds, he inhaled deeply, then let out a long sigh.

"What's wrong?" Trudy asked.

"We don't stand a chance."

"Did we ever?"

"Not really."

"Then what's different now?"

"Kat's alive. Implanted."

"So now you have a reason to survive."

"You're reading my mind."

"It's not hard. I've been doing it for years."

Ben ran a taut hand through his hair. "I feel the violence payload. It says attack, attack, attack. It's hard to think about anything else."

"Yeah. Same here. But we can help each other concentrate."

"Okay. What are our options?"

Trudy drummed her fingers against her thigh. "Well, we have tanks without fuel, missile launchers with no way to move them, probably a couple hundred dead soldiers and their weapons. And another plane somewhere. I heard two engines when they deployed the contagion."

"It probably crashed. But maybe some of its payload is still intact."

"Then that's another asset," Trudy said. "The contagion itself."

"And if Jack followed the plan and told the angels at HQ that the vaccine might have killed the rebels, they won't risk getting vaccinated."

"We can use the ultimate mental weapon. Fear. I like it."

Ben turned toward the invasion area. "Another six-mile hike?"

"Unless we can hijack a vehicle. But I don't see any. It's like the place is on lockdown even though it's not Sabbath anymore."

"Ominous. It's like they're waiting for something." Ben scanned the road. "Maybe we can coax a vehicle to come pick us up. We'll let them know we're close."

"Earbuds on?"

"Yep. Follow my lead." Ben turned his bud on and inserted it, as did Trudy.

"Jack," Ben called. "Can you hear me?"

"Yes," Jack said in a near whisper. "Where are you?"

"Near the road in front of angel headquarters. Where should we attack?"

"Too many guards up front. There's a rear entrance that's lightly guarded. I saw it while I was in the tree perch. You'll have to scale a razor-wire-topped fence, though."

Ben sighed. "If we had bolt cutters, we could go through it."

A pause ensued. A few seconds later, Jack continued. "Hang tight where you are. Wait for nightfall. I'll make sure the back fence is cut."

"Okay. Just a reminder. We all got doused with the contagion—hair and clothes. If you see Kat, stay away from her. I doubt that anyone there has been vaccinated. The three of us are plague carriers."

"Understood."

"Signing off." Ben took the bud out, cut the microphone, and motioned for Trudy to do the same. "That last part was for Novada's benefit. We want her to be scared of us."

Trudy nodded. "I guessed that."

"Let's hide in the woods."

As they trudged into the forest, Ben glanced back at the gate. "Watch for a scout to come looking for us. Novada thinks we're hunkered down, not wanting to risk getting spotted. The scout will probably be alone."

"Because she and Laramel won't want to risk infection," Trudy said. "It's easy to decontaminate one scout."

"Right. They're fishing for our location. Then maybe send a missile or a bomber to take us out."

"And Jack would let them?"

"If he's on our side, he's in a squeeze. Since Novada's listening to every word, and he probably knows that we know she's monitoring, he'll hope to lay low until he hears about our location, then send us a message telling us to move."

"And if he's not on our side?" Trudy asked.

"Then all bets are off. I have no idea what he's up to. Either way, we won't wait for him. If we neutralize the scout, maybe we can borrow whatever he's riding."

They took cover, each behind an oak tree about fifty yards from the road. Trudy peered around her tree. "What if they send SkySweep instead of a scout?"

"It's possible, but they know that would spook us and send us running. They want us to stay put."

Soon, a motorcycle exited the gate and rumbled toward them, the rider in dark armor and an angel-logo helmet, long red hair protruding, likely a woman. She rode slowly, her visor raised, revealing a set of goggles over her eyes.

"Probably thermal sensors," Ben said. "She'll spot our warm bodies."

"She's moving pretty slowly." Trudy raised her X99 to her shoulder. "I can take her out."

"She's wearing armor. The only vulnerable spot is the face. Pretty small target."

Trudy shifted the barrel to match the soldier's slow ride. "No worries."

"Be ready to run the moment—"

Trudy fired. The rider jerked back and fell to the road. The motorcycle toppled with her, a wheel still spinning. "She's down."

"Good shot. Let's go."

Chapter Eighteen

Ben and Trudy dashed to the fallen woman. "Get the goggles," Ben said as he grabbed the motorcycle's handlebars. "We might need them."

Trudy crouched at the fallen soldier and slid her helmet off, revealing smooth, ivory cheeks and a bullet hole in her forehead. She couldn't have been older than twenty. Trudy pulled the goggles, ripping out some of the girl's hair as the strap gave way. She slid the strap over her own head down to her neck and let the goggles ride on her chest.

With the motorcycle now upright, Ben straddled the seat, shifting his rifle to make room for Trudy. She hopped on behind him and held his shoulders. With a twist of the accelerator, he took off toward their community, tires squealing.

Trudy glanced back. A lone person ran from the gate toward the fallen soldier, then stopped, likely realizing that she might be contaminated.

As Trudy stared forward again, heat raged within, glazing her vision in red. Everyone on the angels' side was an accomplice to mass murder. Whether the motorcycle rider was implanted or not, she deserved that bullet. No regrets.

At least that's what she hoped to convince herself.

After a few minutes, Ben guided the motorcycle past the wreckage the kamikaze airplane caused and turned onto the forest road. When they reached the path the invasion vehicles had taken through the woods, he followed it to a camo ATV at the tail end of the convoy. At least ten vultures rose from various corpses and flew lazily upward, apparently unaffected by the contagion.

Ben and Trudy dismounted and strode past the ATV. A burly soldier sat slumped over the steering wheel, the window open and traces of vomit on the door panel and his shirt. Ahead, more vultures stood around the corpses, eyeing the new arrivals.

"Trudy, use the goggles to look for warm bodies. If anyone's still alive, we can put them out of their misery. I'll check the fuel gauges in the tanks."

"I'm on it." She slid the goggles over her eyes. Everything took on an aqua hue with bright green sparkles everywhere. Other such devices usually showed warmth in orange or red, but those colors were nowhere to be seen.

She pivoted toward the motorcycle, propped on its kickstand where Ben had left it. Still no signals of warmth from the hot engine. Yet, far fewer sparkles appeared on the fenders and handlebars, though they coated the seat and tires.

"Ben." She stripped the goggles off and hurried to a tank that he had just climbed atop. "These goggles don't detect heat."

"Then why was she wearing them?"

"I think they detect the contagion. It sparkles. Like glitter."

He touched the tank's top. "Is this glittering?"

She set the goggles in front of her eyes and scanned the tank. Green sparkles covered every inch. "Oh, yeah. Like tinsel on a Christmas tree."

"Perfect. When we drive this tank toward HQ, they'll see the contagion. It'll be a death machine rolling straight at them."

Trudy lowered the goggles. "If we can get it running."

"We can patch the leak. Then we'll siphon fuel from tanks that aren't quite empty. It'll take time, but we can do it. With the contagion still hot here, I don't think we'll see any angel patrols for a while."

During the next half hour, Ben found a cut in the tank's fuel line and spliced it while Trudy collected fuel from six other tanks, enough to fill the one Ben was working on.

When he finished the job, he climbed to the top of the tank while thunder rumbled nearby. "Let's board. No one's inside."

Trudy followed and joined him in the tank's three-person turret basket, Ben in the commander's position within reach of a periscope, Trudy in the gunner's seat. Within a minute, rain began pelting the metallic shell. Thunder clapped. Wind howled.

"The forecast called for a storm front," Trudy said. "Shouldn't last more than a couple of hours, but it'll get pretty cold once it passes through."

"I'm worried about the contagion. If rain washes it away, SkySweep's bound to come, and angel bogeys will be all over us."

"And our tank won't sparkle. So much for our plan."

"Unless …" Ben flipped on a computer embedded in the hull. After manipulating the controls for a minute or so, he studied the screen. "I found the second airplane's last reported location. It's close. Easy walking distance."

"I know what you're thinking. More contagion to keep the bogeys away."

"Right. Even if the plane crashed, the canisters might be intact."

"And the contents shielded from the rain."

"We can hope." Ben turned the computer off and settled into the seat. "Might as well catch a few winks. No use searching for the plane during the storm. It sounds pretty rough out there." At that moment, a gunshot-like thunderclap cracked.

Trudy smirked. "You timed that right. Maybe you've got friends in high places."

"Maybe." Ben closed his eyes. "But I doubt it."

Trudy scanned him from head to toe—slouched form, dark circles under his eyes, dirty fingers tightly intertwined—the portrait of discouragement. He needed a boost, but something more than a sisterly kick in the pants. He needed to get in touch with reality, an invisible reality, to be sure, truth he couldn't see with physical eyes. To give him that, she had to come up with her best speech ever.

She took in a deep breath, shot a silent prayer to heaven, and spoke in a matter-of-fact tone. "Yeah, Ben. I know what you mean. We get into HQ, fool the angels, get fake implants, get admitted to the military base, ready to kill the invading force. Everything's perfect. Then Ben finds a shred of decency inside, hoping that someone in the heavens is watching for a hint of faith. He decides not to be a cold-blooded killer. Then what happens? The vaccine he personally delivers to our fellow freedom fighters strips their souls, and they all kill themselves—men, women, and children. How's that for a little help from above?

"Then kindhearted Ben hears Kat's alive. Another glimmer of light, brighter than ever. But then the hammer drops. Boom. She's implanted. A fate worse than death. And what happens next? Ben gets an angel on our side. A real one. An archangel, no less. Then he turns coat and joins the fake angels and takes our brother with him, or maybe sends him into oblivion with the rest of the lost souls. That'll teach Ben Garrison to have some hope of success. Ain't no one on earth or in heaven gonna come and save the day." Trudy paused and took a breath. "Is that about right?"

Ben kept his eyes closed. "If you're trying to make me feel better, you're doing it wrong."

"Oh? You want me to lie to you? Tell you that you should've stayed in killer-Ben mode like your nagging sister kept saying, should've forgotten all about God, and should've injected enough poison into those kids to murder them? Never mind that your decision to show mercy didn't shatter the cosmos. If we had killed them all outright, we never would've learned about how the real vaccine purges souls. Either way, those soldiers would be dead. Either way, the real vaccine would've wiped out our allies. Either way, the angels would still have Kat in their clutches.

"But what do we have now that you showed a little mercy? This tank, for one. And a new plan. A way to get into angel HQ. A way to rescue Kat. And maybe Jack. None of that would've been possible if we had killed those kids with the fake vaccine."

Trudy kicked Ben's leg, making him open his eyes. "Listen to me. I was wrong, and you were right. I still like killer Ben, but sometimes we need merciful Ben. Whether we're getting help from above, I don't know. Maybe. We sure need it. But this I do know. I believe in you, Ben Garrison. I trust you to make the right decisions. And I will follow you to the very end."

Her heart racing, she stared at him, half wanting to hug him and half wanting to slap him. He was such a good man. A good, broken, hurting man.

As he stared back at her, his eyes sparkled. He bit his lip, then whispered, "Okay. Thanks."

"You're welcome." She rose and climbed toward the hatch. "I'm going out to look for the plane."

"But the storm."

"I don't care. I need to cool off." As she emerged, windblown rain slapped her cheek. Within seconds, droplets fell from her hair and dripped over her eyes. No matter. At least angel bogeys wouldn't show up.

When she turned to close the hatch, an X99 slid out, then another. Finally, Ben's head poked through. "You didn't look at the map grid, did you?"

"Nope."

"No clue where to search for the plane, right?"

"Right."

Ben heaved a fake sigh. "All right. I'll help you. Gotta give you some hope of success."

"Hope of success?" She grasped his wrist and helped him climb out. "That sounds familiar."

"Yeah." Ben closed the hatch and stood next to her. "Just quoting a wise woman I know."

She picked up the X99s and handed him one. "Lead the way."

They climbed down and, after strapping the rifles to their backs, walked toward the front of the convoy, Trudy behind Ben as he looked at a compass. When he reached the lead ATV, he turned left and followed the edge of the field where the river flowed. After several steps, he angled back into the forest. Every few seconds, he brushed water from the compass, mumbling something about primitive technology.

Hoping to find a sign of a plane crash, Trudy scanned the treetops as they bent and swayed in the gusts. Stinging raindrops forced her to blink nearly every second or glance down at their increasingly muddy path.

Soon, a break in the canopy appeared. Something had shattered dozens of branches. She shouted over the clattering din. "I see something!" She pointed at the break. "There."

Ben nodded. "Good work, Eagle Eye."

They jogged underneath the spot and followed the path of broken branches as it angled to the forest floor. The plane lay on the ground in several pieces—fuselage, wings, tail, and propellers. A gray cylindrical canister partially protruded from under the fuselage. No corpses appeared to be anywhere in sight. The pilot might have ejected long before the crash.

Ben crouched and tried to pull the canister out, to no avail.

Trudy set her hands under the fuselage. "Let's try to move this."

Ben joined her. "On three. One ... two ... three!"

With a heave, they shoved the fuselage to the side. Ben lifted the canister and hoisted it under his arm. "The storm might end soon. We'd better hustle."

Retracing their steps, they hurried back toward the tank. As they slogged through mud, Trudy put the goggles on. As feared, only a few sparkles remained—tiny glitters here and there as rainwater swept them away.

She slid the goggles back down to her chest. "Faster, Ben. The contagion's almost gone."

He halted at the front of the convoy line. "So now we know water clears the contagion."

"At least the powdery stuff that carries it. It needs a host, and the sparkly powder is a temporary one. When people inhale it, they become the new host."

"How long can the powder act as a host?"

She shrugged. "At least a day or two. It has to be long enough to transport it to the plane and then to the field to broadcast over the target. Why?"

Ben's brow wrinkled deeply, rain dripping into the channels. "I'm getting an idea."

"Think fast. If the angels send a flyover to check for contamination, they'll see it's safe to land and search the area."

He pointed toward their farm. "Go to the armory and get a couple of tranquilizer guns with holsters and belts."

"Okay. I guess I shouldn't ask why yet. Anything else?"

Still holding the canister under an arm, he stroked his chin. "Yeah. Lye soap, two scrub brushes, and an angel-extraction kit."

"What? We're going to do an extraction? I've never done one."

"No, but you've seen the videos. You know what to do."

"Seeing an extraction and doing one aren't even close to—"

"And get the biggest cooling blanket you can find along with a cooler. I don't know if the freezer's still running, but with all the insulation, the blankets are probably still cold enough."

Trudy blinked at him. "Okay. Now I'm asking. Why?"

"Too much to explain. Just go. I'll meet you at our tank."

"Nope. You said you'd keep me in the loop. Spill it."

He sighed. "All right. I want to use the tank to attack HQ and I need the tranquilizers to knock Kat out."

"And the cooling blanket is for hiding the tank from SkySweep?"

"Not sure if that'll work, but yeah. The rest of the plan is still fuzzy."

"Good enough for now." Trudy turned toward the camp and jogged through the pummeling rain and wind, the goggles bouncing at her chest. Holding the X99 over her head, she waded across the river, now swollen to waist level. After jogging past the perimeter defense bunkers, she arrived at the armory and bustled into the one-room building, dripping water from hair, fingers, and clothes to the wooden floor.

Rifles lined a wall along with shelves of ammo. Atop one shelf lay a few all-purpose belts. The captain had given them belts, but these had more pouches and fasteners along with back slings.

She grabbed two belts and wrapped them around her waist, one above the other, then added two X99 ammo magazines to each.

After finding two tranquilizer shotguns on a wall rack and several dart cartridges in a drawer, she fastened them to the belts and the X99 to a back sling, then walked to the massive freezer embedded in a wall. She spun the combination lock, cycled it through the numbers, and shoved the latch down. As she opened the huge door, white vapor streamed out. Apparently the freezer was working. The generators must have been running at the power station.

Still dripping, she hurried in and began picking through the blankets on a low shelf. At least Ben didn't ask for a liquid-nitrogen blanket. If she had gone into that section, she would already be frozen by now.

She grabbed the biggest blanket, left the freezer, and closed the door. After finding a wheeled cooler filled with water bottles, she dumped the bottles, stuffed the blanket inside, and closed the lid, then turned the cooler's thermostat to its coldest setting. The engine on the side hummed, and the digital thermometer reading dropped rapidly, a good sign.

Leaving the cooler behind for the moment, she hurried out again into the driving rain. An extraction kit would be at the infirmary, not far into the community. As she splashed through mud puddles, she passed corpses huddled in the mire, sheets of rain pelting their motionless forms.

She paused at a group of four—parents and small children. She reached out a hand, then drew it back. Biting her lip, she ran on.

When she arrived at the infirmary, she burst inside and shook her head, slinging water. A small table stood at the opposite wall.

A tray of vials lay on top, along with two injector guns next to an empty medical bag. No need for the injectors anymore.

After grabbing the medical bag, she searched a closet filled with cleaning supplies. A bar of lye soap and a scrub brush sat on a shelf next to a bottle of bleach, and a second brush lay in a bucket on the floor. She loaded everything into the bag and backed out of the closet. Now to find an extraction kit.

The door to the surgery room stood ajar. After setting the bag down and taking the X99 from the back sling, she pushed the door the rest of the way open and entered. Dr. Calhoun lay on the operating table, motionless, his white hair askew and his wrinkled face gray.

He turned his head toward her. "Trudy?"

She gasped. "You're alive!"

"An excellent—" He coughed several times. When he finished, blood trickled from his nose and lips. "An excellent diagnosis."

She strapped the rifle over her shoulder, walked to his side, and peered into his bloodshot eyes. "Did you drink the poison?"

"Not voluntarily. No doctor would take that option. Our code is to do no harm, even to ourselves."

"Someone *forced* you to drink it?"

"Not forced." His breaths rattled as he labored through each word. "I merely misunderstood. You see, I told Barks that I was going out to deploy the weapon. When I straddled a spare motorcycle to leave, he gave me his canteen and said to drink it if I felt the vaccine purging my soul. I thought it might be whiskey, you know, to deaden the pain. I didn't understand that he was supplying poison to end my suffering. Such was the brain-scrambling effect of the vaccine on both Barks and me. So, when I reached a point about a tenth of the way to the weapon, I felt a raging headache, and I drank from the canteen. Within minutes, my stomach boiled, and I realized what I had done.

"I induced vomiting, of course, but I grew sicker and sicker. Too weak to go on and not knowing if I would live or die, I reversed course and arrived here right before this storm began. I found everyone dead, and I knew I would be next. So I decided to wait for the inevitable."

"Maybe it isn't inevitable," Trudy said. "Is it possible you didn't drink enough to kill you, or maybe you vomited enough?"

"No, dear Trudy. My organs are failing. I will pass in less than an hour. That's why I decided to lie here. I want to leave this world from the place where I have had my greatest successes."

Tears crept to her eyes. "I'm so sorry, Doc. I wish there was something I could do."

He slowly tightened his hand into a fist. "Just complete our mission. Rid the world of the angel scourge."

"Well … we're trying. And maybe you can still help. Do you have an angel-extraction kit?"

He lifted an arm a couple of inches and pointed. "Two. In the floor cabinet."

"Good." Trudy rushed over, opened the cabinet, and withdrew a white metal box the size of a typical first-aid kit. She set a hand on the other kit. Although this one wouldn't do any good staying here, carrying more than needed across the river made no sense. She left it in place, returned with one kit to the operating table, and set it next to Doc's hip. "I saw the extraction training video. I hope that's enough to get me through one."

Doc harrumphed. "If you care about your patient, you wouldn't rely on that video. Risk of brain damage is too high."

"What's wrong with it?"

"The surgeon in the video kept the extraction forceps at a high setting for far too long, which caused some of the angel's tentacles to snap before they could withdraw. The vestiges remained in the brain stem, leading to severe damage. That patient became unresponsive and died a few weeks later."

Trudy replayed that part of the procedure in her mind. "Why do vestiges kill a patient?"

"The snapping causes the vestiges to become quasi-physical, no longer pure energy. They rot within the brain stem, causing severe infection and eventually death."

"That makes sense. So we can't leave any angel particles behind in the patient's brain."

"Correct." His eyes narrowed to a slit. "By the way, who is your patient?"

"Kat. Jack found her. She's alive, but she's been implanted."

"Kat?" Doc's voice strengthened. "Why didn't you mention that before?"

"Because there wasn't anything you could do for her. You'd just get—"

"There's plenty I can do. I can go over the procedure with you. We can't lose her again."

"Sure. Okay. If you feel up to it."

"My feelings are irrelevant." He took a deep breath. "The video showed the proper first steps—reopen the original implantation incision and insert the extraction forceps as far as possible. Then place the shock-wave emitter against the skull directly over the brain stem, turn it on at the lowest setting, and slowly increase the power. Since both of your hands will be occupied, your assistant will hold the AngelScan above the emitter while you watch the angel's reaction to the shock waves. The moment the shock loosens the tentacles' hold, turn on the extraction forceps and begin drawing the angel toward the incision through the pathway it took to get to the brain."

Trudy nodded. "And that's when it gets tricky."

"Exactly. Too much drawing power from the forceps will snap the tentacles. Too much shock energy to loosen the hold on the stem will damage your patient's brain. Yet, a stubborn angel will require adjustments to the shock setting, sort of like playing a fish with a rod and reel, so the surgeon has to use quite a bit of finesse with both instruments. It can be time consuming and taxing for the surgeon and the patient."

"So monitoring vitals and anesthesia is critical as well."

"To be sure. No patient wants to feel those shock waves. The post-op headache will be torture enough."

"Are there any signs that the tentacles are ready to snap? Like how thin they get when they're stretched."

"Don't rely on thinness. Watch for color. If the angel begins fading from red to pink, then it's straining, ready to snap. Also if it shudders, like a cold shiver. It's time to back off. And even if they don't snap during the extraction from the stem, they might break while on the path toward the incision, so you might have to go back in with the forceps to clean up vestiges after you withdraw the main body."

"Got it." Trudy opened the box, withdrew the extraction forceps, a thin tube with tiny pincers on one end. "How often do the extractions fail?"

"Early on, the death rate was about eighty percent. Recently, we have lost perhaps two out of five, so chances of survival have greatly improved. Too bad the patient in that video was an early attempt. I have been telling the trainers for months to record me doing a proper extraction, but we never got around to it."

Trudy set the forceps back in the box. "Who was the surgeon in the video? I saw his hands but not his face."

"Oh. That was me. Before I learned better. Another reason I want the video changed." He gave her a weak smile. "My reputation is at stake."

Trudy clasped his hand, tears trickling as she smiled in return. "Not if I don't tell anyone. Your secret's safe with me."

"Thank you, dear." He blinked twice, his eyes glazing. "I'm afraid … my long-winded … explanation has spent … my last reserves. I am fading."

Biting her lip, Trudy tightened her grasp. "I'll stay with you, Doc. To the end. You won't die alone."

Tears glistened in his eyes. "Thank you … again. I'm so … so proud of you." He blinked once more, then closed his eyes. "I almost forgot … to tell you. You need my … my password … It's … Gertrude."

"My name?"

"Yes. You were … always special … always."

"Doc …" Her voice cracked. "Thank you. And you're special to me. Really. Like a father. But now I need to know the weapon's location. Can you tell me?"

He breathed a grating word. "Tea."

"You want tea? Of course. I'll go—"

"No." He inhaled with a rasp, then exhaled and breathed no more.

"Doc?" Trudy brushed tears away. "Doc, I'm still here." She lifted his hand and kissed his knuckles. As she let her lips linger, she whispered, "Safe travels, Doc. I will do everything in my power to complete our mission, God as my witness."

As Iona walked her bike through a dense forest, she munched on pecans she had found on the ground under a massive tree, only a handful, but enough to keep her rumbling stomach under control.

Soon, thunder rolled in. A few minutes later, rain penetrated the canopy and pelted her head, getting heavier by the second. Although she had shed a lot of the manure, bits of the stuff clung to her hair, and smears still colored her arms and pant legs. Since Leo would find the odor of a horse worth investigating, it would be a good idea to wash, as long as the heavens continued providing enough water.

She leaned the bike against a tree, shrugged off her backpack, and withdrew a bar of soap. Leaving her clothes on, she washed her body from head to toe, scrubbing the filth out of her hair and wiping away the smears.

As water poured down her arms and legs, manure flowed with it, along with an occasional hair. She pinched an extra-long strand, thick and tough, probably from a horse's tail. That could be useful. She pushed it into her pocket.

Lightning flashed. Thunder clapped, ending in a long rumble. Iona continued scrubbing. It seemed that every molecule of vanquished grime was a victory, like cleansing bad memories, sins of the past.

And many were her sins—lies, thefts, seeds of distrust. Such was the life of a spy, especially a double agent. And now it was finally time to turn away from them. To come clean. To be herself. If only she could remember who that was.

Chapter Nineteen

Trudy set Doc's hand down and gently withdrew hers. Tears flowed. How could she leave him here, after all he had done for her? Yet, she had to go. She had delayed far too long already.

She slid the X99 into the back sling, then, moving quietly except for the brushing of her wet clothes, she picked up the extraction kit and exited to the infirmary's entry room. There she retrieved the medical bag, set the kit inside, and hurried from the building. Fortunately, the rain had eased, though the wind continued buffeting. As she again passed the corpses, she focused straight ahead. Seeing the faces of her dead friends would be too much to take.

After stopping to get the cooler, she waded across the river, holding the cooler high to keep it out of the water, though the butt of the rifle dragged in the current, probably not enough to hurt it.

Once on solid ground again, she jogged toward the invaders' convoy. When she ducked into the forest, the trees blocked the breezy assault, providing some comfort. Not bothering to try to roll the cooler across roots and trenches, she continued carrying it with the medical bag on top.

By the time she arrived at the tank, the rain had stopped completely. Ben knelt next to a tank track, the canister on the ground with its hatch open and the motorcycle on its kickstand a couple of steps away. He looked up at her. "Have some trouble?"

"A little." She set the cooler and the medical bag on the ground. "Miss me?"

"Of course." He winked. "I wrote you a letter and sent it by pony express. Didn't you get it?"

"Don't get your knickers in a knot. I got everything you asked for."

"Good." He nodded toward the canister. "It took me way too long to pop this thing open, so I was busy the whole time you were gone."

"What's inside?"

"You tell me." He reached in and scooped a handful of yellowish-white powder. "Does it sparkle?"

Trudy put the goggles back on. The powder glittered like crazy. "Yep. You're holding pure death. Super risky, considering we got only half a dose of vaccine."

"We have antibodies. We'd be dead by now if we didn't." He dropped the powder back inside. "Let's light up the tank with glitter but leave a path clear to climb to the driver's seat."

"I see what you're thinking. A contagion bomb delivered to their back door. But won't they know the rain should've washed it off?"

"I think fear will overcome logic. It should work."

"But will they see it? I mean, I know their security guards will be watching for an attack, but …" She lifted the goggles. "No sparkles without these."

"True, but with the contagion drop only a few miles away, they must've taken precautions. The goggles are their technology. They'd be stupid if their security cameras don't have a similar lens."

"Yeah, you're probably right."

"Ready to make a sparkle tank?"

"Okay, but first …" As more tears threatened, Trudy shifted her weight from one foot to the other. "I saw Doc."

Ben jerked his head toward her. "Alive?"

She nodded. "For a few minutes. I held his hand till he passed."

"Tell me about it while we work."

"Sure." After Trudy put the cooler and medical bag in the tank, they each scooped a handful of the contagion powder.

"Sprinkle it evenly," Ben said as he tossed a handful across a rear section. "We want to make it look like it got broadcast by an airplane."

While they scattered the contagion, Trudy told Ben about her conversation with Doc, his attempt to get to the anti-angel weapon in spite of his decaying soul, and how he drank the poison in ignorance. Still, he had enough strength to explain an angel-extraction procedure, and he gave her his password to deploy the weapon.

"Gertrude," Trudy said as she sighed. "My name was one of the last words on his lips."

"No wonder. You were like a granddaughter to him."

"And I asked him where the weapon is. He said something about tea, but I couldn't connect it."

"The drink?"

"That's the first thing I thought. I offered him some, but he said no."

"Maybe he meant the letter T. Part of a code."

"Could be, but he died before he could explain. I should've asked him for the location first thing."

"No use second guessing." Ben stared at a handful of powder. "We have one password, and Jack has the other. We'll have to get it from him."

Trudy continued scattering powder over the tank. "After we rescue Kat?"

"Of course." Ben flung his handful clear across the front of the tank, his muscles tense. "She invented the weapon. Like we've said before, she's the only one who can help if we don't have both passwords."

"Um … right. Kat's the priority. Not the weapon itself. No argument here."

When they finished covering about two-thirds of the tank, the hum of an engine drifted from the sky, getting closer.

"A jet," Ben said, looking up. "Maybe a bomber. Good bet they called in special forces to obliterate this place."

"True. Probably won't be long."

Ben nodded toward the tank. "You drive this beast. I'll take the bike. I need to do some reconnaissance, and I'll get a better view that way."

Trudy brushed her hands together, shedding the powder. "Suits me."

"Thought it would." Ben lugged the canister to the motorcycle and set it in a saddle pack, while Trudy scrambled up the tank.

An explosion rocked the forest. Fire erupted near the front of the convoy. The jet engine noise returned, louder than ever.

"Two jets!" Ben straddled the bike. "Let's bolt!"

Trudy dropped into the control seat and shifted the right track forward and the left track in reverse, turning the mechanical beast left as sharply as possible.

Another explosion shook the ground. Scraps of metal rained. Something clanked on the tank's shell. A steering wheel glanced off Ben's shoulder. The bike's back tire spun futilely. As the wheel fishtailed, mud flew this way and that, some splattering Trudy's windshield. Finally, Ben planted a foot, lifted the bike out of the mire, and took off.

A third explosion sent the tank lurching. Trudy shifted both tracks forward and set the throttle to full, Ben still in sight well down the path. To the rear, a fourth explosion boomed, then a fifth. Apparently the jets were concentrating their firepower on the convoy line and didn't see her tank's escape as they zoomed past. But that could change at any second.

Ahead, Ben slipped his earbud into place. Trudy lifted a hip, dug a hand into her wet pants pocket, and withdrew her bud. The moment she installed it, another boom sounded, farther away. "Got my radar powered up, Ben."

"Good. We can talk openly until we get about a mile away from HQ. Then we'll be in Jack's range."

"And Novada's."

"Exactly. We'll take a long circuit around HQ, staying more than a mile away, then come to the back side. I'm sure a tank can knock their fence down. It's just chain link."

"I'll play bulldozer," Trudy said, "so I should take the lead through the underbrush. Probably no paved road to the back side."

"Right. But later. I'll let you know."

"Are we going to ride this tank right into HQ and hope for the best?"

Ben paused for a moment before answering. "Not exactly. I'm still working on the plan. We'll stop when we're out of the contagion-spreading zone, then we'll talk about it."

"Sounds good."

Something moved, forward and to her right. A small mirror had been mounted next to the fuel gauge. The movement was her own head bobbing with the tank's ups and downs.

She leaned closer to the mirror. Mud smears drew dark lines down her cheeks, and equally dark hair had pulled free from its tieback and now looked like ragged sideburns plastered to her skin.

Her bloodshot eyes told more of the story—exhaustion, pain, and stress. And maybe a reaction to the vaccine? That awful stuff was probably doing all sorts of terrible things within.

Still looking at the mirror, she withdrew the AngelScan from her pocket and set it against her forehead. In the reflection, the scanner showed her soul as a dull amorphous blob, not the usual bright white sphere pulsing with radiance. Red dots sprinkled the dark background, likely the violence payload, though they seemed few and far between. Maybe they were fizzling out.

In any case, her soul was struggling. The environment was probably like a toxic waste dump. How long could it survive?

She pushed the AngelScan back into her pocket and drove on. One way or another, she had to use these next few hours, maybe her last hours on earth, to kill as many angels as possible and set Kat free. And then maybe figure out what Jack, or Zachariel, was up to.

They reached the forest road, then headed toward the main highway. Ben drove the bike at a slow pace, allowing Trudy's tank to keep up. As he puttered along, he kept looking into the woods at each side, as if searching for something. After several minutes, he pointed to the right. "There's a good spot. Let's stop. Bring the soap, brushes, and the sparkle goggles."

Ben pulled into the undergrowth at the forest's edge while Trudy stopped the tank in the middle of the road. When she climbed down and joined him, they tromped together into the woods. "I've been watching a stream that runs alongside this road," Ben said. "It looks deeper here than other places."

They stopped at the stream's edge, likely a tributary that flowed into the river next to the camp. At this point, it was about ten feet across and thigh deep, swollen by the heavy rain.

Ben extended a hand. "The soap and a scrub brush."

Trudy retrieved the bar and a brush from belt pouches and handed them over. He broke the bar and tossed half back to her, then began stripping off his shirt. "We need to decontaminate. Not a trace of the contagion's carrier. We'll check our bodies and clothes with the goggles."

They stood in knee-deep water and scrubbed for several minutes. When they finished, they took turns wearing the goggles to check themselves, their clothes, and each other for sparkles. After dressing, they each strapped on a gun belt with a tranquilizer shotgun in a back sling and an extra ammo magazine for the X99. Both now shivering, Ben nodded toward the tank. "Climb in on the clean side and look for contagion on the driver's seat, the cooler, everything. If it sparkles, wash it with lye. I'll clean the bike."

"Will do." She put the goggles back on, grabbed a scrub brush, and climbed in. After checking the compartment thoroughly and finding no sign of the contagion carrier, she stuck her head out through the access hole. "It's clean."

"Good." Ben inserted his earbud and mounted the motorcycle. "Take the lead. I'll guide you by voice. We'll brainstorm the plan along the way." He drove the bike to the rear of the tank.

After adjusting the shotgun's position, Trudy sank into the seat, started the tank's engine, and throttled to full speed, her grip tight on the track controls. Again the violence payload infused rage, a burning desire to slaughter angels and their minions. Killing that woman in armor had done little to slake the inner beast's thirst for death. It had to be tamed.

Ben's voice returned. "Okay. Here's what I have so far. We've got a tank that'll bulldoze the rear fence and head straight for ... wait ... what's the most accessible room back there? You memorized the floor plan."

"Um ... yeah." Trudy loosened her grip on the controls. "The vault's in the back. The exterior wall is concrete, a foot thick. I'm not sure the tank can plow through that."

"Doesn't matter. As long as we make them think it can, it'll work. That'll be our target."

"Because that's where Jack and Novada said they would be."

"Right," Ben said. "And even more important, where Kat will be. That is, Queen Laramel."

"Okay, we're going straight for the jugular. I like this plan so far. But I hope that's not the violence payload talking."

"No worries. There's a lot more to this plan, including how to time SkySweep's searches. If they find out a tank's missing, they'll look for us. Then if we hear them coming, we'll have to stop and cover the tank, the motorcycle, and ourselves the best we can with the blanket, like we talked about before."

"Slows our progress," Trudy said, "but it can't be helped."

"Right. And now I need your expertise again. If the vault is attacked, where would they take Kat to keep her safe from the contagion? Give me the route and estimated time to get there."

"Okay. Remember the hallway that leads to the vault? From the front entry's anteroom to the intersection with that hallway, the distance is about ..."

As the conversation continued, Trudy allowed herself a smile from time to time. It felt so good to have her brother's complete trust. She wasn't just a kid-sister tag-along. She had become his fellow field agent, his medical expert, his go-to consultant when he needed an extra brain. That was all good.

Still, she might die on this crazy mission. But it was worth it. At least that's what she constantly tried to convince herself. The entire world needed help, whether they realized it or not, whether they deserved it or not. She and Ben would be there for them, together.

Iona stopped the bike at the top of the hill and looked out over the darkening twilight. Angel headquarters lay nestled in the valley below, its many lights illuminating the buildings.

She exhaled. Finally. After following a crazy zigzag course to elude the huntsmen, she had arrived. Now the hard part—how to get inside the building to search for clues to the whereabouts of that agent. Without a name, the task seemed nearly impossible, but he might show up on the camera-feed database. It was a long shot, but no other choice came to mind.

No matter what, however, any stealthy search would have to wait until the middle of the night. It was time to catch a nap, but this crest would be the worst place. Too exposed.

A cold breeze punctuated the thought. If not for the kind lady who had let her come in after the rainstorm and stand in front of a blazing fireplace, she would still be wet and in danger of freezing. Yet, she wasn't able to stay long, not with Leo still on her tail.

She pushed off and glided downhill toward angel headquarters. When she came to a dense part of the forest to the right, not wanting to deposit her scent on the ground, she rode the bike straight into the foliage, enduring the roots, stones, and ruts until she came across a flat area out of view from the road. She stopped, dismounted the bike, and laid it down, then shrugged the backpack off and pulled the small blanket out, careful not to spill the gun.

After spreading the blanket on the ground under a pine tree with low-hanging branches, she found a freshly fallen frond and rubbed the green needles over her face, arms, and legs. Although sticky, this stuff was better than the horse manure from the night before. She broke the frond and scattered the needles on the blanket, then, after retrieving the gun, she lay on her back and pulled the thin material over herself as she rolled to her side.

Now in darkness, she turned toward the road, the gun in her grip. More than likely, the huntsmen would soon pick up the trail at the top of the hill where she set her feet down. Whether or not the pine would keep her scent out of the wind remained to be seen. Closing her eyes, she tried to sleep, telling herself to wake up in three hours. That would be about right.

Soon, forest sounds filtered in. A twig cracked, too quiet to be from a human foot. A rodent squeaked, maybe ten paces away. No problem. Treetops rustled. Not good, an audio mask for an approaching enemy.

She sighed. Being ultra-vigilant robbed so many nights of sleep. Oh, for the days when life wasn't like this, back when Father guarded their farmhouse with his strong hands clutching his weapon, an axe with which he had just hewn trees to build a cattle fence, back when Mother bustled around, busying herself with everything from plowing furrows to sowing seeds to milking cows to harvesting pecans from their farm's stately trees. And giving birth to Little Brother, the sickly baby they never named, thinking it would be easier to grieve for a nameless child if he were to die ... which he did, at six weeks old.

Tears creeping in, Iona clutched the blanket closer. Little Brother's death marked the beginning of the sad days—when blight destroyed the grain, when fire consumed the farmhouse, when the plague took Mother and Father. And then when the angels came, though that seemed like a benefit at first.

Alone and trying to survive on the pitiful crop of pole beans, red potatoes, radishes, and pecans as well as the salted remains of the milk cow, how could life get worse? It couldn't. She prayed for help … or death. Either would be better than her miserable existence.

When the final slices of jerky ran out, the fateful day arrived. An angel representative, a kind man wearing overalls and boots, just like the area's farmers, showed up on the doorstep to evaluate her land. He offered to buy her farm with cash and escort her to the temple to become a priestess. She would have funds to buy new clothes, though not enough money to live on her own.

"What would I do there?" she had asked.

"Serve the blessed angels."

"I know. But specifically. What does it involve? It's not like a brothel or anything like that, is it? I won't do that. I'd die first."

"No, no. You would cook and clean. The temple is a big place, a house of worship for every community for miles around. In exchange for your labors, you will have food and housing. You will be safe from all harm."

Well, he was right about the food and housing. Perfectly adequate. But the labor? It started with cooking and cleaning, as he said, but then Constance took her aside and changed everything. She became a spy for the angels. And that was fine. The angels had been good to her, and the excitement of a dangerous new challenge spiked her courage.

But going undercover reawakened her loneliness. For weeks she had to hide her actions, conceal every secret she had stolen, except to stealthily send them to Constance, an angel who would slit her throat at the slightest suspicion. And when she experienced the goodness of her targets, the mercy in the heart of Commander Barks, the generosity of families in his community, the reality of her foolishness finally came through, first as a trickle, then a flood.

Spying for both sides had made her a friend of both evil and good, and an enemy of everyone, including herself. She had violated her parents' teaching, refused to listen to the warnings of her conscience, and betrayed the only people who had been kind to her.

And now she had to beg them to take her in.

As more tears crept to her eyes, Iona bit her lip to keep from crying until she fell asleep.

Chapter Twenty

Jack landed feet first on a two-lane road with a yellow stripe down the middle. People of all shapes, sizes, and colors walked single file on each side, half going one way and half going the other, all plodding at a slow pace. Some wore summer clothes, others winter, though the temperature seemed neutral—neither hot nor cold.

A gray-haired man wearing suspenders, jeans, and work boots waved an arm. "You best join us. You won't like what happens if you stand still for too long."

"What happens?" Jack asked.

As the man walked away, he called, "You'll find out."

Something sizzled below. Pain riddled Jack's feet. Tongues of flame shot out from under his hiking boots. He leaped away and walked with the crowd on one side of the road.

After scanning the unfamiliar faces, he accelerated, glancing at each person as he passed, calling, "Sophie? Sophie Garrison? Alana?"

When he caught up with the suspendered man, the man said, "Save your breath. We're in hell. Who cares if you find your loved ones or not? You'll just see them suffer on this never-ending road."

A woman farther ahead cried out, "A marker! Only one to go!"

Jack looked at the green signpost with a white numeral one on the front, as well as a few unrecognizable characters underneath, maybe non-Arabic numerals. Several in the crowd cheered, while many spoke excitedly in foreign languages. Yet, the people walking in the opposite direction kept right on walking, as if they hadn't heard the good news that a destination lay in the other direction not far away.

Jack scanned their forlorn faces. Hadn't they come from that direction? They would know what lay only one mile away, wouldn't they? And nobody in his line seemed to want to call out to the other line to tell them the news or ask them what they had seen.

Then another thought rose. Was it one mile to go? Maybe it was one kilometer, or one fathom, or even one parsec. The sign didn't say, and the people didn't bother to guess the units, at least not verbally.

Jack jogged faster, checking faces again and calling for Sophie and Alana as he passed hundreds of travelers. After what seemed like at least a mile, Jack slowed again, leaned toward the center of the road, and looked ahead. The road went on and on into a distant horizon.

A man called, "Look! A marker! Only one to go!" Again the crowd cheered, and again voices in other languages buzzed.

Jack spotted the new marker, identical to the previous one. Didn't these people remember?

He ran on, once more calling and scanning faces on both sides of the road. Soon, a woman going in the opposite direction, holding a little girl's hand, turned toward him and smiled. "Jack?"

"Sophie?" He leaped across the street, caught up with her, and walked at her side. "Yes. It's me."

Still walking, Sophie reached her free hand toward him. "We can't stop."

"I know." When he touched her hand, sparks flew.

She jerked back and blew on her fingers. She stared at him, her brow cut with deep furrows. "What happened?"

"Sorry. You can't touch me. I have some kind of shield around me that no one else has."

"Why?"

"Too much to explain. Just listen. Do you know where you are?"

She leaned close and whispered, "Hell, I think, but Alana doesn't know. I keep telling her we're trying to find heaven."

Jack eyed Alana as he whispered in return. "She hasn't even looked at me."

"She's obsessed with the signs. She hears people announce the one on the sign, and she gets excited, saying we're almost there."

"Do they all have a one on them?"

Sophie nodded. "But Alana doesn't seem to remember. In fact, no one does. Or maybe they do remember, and their only hope for escaping this madness is to believe that the newest marker is telling the truth, even though the others, I guess thousands of them by now, were wrong. It's the only way to keep their sanity."

"But you obviously don't believe the signs."

"No, but you know I've never been one to go along with the crowd." Sophie faced forward. "Stubborn as a mule."

"One of the things I love about you." He kept his gaze on her determined profile. Love for Alana was probably the only thing keeping her sane. "Anyway, we're not in hell. Your souls went through the Oculus Gate, and this is a new prison for souls both good and evil. I was sent here to let you know. Give you some hope."

She gazed at him, tears in her eyes. "Hope? Like the ones on the signs? Are you another lie? I can't even touch you. The real Jack would've taken my hand. Caressed my cheek. Kissed my lips." Her voice took on a hard edge. "I don't believe you're Jack. It's all a lie, and we're in hell."

He spread out his hands. "Trust me. I would do all those things if I could, but this shield around me is the only thing that'll allow me to go back to earth to try to get you out of this place."

She faced forward again. "All lies."

"What can I do to prove to you that I'm really Jack?"

She shook her head. "Nothing ... Wait ... No." She looked straight at him, tears now trickling down her cheeks. "If you can get Alana and me out of here, then I will believe you. Then this wouldn't be hell, because there's no escaping hell."

His own tears welling, he hovered a hand over her cheek. "I swear to you by God and all that is holy, I will get you two out of here. Just wait for me next to one of the markers. March around it if you have to keep moving."

"How will you know which one we choose?"

"I think we might be walking in a big circle, like there's only one marker in each direction. But don't worry. Even if there are a million of them, somehow I'll find you."

She brushed a tear with a knuckle. "Okay. I'll force myself to believe you. Even if it's all a lie, I need it to keep me sane."

"It's the truth, but listen, after I get you out, I don't know when I'll see you again. You might go straight to heaven, and I'll go back to earth. When you get to heaven, remember that you saw me. Then you'll know it's not a lie. And neither is this." He kissed his hand and blew over his palm. "Catch it, Sophie Anne Garrison, my sweet cupcake. It's the only way I can kiss you."

"Cupcake?" She touched her cheek. "Jack? It's really you?"

"It's really me. Goodbye for now." He leaped into the air and willed his body skyward. As he entered the downward tugging vortex, he plowed through it and surged higher and higher.

Within seconds, earth came into view. As he drew near, he focused on the continent he had left behind, then the country, then the region—the area the angels called Queen's Veil, the same place humans called Kentucky so long ago.

After several more seconds, he entered the atmosphere and flew straight toward angel HQ. He passed through the roof and three stories before landing on the floor at the first level near the front entry door. Guessing that no one but Zachariel could hear him, he called, "Zachariel. It's Jack. Where are you?"

An odd, high-pitched hum rode the air. Jack turned toward the sound and followed it through a corridor that ended at a vault-like door. Walking through the door, he entered a room with side walls that looked like stacks of drawers with vapor leaking out the edges.

At the far end, a huge screen hung on the wall, displaying an array of lights that resembled the Oculus Gate. Below that, a man and a woman sat in chairs at a long table in front of the screen while two winged women and himself in winged form stood nearby, all facing the glittering cluster of lights.

Jack floated toward his body. When he drew close, Zachariel's voice entered his mind. *Just leap in. The vaccine's toxicity has sufficiently diminished. I will do the rest.*

Jack jumped into his body. Something grabbed him, rolled him into a ball, and forced him upward into his body's head, squeezing him tightly. Then, like a light switch flicking on, he was back, looking out through his own eyes, moving his hands, and even shifting his wings.

Beware, Zachariel said in Jack's mind. *I am feigning cooperation with the fake angels. Do not speak unless you say the exact words I feed you.*

Jack responded with the slightest of nods, guessing Zachariel could see the gesture. He studied the two women to his left—Novada and Kat, or Laramel, as she called herself. Novada, still dressed casually in jeans and polo shirt, fingered her pendant, as if petting it. Laramel remained in camo, as fit and strong as ever. If he had thought to notice her physique earlier, he might have questioned her lack of atrophy from months in prison, but he'd missed that sign.

Laramel pointed at the screen. "There. Did you see the flash? Upper righthand section. It's exactly like the signal I predicted."

The seated man tapped on a keyboard and looked at a smaller monitor on the table. "I am focusing our instruments on the spot. I will have a reading in a moment."

Novada smiled. "You were right, Laramel. They are coming soon."

"Yes. Quite soon. Maybe even tonight." Laramel gave Novada a dark stare. "Are your methods of persuasion working? Has your human been forthcoming?"

Novada's head drooped. "Not yet, my queen. When she volunteered to be implanted, she seemed extremely pliable. I am beginning to think she doesn't know where the weapon is. Maybe she never has."

Laramel's tone sharpened. "You had better be certain. Allowing our allies to advance without the weapon's destruction is extremely dangerous."

"As we all realize. I am considering other forms of persuasion. When the time gets closer, I can resort to torture if necessary."

"Consider it necessary." Laramel eyed the smaller monitor. "Let's see. It's seven-fifteen. It will be getting dark soon."

The seated woman studied a phone screen. "Sunset was thirty minutes ago. Twilight is fading."

Novada crossed her arms. "You're wondering about the two missing rebels."

"Of course." Laramel's eyes seemed to crackle with fire. "I won't be confident until Benjamin and Gertrude Garrison are in custody, and then either executed or implanted."

Ask for an update on the clean-up effort.

Jack cleared his throat. "Do we have an update on the cleanup?"

Novada frowned. "We sent a doctor wearing a protective suit to check some of the dead rebels. He determined that they did not succumb to the vaccine but rather to poison. Also, the air attack destroyed every vehicle they found in the convoy. Then they dumped the fuel and burned the area. But when ground troops dropped in, they discovered that one of the tanks might be missing. If so, the remaining Garrison siblings are alive, which means they received the real vaccine, and it worked safely on them. Either they somehow managed to avoid losing their souls, or the violence payload and vestiges of anti-angel fury are driving their empty brains. In either case, we will find them. We have three SkySweep drones canvassing the area between the invasion region and headquarters, so it won't be long. The tank isn't fast, and its heat signature is large. It won't be able to elude our drones."

Jack nodded but said nothing.

Laramel looked him in the eye. "What do Jack's memories say about his brother's typical strategy? Will he attack this building to try to retrieve his wife?"

Tell her that his strategy is unpredictable since the vaccine infused a violence-inducing payload.

Jack repeated Zachariel's response nearly word for word.

"Which means," Laramel said, "that a direct attack is more likely than a stealthy approach. The urge to strike will not allow for patience or planning."

"I have the reading," the man in the chair said. "The pulse is within the parameters you expected. The decoded message says that our allies should be able to penetrate the barrier sometime tomorrow."

"Excellent." Laramel pointed toward one of the monitors. "Contact our agents and let them know. If all goes well, I will no longer need Katherine Garrison. I can take the vaccine and force her out."

While the two operators followed her commands, Laramel and Novada looking on and giving advice on the message's phrasing, Zachariel spoke to Jack in his mind. *I am sure you are wondering who these allies are and what they will do when they arrive. Obtaining this information is the reason I am feigning cooperation, but the fake angels have been tight-lipped about it. They assume I already know, that I was infused with the information before coming out of the hive. But that is not the case. With regard to Laramel's obsession with learning the whereabouts of your anti-angel weapon, I searched your mind and was unable to find the location, so I let Novada conduct a probe, and she verified that you do not know. Fortunately, Katherine has valiantly resisted Novada's discovery efforts so far.*

Again Jack nodded, suppressing a smile. Kat was always the toughest of the bunch.

Also, Zachariel continued, *everyone here knows that you have taken the vaccine, thereby purging your soul, which Novada verified with an AngelScan. They are unlikely to test you again.* He seemed to sigh. *That's all. I trust that you can speak on your own now. You know as much as I do.*

Jack nodded once more.

"Are you not well?" Novada asked him. "You have been nodding. Perhaps your host body is weary."

"It is true," Jack said, trying to mimic Zachariel's manner of speech. "I think this body has endured a great deal of trauma in recent hours."

Laramel grasped Jack's forearm. "Then sleep. There is time to rest." She glanced at Novada, then returned her gaze to Jack, an evil smile emerging. "Actually, I will go with you. This might be an excellent opportunity. Katherine has resisted torture to herself. Perhaps she will give in if she sees her brother-in-law tortured."

Jack touched his chest. "You wish to physically harm my host's body?"

Laramel huffed. "Are you as dimwitted as he is? Of course."

"Ah," Novada said. "And if I am there to probe her, I can take advantage of her mentally tortured state."

"Then we will all go together." Laramel hooked her elbow through Jack's. "Come with me."

Concealing a swallow, Jack went along with Laramel's pull toward the vault door. "Novada," she said, "we will give Katherine one last chance to provide the information we seek. Her resolve is still strong, but I think it will crumble when she understands the pain we'll force her to witness."

As they neared the door, Jack called in his mind. *Zachariel? Can you think of a way out of this mess?*

Not yet. But if you make an excuse to escape, it will have to be a clever one. She is the queen. If you fail to acquiesce with complete submission, she will know you are a fraud. In any case, I will pray for divine intervention.

Make it quick. I'm almost out of time.

When Novada opened the door, Laramel guided Jack through and turned him toward the front entrance. "This way."

"Wait." Jack set his feet, forcing her to stop. "Perhaps there is another means by which you can gain the information."

"Why another means? This will work quickly." Laramel narrowed her eyes. "Zeebach, you're sweating."

"Oh?" Jack used a finger to brush beads of wetness from his forehead. "I assume the room's heat—"

"That room is quite cold. Perhaps your host body is ill."

Novada laid a palm on his forehead. "Cool and clammy. He has no fever."

"He's suffering from a bout of cowardice," Laramel said, crossing her arms.

Jack gently grasped Novada's wrist and drew back. "Perhaps I am somewhat nervous. I can feel my host's pain. Of course, I will do whatever my queen wishes, but—"

"Queen Laramel!" the man at the display table shouted. "Our security cameras are showing a tank approaching the rear fence!"

Everyone looked into the vault room. On the big monitor, a military tank rumbled from right to left. Green sparkles coated the tank as if someone had scattered cake sprinkles over its shell.

"It's carrying the contagion!" Laramel shouted. "Sound the alarm! Send the guards to the rear entrances!"

A siren blared. Footsteps pounded in the hallway. At the front entrance, at least fifteen uniformed guards with plasma rifles stormed in and ran toward the rear of the building, though one stationed himself at the front door.

Novada gripped Laramel's arm. "I must get you to safety."

Laramel shook free. "We have sufficient firepower. The Garrison siblings are reacting to the fury the payload incited, which made them overestimate their chances. When we capture them, we can use torture of Katherine's husband to gain the information. That will be more effective than torturing her stupid brother-in-law."

"My queen, the recent rain would have washed the contagion from the tank. The Garrisons must have applied more, which means they have a supply that they probably plan to broadcast once they break in. Since we are not vaccinated, we should get safely away or our hosts will die. There is no time to obtain an injector and wait for antibodies to develop."

"Very well. We'll go to the front and fly to safety." Laramel faced Jack. "Surely your host human knows how to operate a plasma rifle."

Jack nodded. "He is well trained in weaponry."

"Then come with us. You will be my rear guard. I will find a rifle for you."

As the two winged women hustled toward the front entrance, Jack trailed them by several paces. When the corridor widened into the main lobby, he looked toward the rear of the building, though a wall and a pair of closed doors blocked his view. Shouting, crashes, and the telltale whoosh of plasma rifle blasts penetrated the barrier. The assault tank had arrived.

At the front door, Laramel took the remaining guard's plasma rifle and threw it toward Jack. He snatched it out of the air and looked it over—the newest model, loaded with a hundred rounds.

"Stay there until Novada and I are safely airborne. Then follow. Novada's pendant glows. You should be able to see it. When the battle is over and the area is decontaminated, we will return to deal with the attackers."

Jack cocked the rifle, loading a plasma sphere. "Understood."

When they exited, he glanced between their retreating forms and the door leading to the rear of the building. It would be so easy to shoot Novada in the back, then try to take Laramel captive, but Laramel's power was too great, and once she figured out who was in control of his body, she would know he would never shoot her, not with Kat still inside. The best option had to be assaulting the guards from behind and taking out as many as possible. That was the only way Ben and Trudy had a chance to survive. Still, someone had to keep track of Kat. Ben and Trudy certainly couldn't.

Jack blew out a sigh. *I need some more divine help, and I need it now!*

Chapter Twenty-One

Ben crouched behind the angel-royalty hovercraft in the HQ parking lot, a hand on the motorcycle as it leaned against the craft's side panel, Trudy next to him. With his X99 lying on the pavement and a tranquilizer shotgun in hand, he straightened slowly and reached the gun's barrel over the vehicle's wing, aiming at the entry gate where the security drone hovered in front of a line of sixteen armed guards. As deepening twilight shadowed her features, Trudy copied his every move.

"What's your guess on timing?" Ben whispered.

"Fifteen seconds till the tank is in camera view, then twenty more till it hits the fence. Unless it runs into something we didn't notice. The path looked clear."

"Only ferns. Shouldn't be a problem." He mentally measured the distance to the gate. "The tranq cartridges have enough powder to send a dart through a bear's hide at close range. That's why I picked a sniper spot so far away from HQ."

"Yep. I guessed that."

Ben studied her posture as she held the shotgun, her arms unwavering. "Any worries about hitting someone with a dart from this distance?"

"Nope." She closed an eye and peered through the aiming sights. "I could shoot a flea off a dog's tail from here."

"Remember, I'll hit Kat. You take out whoever's closest to her."

"Probably Novada."

"Right."

"Got the AngelScan?"

Ben patted his pants pocket. "Check."

"Good. You can finally fix my mistake if you still want to risk it. Blast Novada's skull open. But you'll have to hurry. Not because the tranquilizer will wear off. It should last. But they'll probably have an armed guard watching their flank."

"Shouldn't be a problem." Ben nudged the X99 with his shoe. "I'll switch to the rifle and shoot the drone, and you shoot any guard you see behind them. With all the commotion the tank causes, no one's likely to hear the gunshots."

Trudy licked her lips, her eyes still on the sights. "Got it."

Shouts rose from beyond the HQ building. A radio crackled. One of the guards near the entry gate snatched a radio from his belt and held it to his ear. After a moment, he nodded, then shouted, "Everyone to the rear posts!" The guards dashed to the building and disappeared inside.

"Party's just getting started, boys." Ben looked through his sights. "Sorry to see you leave so early."

With the guards gone, the drone floated from side to side, as if taking over sentry duty. Shooting it down now would be convenient, but that would alert the security team. They were still too close.

Sweat trickled down Ben's cheek in spite of the cool air. "Should be any second now."

"Good. My clothes are still damp. I'm forcing myself not to shiver."

"Steady, Sis." Three winged forms flitted in the lobby, visible through the glass doors. "I see triple bogeys. It's show time."

Two women rushed out of the building, their wings boosting them as they hurried toward the gate, unable to fly because of the overhanging portico that extended to the gate.

"Steady ..." Ben said again, stretching the word.

"Open the gate," one of the women called. Now closer, their identities became clear—Novada and Laramel, likely still housing Kat's soul.

The drone scanned them through the chain links. "Access granted."

"Steady ..." Ben whispered.

The gate jiggled, then dragged slowly to the side.

"Steady ..."

The moment the gap grew wide enough, Novada led Laramel through, clutching her wrist. When they extended their wings, Ben let out a sharp, "Now!"

Ben fired a dart. Trudy fired hers. The twin *pops* combined in a single sound. Ben's dart plunged into Laramel's shoulder. Trudy's struck Novada's throat.

"Go!" Ben dropped the shotgun, grabbed his rifle, and ran toward the gate, the sound of Trudy starting the motorcycle well behind.

The two angels collapsed, giving a clear view to the drone. Ben halted, aimed the X99 at it, and fired. Metal clanked against metal. The drone flew back and collided with the closing gate, then dropped to the ground. Ben shot a security camera at the roof line, then shot another at the gatehouse.

After sprinting the rest of the way to the gate, Ben dropped to a knee next to Laramel, plucked the dart out, and tossed it to the side. Seconds later, Trudy arrived on the motorcycle and stood it on its kickstand, leaving it running. With her X99 ready, she scanned HQ. "The third bogey's still inside."

"Good." Ben slid his hands under Laramel and lifted her in his arms, holding her wings in place with his hands. "Help me set her on the bike."

"Just a sec. A man with wings is coming out. He's got a plasma rifle." Trudy raised the X99 and fired three shots. "Can't get him. He's tucked behind a column."

"He'll call for backup. He won't shoot and risk hitting their queen."

Trudy strapped the rifle on, kicked up the bike's stand, and straddled the seat. After revving the engine, she twisted in place and lifted a pair of straps behind her. "Ready."

Ben set Laramel upright. While Trudy reached the straps around her limp body, Ben grabbed them, crossed them over Laramel's back, pinning the wings in place, and handed them to Trudy. She took one in each hand, turned forward, and tied them together at her waist. "Secured."

"Go. See you at the rendezvous."

Trudy's brow dipped low. "You're still going to scan Novada? What about the guard? He'll fry you."

A radiant sphere zipped over their heads and rocketed into the parking lot.

Ben slapped the bike. "Go!"

"All right. Just don't die." Trudy took off, the engine noise fading as darkness enveloped her.

Trying to make himself a small target, Ben crouched low next to Novada. He withdrew the AngelScan from his pocket and set it on her forehead. As he waited for it to work, he glanced at the columns near the entry doors. So far, the guard hadn't shown himself.

The disk glowed, revealing Novada's brain. At the stem, red tentacles impaled a white blob that pulsed and wiggled, as if trying to escape.

Ben put the scanner away and rose slowly. Wary of the guard, he lifted the X99 and set the barrel close to the back of Novada's head. The dart lay in view, broken on the pavement in a puddle. Scratches marred her throat, as if she had clawed at the dart to get it out, which meant that some of the tranquilizer hadn't entered her bloodstream. No matter. She would be dead in seconds. "I should have cracked your skull open before," he said, though she probably couldn't hear. "I won't make the same mistake this time."

The moment he touched the trigger, someone shouted, "Ben! No!"

He pivoted toward the voice. Wings fluttered. A man landed next to him, grabbed the rifle's barrel, and pushed it to the side. "Ben. It's me. Jack. I tried to signal you with a plasma sphere, but you didn't look."

Ben blinked at him. "Why are you stopping me from blasting this bogey?"

"Because she's someone important." He shifted a plasma rifle strapped at his shoulder. "Novada's been trying to get her host's soul to spill secrets."

"All the more reason to dispatch her. The dead tell no tales. And since when does rank make a difference? We set souls free no matter how many stripes they have."

"She can help us. The soul inside Novada might know what Novada knows, like about angel allies coming through Hell's Gate, which, by the way, we have to figure out how to destroy. I'll explain why later. Maybe this person holds the key."

"All right. You win." Ben slung the X99 to his back and slid his hands under Novada's arms. "Get her legs. We have to hustle to the woods. SkySweep will be all over us."

Jack grabbed Novada's ankles and lifted. "Yeah. I had to deal with a guard in the lobby. Someone will find his body soon."

As they hauled Novada across the parking lot, Ben eyed Jack closely. His expressions and way of speaking seemed more like him than earlier, but maybe the angel had enough practice by now. A test might help. "How do I know Jack's really behind that ugly rat face of yours?"

"A rat's face ain't as ugly as the other end, rat butt."

Ben cracked a smile. "Okay, that was pretty quick."

"Look." Jack grunted as they descended a slope that led into the woods. "I get that you're suspicious. You can scan me when we stop. I saw the disk you used on Novada."

"Yeah. It'll clear the air." Walking backwards, Ben took the lead, dodging trees while glancing to his rear. "Just another hundred yards or so."

"How do you plan to control Laramel when she wakes up?"

"Trudy's prepping to do an extraction. We brought the tools. If all goes well, Kat will wake up, not Laramel."

"Then we'll have to do the same for Novada," Jack said. "I don't know her human name."

Ben arched his brow. "You're really fired up about saving her. What's the deal?"

"I'm not sure you'll believe me. It sounds impossible."

"Try me. I've seen more impossible stuff in the last few hours than most people see in their lifetimes."

"Cool your jets a minute. I'll tell you and Trudy at the same time."

Soon, they arrived at a grassy glen. Barely visible in the moonlight, Trudy knelt next to Kat as she lay on her stomach, her face in a hole carved out in a pillow. A green sterile sheet the size of a hand towel lay draped over the back of her head with a pair of holes at the surgery sites, one behind the ear and one at the base of the skull.

Ben and Jack laid Novada on the ground next to Kat. "Another patient," Ben said.

Trudy straightened her torso and looked at them, drawing her head back. "Oh. Jack's here."

"Yeah. We'll tell you more in a minute." Ben nodded toward Novada. "Can you do two extractions?"

"Maybe. A lot easier if I'd brought two kits, but I didn't think we'd need a second one."

Ben looked at the white box that lay open near her knee. "What might run short?"

"Hard to say, but using the same tools on two people is an infection risk. After I insert the forceps into one person, they won't be sterile for the next. I'm not sure if swabbing them with alcohol will be enough. Fortunately, I have two scalpels. But I don't know about the consumables, like suture thread, anesthesia, absorbent pads. Stuff like that."

"So do Kat first. We'll risk infection in Novada. Besides, you have antibiotics, right?"

"Plenty."

"Good. Let's get started."

"Flashlight." Trudy snapped surgical gloves over her hands.

Ben took a flashlight from his belt and trained the beam on Kat's head.

"That's good," Trudy said. "Keep it right there."

While she used a scalpel to cut open Kat's implantation incision, Jack told about his soul's visit to the Never-ending Highway. As he spoke, his voice spiked with emotion, especially when he talked about his wife and daughter. Leaving them behind was pure torture.

"So," Ben said to Jack, "you think Novada might know how to destroy Hell's Gate and send Sophie and Alana to heaven. That's why you didn't want me to blow her skull open."

"Right. She might be my only hope."

Ben snapped his fingers. "Almost forgot. Do you have Barks's password to use the weapon?"

"Right here." Jack tapped himself on the head. "I burned the paper it was written on, but I've got it. We're good."

"The extraction forceps are in," Trudy said. "Now one of you hold the AngelScan for me."

Jack knelt next to Trudy and held the scanner an inch or so over the back of Kat's head. Trudy set the tip of a pen-like wand against the base of Kat's skull and flicked it on. "Okay. The angel's starting to react. Turning up the heat now."

Ben averted his eyes, keeping the flashlight in place. Better to listen than to watch. Otherwise his hands would shake.

"The angel's as mad as a hornet, but the tentacles are releasing. It's stretching toward the forceps. Won't be long now."

Ben tightened his jaw and gazed at the sky. Stars twinkled. Behind the trees, the partial moon shone through the branches. Lights blinked toward the HQ building, drawing closer. SkySweep?

"Tentacles released without snapping. Setting the forceps to maximum suction. Come to Mama, you little witch. ... Okay. Got her. Putting Queen Laramel in her new home."

Ben turned toward Trudy. With light-energy forceps in hand, she pinched a tiny pulsing red light and inserted it into a glass vial. When she dropped it in, she set the forceps down, capped the vial, and laid it in the extraction kit. "Some pieces are still in there. The suction broke the tentacles apart on the way out." She reinserted the forceps and withdrew a tiny wiggling red light and put it in a plastic bag. "A few more to go."

"Something's flying this way," Ben said. "Can't tell what it is yet. Could be SkySweep."

Trudy dropped several more wigglers into the bag and set it in the kit. "Still gotta close the incision. I put the forceps in pretty deep to get the vestiges, so she's bleeding quite a bit." She began stripping another plastic bag open. "Just one suture package. It'll have to do for both of our patients."

"Right," Jack said as he lifted the AngelScan from Kat's head. "You still have to extract Novada. We can't bug out and leave her here."

Ben looked at the sky again. The lights continued drawing closer. "If you have another plan, let's hear it. Assuming it's SkySweep, we've got about a minute, max."

"I'm thinking. I'm thinking."

Trudy withdrew a needle and attached thread from the package. "I'll do a few quick stitches and come back to shore it up after I extract Novada."

From the approaching lights, a red beam flashed down into the forest about a hundred yards away. The drone, the size of a mobile home, cast a moon shadow over the treetops as its huge propellers tormented the leaves with violent gusts. "It's SkySweep. Trudy, how much longer?"

"Five minutes at least. Ten is safer."

His hand tiring, Ben shifted the light. "We have thirty seconds, maybe."

"It's not safe to hurry. Kat could lose a lot of blood. And keep the light steady. Surgery isn't as easy as it looks."

"Do you need the AngelScan anymore?" Jack asked.

"No. I'm good until I start on Novada."

He laid the scanner in the extraction kit. "I'll stall the drone."

"How?" Ben asked.

Jack grabbed the plasma rifle from the ground. "Brute force." With a flap of his wings, he launched into the air and flew straight toward the drone.

"Those drones are triple reinforced," Ben said as he watched Jack fly. "Bullets won't penetrate. I've shot one myself. Didn't faze it. Though I'm not sure what one of those souped-up plasma spheres would do."

"We have to believe in Jack." Trudy's breaths rose as white vapor. "Getting cold. Just a few more stitches."

"I do believe in Jack," Ben said. "Without question. But I need a scan to see if it's really him."

"Are you kidding? You heard his story. No phony could talk about Sophie and Alana that way. Impossible."

"Yeah. I guess you're right."

The SkySweep drone's red light flashed again, this time illuminating Jack flying directly underneath it. He took off to the right. The drone followed, picking up speed.

Ben exhaled and watched Trudy. Using traditional forceps, she pulled a needle, trailed by a short thread that slid through Kat's skin behind her ear. "Okay," he said. "Jack bought us some time. No idea how much."

"Good." She dabbed at the area with blood-stained gauze. "I need every minute he can give me. I don't have an assistant."

Ben stepped closer. "Anything I can help with?"

She shook her head. "The light will do. Besides, I have only one more set of gloves. I'll need them for Novada."

"Are you tracking vitals?"

"Pulse and respiration every once in a while. Kat's stable."

"I wonder why her wings aren't shrinking. I saw Doc extract a Gen Two, and the wings started withering right away."

"I don't know. Maybe because Laramel's a higher level." Trudy straightened on her knees and flexed her fingers. "That should hold." She looked at Ben. "So do we prep Novada?"

He nodded. "Like you said. Believe in Jack."

"Okay. You can put the light down and help me turn Kat to her side. I'll need the face pillow for Novada."

After they turned her, taking care not to bend her wings too much, Ben rolled up the cooling blanket, now no longer cold, and pushed it against Kat's back, holding her in place. He knelt at her side and pushed strands of hair from the bandage. "Any thoughts on possible brain damage?"

Trudy peeled off her surgical gloves. "Everything went smoothly, but no way to be sure until she wakes up. That dart would've put down a stallion, so it'll be a few hours. And I gave her an injection of antibiotics. We'll see how it goes."

Ben leaned close and kissed Trudy's forehead. "You really are amazing."

She smiled. "Thanks, but now I have to be even more amazing and extract Novada without giving the host an infection, whoever she is."

Ben picked up the flashlight. "Okay. Let's get it done."

Dr. Elder stooped next to the smashed gate drone and lifted one of its propellers. She looked up at Kyle, the head security guard, a tall man wearing only a T-shirt on top, his outer shirt removed for decontamination. "Something violent happened here," she said. "The queen and Novada might be in danger."

Kyle crouched next to her and set his plasma rifle down. "Security footage indicates that Zeebach disabled the guard we left at the front door. The cameras out here were destroyed."

Something glimmered on the pavement nearby. Dr. Elder scooted over. Novada's pendant lay there with its attached necklace.

She lifted the chain and showed it to Kyle. "The princess would never leave this behind. She once told me that it's called a homing orb, a priceless heirloom."

Kyle eyed the pendant closely. "If she were kidnapped, why would the villain remove it? That makes no sense."

Dr. Elder set the pendant in her palm. "Maybe Novada feared that it would fall into the wrong hands, and she removed it herself. She knew we would sweep the grounds and find it."

"Then you're right. They are in danger. Novada did what she could to protect her treasure and tell us about her capture at the same time."

Dr. Elder closed her fist around the pendant. "Call out SkySweep. Find Zeebach. But don't kill him. Wound him, burn his wings, whatever it takes to bring him in."

Kyle detached a computer pad from his belt. "I'll enter the update in the system."

"No. Wait. Enter Zeebach as rogue. It's the only way to get clearance to send SkySweep after him. But we'll keep the kidnapping to ourselves for now. With the contagion scare, no need to spread further panic. Once we catch Zeebach, we'll find our beloved queen and princess."

Chapter Twenty-Two

Jack beat his wings with all his might. On his tail, the SkySweep drone fired a plasma sphere. It nicked a wing, singeing an edge. He grimaced. *That really hurts!*

Wings have many nerve endings, Jack. Their sensitivity is acute.

"If you have any ideas, Zachariel, I'm listening." Jack flew up, down, and side to side while radiant balls zinged past every few seconds. "I can't believe they haven't blasted me out of the sky already."

I agree with your assessment. You are flying with excellent agility, but their aim has been surprisingly poor. My advice is to lead the drone to the headquarters building. It's not far.

"What? Are you nuts?"

Certainly not. The drone will avoid shooting its plasma gun there.

"Good point." Jack angled that way, still flying like a crazed bat. "But what then?"

I have an idea. How is your courage level?

"I know what you're thinking. Do a one-eighty, fly straight at it, and try to bash it somehow."

Yes, that is what I am thinking.

"Dangerous. Ridiculously dangerous." Jack heaved a sigh. "But you're right. If it stops shooting because of HQ, I have a fighting chance."

With the headquarters compound in sight about a hundred yards ahead and the same distance below, he dove toward it. When the plasma blasts ceased, he whipped around and, beating his wings to stay in place, wielded the rifle like a baseball bat.

The drone surged straight at him. Jack dropped and swung at a propeller under the fuselage. The rifle's butt struck a blade, bending it. The drone flew on in a slow spin as it continued diving toward HQ.

"Now for good measure." Jack flipped the rifle around and fired a barrage of plasma blasts. The first zipped past the drone, but three others nailed its central hub in quick succession. The drone accelerated out of control and crashed into the HQ's main roof.

Jack strapped the rifle to his shoulder and circled over the building, breathless. "The drone probably reported where it spotted me. They'll send another."

True, Zachariel said. *You might have to repeat your stellar performance.*

"And if they send five drones and a hundred guards with plasma rifles?"

Then you will have to devise another plan.

"Thanks, Captain Obvious."

Considering your tone, I assume that is not a complimentary title.

"Ignore me. I was being a jerk."

Duly noted.

"Let's see if I can avoid a new search." Jack flew to the roof and landed next to the drone. Dodging a still-spinning propeller, he opened the hatch and ducked inside to a spherical compartment, large enough for three to four people. A control panel with radar screens and communications equipment lined the perimeter. He found the main terminal screen and read the drone's output. It had, indeed, transmitted the location where it first spotted him.

"Now to send an update before any bogeys show up." He began typing on the terminal's keyboard, using the terminology he had already read as he whispered each word. "Target escaped toward the northeast. This unit has malfunctioned and cannot pursue. Scanner readings indicate no other life forms at original detection point. Recommend dispatching units to follow the target's last known vector."

He sent the message. Seconds later, an LED light flashed, probably an acknowledgement signal.

Jack scanned the board once more and tested various dials and sliders, all locked in place. At waist level, a rectangular plug-in module half the size of his hand protruded from a port. A strip of tape adhered to the top, a makeshift label that read, "Starter Sequence – 43854."

He muttered, "That's not secure. Lazy mechanic."

A switch stuck out at the upper left corner of the board, its toggle angling to the left. Jack flipped it to the right. Several clicks rose all across the board. He tested a dial he had tried before. It moved. The switch must have toggled the drone out of remote-control mode. Now he could run the unit manually if it could get off the ground.

A message flashed on the screen. "Self-destruct sequence activated." The screen cleared, and the numeral five filled the view, then a four.

"Uh-oh." Jack yanked the starter module out, leaped from the drone, and vaulted into the air. An explosion erupted below, a small blast, powerful enough to blow the drone apart, but not enough to damage the roof.

He stuffed the module into his pocket and flew toward the clearing where he had left Ben and Trudy. After a few minutes, he found the spot, guided by Ben's flashlight at ground level. He landed in a run and stopped next to Kat. She lay on her side, motionless, her wings still full, though bent to accommodate her position. "How is she?"

"Stable," Trudy said as she inserted the forceps tube into Novada's incision. "You're just in time. I need you to hold the AngelScan."

Jack set the rifle down, plucked the scanner from the kit, and knelt next to her. "I think I bought us some time."

"Good," Ben said, the flashlight still trained on Trudy's hands. "We need it."

The trio continued the surgery, using the same procedures they had with Kat. When Trudy finished the final stitch and applied the bandage, she flopped to her back and moaned. "This girl is done!"

"Good work." Ben turned the flashlight off. "You deserve a medal."

"Can I have pizza instead? And a beer?"

"You don't drink beer."

"I know, but after pulling angels out of two brains, I might start."

"And you didn't run out of anything?" Ben asked.

"Almost. I had to scrimp on the suture thread. I managed to sew them up pretty well, but it's gone now."

Jack walked close to Novada and studied her back. In the moonlight, it seemed that her wings had already shrunk quite a bit. "Why aren't Kat's wings getting smaller like Novada's?"

Ben flicked on the light and shone it on Novada's wings, now the size of an eagle's. "We've been talking about that. Probably because Laramel was the queen."

Novada groaned. "Oh, my head!"

Jack laid a hand on her shoulder. "Don't move. You're recovering from surgery."

"She can move," Trudy said, still lying on the ground, "just super slowly till the tranquilizer wears off."

"Let me help you." Jack guided Novada to a sitting position. "How are you feeling?"

Novada rubbed her eyes, then blinked, looking at them in turn. "Who are you? And where am I?"

Ben turned the flashlight on himself. "Do you recognize me now?"

She nodded. "Ben Garrison. Rebel field agent."

"Right. I'm here with Jack and Trudy." He shone the light on them in turn. "Who are you?"

"Chantal. Another rebel field agent."

"Okay. That explains a lot."

She grimaced. "Oh! Worst headache ever."

"Yeah," Trudy said. "Sorry. I hit your brain with intense shock waves."

Chantal squinted at her. "You what?"

"We extracted your angel," Ben said as he shifted the flashlight beam toward Kat. "Now we're waiting for my wife to wake up, but we might have to leave before she does. She got a bigger dose of tranquilizer than you did."

"Okay. Okay. It's all coming back now." Chantal looked at Kat. "Did Trudy extract Laramel from her?"

"Right before your extraction," Ben said. "I guess you can't tell because the wings haven't shrunk yet."

Chantal flapped her own wings, nearly withered away. "So what Laramel said was true."

"What?" Jack, Ben, and Trudy said at the same time.

Chantal faced them. "Laramel is the hive queen. She is a replicator. She can duplicate herself in a host. When she felt you extracting her, that's probably exactly what she did."

Trudy sat up. "Are you saying that witch is still inside Kat?"

"A copy of her. It gives Kat angel powers, like the wings, but it has no information. All hive spawns need an infusion. This new version of Laramel is like an infant. You probably couldn't even see her in a scan, but it will eventually attach to Kat's brain stem and grow to maturity."

"How long till the spawn matures?" Ben asked as he stroked Kat's hair. "And what will she do?"

Chantal shrugged. "No idea."

"So I have to extract her again," Trudy said. "The spawn, I mean."

"Only if you can find her. She's tiny. You probably have to wait until she instinctively crawls to the brain stem and attaches. It could take a while."

Trudy threw her hands up. "I can't believe it! Everything's kaput. After all the planning. And I can't possibly use the same kit. It's contaminated. And I'm out of suture thread. Not only that, the other kits were probably destroyed when the jets raided our base."

Jack made a shushing sound. "You're right, Sis, but getting bent out of shape's not going to help. If we have to, we'll go to another base and pick one up there. By then we'll know what's going on with Kat, and you can do the surgery again."

Trudy huffed and wrapped her arms around her knees in a sulking pose. "Easy for you to say. You're not doing the surgery. And the nearest ally base is more than two hundred miles from here. That is, if it still exists. We haven't heard a report from them in weeks."

"Speaking of allies…" Jack turned to Chantal. "What do you know about the angel allies that are supposed to come through the Oculus Gate?"

"Quite a bit." She grimaced once more, then took in a deep breath. "Laramel called them Refectors. It comes from the Latin word that means *restorer* or *renewer*. You see, when they come, they'll indwell the people who have been purged of souls and take control of their bodies. The Refectors claim that the human bodies will be renewed with a better inner spirit than they had before, so Laramel coined that term for them. I don't know what the Refectors call themselves."

"But why do the angels need them?" Jack asked. "Our rebel allies have been crushed. We're the only pocket that hasn't collapsed."

"Good question. Laramel said another force has already come to earth. Quiet. Hiding. Biding its time. She never mentioned its identity, at least not while Novada was indwelling me, but it's clear that Laramel feared it."

Jack whistled. "Let's hope it's on our side, whatever it is."

"Amen to that."

Jack sent a thought to Zachariel. *What do you know about this other force?*

Nothing. But I do know that there are many forces in the cosmos, some for good and some for evil, and a few are more powerful than any you have faced before.

Okay. Add another worry to the pile. "Here's the bottom line," Jack said. "The angels didn't want zombies. They wanted empty bodies for the Refectors."

Chantal nodded. "And they also want to destroy our weapon. Novada kept trying to read my mind, asking about its location again and again. I told her I didn't know, which is true, and I reminded her that I was a volunteer, that she could trust me."

Trudy furrowed her brow. "A volunteer to be implanted? Why on earth would you do that?"

"To become the ultimate spy. I saw everything Novada did. Heard everything she said. Even shared her thoughts. Since I volunteered, she allowed me to stay near the surface most of the time. Being compliant gave me a lot of liberties I wouldn't otherwise have had."

"Is that so?" Trudy crossed her arms. "So what did you learn, ultimate spy?"

Chantal fingered the stitches on her neck scar. "One of the secrets …" Her eyes flared. "It's gone!"

"What?" Ben and Trudy asked.

"The … uh …" Chantal shook her head. "Never mind. It's not important."

"Not important?" Trudy said. "It's important enough for you to nearly have a stroke a second ago."

"That orb pendant." Ben pointed at Chantal's neck. "You were wearing it."

Chantal lowered her hand, though it trembled. "It's all right. I just thought we might use the orb as leverage. But Novada's gone. It might not be valuable to any other angel."

"Fair enough." Ben began pacing slowly. "Let's review and put our knowledge together." He gave a quick summary of recent events, including the contents of Iona's note, Trudy filling in a few details. When he finished, he added with a sigh, "And we could've stopped the vaccine's damage, but we didn't read Iona's disk in time."

"So what's the best option?" Jack asked. "Deploy the weapon or figure out where the Refectors are going?"

"Deploy the weapon," Kat said. "But I doubt that's possible."

Everyone turned toward her. "Kat?" Ben set the flashlight beam on her chest, illuminating her face as he sat next to her and grasped her hand. "Are you all right?"

"Now that you're with me." She compressed his hand. "But it feels like everyone on a sports team took turns kicking my head for a goal."

Jack laughed. "That paints a vivid picture."

"Too vivid." Ben leaned over and kissed her. "I missed you so much."

"Double for me." Kat turned her head toward Trudy. "My thanks to the brilliant surgeon who removed that crazed demon from my brain."

"You're welcome, but you still have wings. We're worried that you might have an angel spawn inside. Like a zygote, compliments of the queen."

"Yeah. The witch dropped a bomb in my brain. I heard Ben tell the story. I guess getting accustomed to being mentally submerged has its benefits. I heard pretty much everything."

"If the spawn attaches," Trudy said, "I can take it out, but with no suture thread, it'll be super risky." She scooted close. "Let me do a wound check before you move too much."

While Trudy peeled the bandage back, Ben kissed Kat's knuckles. "I'm not letting you out of my sight again."

"Better not." Kat smiled. "I want to keep looking into those beautiful eyes."

"Gag me," Jack said, laughing. "Good thing we're outside. The room would be steamed up by now."

"I don't like the looks of this," Trudy said. "It needs more stitches."

"Any substitutes for suture thread?" Ben asked.

Trudy removed the gauze pad and plucked another from the extraction kit. "Well, it has to be thin, yet strong at the same time. But nothing comes to mind."

"How badly does she need it?"

"I wouldn't want her to travel without it. The wound could break open, and she'd be in a world of hurt." Once Trudy had taped the gauze in place, she looked it over. "That should do for now."

"Okay, Kat," Ben said, still holding her hand, "back to the subject. Why do you think we should deploy the weapon?"

"To kill the angels." Kat pulled on his hand. "Help me sit up. These bent wings are painful."

Ben helped Kat rise to a cross-legged position. "Anyway," she continued, "it was supposed to be our ultimate weapon to kill every last angel, but I never finished it. So I don't see how it could possibly work yet."

"Doc thinks it works," Trudy said. "He tried to get to it before he died."

Kat nodded. "I heard that part of the story. Doc's smart. Maybe he completed my work. If he did, I say deploy it. But back to what the angels know. I've been tied to Laramel's brain for months. She's super precise with her words and she's deceptive. She once said, 'Allowing our allies to advance without the weapon's destruction is extremely dangerous.' But dangerous how? And to whom? Certainly to the angels, but they wouldn't fear it unless they knew what it's for. Laramel tortured me for information, but I'm pretty sure I kept the weapon's real use from her."

"Maybe they think the weapon's dangerous to the Oculus Gate," Chantal said. "They monitor that thing like it's God himself. They might be worried the weapon will blow it up before their allies can get here."

Kat pointed at her. "Exactly. My theory is that the Oculus Gate is a source of power for the angels, and I designed the weapon to destroy it."

"Destroy the Gate …" Trudy slashed a finger across her throat. "Destroy its demon spawns."

Ben looked at Kat. "So where is the weapon?"

She shrugged. "I don't know."

"You don't know? You invented it."

"Really?" Kat nudged Ben's ribs. "Thanks for the update, Hubby."

"Okay, I'll bite. How could you not know where it is?"

"Barks didn't want the information tortured out of me, so I was always blindfolded when he brought me to the work area."

"Then we're back to square one. The map region Iona gave us is about eighty miles away, and we don't have air transport."

"Actually," Jack said as he pushed a hand into his pocket, "we do." He withdrew the drone's plug-in module and displayed it in his palm. "This dongle should start a SkySweep drone's ignition. If we can commandeer one, I think we can all squeeze in. It'll be tight, and the smell might be bad, but we're all friends, right?"

Trudy sniffed her armpit. "Friends or not, I smell like a blend of pigsty and lye soap. During surgery I sweated like a roofer in August."

Ben smiled. "Duly noted, Stinky, but we still have to hijack a drone. No easy task."

Chantal raised a hand. "I know where they store them at HQ. But I have no clue how to fly one."

"So we both need to go in," Jack said. "If you still had your wings, it would be a breeze. I could pose as your prisoner. I'm on the angels' bad-guy list now."

"Not a problem. If someone stops us, I'll say Novada could retract her wings."

Jack lifted his brow. "I assume she really can't."

"No," Chantal said, "only Laramel can. Just get us into HQ from the air so we can bypass the gate's security drone, and I'll do the rest."

Kat shifted her wings. "These are retractable?"

Chantal nodded. "That's why Laramel was able to pose as you."

"Nice. If I can figure out how."

May I make a suggestion? Zachariel asked.

Jack raised a finger so everyone could see it. "Sure, Zachariel. What's your suggestion?"

Take Queen Laramel's vial with you. She might be able to help you get through scanners, and if you encounter great danger, she will be valuable leverage.

"Okay. That's cool. Having an archangel in my head is paying off." Jack snapped his fingers toward the extraction kit. "Trudy. I need the vial with Laramel in it. She's going with Chantal and me."

"Yeah. I get your drift." She crawled to the kit and withdrew the glass tube, eyeing the red light within as she walked it to Jack. "Vile angel in a vial, coming up."

When he took the tube, he rolled it between his finger and thumb. "I need some padding."

"I've got that." Chantal removed a pen and small notepad from her polo shirt, slid them into her pants pocket, and stripped the polo off, revealing a blue tank top. She handed the shirt to Jack. "Use this."

"Works for me." He wrapped the shirt around the vial and pushed the wad into a deep pocket in his cargo pants. "What about your appearance when you take me prisoner?"

"They've all seen Novada in her workout clothes. We'll say I had to fight you, so I took the shirt off for battle. They have a sparring ring at HQ. Novada boxes every day in public view."

Jack scanned Chantal's toned arms, easily apparent in spite of the low light. This woman worked out a lot.

"Jack," Ben said, laughing. "Stop staring. Your eyes are about to pop out of your head."

Jack's cheeks warmed. "Uh … yeah … right. I was just thinking the air's kind of cold for what she's wearing."

Chantal hooked her arm in his, smiling. "Thanks for being so concerned about me."

"Okay. So I got busted for staring, but I really am wondering about the cold."

"No worries. I trained outside all last winter. I'm used to it."

Jack turned toward Ben. "Any last-second suggestions?"

"Just watch for Iona. If not for her, we'd be at a dead end. Double agent or not, she stuck her neck out for us. She's one of us now. And maybe she knows more than what she wrote. We need her skills and intel."

Chantal grasped Jack's arm and faced him. "One more thing. Hit me."

Jack blinked. "What?"

She raised her chin and pointed at her cheek. "Hit me. Right here. I need a bruise if we're going to sell the fight story. Kat punched me a while back, but it didn't leave a mark."

Jack shook his head. "Uh-uh. No way. I can't hit a woman. Never have. Never will."

"I'm a boxer, Jack. I can take it."

"I got this." Trudy strode over, pushed Jack away, and punched Chantal across the jaw.

The force of the blow bent Chantal to the side. Touching the spot with a pair of fingers, she straightened and smiled at Trudy. "Good jab you've got there. We should spar sometime."

"I would love it." Trudy eyed Chantal's jaw. "The bruise is turning dark already. You're all set."

"Okay," Jack said, "so I'll fly Chantal over to—"

"Not so fast, big brother." Trudy faced him and raised a fist. "It's your turn."

Jack rolled his eyes. "Really, Sis? Do you think you can bruise my—"

She landed a right cross against his jaw, then a left jab to his chin. He staggered backwards, pain ripping from chin to skull.

Ben caught him and balanced him on his feet. "She bruised you, all right."

"Yeah." Jack rubbed his chin. "My ego's on life support."

Trudy massaged her fist, grinning. "You're welcome."

"Thanks for rubbing it in." Jack turned toward Ben. "Meet you here when we're done?"

"Sure. Kat needs more recovery time. The stitches are kind of iffy."

"And because she had more tranquilizer than Chantal," Trudy said. "The surgery causes a humongous headache, and when the local anesthetic wears off, the headache will triple, at least."

"Okay, then," Chantal said. "We'd better go." She turned her back toward Jack and raised her arms. Her wings now completely gone, twin holes in her tank top revealed where they once protruded, small raised ridges on her skin. "I'm ready if you are."

"You got it." He slid his arms around her waist, and, beating his wings, lifted off the ground. "Let me know if I should adjust my grip."

As they ascended, Chantal grasped his hands at her waist. "Just hold me however you need to. We have to get there as fast as possible."

Something snapped. Iona opened her eyes to darkness, regripped the gun, and set her finger on the trigger. Staying perfectly motionless, she listened.

A gruff voice drifted in on the cool air. "The little bird is around here somewhere."

Iona stiffened. *Leo!*

"What scent are you picking up?" one of the others asked.

"The soap the priestesses bathe with. Constance noticed a bar missing. She gave me a whiff before we left."

Iona cringed. The soap she had used to wash off the manure had given her away. But the manure would have done the same. It was a lose-lose choice.

"Good thinking, Leo."

"Standard procedure, boys. Standard procedure."

Their footsteps drew closer. Sketched by moonlight, their silhouettes came into view only ten paces away. Two of them each held something long in one hand, maybe a rifle, and one of that pair held a flashlight in the other hand that sent a beam knifing close.

Breathing as quietly as possible, she prayed for a miracle. Taking down three trained men with only two bullets would be impossible. Only God could help her now.

They halted again. "Close," Leo said. "Very close. She's hiding. Watching our every move. She has to stay motionless or risk us hearing her."

The flashlight beam swept toward her and danced around, barely missing her with each arcing movement.

"Give me that." Leo snatched the flashlight. "And both of you hold your breath. I hear something."

Iona covered her eyes and held her own breath, but her heart thudded, seeming as loud as that gelding's hoof beats.

Leo's footsteps rustled, marching straight toward her. The moment she hid the gun in the folds, the blanket whipped away from her face. The light shone directly into her eyes.

"So there you are," Leo said with a chuckle. "The little bird is finally in hand."

Chapter Twenty-Three

Leo eyed the girl. In the photo provided by the angels, she looked older, late teens or early twenties. Now with pigtails and no makeup, she appeared to be much younger.

He snapped a handcuff over her wrist and locked it. "Sit up." When she obeyed, he fastened the other cuff to a low tree branch, forcing her to raise her arm, though she stayed seated on the blanket. He inserted an earbud. "Now to report your capture."

Pisces cleared his throat. "Before you do that, Leo, I've been thinking about something. Is it really fair that you get half of the bounty while Scorpius and I split the other half? After all, this is the biggest bounty we've ever been offered."

Leo glared at him. "By Orion's belt, Pisces! You knew the arrangements when you signed on. Why bring it up now?"

"Because I wasn't sure we'd catch her. And I heard you giving an update to Constance when you thought I wasn't listening." Pisces aimed his rifle at Leo. "You're planning to fire us."

"After the bounty split, you idiot." Leo waved the flashlight as he set a hand on his hip, inching toward a knife on his belt. "And I'm firing you for incompetence. You couldn't smell the difference between tuna and teriyaki. You're both worthless."

Scorpius pointed his rifle as well, smiling. "Not worthless for long."

"We'll report that you died in a fall," Pisces said. "And the girl is wanted dead or alive. She'll tell no tales."

Leo spat on the ground. "A huntsman never kills except in self-defense. How can you possibly justify murdering this girl without a trial?"

"We'll think of something." Pisces set an eye to the rifle's sights. "After all, almost anything can happen on a cold night in the forest. No one will hear her scream."

"You'll burn in hell. I'll see to it from my grave." Leo dropped the flashlight, grabbed the knife, and slung it at Pisces, then leaped into the darkness and rolled on the ground.

Four shots rang out, milliseconds apart. Leo looked back toward the fools. The flashlight lay nearby, illuminating a pair of motionless forms, one with a knife protruding from his chest. He whispered, "What the …"

"Leo," Iona called. "It's safe. I think they're dead."

He climbed to his feet, picked up the flashlight, and shone the beam on the men. Blood trickled from a head wound on each. He shifted the beam to Iona. She sat on her blanket, one hand high, the wrist still shackled, the other holding a smoking revolver.

Leo sputtered, "*You* shot them?"

"Obviously." She aimed the gun at him and nodded toward the branch. "Now unlock this cuff."

"All right. Just stay calm." After setting the flashlight on a nearby log, he withdrew a key ring from Pisces's pocket and walked toward her, eyeing her gun hand—steady, finger firmly on the trigger. This girl had ice in her veins.

As he pushed the cuff key into the lock, he spoke in a friendly tone. "Those two wouldn't have treated you kindly." He opened the cuff and let it down gently. "They were slavering dogs."

"I know." She extended her arm. "Now this one. No false moves."

"Trust me, Miss Deadeye, I want to keep my hide from being ventilated." He unlocked the cuff and pulled both away. "There."

She gestured with her head. "Now get your flashlight and take five steps back."

As he did so, the cuffs still in his grip, she climbed to her feet, the gun trained on him. "I assume you still want to take me to the angels."

He shone the beam on her. "You're a fugitive, and I'm a huntsman. Tracking you is my job."

"So if I run, you'll keep tracking me. My best option is to shoot you."

"Unless we make a deal. I could promise not to track you."

She shook her head. "I can't trust your word."

"Ah, but you should. A huntsman's word is golden."

"Says the man whose life I saved from two traitor huntsmen."

"Touché, Sword Maiden. Well struck. Yet, I'm not like them. I risked my life to keep those dogs from killing you."

"Yeah. I saw how you dove for cover while I was still in handcuffs." Iona aimed the gun at the ground, though her finger stayed on the trigger. "But if you really want to help me, I'll give you a chance to prove yourself."

Leo nodded. "If it's in my power."

"It's your specialty. I need to find a man I met at the city temple. I saw you waiting outside while I spoke to him."

"I remember. A farmer, I'm sure. The odors of chicken manure and alfalfa were easy to detect."

"Then you can find him?"

"Once I pick up the scent, certainly, but the farmer's trail from the temple is cold by now. I wouldn't know where to begin."

"Begin here. He was supposed to go to angel headquarters. We're pretty close."

"That we are." Leo inhaled through his nose. The faint aroma of soap entered, but it was different this time. "Strange. I tracked the scent of your soap here, but I'm smelling a different soap blending in. Is it lye?" He nodded. "Yes, it's definitely lye."

Iona shook her head. "I've never used lye soap."

"Someone nearby has." Leo half closed an eye. "Listen, Miss Lye-less, if you'll put that gun away, I'll help you find the farmer, and I won't take you back to the angels. You saved my life. I owe you that much."

"On one condition." She nodded at his hands. "Put the cuffs on and give me the key."

Leo rolled his eyes. "If you insist." He fastened the cuffs, set the key on the ground, and backed away. "But, trust me, I'm a better aid to you uncuffed."

"Maybe you'll earn my trust." Iona tucked the gun behind her waistband at the back and picked up the key. "Now let's get to work."

"Very well." He inhaled again. "The lye scent makes me curious. Clearly homemade. Cherry wood ashes and mutton tallow."

"Mutton? Then whoever made it has sheep. A farmer."

"Exactly. And it won't take long to locate the source." Leo marched toward the scent. "Come along, Princess Pine Needles. Let's find your farmer."

Ben sat on the ground with Kat and Trudy. Trudy examined the bandage again while Ben aimed a flashlight at Kat's wound. "How are you feeling?" he asked.

Kat sighed. "Better. Headache's awful, but no dizziness anymore."

"And what does your surgeon say?"

Trudy let out a tsking sound and drew back. "Still bleeding too much. I think she can get up and walk around if she's careful."

Kat raised her arms. "Then help me up."

Ben and Trudy each grabbed an arm and hoisted Kat to her feet. The moment she gained her balance, gunshots cracked in the woods, then all fell quiet. Ben tossed the flashlight to Kat and scooped an X99 while Trudy snatched a plasma rifle. They stood side by side and listened, both with barrels aimed toward the trees, fingers on triggers, while Kat scanned their surroundings with the flashlight beam.

"Four shots," Ben said. "At least two guns."

Trudy nodded, her voice low. "Three guns. One was large caliber and fired two shots."

"We're in the open. Sitting ducks." Ben waved toward Kat. "Douse the light."

The beam flicked off, casting them in darkness. Ben leaned close to Trudy. "If someone's looking for us, why the shooting?"

"Thought they saw us, maybe? Who knows? And these aren't hunting grounds. Not this close to HQ. The reason can't be good."

"Agreed. Kat, stand close with the flashlight ready. Let's go silent and listen."

While they waited, an owl hooted in a nearby tree. A ground animal chittered, probably a raccoon. A gentle breeze blew the foliage about, raising a faint rustle. A minute or so later, louder rustling noises rode the air, something trudging through forest debris.

Ben tightened his grip on the rifle. Three armed men likely approached, all with trigger fingers. The situation called for split-second quickness—turning the light on, identifying the men, and deciding whether or not to shoot them.

He sidled close to Kat. "Lights on my word."

She nodded, nearly invisible in the faint moonlight, her wings fully extended.

The rustling drew closer, blending with an odd, metallic squeak, its rhythm in time with the trudges, then silence.

Ben whispered, "Now."

The beam flashed to life, shining on a lone figure. A pigtailed girl wearing a backpack stood at the edge of the clearing, a bicycle at her side, her eyes filled with terror. "Don't shoot. Please."

"What?" Ben lowered his gun. "Who are you?"

Wearing torn jeans and a gray jersey, she looked past Ben and Trudy. "Why are you siding with the angels?"

Trudy leaned close to Ben. "Kat's wings."

"Yeah. I guessed that." He focused on the girl's face. It seemed so familiar. "Tell us who you are, and we'll tell you who we are."

She scrunched her brow. "Don't you recognize me?"

Ben stepped closer. Although the outfit made her look no older than twelve, the red hair and freckles finally gave her away. "Iona?"

"Yes." She set a fist on her hip. "Your turn."

"I'm Ben Garrison." He nodded toward Kat, then Trudy. "My wife, Katherine, and my sister, Trudy. We are most definitely not on the angels' side."

"Says the man married to a winged woman."

Kat kept the light trained on Iona. "The angel queen was implanted in my body."

"*Was?*" Keeping her distance, Iona frowned. "The wings say *is.*"

Kat sighed. "It's a long story."

A man's voice punched into the clearing. "A good one, I'll wager."

Ben and Trudy both raised their guns. Leo, wearing a long cloak, walked out of the trees, his hands cuffed as he sidled next to Iona. "You were right, Petite Prophetess. You going first kept them from shooting me on sight."

"The alpha huntsman," Trudy said. "We saw him at the temple."

Ben looked at Iona. "Is Leo your prisoner?"

"He was." She unlocked the cuffs and let them drop. "Now he's yours."

"Did you frisk him?" Trudy asked.

"No. I had a gun on him until just before you saw me. And I didn't want to get that close to him, not without someone else watching."

"Fair enough." Trudy strode toward Leo. "I'll do it."

Clutching his wrist, she led him back to Ben. "Raise your arms." While Leo did so, she reached past his open cloak and felt around his belt. "Let's see. A flashlight, a key of some kind, and …." She withdrew a long serrated dagger, a shorter knife, and a small pistol, dropping each as she found them.

"As you can see," Leo said to Iona as she stood at the edge of the clearing, "I could've shot you when you walked ahead of me. I think I've earned your trust."

She half closed an eye. "Maybe."

Trudy checked Leo's pockets, removing an AngelScan, a metal flask, and a foil pouch with a tobacco leaf emblem on the side.

"My trail drink and pipe tobacco. The pipe's in the pouch. When a fire's too risky, a fellow has to stay warm at night. And the disk is a—"

"I know what an AngelScan is." She slid the disk into her pants pocket. "It tells if a soul or an angel is present in someone's brain."

"Oh, more than that. Every angel implant has an ID. That scanner reads the ID and looks up the angel's name. Shows it on the screen. I downloaded the latest data before I left."

"That might come in handy." Trudy set the flask and pouch back into his pocket. "You can lower your arms."

"Thank you." Leo withdrew the flask, uncapped it, and took a drink. After swallowing and recapping, he unfastened the flashlight from his belt and aimed the beam at Iona, still at the clearing's edge. "I needed a boost from my bottle. I chased that orange-headed squirrel all night."

Ben huffed. "I'll shed a tear for the mighty huntsman." He gestured toward Iona. "Come closer. We've disarmed him."

Her skeptical frown deepened. "I'm still worried about the angel queen, but I guess I don't have much choice." She wheeled the bike next to Ben and Trudy and propped it on its kickstand.

"Did you ride that rickety thing all the way from the temple?" Trudy asked.

"Sure did. It's part of my disguise." She flipped up one of her pigtails. "That's how I escaped. No one bothers to stop a little girl on a bike."

Ben grasped a handlebar and gave the bike a shake, making it rattle. "We're at least fifty miles from the temple."

"Yep. I had to sleep in a pile of manure last night, but I made it."

Leo rolled his eyes. "So that's how you ..." He shook his head. "Never mind."

Iona swung the backpack off and set it on the ground. "Do you have any food? Maybe trail mix or jerky? I've had only a few pecans since I left."

"I think Trudy has snacks." Ben touched Iona's arm. "You mentioned side effects in your note. Were you able to avoid getting vaccinated?"

She nodded. "Risky, I know. But I figured getting the vaccine was riskier."

"Good call. We discovered what the side effect is. The vaccine purges souls."

"Purges souls? That's disturbing."

Trudy tossed an energy bar to her. "We heard gunshots."

Iona caught the bar and began unwrapping it. "I had to kill Leo's henchmen and make him my prisoner." After taking a bite, she withdrew a revolver from her waistband and put it in her backpack. "If I hadn't, I might be dead."

Ben stared at her. How odd. This girl seemed to contradict every stereotype. "How did you find us?"

Leo raised a finger. "Allow me to explain with a demonstration." While sniffing the air, he glanced at Ben, then Kat, then Trudy. "Ah. It's you. Lye soap residue in your hair."

Ben nudged Trudy. "You didn't rinse."

"I rinsed," she said, scowling. "I have longer hair than you do."

"Okay. Back to the topic." Ben turned toward Iona. "Now we know *how* you found us. *Why* did you find us?"

Iona chewed another bite. "Because I gave you the esoterica. I want to talk to you about using the weapon to kill the angels."

Leo raised his hands. "Whoa! Stop right there. Don't say another word. I don't want to know what you're up to."

"Too late." Ben gave Iona a scolding stare. "You're a spy. You know better than to spill a secret like that."

"I know exactly what I'm doing." She slid her hand into Leo's pocket and withdrew the foil pouch. "First, you believed him when he said this held tobacco." She opened the top and peeked inside. "Nope."

Leo growled, "Little snitch."

She rolled several plastic spheres into her palm. "Mini bombs."

"My error," Trudy said as she took the pouch and looked it over. "How did you know?"

Iona pinched one of the spheres. "The pouch has tiny round protrusions that tobacco couldn't make. Because the bombs are plastic, the weight is about right. You just believed the label and this huntsman's lie."

"Merely trying to protect myself," Leo said. "They're defensive weapons. More smoke than anything. Gives me a chance to escape danger."

"And escaping is exactly what I don't want you to do." Iona poured the bombs into the pouch and took it from Trudy. "Which brings me to the second reason I mentioned the weapon. I came to find Ben because I remembered more information that I didn't include in the esoterica. The region to search is large, so we need to narrow it down. Right before I entered the place where the weapon is stored, I smelled something pungent, like what we use at the temple to clean the floors."

Ben looked her in the eye. "If you smelled it again, could you—"

"Stop," Leo said, pushing Ben out of the way. "This is my expertise, Farmer Jones."

"Be my guest, huntsman."

Leo faced Iona. "Did the odor burn your eyes?"

"A little."

He touched his throat. "And the back of your throat. Did you taste something metallic?"

"Yeah. Kind of."

Leo firmed his lips and nodded. "Ammonia. Since it burned her eyes, she was close to the source. Within a mile."

"What might be around, then?" Ben asked. "A factory that makes floor cleaner?"

"More likely livestock production. Urea buildup." Leo wrinkled his nose. "Nasty business."

"That region has several farms. We can't use the smell to pinpoint the location."

"There's another option." Leo crouched in front of Iona and touched his nose. "Did you notice a scratchy sensation in your nose or throat? Like you breathed something dusty?"

She rolled her eyes. "First, stand up. Don't treat me like a kid. Second, yes, but I thought it was dust. I heard Barks say it was dry and dusty that day."

"Interesting." Leo straightened. "The evidence points to a fertilizer plant. I imagine there aren't many of those around. Look them up in a directory. You'll find them."

"I buy fertilizer for our farm," Ben said, "and I know where all the outlets are. There aren't any listed in that region."

"Then I guess you're out of luck." Leo set his feet as if ready to leave. "Since I can't be of any use to you—"

"No," Iona said. "You missed my point. I spilled the weapon information so Leo would know too much to let him go. He has to stay with us and find the ammonia scent with his talented nose."

Leo glared at her, then looked at Ben. "I promised my pigtailed captor that I would help her find you, but honoring that vow led me into quite a fix. If I refuse to help you, I'm a dead man, because you'll kill me to keep me from ratting to the angels. If I go with you on this impossible mission, when we're captured by the angels, I'm a dead man for being a traitor." He squared his shoulders, keeping his stare on Ben. "My guess is that you consider yourself to be a man of principle. Is this the kind of dilemma you would shackle me with? Remember, I came here to do a legal job that had nothing to do with you. I am not your enemy."

"Ben," Kat said, touching his back. "He has a good point."

"I know. I know." Ben sighed. "Do you have a solution?"

"Maybe." Kat touched Trudy's pocket. "Read my brain with that AngelScan."

"Uh ... sure." Trudy withdrew Leo's scanner and set it against Kat's forehead. The screen turned on and showed a white sphere— Kat's soul—but no red, tentacled monster. The disk beeped, and a name appeared at the top of the screen—Laramel.

Trudy removed the disk. "It says you're Laramel. I guess the spawn's too small to see, but the scanner picked it up."

"Then I'll be Laramel." Kat spread an arm toward everyone in the group. "And the rest of you will be my entourage. If we're accosted by angels, they'll believe that I am their queen. Leo, therefore, will be in the clear if he joins our mission."

Leo scrunched his brow. "Forgive me, but I don't understand how you can be Queen Laramel and not Queen Laramel at the same time."

"I'm with Leo," Iona said, a fist on her hip. "My father used to say, 'When two and two don't equal four, something ain't right.'"

Ben nodded. "You deserve a full explanation. While we're waiting for our transport, I'll tell you the story."

"But we still need to stitch Kat before we leave," Trudy said. "Where are we going to get suture thread?" She turned toward Leo. "Got anything in one of your pockets that we can use?"

"Not me, Miss Nosey. Fresh out of thread."

Iona untied a rope from around her waist. "Can you get fibers from this?"

"Maybe. They might be too short and brittle, though."

"Then how about"—Iona dug into her pocket and withdrew a long, dark thread—"a hair from a horse's tail?"

Trudy blinked. "Uh ... yeah. I can sterilize it with alcohol. Maybe double it to make it stronger."

Iona gave her the hair and sat with her legs crossed. "Okay, Ben Garrison. You tell me your story, and I'll tell you mine."

Chapter Twenty-Four

Jack flew with Chantal over angel headquarters and slowly descended. With his wings carrying her weight as well as his own, he huffed and puffed, nearly out of gas. This flight would have to end real soon.

Chantal pointed toward their two o'clock direction. "That building. The small one with the angled roof."

"I see it." He turned that way and dropped quickly.

Chantal gasped, then held her breath. When they landed on the apex, she smiled. "Well, I must say that you know how to show a girl a good time."

"I do my best." Jack released her, pivoted carefully, and walked to the end of the roof. A concrete pad lay below, maybe a takeoff and landing site for the SkySweep drones. Flapping his wings to keep from falling, he leaned farther out and looked back at the wall below. It appeared to have a large vertical entry, like an airplane hangar's roll-up door. This had to be the place.

After righting himself, he turned toward Chantal. "What's your read? Is security high?"

She angled her head, listening. Jack did the same. Something tinkled, like breaking glass, close, but probably in another building. Then a voice came over a PA system. "The contagion threat is still ongoing. Stay where you are and keep all doors and windows closed. The next update will come in one hour."

"There's your answer." Chantal held out a hand. "I'll try the pass key."

Jack pulled the polo shirt from his pocket and carefully unwadded it, exposing the angel vial. It glowed brightly in the night's darkness. She took the vial and lifted her arms. "Let's do it."

Jack stuffed the shirt into his pocket, embraced her again, and flew to ground level. When they landed in front of the hangar, Chantal set the tube in front of a sensor next to the door. It beeped, and a computer said, "Queen Laramel. Access granted."

Chantal pushed the open button. The door rose slowly with barely a sound. She walked in and flipped a switch on the wall. Lights flashed on at the high ceiling, revealing three SkySweep drones sitting in a triangle in the massive chamber.

"We have to hurry," she said. "The security system might alert someone that the queen accessed this building. With a lockdown underway, we don't know if she's been reported missing. Someone might check."

Jack stepped to the closest drone, opened its entry door, and peered inside. "Do you think five adults can fit comfortably in there?"

Chantal set a hand on his shoulder and peeked around him, her hair tickling his ear. "Not when two of them have wings. One set can be retracted, but I heard it's uncomfortable."

"Good point. Maybe we can take a second drone."

She turned toward him, their eyes only inches apart. "Are you expecting me to fly one?"

Jack drew away a bit. "It's not hard. I'll program the destination and set the autopilot. You just sit and let the drone do the rest."

"Okay. That I can handle. But if it flies by itself, I don't have to be inside at all. I can go with you."

Jack touched the seat. "Pressure sensitive. If no one's sitting here, it won't fly unless someone's running it by remote control."

"Then we'll find something to lay there." She turned. "I'll look for a—"

He grasped her arm. "Hey. Where's your sense of adventure?"

"Sense of adventure?" She cocked her head. "A few minutes ago, I let you fly me back to the place that implanted me with an angel, and you're asking me about my sense of adventure?"

"Okay." He released her. "You win. We'll find a weight."

Smiling, she shook her head. "You don't get it, do you?"

"Get what?"

"Never mind." She climbed into the drone and sat in the seat. "I'm ready. What do I do?"

Folding his wings as much as possible, Jack vaulted into the compartment with her and looked at the dongle port—empty. He withdrew the starter module from the crashed drone and plugged it in. Then, leaning over Chantal's shoulder, he entered the code into the computer and waited for it to respond.

Her lips next to his ear, she whispered, "How long ago did she die, Jack?"

"What? Who are you talking about?"

"Your wife. When did she die?"

The computer beeped. A message appeared: "Ignition sequence activated." A hum rose, and the drone vibrated.

Jack punched in the destination coordinates and crouched next to her. "How did you know about my wife?"

"When Laramel implanted you, she told me you're a widower, but I could tell anyway. You have the eyes of a heartsick man, so I was wondering how long it's been."

"A while. A plague. It got our daughter, too."

"I'm so sorry. What were their names?"

"Sophie and Alana." As she gazed at him, her lips softened, opening a slit. Jack tightened his own lips. This couldn't happen. At least not yet. "Okay," he said as he backed away and climbed out of the drone. "I get it now."

She blinked. "Get what?"

"You said I didn't get it. Now I do. But I can't. Not yet. Not while Sophie and Alana are in that horrible place. I have to get them out before I …" He shook his head. "Never mind. Let's get going."

"But, Jack, what horrible place? They really are dead, aren't they?"

"Yes, they're really dead." His heart pounding as he stood on the hangar floor, he set a fist against the drone's doorframe. "Listen, Chantal, I like you. Really. You're smart, compassionate, courageous. And drop-dead gorgeous. But I'm on a mission, and I can't think about anything else until it's done. I don't expect anyone to understand, but that's the way it is. My loved ones are suffering in a ghastly eternity in the Oculus Gate. I can't leave them there." His voice cracked. "I *won't* leave them there."

"What do you have to do to get them out?"

"Destroy the Gate. It's the only way."

As she stared at him, a tear trickled down her cheek. "Let me help you. I'll do anything."

"You are helping me." He reached in and pulled the dongle out. "Just follow me in this drone."

"Queen Laramel?" a man called.

Jack turned toward the voice. A burly man wearing an angel-HQ polo shirt with a Security Team badge stood at the hangar opening, a handgun in a belt holster. "Who are you?" the man asked.

"He is my prisoner," Chantal said as she stepped out of the drone and grasped Jack's arm. "Who are you?"

The guard gasped. "Princess Novada?"

"Obviously."

"What happened to you?" He touched his cheek. "Did something hit you?"

"Again, obviously." She scowled. "Who are you?"

The guard fidgeted. "Hiram. A security guard. The system said that Queen Laramel accessed the entry lock. I came to see—"

"She is nearby." Chantal's brow loosened. "Why are you here? Aren't you worried about the contagion?"

"I was vaccinated yesterday. Everyone in my department was."

Jack read his eyes—lost and vacant. A soulless zombie. But by what magic was he able to do anything? What guided his actions? Instinct plus memories?

"Well, Hiram," Chantal said, giving Jack a hard shake, "I am taking Zeebach in a drone to an offsite facility for questioning."

"Zeebach?" Hiram looked at a computer tablet and tapped on the screen. "It says here that he's gone rogue."

"Which is why I have him in custody. You can see that I had to subdue him."

Hiram smiled. "You're quite a fighter. I've seen your workout videos." He leaned to the side. "But where are your wings? You always used them so well while fighting."

"I retracted my wings. Is your knowledge of my traits lacking?"

"I … I can't remember everyone's traits, but I thought I knew yours. It's hard to miss your … well … never mind."

"Never mind your ignorance?" Chantal extended her hand. "Give me your pad. I'll show you my file. I have a video of my wings retracting."

Hiram eyed the pad, his tone sheepish. "I'm not supposed to give it to anyone outside my department. And I've seen all your videos. I never saw one with your wings retracting."

"Because, as you might imagine, with my shirt off, it's rather intimate. It's in the private section of my file. You have no access."

"Oh. Well, then, I suppose it's all right." He walked to her and handed the pad over.

"Thank you, Hiram." She set it on her palm and tapped on the screen. "I see that my access is still intact."

"Of course," Hiram said. "When no one could find you or Queen Laramel, we assumed you escaped to your bunker tunnel to avoid the contagion. We were all worried about you."

"To set everyone's mind at ease, you may tell them that I am on a mission to deal with this rogue angel, though I won't divulge the purpose. He has promised to be compliant in order to avoid severe punishment."

"And the queen?"

"She is coming as well and has already settled inside one of the drones, and she doesn't wish to be disturbed. When we leave, make sure that the drone team knows that these two units are to be left alone, no matter where they fly."

Hiram backed away. "Understood, Princess."

Chantal lifted the pad. "And I am taking this with me."

"If you say so, Princess."

Jack whispered to her, "Push the autopilot button, and we'll get going." He hopped into another drone, plugged the dongle in, and entered the code, talking to himself. "Let's hope it works on more than one drone at a time."

When the computer beeped and the control-panel lights flashed, he toggled manual control on and called, "Ready, Princess."

Propellers whirring, Chantal's drone lifted and floated slowly out the hangar door. While Jack followed at the same pace, Hiram jogged behind, calling, "What about the video?"

By the time Ben finished his story and Iona added her tale, Trudy had stitched Kat's wound with the horse's hair and applied a new gauze pad. Kat curled her arm around Ben's. "I had no idea you've gone through so much."

He kissed the top of her head. Her tight clutch felt so good. "Not nearly as much as you have."

"Not bad for a farmer." Leo clapped Ben on the back. "Or should I call you a warrior?"

"Well, I'm on the warrior's team," Iona said. "But I'm still worried about Kat. Who knows when that angel spawn will take hold?"

Ben gave her a conciliatory nod. "We'll keep scanning, and we'll extract it as soon as we can." He looked at Leo. "Are you in?"

"Well ..." He turned toward Iona. "I found your farmer. Do I have your trust now?"

"I guess so, and if you'll help us find the weapon, you'll have my trust forever, but I don't see why that's so important to you."

"Not for you to know the reasons why." Leo refocused on Ben. "My services and my nose are yours to command."

"And you …" Trudy lightly punched Iona's arm. "A revolver? In the dark? Kill shots to the head? I'm in awe."

"Shhh!" Leo furrowed his brow and looked skyward. "I hear SkySweep drones. Two of them. I thought your brother was bringing only one."

"Let's hope he changed his mind," Ben said. "It's too late to run."

Lights appeared over the treetops, slowly descending. As everyone backed away, the twin drones landed. The moment the engines stopped and the propellers slowed, Jack jumped out and hustled to the other drone. "Any problems?" Jack asked Chantal as he helped her climb out, a computer pad in her hand.

She pushed her hair back. "None. It flew perfectly on its own."

Jack turned to Ben. "We're on easy street. Chantal got these two drones officially assigned to her, and angel security believes she's on a secret mission with the queen. No one will harass us. And she connived a computer pad that communicates by satellite. We can monitor everything the angels do." He gave Chantal her polo shirt. "You should've seen her acting performance. It was for the ages."

Ben flashed a thumbs-up. "I admire undercover agents. I could never pretend like that for so long."

"Thank you, Ben." Chantal pulled the polo shirt on and shook out her hair. "I appreciate your confidence in me."

"And it's a good thing you brought an extra drone." Ben nodded toward the newcomers. "Jack, Chantal, the girl is Iona. I told Jack about her. And the man is Leo. Jack's seen him."

"Yeah," Jack said. "Our temple mole and the huntsman. What are they doing here?"

"Tell you about it on the way." Ben scanned the group. "Now I have to figure out who goes in which drone."

"Leo and I should probably be together," Iona said. "To track the scents."

Leo picked up one of his daggers and slid it into a belt sheath. "Agreed, and I think the feisty woman with the soapy hair should ride in the other drone. Her ... how shall I say it? Her blend of fragrances would make my job a lot harder."

Ben draped an arm around Kat. "We'll go with Leo and Iona. Jack, Chantal, and Trudy will fly together. That way we'll have someone with wings in each drone. Angel safety nets."

"Take Chantal's drone," Jack said to Ben, pointing. "You'll figure it out. It's a lot easier than a chopper. It's still running, so you just have to start the props."

Trudy raised a hand. "Wait. I'd like to split us up differently. Ben, Leo, and I in one drone, and Jack, Chantal, Kat, and Iona in the other."

Ben squinted. "But that puts two winged people with two other people in the same drone."

"Too crowded?" Trudy gave Iona a long stare. "Okay. We'll take Iona."

Iona crossed her arms. "I feel like I got picked last for a sports team."

"Sis," Ben said to Trudy, "what's this all about?"

"Please, just trust me."

Kat shrugged. "I'm okay with it. And I can try retracting my wings."

Iona tightened her arms. "Listen, if Trudy doesn't want me with her, I'll go with the others. I'm small. It shouldn't be a problem."

"No," Trudy said, touching Iona's elbow. "I changed my mind. I was wrong. Please come with us."

Iona scrunched her brow. "Are you always this strange?"

"Yeah. Pretty much. Sorry."

She loosened her arms. "All right, then."

Ben leaned close to Trudy. "I hope you know what you're doing."

"Me, too. I'm kind of winging it."

After everyone relieved themselves in the forest, Ben and Trudy gathered their items, including the cooling blanket, the spent extraction kit, the rifles, and the medical bag. Ben helped Kat get into Jack's drone, letting her take the driver's seat, then hopped into the other drone and sat at the control panel. While he surveyed the controls, Leo collected his remaining weapons and boarded, seating himself on the floor behind Ben.

Wearing her backpack, Iona climbed in behind the driver's seat. Trudy extended her hand toward Jack, an earbud in her palm. "This was in Chantal's ear. Do you need it?"

"Nope." He touched his ear. "Still got the other one."

"Then we're set." She pocketed the bud, grabbed a medical bag, and joined Ben in his drone. She sat between Iona and Leo, the bag in her lap.

When Jack signaled from the other drone that they were ready, Ben started the propellers, grasped a protruding joystick, and pushed a slider that increased the power as well as the humming noise.

As they lifted off, Ben called, "Jack, can you hear me over all this racket?"

"Barely," Jack said through the earbud.

"Good enough." Ben guided the drone to the highway that led from HQ toward Camp Rogers and followed the route from about two hundred feet above. "Jack, I'll fly lead. I know approximately where we're going, and I've got the bloodhound on board."

"Yeah. Sounds good. Let me know when our sniffer gets a hit."

"Will do." Once Ben had set the controls at a steady cruising speed and altitude, he took out his earbud, switched it off, and turned to Trudy. "All right, Sis. Time to spill it. You're acting weird, even for you."

As Ben stared at her, Leo and Iona turned toward her and added their stares.

Trudy sank a bit and pulled the bag close to her chest. "Uh … give me a minute to put my thoughts together."

Leo withdrew the flask from his pocket. "Here. This'll give you some gumption."

Trudy took the flask and squinted at it. "The strongest drink I've ever had is a glass of wine. And that was only twice."

"No time like the present." He unscrewed the cap. "And get ready for a kick."

She looked at Ben, her brow raised. He shrugged. "You don't need my permission. Besides, one swig won't hurt you."

"All right, then." She tipped the flask up, took a mouthful, and swallowed, then blinked. "It's coffee."

"Not just any coffee. It's triple caffeinated. Perfect for staying alert." Leo took the flask and recapped it. "Now let's hear what's on your mind."

Hiram reached for the hangar's light switch and eyed the single drone still in the chamber. Something on the floor sparkled. Squinting, he walked to the spot. A glass vial lay where Novada's drone once sat, a scrap of paper underneath.

He pinched the vial and set it close to his eyes. A red blob glowed within, like a miniature lava lamp from the old movies. He picked up the scrap and read the neatly handwritten note. "This vial contains an angel. Take it to Dr. Elder. She will know what to do with it. Tell her Chantal is on the trail of the weapon and needs the homing orb. Follow the drones that I took from the garage."

Hiram jogged to the door's security sensor and held the vial close. It beeped and said in its mechanical voice, "Queen Laramel. Access granted."

He gasped. "Queen Laramel?" He slid the vial gently into one pocket and pulled a phone from the other. With trembling hands, he pressed the speed dial code for the angel hive room. As he waited for an answer, he paced in a circle.

"Dr. Elder here."

"Oh. Dr. Elder. Perfect. It's Hiram from Security. Listen, I'm at the SkySweep drone hangar, and I found a glass vial on the floor with light energy inside. A note says it holds an angel. So I set it against the door sensor here. The computer said it's Queen Laramel."

Dr. Elder's voice spiked. "What? That's impossible!"

"No. Listen." Hiram read the note to Dr. Elder. When he finished, he added, "I came to the hangar because I got a notification that an angel accessed the door. It said it was the queen, so I rushed over to investigate."

"And what did you find?"

"Princess Novada was here with that new male angel. Zeebach. The system says he's rogue."

"Zeebach. So she *is* with him, but apparently of her own accord."

"She said he was her prisoner. They both had bruises. I've seen her fight, so I didn't doubt her story. Anyway, Princess Novada said she and Queen Laramel were going on a secret mission in two drones. But now I have Queen Laramel in a vial. What do you think it means?"

"Obviously Queen Laramel has been extracted from Katherine Garrison, and Princess Novada and Zeebach had the queen in their possession."

Hiram gasped again. "The princess and Zeebach were kidnapping the queen?"

"No, you moron. The princess left the queen in the hangar for us to find. She's loyal."

"That brings up another question," Hiram said. "Princess Novada didn't have wings. She said they're retractable, but I never heard that. I thought only the queen has retractable wings."

"You're right. Only the queen has them. Chantal was Princess Novada's host, an angel loyalist, which means Princess Novada was extracted, too."

"Okay, but who is Zeebach's host?"

"Jack Garrison. A rebel agent. I was suspicious of Zeebach. His glow was a bit off when I implanted him."

"So why would a loyalist leave the queen behind and then take off with a rogue angel?"

"How should I know? The angels don't keep me in the loop. They demoted me to their obedient little scalpel girl."

"What should we do?"

"Track them with our drone team, but give them space. Don't get close enough to let them know you're following."

"Agreed. Anything else?"

"Bring the queen to me. She needs to be implanted right away. And I know just the human who should host her."

Chapter Twenty-Five

Trudy folded her hands over her medical bag. "Okay, here's the deal. First, what I say has to be between the four of us. Ben, I understand the husband and wife you-gotta-share-everything idea, but this has to be an exception."

Ben eyed her expression—her I'm-being-super-serious face. "This sounds really intense."

"It is. Listen. In my view, everyone but Ben is compromised. Kat's hosting an angel spawn, and we have no idea when it's going to latch on and take over." She turned toward Iona. "And you're a double agent. Now, don't get me wrong. I admire your skills. You're an actress extraordinaire. And you're super resourceful. But you have to understand. Since you've worked both sides successfully, it's hard for us to trust you."

Iona's reddish eyebrows dipped. "Okay. Go on."

Trudy turned toward Leo. "And you're a freaking huntsman. Like with Iona, don't get me wrong. You're as skillful as they come. I mean, you could sniff out a soap bubble a mile away on a windy night. But you're a mercenary. You're loyal to whoever pays you, whether angels or rebels."

Leo gave her a hard stare. "You never had friends growing up, did you?"

"No, but that's not important right now. Let's move on to the others. Jack is possessed by an angel. Yeah, Zachariel says he's an archangel from God, but how do we know that for sure?"

Iona raised a hand. "Um … I think I'm out of the loop on that one. You actually believe Jack has a real angel in his brain?"

"Maybe. Jury's still out. My point is we're not sure, so he's compromised, too."

"Okay. I'll go along with that. Never trust an angel."

"And Chantal?" Ben asked.

"She's my biggest worry." Trudy zipped open the medical bag and withdrew the extraction kit. "Remember Chantal took Laramel's vial to the hangar to get the drones?"

"Yeah. Sure. For security clearance."

"Well, check this out." She opened the kit and picked up a vial filled with a red glowing blob and set it in the light coming from the drone's control panel. "Look familiar?"

"Very." Ben pinched the vial and drew it closer. "Laramel, right?"

"Right. I checked it before we left." Trudy set the vial back in place. "Where does that lead us?"

"I can help with that," Leo said. "I watched Chantal check a vial with my scanner, I assume the vial she took with her. It holds Queen Laramel, if the scanner is to be believed."

"I see no reason not to believe it." Trudy turned toward Ben. "And do you remember the tentacle vestiges I extracted?"

"Yeah. You put them in a plastic bag."

She nodded. "But now the bag's gone."

"Okay," Ben said. "This is leading up to a big theory. Just lay it on me."

"Bottom line? Chantal needed Laramel to access the security system, so she took a vial with her, thinking it's Laramel because of Leo's scan. But the scanner says the one we have here is Laramel. We know Novada is Laramel's daughter and that the spawn in Kat registers as Laramel."

"So Novada would also show up on the scanner as Laramel," Ben said. "But which one is the real Laramel? The one we have or the one Novada took?"

Leo raised a hand. "The one you have is Laramel. When my scanner checked Kat and the vial Chantal took, it paused a good two seconds before identifying them. It probably noticed some minor differences between the real Laramel and the spawns, but the programming concluded that they were a close enough match. It identified the vial you have in a snap."

"Did Chantal know that?" Trudy asked. "Being the ultimate spy, as she called herself, she probably knew that the scanner would identify Novada as Laramel. Why do the scan if either vial would show the same result?"

"She watched real closely." Leo narrowed his eyes to slits. "Like this. When the scanner delayed, she seemed relieved. I think she knew who she had."

"Okay," Ben said, "but why would Chantal want Novada instead of Laramel?"

Trudy refolded her hands. "I'm still working on that one, but Chantal volunteered to be implanted. That worries me. I'm not convinced by her excuse. She must've been communicating with Novada in their blended mind. Why else would Novada know to meet us at the staircase after our implantation?"

"But Novada didn't give the passcode," Ben said. "And she wasn't aware that we were spies. If Chantal were a turncoat, she would have tipped Novada off. I'm sure Novada would've wanted to avoid getting her throat cut. And so would Chantal."

"Good point. But have you seen her making googly eyes at Jack? She's trolling for him, and he's sniffing the bait."

"Trolling?" Ben frowned. "Maybe she's just attracted to him."

"That's not my read, but what do I know? I don't have a romantic bone in my body."

"My turn." Iona raised her hand. "Jack's a head turner. I mean he's smart, brave, and good looking, but Chantal's playing him. I can see right through her scheme."

"Then if Chantal's not a turncoat," Trudy said, "what's she up to?"

Ben shrugged. "Could she be a lone ranger? Maybe she thinks we're all compromised, and she has to complete the mission alone."

"Doesn't work. She had free access to Laramel. We wanted her to take Laramel with her. But she took Novada without letting us know what she's up to."

"From my experience as a double agent," Iona said, "if you confront her without evidence, she'll just go deeper undercover. You'll never catch her. You need to do something to show you're not suspicious of her at all."

"And maybe she'll get careless," Trudy said.

"Exactly my point."

Leo withdrew a small dagger from his belt and showed it to everyone. "The best weapon in a battle of stealth is a small one, a blade you can hide, an edge unseen by the enemy, yet razor sharp, able to cut a jugular in a flash, then escape in a puff of smoke. And that's why, I'll wager, Miss Trudy gave in to bringing Iona into her confidence. Am I right?"

Trudy gave him a conceding nod. "You nailed it."

"I thought so." Leo put the dagger away. "Then why have I been invited into the fold? I have an idea, but I want to hear you say it. I expect to be entertained by your explanation."

Trudy paused, staring at Leo, then drew a deep breath. "I want to make it look like we suspect you of being a spy."

"I knew it! Blame the creepy huntsman. Make him the scapegoat." He laughed with a bellow. "This is rich!"

"Does that mean you won't cooperate?" Trudy asked.

"No, no, Miss Fists of Iron. I'm glad to. Even though I'm a greedy mercenary, I hate traitors. If Chantal's betraying you folks, I want to expose her."

Iona pointed at herself. "So am I the sharp dagger that cuts a throat and disappears in a puff of smoke?"

Leo waved a hand. "That wasn't meant as an insult. The way you eluded me on the trail, you have skills—"

"I didn't take it as an insult." A smile emerged on Iona's impish face. "I kind of like the idea."

Ben kept a hand on the steering joystick while glancing at the crew. "Well, whether or not Kat's compromised, while she's in her right mind, she'll figure out what we're doing. She's as smart as they come."

"No worries," Trudy said. "Laramel's spawn is the problem. It's her we want to fool. As long as Kat's in control, we're good. And I think it would take a long time for a rookie spawn to read Kat's mind well enough to become her. If it tries to take over, we'll know."

Leo focused on Trudy. "So how do we pull off this deception?"

"I'll have to figure it out along the way, you know, watching to see what Chantal does, but you and Iona are both smart and experienced. You'll be able to follow my lead when the time comes."

"Ah, that we are," Leo said. "We can ..." He blinked, then inhaled deeply through his nose.

"Ammonia?" Trudy asked.

"Just a trace." He pointed toward their ten o'clock direction. "That way."

Ben turned his earbud on and reinserted it. "Hey, Jack. We got a hit. I'm changing course." He shifted the propellers and increased the power.

"Ben," Jack said through the earbud, "I tried to call you a second ago, but you didn't answer. Chantal's been watching activity on the security guy's computer pad. They're on our tail."

"How far behind?"

"Three miles and closing. Hey, I was about to catch up and get in your face. Why didn't you answer?"

"I had to investigate a security matter, so I shut the bud down for a minute."

"Oh, I get it," Jack said. "Leo's kind of squirrely, isn't he? I wouldn't trust him either. Or is it Iona?"

"Talk to you about it later. Just keep me up to date on the HQ drones."

"I will, but I'm wondering about angel HQ knowing we have a computer pad. We might be getting bad intel."

"In other words, they might be a lot closer or coming from another direction."

"Exactly."

"Can we feed them bad intel?" Ben asked. "Make them think we're somewhere we're not?"

"I'll work on it. But maintain speed. We don't want them to think we're spooked."

"Got it."

After a minute or so, Leo shifted to his knees and looked out the front window as he continued sniffing. "Veer a bit more to your left. We have about three and a half miles to go. That is, if it's a fertilizer factory. If it's a farm with livestock, it's much closer, perhaps a mile."

Ben repeated the information to Jack.

"Good," Jack said, "but feeding them false locations isn't getting them off our tail. Better for you to land, shut down, and let me lead them away."

Trudy shook her head hard. "That's divide and conquer. Don't do it."

"Agreed," Leo said. "The worst strategy. Better to both land. We can walk the rest of the way."

Ben turned the earbud off. "But they'll track our heat signatures. We can't get away from them on foot."

"They won't scan for us if these drones take off like scared jackrabbits, if you know what I'm saying."

"Program them to scat on their own."

Leo winked. "Farm Boy's got some serious brains."

Trudy raised a finger. "But don't tell Jack what we're planning. Just tell him to land."

"I'm with you," Ben said as he searched the controls. "I'll program this drone to go in one direction, then when we land, I'll program the other to scram in another direction."

Iona pressed a thumb against her chest. "And I'll watch Chantal to see if she squeals to HQ on the computer pad."

"Be careful," Trudy said. "You can't just peek over her shoulder."

"You're right about that. I'd have to stand on a stump to see over Miss Statuesque. But don't worry. I've got it covered."

Ben powered up the earbud. "Jack, I'll find a place to land. Join me there."

"Then what? The drones are within two miles now. If we stop, they'll be on us in a flash."

"Trust me. I have a plan."

"Okay, Ben. You're the boss."

Ben scanned the forest treetops. Soon, a small clearing appeared, barely visible in the scant moonlight. "I found a spot. Everyone get ready to gather your stuff."

He veered the drone into the clearing and landed. The moment they touched down, Trudy, Leo, and Iona collected the rifles and the medical bag while Ben finished programming the drone. A moment later, Jack's drone settled next to theirs.

Ben set his drone to take off in twenty seconds, then, a flashlight in hand, ran to Jack's and waved an arm. "Get out! Hurry!"

In a rush, Jack, Kat, and Chantal climbed out, Jack's wings snagging in the doorway for a second in the rush. Ben leaped in and programmed the drone to fly away. As it began to rise, he jumped to the ground.

One second later, his own drone rose, and the two units turned in opposite directions and zoomed away.

Jack waved his arms at Ben. "What in blazes are you doing?"

Ben glanced at Chantal as she bent low while Iona spoke into her ear. He pointed a rigid finger at Leo. "He tipped off SkySweep. He's been dropping his little smoke bombs like a trail of breadcrumbs. I set our drones to send them on a wild goose chase."

Jack stormed over to Leo and glared at him nearly nose to nose. "Who's paying you to sabotage us?"

Leo backed away. "All lies. Your brother discovered that the bombs were missing from your sister's stash. They thought I've been dropping them because they can't explain why we're being followed."

"Then where did you put them?" Trudy asked, her voice hard.

"Nowhere, Miss Muscles." Leo flicked on a flashlight. "I haven't seen them since they were confiscated."

Jack waved a hand. "Never mind. We have to bug out. The other drones know where we landed, so one of them will do a quick scan here before it joins the chase for the other two."

Leo whispered to Ben, "Stick to the same heading."

"Got it. Stay at my side." Ben slung on a plasma rifle while Trudy grabbed an X99. He hurried over to Kat and guided her to the front of the group, her gait still a bit wobbly. "Everyone follow me."

He marched ahead. When they left the clearing, they trudged into a morass of smilax and scrub trees that snagged and scratched their clothes.

Far to the rear, the hum of a drone filled the air. Ben looked back. The familiar red light flashed into the clearing, too far away to detect the troop of fugitives. After a few seconds, the light turned off, and the drone zipped into the darkness.

Leo caught up with Ben and Kat and walked at Ben's side, saying nothing as he stared straight ahead.

"Follow your nose?" Ben asked.

"If you trust me, Farm Boy, yes."

Ben raised his voice a notch so the others could hear. "I'm not sure if we can trust you, but we don't have much choice."

Kat hooked her arm into his and whispered, "I know you, Ben. And Trudy. You can't hide anything from me. Just remember, Jack's not stupid. He's going to figure this out before long."

Ben turned off his earbud and lowered his voice. "He's not the one we're worried about."

"But the one you are worried about has her hooks sunk deep into your brother. I know. I rode with them. But I'll see what I can do to keep the two separated while Iona works on Chantal."

Ben smiled. "I told my coconspirators that you'd figure it out."

"It's not hard. Your acting won't win any awards, but Jack's not focusing on you, so we'll see how long the charade will last."

"Chantal," Iona said in a low tone as she picked up her pace to walk next to the taller woman, "did Jack tell you about me? I mean, my dark side?"

Chantal kept her voice low as well. "That you were a double agent? Yes, he mentioned it. Why?"

"I don't think they trust me. The Garrisons, I mean. You know, like maybe I could turn on them at any minute."

"I can relate. They're really tight. If you're not in their inner circle, you might feel like an outcast."

"Yeah. An outcast. I definitely feel it." Iona gave Chantal a quick visual scan. Although neither had a flashlight, the moon offered enough light to provide a decent view. She appeared to be carrying no weapons, but something small caused a slight bulge behind her shirt at the back near her pants waistline. Also, she kept glancing at the computer pad in her hand as if she wanted to use it.

Iona concealed a grin. *Too bad, honey. You're stuck in this conversation until you let something slip.* "Is that why you're kissing up to Jack? To get into the inner circle?"

Chantal laughed under her breath. "My, aren't you the tactful one."

"Just being honest. I know I look young, but you can't survive in our business without pulling whatever strings you need to pull."

"*Our* business?" Chantal huffed. "I'm not a double agent, Hon. I've been on the rebels' lead field squad ever since the angels showed their glowing little butts in our world."

"That's cool. And it must be nice. I'm too new on the rebel side to be trusted." Iona shrugged. "Anyway, if you snag Jack, that's a nice prize. He's pretty hot, and you'll automatically get into the inner circle."

Chantal gave Iona the kind of smile a spy uses to hide her feelings. "So you think he's hot?"

"Well, yeah. Any girl can see that. Not that I'm trying to muscle in, though. I'm too young, and you're both out of my league."

Chantal glanced at the pad, then looked straight ahead and chuckled. "Okay, kid, what's your game?"

Iona concealed a wince. She had overplayed her innocence routine. Chantal was too experienced to fall for it. "My game? What do you mean?"

"Don't play dumb. Like you said, you can't survive in our business without pulling strings, and you're tugging on mine like a bulldog. What's your angle? What are you fishing for?"

"I want them to trust me. I figured you got your foot in the door. Maybe I could squeeze in behind you before it shuts."

"But why do you need in? You're already in the game. You're participating."

"I'm just tagging along because I showed up. You know, the lost little girl who escaped the huntsmen. An abandoned puppy. I want them to trust me to do something big."

"Like what?"

"I don't know yet. But when the time comes and I volunteer, I want one of them to point at me and say go for it."

Chantal thinned her lips. "Okay. I can buy that."

Iona looked her over once more. Her facial muscles were still tense. She didn't really buy it. Not yet. "What about you? Why are you trying to get in?"

Chantal continued staring straight ahead. After a long moment, she sighed. "Because Jack Garrison needs me."

"Needs you? Why?"

She shook her head as if casting off a thought. "Never mind that. But you can keep clinging to me like a leech if you must. If Jack lets me into their inner circle, I'll help you get in."

"Okay. Great. When do you think you'll know you're in?"

Chantal halted, crouched, and pulled Iona down with her. Her strong hand clamping her wrist, she whispered with a hiss. "Listen, kid. I'm on to you. I know you already have an in. You've been to the weapon location. The Garrisons need you. So why are you grilling me?"

Iona bit her lip hard. *Busted!* Ahead, the others were nearly out of sight in the dark forest. This recovery would have to be quick. "Once they find the weapon, they won't need me. They'll cast me off like used toilet paper. I want to be a permanent part of the team."

Chantal rolled her eyes. "Yeah, right. Give me a break. I know your kind. You're a solo artist, and you love it."

"Oh, really?" Iona flashed her a hot stare. It was time to go for broke. "Then why did you take Novada instead of Laramel?"

As Chantal blinked, her mouth dropped open.

Iona firmed her jaw. Time to reel the fish in. "You thought no one knew the difference, didn't you? Well, I guess you're not the super slick spy you think you are." She held her hand out. "So where's the vial? I think we should scan it again."

"I ... I don't have it. I left it at angel headquarters."

Iona drew her head back. "You did what?"

"Shhh!" Chantal pulled Iona to a standing position. "You can't let anyone else know."

"Well, they're out of earshot, so no worries about that. And we'd better get going or we'll never catch up."

"All right." Chantal began striding through the underbrush. "Stay with me, and I'll explain."

Iona jogged behind her, eyeing her long legs and the bulge at the back of her shirt. She closed the gap and tangled her legs with Chantal's, and they toppled into a headlong fall. When they hit the ground, Iona reached behind Chantal and pulled the object from her waistband, a small plastic bag with tiny wriggling red worms that seemed to glow. She stealthily tucked the bag into her pocket.

"I'm so sorry," Iona said as she leaped to her feet and extended a hand. "It's dark, and I was trying to catch up."

"Yeah. I know. It's okay." Grabbing Iona's wrist and jeans pocket, Chantal climbed to her feet. "But we still have to hurry." She broke into a fast march, her jeans brushing against dense foliage. "Now listen carefully. My story is complicated."

Iona jogged at her side. "Yeah. I'll bet. This ought to be good."

After Chantal related a quick version of her mission to infiltrate angel headquarters, Iona stared at her. "How did you read the encrypted messages without Novada knowing the real meaning?"

"The messages always had two meanings, a fake one and a real one. I helped Novada interpret the fake message while keeping the real one to myself. The fake ones always led the angels on a wild-goose chase trying to find the weapon. Barks was smart enough to leave clues that made it look like the weapon might have once been where the fake messages led them."

"Okay. That's cool. But what was your exit strategy, your end game? How did you plan to get extracted so you could get the secrets to Barks? I mean, you did get extracted, but you didn't know it was going to happen."

"You're right. I didn't know. But once I was sure about the Refectors ..." Chantal glanced at Iona. "Do you know about them?"

"Just what you said to Ben. He told me the story while you and Jack were fetching the SkySweep drones."

"Good. Well, anyway, I planned to send a message about the Refectors to Barks, encoded the same way. Novada would think I was saying something else."

"So Novada knew you were a rebel agent."

Chantal nodded. "I pretended to become a loyalist, and she made me a double agent, or so she thought."

"Sounds familiar."

"Anyway," Chantal continued, "I didn't think I would ever be extracted, but when I woke up and realized Novada was gone, I noticed that the homing orb was missing. That's why I left her vial at angel HQ to be re-implanted. She's drawn to the orb, so I know she's found it by now, and I need her to bring it to me."

"Why?"

"So I can do what I was hoping to fool her into doing while I was still implanted."

"And what is that?"

Chantal smiled. "You are a nosey one, aren't you?"

Iona smiled in return. "Just trying to learn from the best spy in the business."

"Ah. Flattery at its finest." Chantal's expression turned serious. "Okay, fellow spy, I'll let you in on my plan, but I'd better start at the beginning, four years ago."

Chapter Twenty-Six

Jack checked the path to the rear. Chantal and Iona were nowhere in sight. "Ben. Wait."

The sound of marching feet ceased. "We've lost two. Chantal and Iona."

Ben hustled back. "When was the last time you saw them?"

"Not more than a minute ago."

Leo joined them and sniffed. "They're not far. Maybe fifty paces. And they're together. Getting closer."

After a few seconds, new rustling sounds drew near. Ben aimed his flashlight that way. Chantal broke between two bushes, followed by Iona. "Sorry we fell behind," Chantal said, out of breath as she arrived. "We got into a conversation and didn't realize we were lagging."

Jack set a hand on Chantal's shoulder. "No harm done, but we'd better pick up the pace. The drone operators know by now that we pulled a fast one on them."

Leo sniffed again. "It's clear to me that the ammonia is from a fertilizer manufacturing outfit, but it is rather stale, as if production has not been recent."

"Probably because growing season is pretty much over," Ben said.

Leo looked at Iona. "When you were in the room with the weapon, did you smell the ammonia there?"

She shook her head. "No ammonia. It smelled like ... tea, maybe?"

Leo threw his hands up. "By Orion's belt, why didn't you mention that before?"

"I just thought someone was drinking tea nearby."

"Have you detected the aroma of tea?" Jack asked Leo.

He nodded toward Chantal. "On her breath. Angel tea. She probably drank some in the last several hours."

"I did," Chantal said. "All the angels drink it. Supposedly it makes the implantation firmer. And it's excellent tea, the best in the world. Expensive, though. Difficult to grow, I hear."

"Any source other than that?" Jack asked Leo.

"No, but if I had smelled tea, I wouldn't have mentioned it. It wasn't on my list of things to smell for." Leo glared at Iona. She seemed to melt under his fierce stare. "I will now, seeing that our firecracker decided to leak a little more information."

Jack, Zachariel said, *the issue is plain to see. Iona is slow with dispensing information because she thinks when she tells everything she knows, she will no longer have any value to our cause or to the people here.*

Jack nodded. *Got it.*

"Okay, Iona," he said, bending to look her in the eye. "you need to come clean. What else do you remember? Don't keep anything from us."

She pushed a stray lock of hair back and took in a deep breath. "I've told you everything I know."

Jack crouched and caressed her cheek, the same way he used to with Alana. She flinched for a moment, then let the touch continue. "Iona, I once had a daughter, and I loved her very much. I still do and always will even though she's out of my reach. Trust me, no matter what, I won't forsake you. Please, think again. Put yourself in that room. What did you see, hear, smell, or feel?"

"Okay. I'll try. But I'm sick of being treated like a kid." When Jack withdrew his hand, Iona closed her eyes. "I'll replay the day in my mind."

Ben leaned close to Jack. "I hope this doesn't take too long. Those drones won't give up."

"I think it'll be worth the time."

"I'm ready." Iona kept her eyes closed. "Like I told Ben in my note, I was spying for the angels, and I got wind that the weapon location was in the map area I sent to Ben. When Commander Barks and a big rebel soldier found me in the forest, they blindfolded me and took me in a jeep to a place they called the bunker.

"Before they guided me in, the sun warmed my right cheek, and a breeze cooled my left. The ammonia odor came and went as the breeze strengthened or slacked off. The tea smell, though, was always there. When we walked through a door, it got darker and cooler, and we went down some stairs, maybe twenty or so. They felt like wood, but I had shoes on, so I'm not sure. But I remember that most of them squeaked. The handrail was definitely made of wood, rough and splintery, not real solid. The floor at the bottom felt uneven but hard like concrete. The air was cool. No sun or breeze, of course, because we were probably underground.

"I heard a man ask who I was, and Barks said he'd tell him later. That man had kind of a deep voice, like he was older. I'm not sure. Anyway, they led me through what felt like another doorway, maybe to a hall. I had to step up, and I felt the lighting dim a little. Then they turned me to the right. A door closed, and someone took the blindfold off. The room was small with a low cot, a thin pillow, a table with a battery lamp, and a wooden chair next to the cot. Commander Barks sat in the chair holding the blindfold. He nodded toward the cot and told me to sit.

"So I did. That's when we had our talk about me becoming a spy for the rebels. It didn't take much persuading. I was already being mistreated at the temple and felt like a prisoner there except when they sent me out on missions. And Barks was nice to me. He could've had me killed. I'm sure the angels would've killed me in the same situation.

"Anyway, after we finished talking, I laid on the cot and tried to go to sleep. I smelled the tea but no ammonia. I suppose they might have been drinking tea in another room. It was pretty strong. Since I was exhausted, I went to sleep quick. After maybe five hours, Barks woke me. He gave me a slice of cornbread on a paper plate and a bottle of water. I didn't smell any other food or even tea, so I guess that's all he had to give me.

"Then he blindfolded me again and led me out. I didn't hear anyone else. After we climbed the stairs, we went back outside. I smelled ammonia and tea again but not as strong as before. Then Barks helped me get back in the jeep. He drove me to the city limits, and I walked to the temple from there."

Iona opened her eyes. "Does any of that help?"

"Concrete floor was rough," Ben said. "Quick slab pour with no trowels. They did it in a hurry."

"The stairs weren't reinforced," Jack added. "No sanding of the rail. Another sign of hurry."

Trudy raised a finger. "The deep-voiced man had to be Doc, and the brewing indicates an electricity source. We can work that angle."

"Did you hear a generator?" Ben asked Iona.

She shook her head. "I didn't smell one either."

"Then maybe a long electrical cord to Barks's jeep."

"Or another vehicle that Doc had there," Trudy said.

Leo stroked his chin. "Okay, then. I will see if I can follow ammonia, tea, and a vehicle, which means fuel, grease, and motor oil. But it's a long shot."

"Since they did the job in a hurry," Jack said, "they might have sawn boards scattered around. The stairs squeaked and the rail had splinters, so maybe pine."

"The pine will be easy if the boards have been sawed recently. If not ..." Leo shrugged. "I'll do my best."

Chantal sidled close to Jack. "That was really impressive. No wonder you and your siblings were assigned together."

Jack smiled. "Yeah. We're pretty much inseparable. We know how each other thinks."

"I wish I could be in a group like that." Chantal gestured toward Iona. "She and I hit it off. I think we'd both be a great part of your team. Maybe after this is over we can talk about ongoing alliances."

"Um ... sure. But we'd better stop talking and—"

"Kat?" Ben hustled toward her. She sat on a fallen log, her head low. He knelt in front of her and rubbed her shoulder. "Are you all right?"

She massaged the back of her head. "I feel it. The spawn thing. It's attaching."

Ben turned to Trudy and snapped his fingers. "Leo's AngelScan! Quick!"

"On it." Trudy grabbed the medical bag and dug through it. When she fished the scanner out, she crouched next to Ben and set the disk on Kat's forehead. The light flicked on, and Trudy set her eyes close. "I see the little demon. It's still small, but it's attaching." She drew back, blinking. "The scanner says it's Laramel."

Jack eyed Trudy's expression. Her surprise seemed kind of fake.

Chantal edged closer. "The spawns have the same ID code. The scanner can't tell the difference."

Jack joined her. "How many other spawns has Laramel produced?"

"Novada's the only one I know about."

"You had a Laramel spawn in you?" Jack asked.

Chantal nodded. "The queen's spawned princess. It's why the two were so close. In fact, Novada is able to locate her mother with a sixth sense sort of power. That's how she found Jack in the refuge."

"Good to know," Ben said.

Trudy removed the disk from Kat and showed it to Chantal. "So the angel inside you would've scanned as Laramel on this."

"I assume so. Is that important?"

"It confirms a theory, but I can't worry about that now." Trudy dug into the medical bag and withdrew the used extraction kit. "We need a fire to sterilize the instruments."

"A fire will reveal where we are," Leo said. "Risky."

"Hang the risk. Kat's life is at stake. Just give me fire and one assistant."

264

Ben raised his flashlight. "I'm staying. The rest of you keep heading for the bunker. And hurry. This place won't be safe in a few minutes."

"You're right." Jack waved a wing. "Everyone else, let's hustle."

Leo pointed into the forest with his flashlight. "I'll lead the way. I've got a good fix on the ammonia." He jogged into the underbrush.

Jack hustled behind him, tearing vines with an X99 as he glanced back. Chantal and Iona followed, whispering to each other as they high-stepped over the trampled plants.

As Jack faced ahead again, Zachariel spoke up. *Your conversations have been intriguing of late. Are you concerned?*

Jack continued hacking at the thorny vines. "Should I be?"

Trudy is concerned. Perhaps her anxiety is related to her insistence on how to divide your team into the two drones. She clearly lacks trust in Chantal, and when Chantal revealed that Laramel's spawns have identical identification coding, it raised an alarm in Trudy.

"I noticed the alarm. But it was weird. I haven't had time to figure it all out. I know Trudy doesn't trust most people, especially people who want to break into our little huddle. She's kind of … possessive, I guess. Ever since our parents died in the plague, she wants us three to be together as much as possible. No outsiders."

And Chantal wants in, so Trudy has an immediate distrust.

"Exactly."

And Iona? You opened a door to her that you cannot possibly close now.

"Yeah. I realize that. No regrets. I like her a lot. Like a little sister, I mean. Or a daughter. I haven't figured out how old she is yet."

I suspect that she is younger than twenty. My point, however, is that Trudy does not seem suspicious of Iona. She allowed Iona into the same drone with her and Ben. Therefore, she is suspicious of one newcomer and not the other. Her reasons are likely sound.

"Are you saying that I should be suspicious of Chantal?"

Not necessarily suspicious. Watchful. Wary. You might have noticed that her attention toward you has been beyond the norm.

"I noticed. And I'll be watchful, but I think you're off base. At the end of all of this, you'll see."

I am the angel of last chances, so I am not one to judge prematurely. I agree that you should let events play out. She is risking her life being with you, which is a positive sign.

"More than just a positive—"

"Shhh!" Ahead, Leo raised a halting hand, then turned his flashlight off.

When the others joined him, he gathered everyone into a huddle and whispered, "Human scent plus wings other than Jack's. We have an angel patrol ahead."

"How far?" Jack asked, his voice so quiet he could barely hear it himself.

"No more than a hundred paces. And I smell the tea. It's not brewed. It's alive. Growing."

"A tea farm?"

Leo nodded. "I'm not the boss here, Wing Man, but maybe you could get an aerial view. See what we're up against."

"Can't argue with that." Jack scanned the sky toward the east, mostly blocked by treetops, though it appeared to be lighter than before. "I'd better hurry. It'll be dawn soon." Beating his wings, Jack launched into the air, dodged the bigger limbs, and pushed past smaller branches until he broke into the clear.

The moment Jack flew out of sight, Iona looked at Leo and Chantal. "So do we just wait here?"

"What choice do we have, Fireplug?" Leo sat on a flat boulder. "The soldiers wait for reconnaissance. It's standard procedure to get a safety clearance."

"We can't wait," Chantal said. "She's coming. I can sense her."

Iona squinted. "*She?* Who's *she?*"

"Someone I didn't tell you about. All you need to know is that I'm being followed, and I have to keep moving." Chantal strode away. "Leo. Iona. If you want to join me, come. I can smell the ammonia myself now. I'm going to find that weapon."

Iona looked at Leo. "Should we go with her?"

"Well, we can't let her go alone." He rose from the boulder. "I'm sure Jack can find us. He'll have a bird's eye view."

They jogged after Chantal, Leo leading the way. Iona looked into the sky, but Jack was nowhere in sight, and darkness would make it nearly impossible for him to find them. She had to leave a trail, something easy to see.

With Chantal now in sight and Leo seconds away from catching up with her, Iona slowed to a quick walk and withdrew the bag she had taken from Chantal. She tipped out one of the glowworms and set it on the ground, hoping it would stay in plain sight, then resumed jogging, staying several paces behind.

Iona eyed Chantal's marching form—quick and unyielding. Whatever she was up to, it had to be super important, and leaving a trail for Jack while jogging to keep up wouldn't be easy. But it had to be done, and no one else could do it.

As Jack flew higher, the forest border came into view, dim in the morning twilight. Beyond it lay at least ten acres of greenery with cultivated plants in neat rows, most likely tea plants. At a swath of bare terrain between the forest and the farm, a winged man paced with a rifle in hand as if on sentry duty.

Jack reversed course and looked in the direction they had come. No drones flew in sight. By now, the angels knew they were in the general area. If this tea farm was important enough to guard, maybe the angels thought it was the target of the rebels who had stolen two drones. If so, they should have beefed up their defenses by now. An ambush was not out of the question.

"Ben," Jack said, "got your ears on?"

"Yeah, but it's scratchy. You must be more than a mile away."

"Close to two. How's Kat?"

"Anxious. In pain. Trudy's prepping her for surgery now."

"What about suture thread?"

"She'll try to reuse what's already there, saving what she cuts. It's the only choice we have."

"Keep me informed. I'm flying reconnaissance and found a tea farm with an angel guard. I'm going to have a chat with him. Just wanted to let someone know."

"Got it. Call back when you can."

"Will do." Jack flew across the remaining expanse of forest and descended toward the angel guard, calling, "Don't be alarmed. I am an ally."

The guard backed away, holding the rifle with both hands. Young and trim with his face aglow, he was probably a Gen Two. "Who are you?" he asked.

Jack landed in front of him. "No time for pleasantries. I am on a special assignment from Queen Laramel. How many guards are here?"

"I'm the only one. It's just a tea farm, but we have to make sure the rebels don't try to infuse something toxic into the crop."

"Have you had to chase any away?"

He shook his head. "I think this would be a low-priority target. They test the tea after it's harvested, so my job is kind of redundant, more like a punishment than anything. I doubt that the rebels even know about this little farm."

"Yeah. It's kind of innocuous." Jack inhaled. The ammonia odor was strong here. "Except for the smell."

"A special kind of fertilizer we manufacture for the plants." He nodded toward a small building on one side of the farm. "Over there. Stinks to high heaven. I stay away. I mean, fertilizer would never be a rebel target, right?"

Jack smiled. "No. It's really just bags of crap."

"True." The guard rested his rifle on his shoulder. "So why are you here?"

"I am rounding up everyone who is on nonessential assignments. We need to quell an attack at headquarters. The rebel vermin broke our communications encryption, so we can't call through normal channels. You are to fly at once to HQ and join our forces to squash the rodents once and for all."

The angel smiled. "That's great. I'll be glad to get away from the stench."

"I don't blame you. And whatever you do, stay off the normal comm channels. We don't want the rebels to know that we're massing everyone to put them down for good."

He beat his wings and rose slowly. "What are you going to do?"

"Fly to a remote station to recruit another soldier. I will be there soon."

"Hail to the queen!" He flew off over the forest.

Jack shook his head. "Gullible freak."

Remember that a human soul likely resides within, a victim imprisoned by a monster.

"Yeah. Keep reminding me. It's hard to see past the monster." Jack vaulted into the air. "Ben, the farm's clear. There's a building where they manufacture a special fertilizer for the tea. That's probably what Iona smelled and what Leo's following, so the weapon location has to be nearby."

A reply crackled in his ear, too scratchy to distinguish.

"Ben, I didn't read that. Are you there?"

More wordless static responded.

"Can't worry about that now." Jack beat his wings harder and zoomed back to the spot where he had left the others. When he landed, he scanned the area. They were nowhere in sight. Why would they leave? Maybe they heard someone coming, and they had to bolt.

He searched the ground for clues. Gaps in the debris led in the direction they had been traveling. As he followed the trail, he came across something that glittered.

Bending, he snatched the tiny object and set it on his fingertip. A red wormlike creature wriggled on the pad, no larger than a curve in his fingerprint. With his thumb, he squeezed the creature, but it continued wriggling, unaffected by the pressure.

He sloughed it off and continued following the trail, but when he came to a clear area, the lack of debris made the trail vanish. Yet, another red glimmer appeared several paces ahead.

Jack scooped it up—the same kind of glowing worm. A closer look revealed that one end had a ragged break. This was a piece of a larger creature.

"Zachariel, am I dreaming or is this part of an angel? You know, a piece of a tentacle."

I am no expert on fake-angel anatomy, but based on its semi-physical appearance, I think you're right.

"Chantal had an angel in a vial. I think she's leaving me a trail." Jack forged ahead, his stare on the ground as he searched for more red glimmers. A third came into view atop a stone. Not bothering to pick it up, he continued. A fourth lay on an exposed root. It seemed that she was placing them where they would be easy to see. Good for her. He could pick up the pace.

As he plowed through the forest, he glanced between the ground and the woods ahead. Whether or not they were fleeing or were in the hands of captors, they couldn't have gotten far. Of course, he could fly and try to intercept them somewhere, maybe the tea plantation itself, but if they were captives, they might not be heading in that direction, and staying on foot was the only way to find the trail.

No matter. He would probably catch up soon, and with a plasma rifle strapped on, he would be ready to do a lot of damage.

Chapter Twenty-Seven

Ben added twigs to their campfire, a circle no bigger than a hand's breadth. Kneeling, Trudy drew the end of the scalpel out of the flames. "I hope it's sterile."

"Is that the last instrument?" Ben asked.

"Yep." She rose and walked toward Kat where she lay supine on the ground, both hands over her eyes. "I'll sedate her and get started."

"Good." Ben stamped out the fire and scattered the embers. "Let's get it done."

Trudy knelt at Kat's side. "I'm running on empty, but I'll manage."

Ben looked up at the brightening sky. "It's almost daybreak. We've been up all night."

"And no rest in the near future." Trudy touched Kat's shoulder. "It's time. I'll help you roll over."

When Kat turned to her stomach, Trudy withdrew a sterile pad from the extraction kit and swabbed behind Kat's ear at the same spot she had cut earlier. "Ben? Have you heard from Jack lately?"

"Got a surge of static. He must be out of range." Ben knelt next to Trudy with a flashlight in hand. "I'm ready to assist."

"One second." She put the pad away and picked up a tranquilizer dart. "Since we don't have the shotguns anymore, I removed the darts from the cartridges. It took only one to keep her asleep last time, but I wanted to be sure, so they're all available. One dose doesn't last very long."

"Just put me under and get it done," Kat said. "That spawn's clawing at me like a maniac. Maybe it's too young to know what it's doing."

"We'll have it out in a few minutes. Get ready for a sting." Trudy injected the anesthetic into Kat's neck, raising a twinge in Kat. Seconds later, her body relaxed. "She's out." Trudy put the dart away and lifted the scalpel. "Okay, demon seed, here I come."

A new voice broke in. "Don't you dare!"

Ben whipped the rifle off his back and jumped to his feet. A woman stood nearby, three armed guards at each side. Although her face glowed, she had no wings. "Drop your weapon," the woman said calmly. "If you fight, my guards will shoot. Your sister will be the first target."

Ben set the rifle on the ground and eyed the newcomer. She looked like the surgeon who was supposed to implant them. "Dr. Elder?"

She smiled. "I am no longer the surgeon you knew. Yet, you do know me. I am royalty."

Ben spotted the glowing spherical pendant dangling at Dr. Elder's chest. Apparently, Chantal had delivered Novada's vial to the angels, too recently to allow time for wings to grow on the new host. "So Princess Novada, what do you want from us?"

"My mother and my sister. I arrived in time to overhear that you extracted my mother, but not before she replicated. Of course, I had to stop the surgery. And now it will be good to have Katherine on our side again."

Ben turned toward Kat, still lying on her stomach. Trudy cast a glance at the extraction kit, then gave him an alarmed stare. What had she noticed?

"Come, my sister," Novada said to Kat. "We will be reunited with our mother soon."

Trudy set a hand on Kat's back. "She can't get up. She's sedated for surgery."

"I will verify your claim."

As Novada walked closer, Trudy rose and sidled to Ben. "The vial holding Laramel is gone. And one of my scalpels is missing."

He nodded but said nothing.

With the armed guards watching, Novada crouched at Kat's side and looked her over. "My sister has attached. Maybe she will be able to awaken her host soon." Novada straightened and held out her hand. "Give me my mother."

"She's not here," Ben said, "but we know where she is."

"Do you expect me to fall for that ploy?" Novada gestured toward her men. "Three of you stand guard while the other three search them and their belongings as well as the surrounding bushes."

A trio of guards rifled through the medical bag, patted Ben and Trudy down, and combed the area while one confiscated Trudy's X99 and searched the bushes for other weapons.

When they found no sign of Laramel, Novada clenched her jaw. "I assume you realize that I can extract my sister from a corpse."

Ben glared at her but said nothing.

"Yet, I prefer to persuade you in a less messy way." Novada barked at her men. "Strip search them both. Start with the girl."

Ben lunged for Novada. One of the guards fired a plasma sphere that splashed on the ground at his feet and sent arcs of radiance across his legs and abdomen. The energy burned holes in his pants and shirt and sizzled on his skin like boiling oil.

"Argh!" He swatted at the burning spots, rubbing his clothes across the wounds. "If you strip search my sister, you'll never learn where I put Laramel. I swear it."

Novada hummed a laugh. "Your sentiment is quite touching to humans, I'm sure. I don't care about your feelings one way or another, but there are ways to learn what I need to know without a strip search. I have the ability to read your mind."

"All right," Ben said. "If that's the choice. Go ahead."

Trudy scowled. "Ben, you don't have to protect me. I can handle it."

"I know, but when they don't find Laramel, Novada will just make more threats. Maybe when she sees that I'm telling the truth, she'll stop."

"The truth," Novada said, "is all I seek." She turned toward a guard. "Cease the search. Have your weapons ready while I probe this rebel for answers."

Novada strode to Ben with a confident gait. As she looked at him, their eyes connected in an invisible lock. Her orbs seemed to elongate and pierce his own, warm and moist, like a saline eyewash. Seconds later, her voice penetrated, at one moment near his left ear, then another moment at his right, as if echoing in stereo, a feminine tone more soothing than Dr. Elder's.

Benjamin Garrison, where is Laramel? If you know, as you have stated, I will learn eventually. Make this process easier for both of us.

Ben set up a blockade in his mind, allowing only his whispered words to escape. "We had Laramel in a vial, but someone took it. We're not sure who."

Interesting. I sense that you are telling the truth but not the whole truth. You have a suspect. Who do you think took the vial?

The answer slipped through Ben's blockade, but he pushed the name into a different context. "When you were implanted in Chantal, you tried to kill us. If I tell you everything I know, you'll try again."

I wounded your sister. I was trying to capture you, not kill you. Then it was you who sliced my throat. And it was you who deceived our soldiers with fake vaccine with the intent to kill them all. If anyone is ruthless, it is you.

"I was defending my family and friends. The soldiers were going to kill us."

And I am trying to rescue my family from you, which is why I arrived here with a threatening posture. I apologize for that. Give me Laramel, and I will take every angel to another world. We left ours because it became uninhabitable, and we came here, but we could not survive the environment without possessing human bodies. I have located another world where we can live in peace without possessing anyone.

"How can I believe you? How do I know it's not all a lie?"

By a pledge. I will allow you to extract my sister spawn from your wife. You can keep her in a vial. In exchange, you will tell me where my mother is.

"What happens when you retrieve your mother? Do you expect me to give your sister back to you?"

Yes. Not implanted in your wife, of course. The vial will do. In fact, once we are reunited with our family and allies, my forces will fall back, a move that you can verify. Then you can leave the vial in a safe place and retreat to whichever hideaway you choose. Once we collect it, we will leave this world, and you will never have to concern yourselves with us again.

"How will you travel to the other world?"

By the same means we traveled to this one. Through the Oculus Gate. Your own commander and the very same Dr. Elder I am inhabiting combined their knowledge and that of a brilliant scientist. The trio created a conduit to bring our species here. I have deduced that the technology is the basis for the weapon we have been seeking. My mother wants to destroy it. I want to use it to help us leave. My guess is that the weapon would break our connection to the Oculus Gate, which would bring about our demise.

"And what of the Refectors we heard about?"

They plan to come by the same conduit, which would have to stay in place until we leave. If you destroy the conduit, you will kill us all, and we would not be able to escape your world.

"I don't see the downside to that option."

If the conduit fails, every human that we inhabit will also die. If you follow my plan, I will be able to use the homing orb to draw all of us to the queen. They will peacefully leave the humans they inhabit and join us. Otherwise, a broken conduit will cause them to die within the human brains, which would kill the hosts.

"How does that work? I mean, how does she draw all the angels?"

Once the queen is in the conduit's energy, the homing orb, which houses material from our native world, irresistibly draws all angels to her. They emerge from the bodies they inhabit and stream to her in mere seconds.

A hive reforms around her, and the angels inhabit its cells until we can disperse again in the other world.

"And what will your mother say about your plan?"

She need not know. Once we get to a new world, I will deal with the consequences of my actions.

"So you want to become my ally. The alien who ordered a strip search of my sister will be on the same side with the man who slit her host's throat. And I'm supposed to believe that?"

Humans have a saying—desperate times call for desperate measures. I am willing if you are willing. Remember, if you accept this arrangement, I will allow you to extract the spawn from your wife, and you will have her back in your arms. My perception is that you value her above all others.

As Novada's soothing words penetrated, Ben steeled himself. She was powerful, persuasive. If his mental training was ever going to rescue him, now was the time. Since all angels were liars, he had to focus on what was true and search for a way to escape. "You're right. I do value my wife over all others."

So are you agreeing to my proposal?

Ben glanced at the medical bag lying on the ground near Kat. The goons had taken their weapons but maybe not the darts. They would have to serve as his emergency escape device.

Novada spoke with a purr. "I detect that you are plotting an escape. Do you think you can win a fight against an angel and six armed men? You will lose, and I will make sure your sister suffers great pain. Give me the information I want, and all will be well."

"You've really put me between a rock and a hard place."

"Another appropriate human saying and quite true, but the time for negotiating is over. I want your answer now."

"Well, we humans have yet another saying." He took a deep breath. "When pigs fly, you wingless sow."

Ben broke free from her eye lock, grabbed Trudy by the arm, and dashed with her to the medical bag. He snatched it up and sprinted with her deeper into the forest. The moment they ducked behind side-by-side trees big enough to cover them, plasma spheres rocketed in, some zipping past and some blasting the trunks, eating away at the bark.

Ben found five darts in the bag, leaned into the gap between himself and Trudy, and handed her two. A plasma ball zoomed by, heating his ear. Grimacing, he drew back.

"What now?" Trudy asked as she dodged plasma splatter. "We can't throw the darts that far."

"We just need to knock out Novada. The men are like robots. My guess is they're vaccinated. No implants. No souls. Once their master's on ice, they won't know what to do."

"Are you sure?"

"Not in the slightest. But even if they fight us because of the violence payload, they'll have no purpose. We can try to escape. I don't think they'll chase us."

"And you're not sure of that either."

"Nope."

Trudy sighed. "Best plan we've got. If we run and they do chase us, they probably have a speedy transport somewhere, that cruiser for royalty we saw."

"Right. We won't get far. And I'm not leaving without Kat. I don't think she's in danger at the moment. The sister spawn's still inside her."

"So do we pretend to surrender and throw the darts when we get close enough?"

Ben nodded. "And we don't have to be real close. I've seen you throw darts in the rec room."

"Within thirty feet ought to do it. I'll hit Novada. You go for one of the guards. I'll wait for your cue. Then we'll dive, roll, and the rest will be ad lib."

"And the ad lib includes rescuing Kat." Another plasma sphere blasted Ben's tree a foot above his head. The trunk gave way, and the upper portion toppled, hitting another tree and lodging at an angle. He tucked the darts behind his belt at the back. "We'd better do it now. Our trees won't last long."

Trudy did the same with her darts. "I'm ready."

"Wait!" Ben shouted. "Hold your fire! We surrender!"

The plasma balls ceased.

"Come forward with your hands high," Novada called.

Ben and Trudy raised their hands and walked out from behind the trees. A hundred feet ahead, the six men stood next to Kat's unconscious form, their rifles at the ready. To their left, Novada waited, her eyes trained on her new captives.

"Make your mind go blank," Ben said to Trudy as they walked slowly. "You know the training."

Trudy blinked at him. "I have no clue what you're talking about."

"Perfect."

When they drew within twenty feet or so, Novada said, "Halt right there."

Ben and Trudy stopped, their hands still raised.

Novada took a step closer. "Where is Laramel?"

"If we tell you," Ben said, "you'll kill us anyway."

Novada rolled her eyes. "This is getting tiresome. There is no bargaining to be done. Tell me what I want to know, or my men will—"

"Now!" Ben whipped a dart from his belt and slung it at a guard. Trudy plucked one of hers and threw it at Novada. Both darts hit their targets directly in the throat.

Ben and Trudy dove to the ground, Ben to the left, Trudy to the right. As they rolled, Ben looked back. A guard crumbled and fell to his stomach. Novada dropped to her knees. Her eyes blinking, she pointed at Kat, still on the ground. "Kill her. Now."

"No!" Ben leaped up and dashed toward Kat. Just as one of the men aimed his rifle at her, he slung a dart at him and threw himself over her.

Something flowed across his back. His skin burned, worse than acid, worse than flames. He twisted his neck and looked. His shirt was on fire, and the gunman had fallen.

Trudy snatched the man's rifle and shot him and the others in quick succession, then dropped to her knees next to Ben. "Don't worry," she said, gasping. "I'm here." As she slapped at the flames, new pain roared. He grimaced at each blow, gritting his teeth.

While Trudy worked, Ben checked Kat, lying motionless underneath. She breathed evenly, her eyes still closed. She seemed okay.

Trudy batted the last flame, then whistled. "Oh, man. Your back looks awful. Good thing it was a glancing blow or you'd have a hole straight through."

"Yeah. Good thing." He raised a hand. "Help me up."

After she pulled him to his feet, they scanned their surroundings. The clothes of the six men burned, the flames spreading to their bodies. Two lay motionless, while the other four writhed in pain. Ben found his X99 and fired a bullet into each man's head, then marched to Novada.

Lying on her back with the homing orb glowing at her chest, she looked at him, blinking, her eyes rolling as she seemed to be trying to stay awake. "Go ahead." She licked her lips. "You've been wanting to blow my brains out for quite a while, haven't you?"

"Not this time. Now I know you're implanted in a volunteer. You're staying locked inside." He set the barrel close to her chest and fired three bullets into her heart. She twitched, then quivered. After a few death throes, she closed her eyes and lay motionless.

He grabbed the orb and jerked it away, breaking its chain. "Let's search them for their transport's ignition key." After sliding the orb into his pocket, Ben patted down Novada, then helped Trudy check the men, though avoiding the remaining flames and melting skin made the process slow and difficult.

"Found something," Trudy said as she dug into a pants pocket. She withdrew a winged cylinder key and fisted it. "Let's find that cruiser."

Ben grasped Kat's wrists and hoisted her limp body over his shoulder. When her arms slapped against his scorched back, he winced.

"I'll take her," Trudy said. "She's not heavy."

"Thanks, but ..." He forced a smile through the pain. "I'm carrying my wife."

"Suit yourself." Trudy strapped on the X99 and a plasma rifle, picked up the medical bag, and pointed into the forest. "I think they came from this way."

As they walked side by side, Ben looked Trudy over—her strong, lean form, her confident gait, and her hardened expression. She was really amazing. "Great work back there. Thanks for saving me."

"No problem. You would've done the same for me."

"And you were right. You didn't flake out. You're a fantastic soldier."

Her lips firmed as if she were trying to hide a smile. "Thanks for saying so. Coming from the best soldier I've ever seen, that's a great compliment."

"Okay. No more warm fuzzies." Ben focused on the myriad trees ahead. "We have to extract Laramel's spawn, find Chantal, and see if we can figure out how to use the weapon, whatever it is. We've got a long way to go."

Chapter Twenty-Eight

Iona, along with Leo and Chantal, walked out of the forest and into a huge field filled with lush green plants. As they stepped along a divide between rows, Leo inhaled. "Tea as far as the eye can see."

Iona took in a long whiff. The tea smelled so good, and the ammonia scent no longer burned her throat. "This is definitely what I smelled, but the ammonia's fainter."

"The intensity depends on when they're making it, shoveling it into bags, spreading it in the field. This one's nearly ready for harvesting. No need for fertilizer until they plow again."

Chantal halted and pointed to her left. "See that building? The two-story wooden structure behind that line of trees?"

Leo shielded his eyes from the rising sun. "Most likely the fertilizer plant. The source of the odor is in that direction."

"Then it's not what we're looking for." Chantal rotated in place. "We're looking for a small structure, something inconspicuous."

"Are you saying the rebels hid a weapon to destroy all the angels right under the angels' noses? In a field of tea they guzzle by the gallon?" Leo laughed. "That's rich. Excellent irony."

Iona closed her eyes and again reimagined her journey to this place. She had come in the late afternoon when the sun would have been on the opposite side. She turned in the proper direction and opened her eyes. The building had to be that way.

"Follow me." She marched across the tea garden, trampling the plants. Beyond the opposite edge of the field, the forest continued, maybe fifty paces away.

The sound of rustling followed, Leo and Chantal trying to catch up. "Nothing but trees ahead," Chantal called. "That can't be the right direction."

"It has to be." When Iona reached the field's edge, she looked around. The forest lay only ten paces in front, a swath of thick straw separating the field from the trees, likely to keep weeds from growing and infesting the crop. Or maybe it was hiding something.

She slid a foot and swiped straw, uncovering bare ground. "Look for a trapdoor."

"Good thinking." Chantal joined the effort. "Leo, get to work. Your feet instead of your nose."

"Of course, Boss Lady." He began sweeping straw with his feet. "But I will keep my nose wary for unexpected arrivals."

After a minute or two, Iona's sweeping foot exposed a wood panel and handle with an attached rope. "I think I got it."

"Wait," Chantal said. "Don't open it yet." She jogged over and grasped the rope. "Leo, I'm going to open it a crack. Tell me what you smell."

Leo knelt at the panel's edge. "Ready."

When she lifted the door an inch or two, Leo inhaled. "Dried tea. Dust. Nothing alive but cockroaches and not many of those."

"Good." Chantal lifted the door the rest of the way and let it drop on the other side, revealing a set of wooden stairs that descended into darkness. "Let's see what's down there besides tea."

"The stairs creak," Iona said. "Let me go first. I'm the smallest. I'll make the least noise."

Leo held his rifle with both hands. "Noisy or not, I'm armed, and I have more battle experience. I should go first."

Iona snatched the rifle. "Now *I'm* armed. In case you think I can't shoot, remember what happened to your henchmen."

"I know you can shoot, Dead Eye, but I can detect—"

"Stop arguing and let her go." Chantal nodded at Iona. "Go on. I'll be close behind."

"Wait till I get to the bottom," Iona said. "If it's clear, I'll let you know."

Her finger on the rifle's trigger, she stepped lightly onto the first stair, then the next, then the next, not bothering to grasp the rail.

The steps creaked more loudly than they had during her blinded visit here. If anyone waited below, he knew someone was coming.

As she descended, her eyes adjusted to the dimness. Near the landing, burlap bags lined the walls, and a closed door stood on the far side. When she arrived at the bottom, she took the remaining three steps to the door and tried to turn the knob—locked. "It's safe," she called.

Chantal hurried down, her steps loud. Then something thudded, and light from above blinked off. "Leo closed the trapdoor," Chantal said as she arrived, now in total darkness.

A flashlight beam knifed in from above, and Leo's clumping footsteps sounded, then his voice. "I couldn't cover the door with straw, so we're not as safe as I would like."

Iona touched the door. "It's locked. This is where Commander Barks took me when I came." She eyed Leo, his face visible in the beam's glow. "So you got us here, huntsman. You've proven yourself trustworthy. I guess you can leave whenever you want."

"Leave?" Leo fidgeted. "Well … you see … I came along out of obligation, but now …"

"He likes you, Iona," Chantal said, smiling. "He's a softy."

Leo sighed. "Okay, Princess Perceptive, so sue me for being human. I lost my sister a year ago. She looked a lot like our sly little fox."

"Now I get it," Iona said as she touched his elbow. "Sorry about your sister, Leo, but it'll be good to have a big-brother type like you around. For example …" She nodded toward the door. "Got any idea how to unlock it?"

"Maybe." Leo withdrew an odd-looking key from his belt. "This opens most locks." He inserted the key and tried to turn it, but it wouldn't budge. He grunted a mild oath, then withdrew the key. "Well, there's more than one way to peel a potato."

He lifted a foot and slammed it against the door. In a spray of splinters, his foot burst through the wood. As he tried to pull his leg back, he hopped on one foot. "I would appreciate some help, Boss One and Boss Two."

Iona and Chantal each grabbed an arm and guided him back as he withdrew his foot. When he regained his balance, he pushed his hand through the hole and unlocked the door from the other side.

Chantal opened it. "Let's see what we can find."

She walked into a narrow hall, Leo's flashlight beam sweeping the wooden floor and paneled walls. A door stood on each side, both open.

"I slept in the one on the right," Iona said.

"Then we'll choose the other one." Chantal walked into the left-hand room, followed by Iona and Leo. Inside, a desk with a computer and two monitors stood against the far wall. Chantal rolled a chair out of the way, making it collide with its twin. She flipped the computer's switch, but it failed to come on. "No power."

"Short Stuff said she didn't hear a generator when she was here."

"Right," Iona said, frowning at Leo's newest nickname for her. "It was quiet."

"They might have a battery of … well … batteries." Leo shone the beam on an electrical outlet near the floor next to the desk. "An activation switch should be nearby." He set his nose near the wall above the outlet and sniffed.

"You can smell electrical wires?" Chantal asked.

"Dust. It clings to the wires." Still sniffing, he followed the wall until he reached a corner. Then he stepped back and pressed the wall with a finger. A panel popped open. He reached in and flipped a switch.

A fixture on the ceiling flicked on, bathing the room in light. The computer hummed, and the two monitors brightened.

"Perfect." Chantal scanned the room. "I'm looking for a pressurized suit, something airtight to survive in a zero-oxygen environment."

"How do you know they have one?" Iona asked.

"I received an encrypted update from Barks that explained what the weapon needs to work. He said they developed a suit, so it must be here somewhere."

"I'll check the other room," Leo said as he headed for the door.

"While he's doing that ..." Chantal wheeled a chair close and sat in front of the monitors. "See this?" She pointed at the screen to the right. "It shows the Oculus Gate. The monitor on the left is displaying light-emission data from the various points in the Gate."

Iona stepped closer, the rifle still in hand. "How do you know all that?"

"The data feed is the same as what I saw in a similar setup at angel headquarters. Laramel put it together, probably borrowing from Kat's knowledge." Chantal studied the numbers, her brow scrunching. "This is not good. Not good at all."

"What?" Iona asked.

"I assume this is it," Leo said as he walked into the room with a silvery garment over one arm and a helmet tucked under the other.

"Yes." Chantal rose, took the suit, and began putting it on over her clothes. Far too large, the coveralls-like suit, complete with gloves and boots, seemed to swallow her. "The Refectors are trying to break into the transportation conduit between the Oculus Gate and Earth." Her hands now covered by gloves attached to the suit, she zipped the front and took the helmet. "It was Laramel's idea. She thinks the Refectors will be allies who will help her conquer the rest of the world, which is why she prepared human vessels for them. They told her the souls had to be purged before they could inhabit a body."

"That's terrible," Iona said. "And Laramel's a fool to think they'll be allies. Any race that believes it's fine to enslave humans can't be trusted."

Chantal set the helmet on the desk. "She thinks the angels will be more powerful than the Refectors, and she fears another force that's already in this world, so she needs an ally. Either way, it's bad for us humans."

"Any idea how long till they break through?" Iona asked.

"It could be at any moment. We have to destroy the conduit before it's too late."

"How do we do that?"

"With the weapon." Chantal strode to the wall next to the desk and stood at the side of a narrow vertical alcove that ran from floor to ceiling, about three feet wide and the same depth. An object that looked like a missile stood inside, around five feet tall and filling most of the recess. "Obviously this is it."

When she reached her gloved hands into the alcove, light splashed, as if she had thrust her hands into liquid energy. She slid the missile out, laid it on the floor, and knelt at its side near the cone-shaped end. "Let's see if we can get the warhead off."

Iona knelt at the opposite side while Leo crouched at the cone's point.

Chantal set her hands around the cone. As she tried to turn it, she grunted. "Help me. These gloves are slipping."

Iona slid her hands underneath the cone and grasped it while Leo gripped the top. "On three," he said. "One … two … three!" They all twisted the cone at the same time. It popped loose, then turned easily.

Chantal disconnected the cone and extended it toward Leo. "Hold this, Muscle Man, while I look for the conduit activator settings in the computer."

"Of course." He took the cone, rose to his feet, and cradled it at his waist. "Being a huntsman, I am no scientist by any means, but I thought the missile is supposed to deliver the warhead. Why did we remove it?"

"You'll find out in a minute. I learned quite a bit while Novada probed Kat Garrison's mind, especially about weapon specifications." Chantal unfastened and removed a glove, sat at the desk, and tapped on the data-feed screen. Program windows opened and closed as her fingertip flew from point to point. "It has to be here somewhere."

"I heard a noise," Leo said. "It sounded like the trapdoor opening. I think we have a visitor."

"Or maybe more than one." Iona tiptoed toward the hall door, her rifle ready. "I'll keep watch."

As Iona glanced between the hall and the desk, Chantal continued searching. Seconds later, the door at the end of the hall opened, and Jack peeked in. When he saw Iona, he smiled and walked toward her.

"Got it," Chantal said. "The conduit is active, though it's closed for now. Stay away from the wall alcove where the missile was standing."

Iona relaxed her grip on the rifle. "No worries about a visitor. It's Jack."

Chantal's eyes widened. "Jack? Oh, no!" She shot to her feet and snatched the warhead from Leo. "Don't let him in."

Jack walked into the room, his wings folded to let him pass. "Why not, Chantal?"

She backed toward the alcove. "Because you'll try to stop me."

"Stop you from doing what?"

The computer beeped multiple times. Bold red letters flashed on the data monitor. "Conduit breach."

Still holding the warhead, Chantal hustled to the screen and read the data. She whispered, "The Refectors."

"The Refectors?" Jack joined her at the desk. "So they're coming? Now?"

"I'm not sure." Chantal set the warhead on the desk. Her mouth dropped open, and her eyes flared. "I sense the homing orb. It's almost here. I have to hurry."

"Hurry to do what?"

She withdrew something metallic from her pocket and set it behind her ear. "Either help me or get out of the way."

"A scalpel?" Jack reached for it, but Chantal dodged.

"I'll give it to you if you swear to do what I tell you."

He shook his head. "I can't make that promise."

"So be it." She sliced her scalp behind her ear. Blood dripping down her fingers, she set the scalpel on the desk. "Trust me, Jack. This is for you."

"For me? What are you talking about?"

She lifted a vial with a red blob floating inside. "It's the only way to destroy the angels."

Jack eyed the vial. "Who's in there?"

"Queen Laramel." Chantal uncapped the vial and set the opening against the cut she made behind her ear.

"Chantal!" Jack grabbed her wrist and slapped the vial from her fingers. "What the blazes are you doing?"

"Too late, Jack. She's already inside. I can feel her crawling toward my brain." Chantal picked up the glove and helmet. "Get ready, Iona. Just tap on the icon that says Open Access to Conduit."

Iona sat in the chair and studied the screen. When she spotted the red square, she nodded. "I see it."

Chantal put the helmet on, tucked the glove under her arm, and picked up the warhead. After lifting the helmet's visor, she backed toward the alcove. "Jack, trust me. This is the only way."

Jack glanced at the decapitated missile on the floor, then looked again at Chantal. "Is that a warhead?"

"You don't need to know." She backpedaled the rest of the way into the alcove. Light splashed in rippling waves that wrapped around her body.

"Chantal!" Jack lunged to the alcove, grabbed her arm, and pulled her out. "What's going on?"

"Let me go!" She tried to break free, but his grip was too strong. "Laramel's taking hold of my brain. When she does, it will be too late."

"Too late for what?"

Leo stepped toward the door. "Someone's coming."

Iona rose from the desk chair and aimed her rifle at Jack, steeling her body to keep the weapon from shaking. "Let her go! Now!"

"What?" Jack's mouth dropped open. "Iona, what are you doing?"

"You heard me." She set her finger on the trigger. "Let Chantal go."

Ben trudged into the room, a winged woman limp over his shoulder. Trudy followed. When she saw Iona, she aimed a rifle at her. "Iona! Stand down!"

Iona fired. The bullet nicked Jack's forearm. He grimaced, but he kept his grip on Chantal.

Trudy snatched Iona's rifle and tossed it to the floor, fierce anger in her eyes.

"Stop!" Ben called as he laid Kat on the floor. "Someone explain what's going on here."

The computer's beeping alarm shifted to a wailing siren. The onscreen message said, "Life forms entering conduit."

Iona shouted, "Jack, the Refectors are on their way! You have to let her go!"

"Jack," Chantal pleaded. "Remember what you told me about Commander Barks and the suicide pact. I'm not a child. I'm a soldier. Let me dive on the grenade. There's no time for anyone else to get ready."

Jack stared at her, his blood trickling to the floor. Finally, he let her go.

"Thank you, Jack." She hustled into the alcove, again raising splashes of light, and faced forward. She grimaced, then wailed. "Benjamin Garrison! Give me the homing orb! Now! I see it glowing in your pocket."

Ben withdrew the chain and attached orb from his pocket and strode to her. "You've been planning this all along, haven't you?"

Still cradling the warhead under an arm, she nodded, extending an ungloved hand, stained with blood. "Open … open the clasp."

Ben pinched the clasp open and set the glowing sphere on her palm. He eyed her closely. "You look different, but still familiar." Then he nodded. "I remember now."

"It's been four years." She closed the sphere in a fist, squeezing hard until something crunched. She opened her hand, revealing tiny shards and a bluish blob, no bigger than a fingernail. She rolled the blob to her fingertips and pushed it behind her ear.

Ben grasped her arm. "I'm sorry for doubting you. I was wrong. You're the bravest soldier I've ever seen."

"Thank you for saying so." Something sizzled. Chantal grimaced, gasping. As Ben backed away, she lowered her hand and refastened her glove. Her tight expression loosened, though she continued breathing rapidly. A stream of gaseous crimson flowed from Kat's ear and flew behind Chantal's. As the vapor left Kat, her wings shrank, as if deflated by the emission.

Seconds later, dozens of streams flew in through the doorway and funneled to Chantal. As she absorbed them behind her ear, her eyes grew wider and wider. Her arms shook, and her body trembled. Her cheeks cracked, forming a matrix of squares that turned into raised ridges that flushed scarlet.

The moment the last stream entered, Chantal lowered her visor and locked it in place with a snap. She pressed a button on the suit's belt. The garment hissed, inflating with air. "Iona!" she called. "Open the conduit!"

Iona tapped the Conduit Access icon. A message appeared on the screen. She read it out loud. "Enter password number one."

"Oh." Trudy shook her head, as if throwing off a stupor. "Gertrude. It's my real name."

Iona typed it in. Another message appeared. She called out, "Password rejected."

From the floor, Kat spoke with a rasp. "Use all caps."

Everyone stared at her wingless form as she rose to a sitting position and massaged the back of her head. "Don't stand there gawking at me. Enter it again using all caps."

"Okay." Iona reentered the password in capital letters. The computer beeped and displayed another message that Iona read out loud. "Enter password number two."

"Iona," Jack said.

"Yes?" Iona looked at him. "Do you know the second password?"

He gave her a weak smile. "The password is Iona. Barks's note said to tell you, 'Good work.'"

Iona bit her lip. Trying not to cry, she typed her name in all caps. When she hit the Enter key, the computer beeped, and Chantal flew upward as if sucked by a vacuum.

"Wait," Kat said, shaking her head as if in a daze. "Does Chantal know that manual detonation requires a specific series of button pushes?"

"I have no idea," Jack said. "Anyone else?"

Iona shook her head. "Never mentioned it to me."

Kat raised three fingers. "Color-coded buttons. First blue, then green, then red."

"I'm going." Jack lurched toward the alcove. Tucking his wings, he backed into the recess. Light splashed once more. Jack screamed, his eyes wide. A silhouette of radiance rushed into the upward stream, though his body remained.

"Turn it off!" Trudy shouted.

Iona touched the icon. The stream ceased. Jack stepped out of the alcove, his shoulders straight and his face still glowing. He gazed at each person in turn. "Your ally is not here," he said in an even tone, blood dripping down his arm. "I am Zachariel."

Ben stepped closer to the alcove and looked up through an access hole leading to the sky. "Where's Jack?"

"I released him from his body so he can give Chantal the required information to detonate the warhead."

Ben turned toward him. "But won't the explosion destroy Jack's soul along with the Oculus Gate?"

"Jack will be safe. An explosion cannot harm a soul." Zachariel walked toward the hall, his wings bending to fit through the doorway. "Come. Let's see the results for ourselves."

He left, Trudy following.

Ben crouched next to Kat. "Think you can walk?"

"Probably."

Ben and Leo each grasped one of her wrists and hoisted her up. Her knees buckled, and they lowered her to the floor. When Ben knelt to pick her up, Leo did the same on the other side. "Allow me, my farmer friend. It looks like you backed into a bonfire."

"She's my wife. I really should—"

"Ben," Kat said, patting his arm, "it's all right. Let him carry me."

Leo smiled. "Then it's settled." He lifted Kat into his arms and carried her into the hallway.

Ben rose to his feet and picked up Iona's rifle. He looked her in the eye. "You shot my brother."

She cringed. "I know there's a lot of blood, but I just nicked him. If I had wanted to—"

"No. Don't say another word. We'll talk later. Come with me." He turned and walked out.

Iona followed, letting her shoulders sag. Had she done the right thing? She had betrayed Ben and Trudy, shot Jack, and sent Chantal on a suicide mission. And now she was gone, probably soon to be dead, the only person who could fully explain what happened.

She stopped at the stairway leading outside and gazed at the light streaming in from the open door. How could she face them now? After all that Chantal had privately revealed, mounting a defense was easy, but would they believe her? Not likely. She wasn't sure she believed it herself.

She pushed her hands into her pockets and began the long upward trudge. At the bottom of one pocket, her fingers came across something odd. She halted and withdrew a leather cord with a small wooden cross attached, scorched yet intact. A scrap of paper fell out with it and landed on the stair.

Iona picked up the scrap and read the hasty script. *Take courage. The trail of sacrifice has been blazed. Love, Summer/Chantal.*

A sob rising, Iona bit her lip. As she tied the cord behind her neck, a single tear slipped down her cheek. When she finished, she brushed the tear away, squared her shoulders, and marched up the stairs, whispering, "I'm your spy, Commander."

Chapter Twenty-Nine

Jack zoomed through the alcove and into the sky, following a sparkling path at what seemed like an impossible speed. Ahead, a human form raced upward at a slower rate. As he drew closer, the silvery spacesuit clarified. Chantal flew only seconds ahead.

When he caught up, he willed himself to decelerate and fly with her face to face. Her eyes wide, her cratered cheeks scarlet, and blood streaming down her neck, she seemed terrified. Somehow, he had to help her detonate the warhead without killing herself, but communicating from his spiritual state to her physical body would be impossible ... unless ...

He pushed a hand through the helmet's glass visor shield, then flowed inside. After finding the slit behind her ear, he streamed into her head and around her skull to her brain stem. A pulsing red blob wrapped a dozen tentacles around the stem, some long with pointed ends that stabbed the stem's surface and others shorter with ragged ends, apparently torn.

Jack swam to the brain, squeezed between the stem and the tentacles' spikes, and covered it, his entire nebulous body spreading around it. Within seconds, a new form of vision took shape. The sparkles in the conduit appeared. Somehow he was seeing through Chantal's eyes.

The spikes stabbed at him, piercing with incredible pain. "Chantal, can you hear me?"

"Jack? How can you—"

"Never mind. Just listen. Do you know the warhead's detonation sequence?"

"A sequence? I just thought I needed to push the red button."

"Kat says you have to push a blue button first, then a green one, then the red one. Do you see all three?"

His vision shifted to the warhead. A large red button lay recessed in the cone's surface next to two smaller buttons, one blue and one green. "Yes. I see them. Good thing you told me."

"Yeah. Good thing. But maybe we can figure out a way to do this without you killing yourself."

"It's too late, Jack. I can't reverse the flow."

"The conduit isn't a one-way street. The angels came down. Supposedly the Refectors can. That means we can."

"No. According to Barks, the warhead won't explode without someone holding it, so I have to stay with it and end the angels' reign of terror. It's our mission. We swore to it together. Don't you remember? Four years ago? We were together, side by side."

"Were you the skinny teenager? Summer?"

Chantal laughed. "Yes. That was my birth name, and I was rather scrawny then."

"I'm sorry. I didn't mean—"

"It doesn't matter, Jack. I made a solemn vow that day, and I'm fulfilling it. If you want to fulfill your vow, you won't try to stop me."

A spike knifed through Jack and plunged into Chantal's brain stem.

She groaned. "Augh!" Her vision dimmed, as if she had partially closed her eyes.

"Chantal?"

She panted for breath. "Jack, I feel her. Laramel. She's invading my mind."

"Yes, I am," another female said. "You should listen to Jack. It is foolish to kill yourself. Suicide is a coward's way out of her troubles."

Chantal gasped as she spoke. "It's ... not suicide. It's ... sacrifice."

"Semantics. Two words with the same result. I can show you how to reverse course and—"

"Shut up, Laramel!" Jack shouted. "This isn't your call. You invaded our world, subjugated our people, poisoned us with a contagion and a toxic vaccine, and invited another horde to come in and finish us off. You're the enemy, and we're taking you out."

"Right," Chantal said, still gasping. "But I need ... your help, Jack. I can feel her ... trying to take over ... my motor functions."

Jack formed a hand, grabbed the piercing tentacle, and pulled. As it eased out, Chantal breathed a sigh of relief. "Whatever you're doing, it's working."

The view shifted. A highway appeared with two lines of people walking in opposite directions.

"You're standing on the Never-ending Highway," Jack said. "This is where Sophie and Alana are."

"Good. I hoped so. They're one of the reasons I'm doing this. To make sure they escape. Do you see them anywhere?"

"No. I told them to wait for me at a marker, like a highway mileage marker."

The view swiveled from side to side, then locked on a green sign in the distance, only the top half visible because of the line of people in the way. "I see one."

The view bobbed, likely from Chantal jogging, her progress slowed by the cumbersome suit. As she drew closer to the sign, another spike stabbed Jack and snaked into the brain stem.

"Oh!" Chantal dropped to her knees. Some of the people turned and stared at her, dividing to allow a view of the lower part of the sign. Sophie and Alana stood at the base, looking at Chantal.

Taking Alana by the hand, Sophie ran to Chantal and helped her rise. Sophie's lovely blue eyes nearly filled the view. "Who are you? And why are you dressed like this?"

Jack trembled as he spoke. "That's her. Sophie. And Alana."

"I'm Chan ... Chantal. I came to ... help you escape ... this place. Jack ... Jack is with me."

Sophie blinked. "Jack? My husband?"

The view bobbed.

"Where is he?"

Chantal's thoughts came through as well. *Jack, I think I'm running out of air.*

Jack groaned. "I didn't notice before. This suit has no tank."

Right. I have to hurry.

"He's in my brain," Chantal said. "Please ... please don't ask ... me to explain. Just know ... know that he loves you ... and he is ... risking his soul ... to rescue you and Alana."

"His soul?"

"Yes, his soul ... is riding ... in my brain ... to help me ... save you. If not for him ... I would be ... an angel robot. He is ... a good man."

"Yes. Yes, he is." Sophie smiled, tears streaming down her cheeks. "And what about you? You're here in some kind of space suit. Aren't you risking your life?"

"I'm not ... risking my life. I'm ... sacrificing it."

Another spike stabbed into the brain stem. The view dropped, as if Chantal had fallen to her knees again.

"You will not destroy us!" Laramel shouted as the tentacles sizzled. "I can restore your power as a princess by my side."

Chantal set the warhead down and pressed the blue button. *Jack! The pain! It's so awful!*

"Do what I say," Laramel said, "and I will release you from the pain. You will live in comfort and luxury."

Jack grabbed a tentacle with each hand and pulled. They seemed to be sliding out but not fast enough.

Chantal pushed the warhead's green button, then set her gloved finger next to the red one. "Just ... just do what you say ... Laramel?" She gasped for breath. "That's it? And the pain will go away?"

"Yes. Do what I say, and I will lead you safely home. To demonstrate my good will, I will withdraw my influence for the moment."

The tentacles loosened. Jack yanked them out and embraced the brain stem again.

Chantal exhaled heavily. "That's better."

"And your comfort will continue if, as I said before, you simply do as I say."

"Okay ... Okay." She picked the warhead up and cradled it, gasping for breath again. "Before ... before I do what you say ... will you do ... one thing that I say?"

"Perhaps. What is it?"

"Go to hell." Chantal pushed the red button.

Ben gathered straw into a pile and helped Leo lower Kat to a sitting position. "Comfortable?" Ben asked.

Dawn's rays illuminated her wincing smile. "Not too bad. Headache's getting better, and that demon is gone. At least I think it is."

"I'll check." Trudy knelt close, withdrew the AngelScan from the medical bag, and set the disk on Kat's forehead. When the light flicked on, Ben peered over Trudy's shoulder and looked at the screen. A vibrant white sphere hovered within Kat's brain stem, no redness in sight. The identifier flashed with an "Angel Not Present" message. Trudy turned the scanner off and put it away. "You're clean."

Kat lifted her arms. "Then I'll stand."

Ben and Trudy helped her rise. Although she wobbled a bit, she seemed pretty steady. Ben nodded toward the royal cruiser they had taken from Novada and her guards. "Do you want to sit in the transport?"

"No. I want to see if the weapon works." Kat took Ben's hand on one side, Trudy's on the other.

Jack, now Zachariel, pointed at the Oculus Gate, barely visible in the sky, like dim stars in the morning glow. "It shouldn't be long now."

After Iona exited the storage room, Leo hoisted the door panel from the ground and let it fall closed with a thud. She stood with Leo well away from the others.

While eyeing the Gate, Ben whispered to Kat and Trudy, "If what Novada said is true, every single angel went into Chantal's—"

A ball of light exploded at the center of the Oculus. Streams of radiance arced in every direction. As the arcs reached the points of light in the perimeter, they winked out one by one.

Then, the entire Oculus Gate disappeared.

Everyone stared in silence. After several seconds, Ben blinked, trying to refocus on the sky. "Is it gone? Or just too dim to see now?"

Trudy bit her fist. "I hope Jack's all right."

Zachariel turned toward them, his expression blank. "We'll know soon."

"Sir Angel," Leo said, taking a step closer to him. "What about the Refectors? Did they come to earth?"

"That I do not know." Zachariel spread his wings. "But this I do know. As the angel of last chances, I will report that the members of this troop are bright, shining lights. There is hope for your planet yet."

"That's all well and good." Leo set a hand on Iona's shoulder. "But who belongs to the troop? Some of us feel like outsiders looking in."

Zachariel shook his head. "I'm afraid that's not up to me."

Ben looked at Iona. As she looked back at him, tears sparkled in her eyes, but she stood straight, as tall as her diminutive frame allowed. "I know I went behind your back," she said, her voice firm, though it seemed ready to crack. "And I shot your brother. But I had to. Chantal was the only one who knew how to—"

"No. Don't explain." Ben spread his arms. "Welcome to our family."

Iona's mouth dropped open. "You mean …"

Ben spread his arms wider. "Don't leave me hanging, girl."

She ran and leaped into his embrace. As they hugged, Kat and Trudy joined in. Then Trudy reached toward Leo. "Get over here, you big lunk."

"Glad to, Scalpel Maiden." He wrapped his long arms around her and Kat, laughing. "Plenty of body odor, but I think it smells like family."

When they parted, Iona brushed away tears. "I guess I should tell you all of my secrets. I mean, since we're family now, like Leo said."

"Not necessarily," Ben said, "but I would like to know how old you are. Your changes in appearance have made me wonder."

She grinned. "Guess. Everyone guess."

"Nineteen," Ben said.

Kat tapped her chin. "Twenty."

Leo harrumphed. "No woman that smart and tough could be a day younger than twenty-one."

Trudy crossed her arms. "You're sixteen, aren't you?"

Iona's brow lifted. "How did you know?"

"A hunch. Let's just call it a fellow sharpshooter's intuition."

"It is time," Zachariel said, beating his wings. "Goodbye, my friends." A shining humanlike form rose from his body, seeming to take the wings along as it ascended. A moment later, it was gone.

A wingless Jack shook his head hard. "Wow! What a trip!"

"Jack!" Trudy ran to him and wrapped him in her arms, then drew back. "What happened?"

As he gazed skyward, tears tracked down his cheeks. "Well, Chantal didn't know about the sequence, so it's a good thing I went. And I was able to keep Laramel at bay, at least long enough for Chantal to activate the warhead. It destroyed the conduit and the place where my wife and daughter were trapped. The blast killed Chantal, but she, Sophie, and Alana are all safe in heaven. I saw their souls before I left, though I couldn't touch them because of a shield covering me. Anyway, I was able to tell them goodbye and that I'd see them …" He sniffed and brushed a tear, barely able to squeak out, "Eventually."

Trudy massaged his shoulder. "Then you're a hero. Without you, Chantal's suicide mission would've failed. A complete waste of a life."

Jack laughed under his breath, obviously trying not to cry. "Not suicide. Sacrifice. She's the hero."

"You're right," Ben said. "Chantal, or I guess we can call her Summer, is the greatest of heroes. I feel like we stumbled along like a gang of crippled geese. We did some things right. Most things wrong. But Summer saved the day ... and the world."

"Don't worry, dear brothers," Trudy said. "No I-told-you-so snark from me, even though I did tell you so back when we took the rebel oath." She leaned her head against Jack's shoulder. "So I guess it's all over. We won."

"We defeated the angels," Ben said, "but did the Refectors make it to earth?"

Jack shrugged. "Maybe. I couldn't tell if anyone got through the conduit before it vaporized. And what about the other force that's already here, the one Laramel was worried about? We have no idea what it is."

Iona turned toward the forest. "Well, we can find out about the Refectors. We'll go to the city and see if the soulless humans are dead, alive, or possessed."

"Now?" Leo asked, suppressing a yawn. "We've been up way too many hours."

Ben smiled. "What's the matter, huntsman? No stamina?"

Leo wagged a finger, failing to hide a smile. "Listen, Farmer Jones, I've been awake two full nights, one chasing the ginger cat and one making sure you and your company didn't fall into a hole somewhere."

"Fair enough." Ben took Kat's hand. "You can stay in the transport and get your beauty sleep. The rest of us will go to the city without you. I mean, facing those Refectors might be terribly scary."

"Since you put it that way." Leo lifted the trapdoor and let it fall open. "I'm getting a big bag of angel tea, or whatever we're going to call it now. Maybe Flight Fuel. I think we're all going to need it."

Author Note

What would it be like to live in a dystopian world while being part of a resistance faction? What could a small group of people do to topple a seemingly omnipotent tyrannical regime? Overwhelmingly underpowered and outmanned, they would have to resort to extremely clever strategy and unbelievable courage.

While creating this story, I imagined strategies that would make agents from Mission Impossible question my sanity, but the odd situations made for fun scenes. I enjoyed creating characters who would face incredible challenges in believable ways, which made them engaging and entertaining. In short, writing this story was a blast.

Research included consultation with a munitions expert and personally firing guns to get the feel of the experience. Yet, that was the extent of my hands-on trials. Since the adventure takes place in the future, many devices my characters used don't exist at the present time, so I couldn't try out my imagined gadgets.

Regarding themes, I am concerned about our society. In my sixty-plus years, I have never seen as much division and outrage as we have in our present time. Still, there is a worse possible outcome. Suppose a despotic force, claiming to be heaven-sent, offered to restore peace and order. Would people trade their freedom for chains if it meant gaining security? And what would become of those who object? Could they mount a resisting force even though the vast majority opposed them? The possibilities felt troubling but all too real.

Also, the COVID-19 pandemic struck as I was editing this story, long after I included a contagion and a vaccine as danger devices. I didn't realize how relevant it would be for readers until finishing the final draft's edits.

If you enjoyed this book, I hope you will provide a review, whether on a retail website like Amazon, Christianbook.com, in a blog, or in a social media post. I thank you in advance for doing so.

You can connect with me on the Internet in the following ways:

Website – www.daviscrossing.com – You can sign up for my email newsletter there.

Facebook – https://www.facebook.com/BryanDavis.Fans

Twitter – @bryandavisauth

Blog – www.theauthorschair.com

Email – author@daviscrossing.com

I look forward to hearing from you.

BOOK TWO COMING MAY 1, 2021

INVADING HELL

WITHDRAWN

9 781943 959822